THE APEX AGENDA

TRACY TODD

CRANTHORPE MILLNER PUBLISHERS

First published by Cranthorpe Millner Publishers (2025)

ISBN 978-1-80378-269-0 (Paperback)

www.cranthorpemillner.com

Cranthorpe Millner Publishers

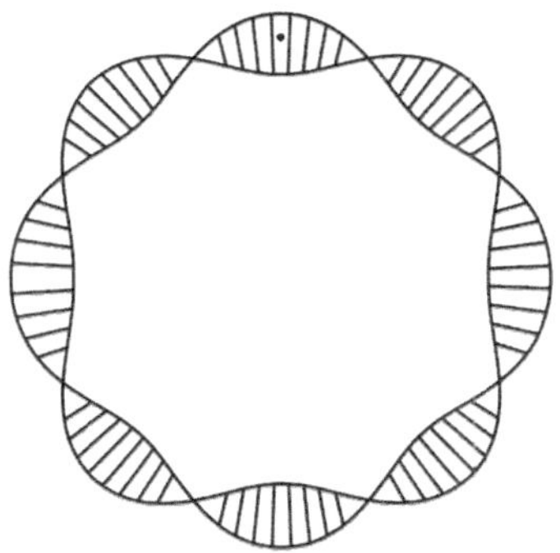

GOODNESS IN PURITY.
GOODNESS IN LIFE.
DEFEND OUR VALUES.
KEEP US SAFE.
REPORT DIFFERENCE.

CHAPTER ONE

I'm what they call a 'late bloomer'. At least, I hope I am. Mum said not to worry, that it runs in the family and that's why I'm small, but that still doesn't make up for all the snarky remarks and the whispers of 'zombie' and 'Golem'. I'm the last one in my class to make the transition and the whole school knows it; the oldest, ungendered, grey-and-white-uniformed oddity. That's me! I stick out amongst a sea of black, blue and purple. Even kids in younger classes have started to wear their new, gender-defined clothing.

Liddy, my best friend, has changed already. She so wanted to be a girl and dressed like one the whole of her life – make-up, nails, frills, the whole lot – but about a year ago, she came to school with red eyes. When I asked her what was wrong, she just pointed to a couple of fine, dark hairs above her top lip.

"So?"

"So? Is that all you can say?"

"Well, I mean…" I felt as if I were to blame. "It's just who you are."

"No, Cam, it isn't who I am. I'm a girl. You know that."

"Maybe it'll go away."

She'd glared at me in horror and stalked off. A couple of months later, after formal testing and several clinical check-ups of physical changes, her family had her coming-out party and proclaimed her a *him*, and immediately began using his middle name 'Lou'. Liddy hated every second of it, and since then, even though he's now so obviously a boy, with boy parts, he still dresses in purple wraps and wears kohl eyeliner. Not only that, but he resists responding to his middle name, which gets him into huge amounts of trouble.

By law, we're all required to have a first and middle name, one female and one male, both beginning with the same letter. It just makes things easier after the Change happens. Some opt for unisex names to avoid the whole thing. Pre-Change, we're permitted to use either name, but after coming out, we have to use the one defining our gender. My middle name is Camden, so Cam works for me.

Liddy gets moody and just ignores me if I try calling him Lou. He's even begun growing his black hair long again. We're all allowed some time to adapt after the Change, but if he doesn't conform soon, his parents will send him to one of those weird 'head doctors'. I wince and tense my stomach muscles, as if someone's about to attack me. I couldn't bear them taking him away. What would I do without Liddy? He's my only friend.

When we were seven, we went on our first school trip together. The teachers sat us around a campfire and told us these scary stories of poor creatures who'd failed to go through the Change properly; how, in the past, they'd roamed the streets, zombie-like figures with white eyes that craved human blood, strange non-humans that were physically and morally corrupt. We'd squealed in delight at the horror, knowing we were safe, that we were pure; physically and morally superior.

Later, I remember, we created a game. One of us took the role of the zombie and went up front. The rest of us huddled behind. The aim was to get as close as possible, taunting the evil creature, knowing at any point it might turn around, grab one of us and then we'd catch the 'lurgy' and turn into a zombie, too. 'Zombie' isn't the official word for the ungendered, but as kids, it was either that or 'Golem'.

I don't feel safe anymore. There are too many eyes watching, too many snide comments. When I walk around school, kids glance and hurry away, as if I've got a contagious disease. Even worse, the teachers have become more cautious. Mum says they won't report me, that she's had a word with them, but parents watch, too. Liddy's father won't let me visit anymore; he hates me. A few months ago, he screamed at me to get out of his house and even told Liddy we couldn't hang out anymore. Liddy ignores him, but he isn't someone to mess with. He works in security at one of those clinics, and anything can set him off. He'd have no problem speaking to the authorities about me.

My breath hitches and I hold my body tight, my fists clenched. In the oval-shaped mirror of my dressing table, I notice my pupils widening in horror. I see what they all see when they look at me. Heck, I totally get it.

I'm an anomaly.

Using my forehead as a drumstick, I tap it against the cool surface of the mirror and rock on my feet, heels to toes, *tap, tap*, heels to toes. A shudder runs through me at the thought of being a Golem for the rest of my life. Our family genes are pure, but still, we know it could happen. It's happened to others.

"Cam, I'm going."

My mum's voice startles me. She's shouting up the narrow stairs. I pop my head around the bedroom door.

"Right, Mum. See you later."

"Don't be late."

"What?"

"For the specialist."

"Oh, yes… okay, I'll be there."

Of course I'll be there. I have no choice.

Walking over to the window, I push the curtain aside and force the air out of my lungs. The glass fogs up. I smear the mist away with the tips of my fingers as I watch my mum open the gate, turn left and stride away, her broad shoulders swinging slightly. She's wearing a smart, purple suit with a pink blouse. Around her neck is her trademark scarf, knotted in front to cover her scar – a bicycle accident from childhood which threw her over the bars into a wall. Her windpipe swelled so much that she was unable to breathe, and the medics had to perform an emergency tracheotomy on the street. It resulted in her having a deeper voice than normal, but she was lucky to survive.

My eyes wander across the road to the squat block of flats for oldies. The faded yellow paint is weathered and peeling. There are ten districts of these 'prefab' buildings in our town, cement and steel-framed, made in a workshop and put up within a week. Ours has been here for at least twenty years. Colours indicate status. Because my mum works as a CEO's secretary at a large energy company, she was allocated a two-up, two-down terraced block in the yellow section. Yellow is about midway, with blue being the most luxurious and cream being single-roomed hovels. Those with jobs graded 'higher-up', such as government officials, are permitted *real* houses, with red bricks and gardens.

I slump in front of my mirror again, watching the person in front of me stare back, nostrils flared, thinking of the appointment. My mum took me for initial testing a couple of weeks ago and we are now going back for the results. She said we needed to show our support for purity by volunteering, rather than have them knocking on the door.

"Just to be sure," she'd said. "Nothing to worry about."

"But what if—"

"You know the Change can happen any time from ten to fifteen. You're not yet past evolving. No good thinking about it until we get the results, Cam."

And so, it's all I've thought about ever since. I'm so ashamed, I haven't even told Liddy we get the results today. What if I am a zombie? What if they just take me away? My chest heaves and tears well up. I scrub my scalp with the tips of my fingers, as if it will somehow help me escape my own thoughts. But I'm still here, still trapped inside this non-human body. I pick up a brush and drag it through knotted, dark hair. My face pinches in pain, but at least it's real, something I can feel in a world that is gradually tilting, like a sinking ship in a great storm.

I close the front door and navigate my way down the street, avoiding mothers and little children, kids chasing each other, and the queue of people at the bus stop. My eyes flick to the new signage flashing on the wall of the bus shelter:

Pure Genes are the ONLY Safe Genes. We are all in Danger. Report Difference.

There's a crackdown going on. It happens at least once a year. Scowling, I hunch over as my stomach churns. I wish Liddy didn't have detention again. He lives around the corner and usually we walk to school together, but he's always in trouble nowadays.

By the time I get to school, I'm miserable. The musty smell in my locker doesn't help. It's been getting worse over the last few days, like something is rotting in it. I tried air freshener, but now it stinks even more. Stuffing my bag in, I grab my history book and head for the toilet. As usual, Liddy's already in there, applying eye make-up. I stop and stare, unable to ignore the fact he's now in a black trouser suit and blue shirt while I'm still in childish grey and white.

He narrows his eyes at me. "What you gawping at?"

"You want another detention?" I glance around at the cubicle doors, making sure no one else is around.

"What for? This toilet isn't as busy as the other one."

He's referring to the fact that he's in the ungendered loo, but is supposed to use the boys' now.

"That's not what I mean. Doesn't your dad say anything about the make-up?"

He skims his lower eyelashes with kohl. "What he doesn't know won't hurt him." He looks down at me, smiling, and flicks his shoulder-length locks behind his ears. "What do you think?"

"I think the teachers will have you wash it off before break, and the note home will have your dad belting you again."

He frowns and sticks out his tongue as I wash my hands. The antiseptic smell of the brown, liquid soap tickles my nostrils. I glance at the speckled mirror, trying to avoid my own reflection. I hate looking at myself. Still flat-chested and skinny at fifteen, I look like a tall twelve-year-old. Last year, I thought it had begun. I was getting the typical hot sweats, my chest ached, my stomach was in agony – all the right signs – but it stopped after a couple of weeks. Mum said it was probably pre-puberty and an indication that the Change was coming, but nothing's happened since. Every morning, I get up, praying for the sickness, the foggy head. Every morning, I'm just the same abnormal me.

The pale green walls of the ungendered bathroom, the low sinks (made for younger children) and the tiny cubicles all seem to mock me, reminding me that I am not like others; not a true citizen in society yet; not a safe part of the whole.

Glancing at Liddy as I pick up my book and pencil case, I can't help but feel a bit envious.

Why does he fight it? I wouldn't care if I were a boy, as long as I was something. He doesn't know how lucky he is.

"Come on, we'll be late."

Liddy and I head for our first class. We walk down the centre of the corridor. As usual, those passing us scoot to the edges, like a wave parting to form a passageway just for us.

Liddy grins and bows his head as if he is a king. "Thank you, my subjects."

I keep my head down. Liddy doesn't have to worry. He isn't like me; he's confirmed.

We enter the stuffy classroom and head for our usual seats on the right-hand side, dumping our books as we slump down. Liddy's legs are so long, they reach into the aisle.

Mr Shu whips his long ruler on the desk, making a cracking sound. "Right, everyone, settle down." He grins at the sudden silence and pushes his thick glasses further up the bridge of his nose. "We have a lot to get through, but first, Joe has something to say."

Liddy and I look at each other.

He raises his eyebrows and mouths, "Who's Joe?"

I shrug in response as Mr Shu opens the door and a gush of cooler air enters the room. A wide-faced boy with dark skin and short, black hair walks in. For a second, I think he must be new, until he lifts his head. I hear several gasps from the room.

Liddy grabs my arm and squeezes so tight a pain shoots up my shoulder.

"Cam, it's Joanna."

Joanna used to hang around with us. I watch Liddy's face pale and then flush a deep maroon.

"When did they take him?" I ask in a whisper. "How long has it been?"

"Six months."

Liddy's leaning so close, I can smell the sweat prickling on his forehead.

None of us thought Joanna would be back. A year after his coming-out party, he'd still had his hair braided and insisted on wearing dresses outside school. Then, one day, he didn't come in. There were rumours, but no one knew for sure, and no one dared ask.

He looks different now. His eyes glaze over as he begins to speak. "Hi. I know you all knew me as Joanna... I mean, Joe." His voice is flat. Flicking his eyes over a piece of paper with a pre-written statement, he starts again, stuttering. "I-I'm better now." His fingers twitch as he strains to say his next words. There's a hoarseness to his tone. He glances over at us and frowns, confused.

"What have they done?" Liddy leans in further. "He's not right,"

I nod. A year ago, Joanna was happy, funny; she couldn't keep still. But Joe is nothing like that. Other than the twitches, he doesn't move. No facial expressions, no widening of his eyes, no grin.

"If I upset any of you before, I'm sorry. But now... I'm... I'm better now."

His arms hang at his sides. He lifts his head and focuses on the back wall, as if he's trying to read last year's essays. They're yellowed with age, like enemy soldiers hanged and left to rot over a medieval battlefield.

Mr Shu's hand folds over Joe's shoulder and he gently pushes him forwards. "It's okay, Joe. Look at this as a fresh start for everyone. Take a seat."

Joe shuffles to an empty desk in the corner. The whole class watches as he drops into his chair and rests his head on his arms, closing his eyes.

Mr Shu clears his throat to get our attention. "Joe will need our support," he says. "The treatment works, helps people become productive members of society, but it sometimes affects memory. In Joe's case..." He hesitates. "Let's give him some time." He waits a second before going into the usual spiel. "Right, everyone. On your feet."

We all obey with a clattering of chairs, dragging our bodies to a standing position, and begin the monotone chant of allegiance we've been saying since we started school.

"I promise to observe the five tenets and never misuse them for my own or another's benefit. I promise to respect and obey my elders and those in a position of knowledge and greater understanding. I promise to champion purity of humankind and the natural world. I promise to serve my country and free it from disease and corruption by rooting out evil and the forces that would destroy us."

Mr Shu nods. "Goodness in purity."

The class choruses, "Goodness in life."

"Defend our values," is his reply. "Keep us safe."

"Report difference," we drone in response.

Immediately, everyone slumps down, Joe already forgotten. Mr Shu quickly begins the lesson, blabbing on about something to do with homework.

Liddy's hand is trembling next to mine. He pulls it under the table; his face is still a maroon colour. I glance at the new poster on the wall. It's red with black writing.

SPOTTING DIFFERENCE

1. DOES NOT LOOK ACCORDING TO GENDER ASSIGNMENT.
2. DOES NOT BEHAVE ACCORDING TO GENDER ASSIGNMENT.
3. DISPLAYS AFFECTION TOWARDS THE SAME GENDER.
4. ENCOURAGES IMPURE LIAISONS.
5. DOES NOT OBEY THE FIVE TENETS.

I scribble a note on the corner of my pad.

You gotta conform, Lid, before it's too late. Y'know there's another crackdown going on.

Liddy leans in and reads the scrap of paper. Sighing, he picks up a pencil and draws a sad face, then turns away as the teacher begins the lesson on civil rights in the 1850s. Normally, I like history, but today I can't focus.

What if they take Liddy for the same treatment? Will I lose my only friend?

My chest tightens at the thought, and I rip a scrap of paper from my notebook, intending to scribble another warning note for Liddy. But as I look at him, I see his eyes watering as he stares at Joe. I change my mind. Scrunching up the paper, I stuff it in my pocket. We can talk later. But Liddy *has* to conform. He can't go on like this. It's just too dangerous.

CHAPTER TWO

The door slams hard as I leave the school reception, echoing across the forecourt. It isn't my fault. The hinge is broken, and unless you push hard, it won't shut. I may have pushed it a little harder than necessary, but I'm on edge. I feel as if tiny creatures are crawling under my skin.

There's a guard at the main school entrance holding one of the gates open. Without a word, he steps aside to let me pass, snapping the lock back into place as soon as I leave.

Hitching my bag on my shoulder, I head for the narrow lane that leads to the bus stop. The clinic is a twenty-minute ride away. Mum and I told the school I had a dental appointment so as not to cause any suspicion, but Liddy knows me too well. At lunch break, he'd slung his arms around me, the soft down from his unshaven chin feeling strange against my cheek.

"It'll be okay, Cammy."

I'd forced a thin-lipped crack of a smile. "Er... yeah, sure. It's only teeth."

He'd stared and tutted. "Fine, if that's how you want to play it."

We tell each other everything normally, but this was just too hard. I figure that later, when I get home, I'll call and laugh it off, tell him how it was nothing, really; that everything's okay.

The warm air smells of cut grass and pink roses. Across the narrow road, a man is wiping sweat from his brow as he takes a break from mowing the wide lawn in front of a red-bricked house. He nods as I stride past. From his clothing, I figure he must be the gardener.

"School out already?"

I feel obliged to respond. Pointing to my mouth, I mumble, "Dentist."

He smiles and starts up the mower again, his day perfectly normal.

Sitting on the bus, the plastic seat hot and uncomfortable, I squint out of the window, protecting my eyes from the glaring sun. Cars whirl past in a noisy blur. A man on a bicycle screeches to a halt, narrowly missing a pedestrian crossing the road. The sound of tinny rap music – something I don't recognise – irritates me, but I daren't turn around to see who's causing the racket.

As the bus pulls out for the third time, we move away from the estate and pass a children's park. A little kid laughs as his mum pushes him higher on the swings, happy just existing; no worries about gender, or anything at all really. I twist my head to watch the scene disappear behind dilapidated, high-rise social housing for those with low earnings. Shortly after, we reach the main high street. Each building has a shop on the ground floor with upstairs living accommodation. I've seen large indoor shopping centres advertised on television, with places to eat, shop and spend money, but they're only in the cities. Small towns have to be self-sufficient, growing their own produce, breeding stock and trading goods. Our leaders give everyone a role, dependent upon gender, knowledge and ability. Gaining approval to have one's own small business is hard – the right connections are needed for a licence – but once obtained, one can live independently.

Wrapping my arms around myself, I cling on as if I need restraints to stop me falling forwards. In gender class, we were taught that the Change is just a part of growing up, that everyone goes through it. Until puberty, we're all the same: phenotypically ungendered.

For Liddy, the Change meant testosterone kicking in and three months away in a support clinic. I know the theory, we all do – boys need more intensive help with the physical transition. After all, they have to grow stuff, and other parts need sealing. Girls are left alone to grow their internal organs naturally.

When Liddy came back, he didn't want to talk about it. Sometimes, he mentally shuts down; that was one of those times. Then, he just started acting the same as he did before the Change, as if nothing had happened.

I was six when we had our first gender class. The nurse asked us if we had any questions, and I'd stuck my hand up.

"If we don't go through the Change, do we grow up?"

He'd laughed and assured me everyone grows up.

I do get it… I mean, I understand that they're keeping our genes pure, protecting the human race from destroying itself. In the past, we tried to change who we are – what we are – to prevent disease and increase health and longevity. Some just wanted perfect little babies. Geneticists played around, awakening junk DNA, testing to see whether it could make a difference. And it did: babies were born healthier and more resistant to disease… until it went wrong. Huge numbers of people just couldn't have kids anymore, others had miscarriages and stillbirths. They thought the human race would become extinct. Then, Baby X was born without a gender. No one knew what to do. There was panic and civil unrest when other newborns had the same genetic fault. It was abnormal, until it wasn't. Soon, most newborns were genderless. Only later did they figure out that gender formation was just delayed, but the damage was already done.

The Diversity Commission now make sure we never mess up again; that we live according to nature and within the bounds of the Holistic Law, which dictates all things physical and moral for us to thrive.

A flashback of Joe's face hits me; the torment in his eyes. He's had it tough… and having to apologise to all of us like that? How could anyone hate Joe?

Liddy's dad pops into my mind. He *would* hate Joe. He hates *me* just for existing, and nothing's been proven yet. It's not fair. But we're not supposed to think like that.

My face heats up as I look around the bus. A man in a dark coat stares a little too long and I flick my eyes back to the front, sure he's delving into my mind.

Don't be stupid!

My right knee jiggles up and down and I stare at it as if it doesn't belong to me, before stopping it with a sweaty palm. I want time to stand still; I want to turn around and go home, hide in my bedroom. I wish something, anything, would happen to stop me having to face the test results, but wishes are silly.

What if I'm a Golem? Will they just take me away, there and then?

I don't know what happens – not really. About once a year, there's this mandatory television programme we all have to watch. They cite facts and figures to keep us informed of their progress in wiping out the anomalies. Our leader reminds us why personal freedoms and preferences can never again be above the law – they are fighting for the moral and physical safety of the human race. Our preventative measures are the only ones with such a high success rate across the globe. Countries have even joined forces to duplicate our processes.

The clinic whizzes past and I know this is my stop. My palms are sweating again, and heat flushes my cheeks. I glance at my watch. It's 1:30 p.m. and my mum will already be waiting for me. Reaching for my backpack, I stand as the bus lurches to a halt. I lurch with it and grab a rail to steady myself, before negotiating my way to the door. My legs are trembling as I step off the bus and watch it move on. The man in the dark coat turns his head to stare at me, his face pale, eyes dark. I shiver, as if some evil spirit has entered my body, and lean against the post, lingering for a while, allowing the warmth of the sun to penetrate the sudden coldness I feel.

Crowds pass by – people heading to work, to lunch, home, shopping – all normal. I crave to be one of them; to choose my gender-related job, earn my living, have a family. Be normal.

I swallow hard and blink rapidly to avoid the brimming tears, my chest tight and heavy, before taking a step towards a solitary grey building surrounded by a high iron fence and wide gate.

The room is stark: white walls, brown furniture, a desk, three chairs. There is an A4 poster with the same mantra I've known all my life:

Goodness in Purity. Goodness in Life

Underneath, in black are the words:

Defend our Values. Keep us Safe. Report Difference

We sit opposite the consultant. My mum – in her purple suit with matching shoes, a bag slung across her shoulder – frowns, then forces a thin-lipped smile. She's always tidy and careful about her appearance, nothing like me. She pushes her broad shoulders back, straightens up and readies herself.

"Thank you for seeing us so soon, Mr Bowne."

"Yes, well, you should have come in six months earlier, Mrs Chadwick. You know the regulations."

I look at my mum. She purses her lips, but says nothing.

The consultant, his hairy moustache creeping me out, makes an effort to look at me.

"Cam, is it?"

I nod, gritting my teeth, knowing he's going to give me a speech.

"The law requires any young person who isn't already undergoing the Change by the age of fifteen to be formally assessed."

My mum shades her blue eyes, looking over at me, the sunlight through the window on my left blinding her. "I just thought a little more time..." She looks back at the doctor. "After all, she did start..."

My limbs begin trembling. I ball my hands into fists and stuff them in my jacket pockets. The touch of my mum's hand on my shoulder doesn't reassure me. Mr Bowne, with his shiny forehead, receding hairline and bushy-slug eyebrows, makes a grating noise at the back of his throat.

"I have the initial blood test results here." He taps a screen on the desk in front of him. "And there's no other way to say this, Mrs Chadwick, but your daughter's hormones are inadequate. She does not have sexual differentiation genes. There are neither fully developed XX chromosomes nor any indication of testosterone to advance into a male gender. We can only assume her genes are faulty. She obviously has Halted Growth Syndrome and will be classified as ungendered."

"HGS. You mean a Golem?" I stutter.

"'Golem' is not a term we use."

"What then? 'Zombie'?"

He grunts and looks at me as if I'm an imbecile, before turning to my mum. *Am I some creature he can't bear to behold?*

"We prefer 'HGS'. Although it seems your daughter's body intended a womb and ovaries, the actual growth of them didn't happen. It's been interrupted – 'halted'. It's rare for the Change to commence and not be finalised nowadays – we've been trying to eliminate it through our purity programme, but it isn't an easy task, as you can well imagine."

A sharp pain cuts across my chest and my heart begins thudding in my ears. *It can't be true.*

My mum's voice is shrill. "But surely you can do something to kickstart it again? Hormone treatment? Anything?"

"Had you brought her in at twelve, there might have been a chance, but it's too late now. Gene therapy and hormone treatment are forbidden at an advanced age. The consequences are just too dangerous. We have learnt from our past mistakes."

Their words fade in and out. '... intended ovaries and womb... Halted Growth Syndrome'. *What's inside me, then? Just a black hole?* My pulse is pounding in my ears and my limbs feel weak. I try to focus on what they are saying.

"But we have no history of problems. I didn't know."

"Her father?"

"He died not long after she was born."

The questions in my head gradually rise to become a shrieking I can't control.

If I'm one of the ungendered, am I a Golem, a girl, a boy, or just nothing? How can I be just nothing? I'm here. I breathe. I'm living. This can't be happening to me.

My whole body simultaneously heats up and trembles. Instinctively, my arms wrap around my centre.

A pinging noise distracts me.

"Ah, a notification for further tests. Expected. They don't like the unknown. As I said, cases of HGS are fairly rare. More research is required to understand how we can eventually eradicate it. I'm sure you understand. We can't have the anomalies of one individual affecting our species or our dedication to protecting the human race."

The room goes quiet. My mum's face has blanched. I'm waiting for her to say something, to defend me in some way, to tell them they must be wrong. She's strong, always has been, but her lips just press more tightly together.

"They're allowing you a night together. That's good. It'll give you both a chance to chat and work through things."

What does he mean? This can't be right. What further tests are they talking about? I'm not a lab animal. I'm no longer in control of my body. My teeth are chattering and my limbs tingling. I hold myself upright through pure determination, focusing on keeping my shoulders back.

"Pick-up is tomorrow at 1:00 p.m. After that, Cam will go through the normal procedures. Everything will be explained after further tests."

He's handing something to my mum and standing up, wanting us out of his office.

"This includes some more information about the tests and how they work. There's a helpline on there as well." He walks around his desk. "I understand this is a shock, although you really should have known something was not right. Regulation means she needs to be removed from school immediately, and then all family members will need checking for faulty genes."

I hear my mum gasp next to me and, for the first time ever, she looks haggard, her cheeks sunken. I can't reach out to comfort her. I can't even speak. The world is unreal. I feel as if I'm in a boxed room, looking out of the window at another person's life.

My mum takes the offered literature and stands. "There isn't anyone but Cam and me."

The doctor clears his throat. "You'll still need checking, Mrs Chadwick. Just procedure. And, of course, when Cam turns sixteen, she'll be taken to a more permanent facility. I've already registered her. I'm sorry, but you know the law."

I can't help myself, can't help the shriek in my voice. "Where is it? What happens there?"

The doctor sneers at me. "That is no longer any of your concern. You should be grateful our leaders provide a safe place for the ungendered to contribute to our society without causing further harm. In the past, people like you were attacked by the masses. Now, we remove you for your own protection, and for the sake of the human race and our purity of life values."

His words hit me hard. I've heard them before, of course – we repeat them constantly at school and in formal assemblies – but now they're like a mallet smashing into my gut. I can't breathe.

The dull voice in front of me reels off dates, times and preparation information as the pounding drum in my head gets louder and louder. There's pain, so much pain. I lean over, clutching my body, trying to hold on. Swallowing hard, pushing the burning acid back down my throat, I close my eyes, attempting to gain control of the waves of sickness, but the chair I'm sitting on begins rocking. The table rises up in front of me, and then the walls crowd in, crushing me.

I gasp for breath, feeling as if I'm drowning. Blind spots flash in front of my eyes; a wail of terror reaches my ears as the tiles soar upwards. Unable to keep my balance, I pitch forwards, my head hitting the hard floor. I'm aware on some level of voices, words with lost meaning, squinting eyes, confused faces and tears, and then a dark and welcome silence takes me away from the unbearable horror film I've just plunged into.

CHAPTER THREE

A cold pressure on my head – pain. I reach up, squinting. Someone pushes my arm down.

"Cam, it's okay."

My mum's voice. She's leaning over me. Dark circles surround her eyes. There's a worried look, a sadness... and fear. It oozes out of her as she leans over me, like the odour of rotting cabbage.

She tries to hide it by smiling. "How's your head?"

My brain doesn't connect with my vocal cords quickly enough, so she answers my unspoken question.

"You fainted, but you're home now." She's stroking my hair. "Everything will be okay."

The blue ceiling comes into focus. "Fainted? At school?"

My throat is sore and voice quiet. My head pounds and a throbbing reverberates in my ears.

"Drink some of this. It will help you sleep."

My mum is holding a yellow container with a straw in it. She places the straw in my mouth, and I suck. The cold, bitter liquid dribbles down the back of my throat, cooling the burn.

"Not too much at once. Don't want you to be sick again."

"I was sick?"

"Yes, but it stopped a few hours ago. The doctor said it was from the fall – you hit your head hard."

My brow wrinkles. "I don't remember. What happened?"

"Don't worry about it now. Just rest."

"What time is it?"

"Two o'clock."

The curtains are drawn. Outside, the sky is dark.

"In the morning?"

She nods, her pale face lined with tiredness. "Sleep Cam, rest. You'll feel better tomorrow."

My eyelids are so heavy, I can't fight it.

Gradually, my mind falls into a fitful slumber.

I wake with a start, gasping, sure there's someone in my room, but there isn't. My head feels dull, and I groan as I lean towards my bedside cabinet, switch on the lamp and pick up my phone. There are twenty missed calls, three voicemails and five messages, all from Liddy. Grunting, I flick through the messages:

What's up?

Answer your phone.

Look, we need to talk. Something's happened.

Cam, call me back when you get this.

Call mee!

My brain's still fuzzy, as if a blanket of cloud is sweeping through it, numbing pain and blocking memory. The date and time make no sense, but out of habit, I press the recall button. The phone rings twice before Liddy answers.

"Where have you been?"

"Sick."

"Sick? I thought you went to the dentist."

"Dentist?"

I hear his dad's voice in the background.

Liddy begins whispering. "Cam, I'm not supposed to speak with anyone," he sniffs, "but I had to speak to you before they take me away."

"Take you away?" Nothing's making sense. I roll over and lay on my back.

"Didn't your mum tell you? I called last night."

"No. I think I fainted. Banged my head." I rub a tender lump on the side of my temple and wince.

He sniffs again. "Fainted?"

"Are you crying? Lid, what's up?"

There are a few seconds silence before he responds.

"Listen, I can't stay on the phone long. The school reported me. They're taking me to the reconditioning centre for treatment."

"What?"

His heavy gulps of breath make him stutter. "My dad brought them in. Signed the paperwork when I was at school. I should... I should have listened... to you. Acted like... like a boy."

I push myself up. Pain shoots through the side of my head. Something's nagging at me; something I need to tell him. I'm finding it hard to concentrate.

"But they can't do this." Now my voice is screechy. "You just needed more time to adapt."

A ghostly, dark image reflects back at me from the mirror opposite. I start, before feeling silly. *It's me.*

"They can, Cam. You know they can. They're coming on Monday at 10:00 a.m." He's sobbing silently into the phone now. "I won't be me anymore. I'm sorry."

"What are you saying sorry for?"

But I know why. Liddy's always been the strong one, always upbeat, always supporting me. Ridiculously, he feels he's letting me down.

"You will," I affirm before he can continue, crossing my legs and leaning forward. "Nothing will change who you are. I'll make sure of it."

He's quiet for a few seconds; seconds I want to fill in, but don't know what to say.

"You don't get it, Cam. I spoke to Joanna." His voice is trembling, and there's a whispery echo on the line, like he's cupping the phone. "They do something to your brain. Force you to change. She's on monthly injections to keep her from fighting back. It's all a lie..." Liddy's voice cracks again, as he battles for control. The gulping slowly lessens. "I'll try to remember you, try to be me, I promise. But I'm scared."

I swallow hard as tears fill my eyes. The thought of Liddy not remembering me makes my chest tighten so much I can barely breathe. "I'll help you. I won't let them change you, Lid. We'll record videos of you before you go, then when you get back we'll—" I know I'm grasping at straws.

He doesn't reply for a few seconds. I hear a snort, and a sound as if he's rubbing his nose.

"Your eye make-up will run." It's pathetic, I know. I just don't know what else to say; I don't know how to comfort him.

"Nah, washed that off before I got home." He's changing the subject. Shutting down. He doesn't do sympathy very well. He wants a distraction. "So, how did your dentist's appointment go? What's this about fainting?"

"Dentist?"

"Y'know, the appointment yesterday."

"My mum said I fainted. Head hurts a bit."

"Cam, did you really go to the dentist? You can tell me. I'm your best friend. Besides, I'll probably forget it by the time I come back, anyway."

I roll my shoulders, cringing at the thought. Glancing at my grey, distressed dressing table, I see for the first time the large bruise on the side of my head. I reach up to touch it, wondering how it was caused. Something about the gesture causes the walls to zoom in, crashing towards me as my stomach rolls in waves of sickness.

"No!"

"What?"

"No, no..." My voice is a shriek.

"What, Cam? What's going on?"

My chest heaves as I remember the consultant meeting and the test results. Unable to catch my breath, I gulp air as if I'm swallowing water.

Liddy's voice is distant. "Cam? Cam... you're scaring me."

Phone still in my hand, I rest my head on my knees, tears flooding down my cheeks.

The tinny voice of my friend screams down the phone. "Cam!"

I whisper the detested words, not sure if he'll hear. "Golem. I'm a Golem."

I press the disconnect button, unable to bear his response.

The car is dark with blackout windows, typical of official vehicles. No one can see in, but I can see out. Another sunny day; people going to work, shop, eat, spend time with family – normal stuff. I sigh and look at the broad-shouldered man sitting opposite me. His brown, dead eyes stare blankly ahead. I know what he is – I've seen a few of them around before, but never dared get close – a reconditioned Golem guard, like one of the zombie horrors we played as kids, given the choice to serve the community. I wonder who he was before he made that choice and whether I'll be given the same option.

Would I take it? Forget everything about myself? No 'me' ever again, living without memory or emotions?

Why would he choose to live like this if the compound is a humane place? And if the segregation is necessary to maintain the Holistic Law, why did they give him a choice in the first place? Surely, they wouldn't even let him back into society if he was dangerous? I'd never given much thought to it before, but now the questions bombard me. My face heats up as I consider these alien ideas.

Dead Eyes hasn't moved, not even a twitch. His duty is to escort me to the test centre. They say escort, but really, it's just to make sure I don't run. Some do. I've seen them on the news, shackled and dragged into police cars, local leaders assuring us we are all safe once more.

Safe from what? People like me.

Last week I was a school kid taking history, and this week I'm spreading genes of destruction, destroying our society, breaking the law. If I'm ungendered, how can that be possible? I can't have kids, and it isn't as if genes are a disease. Nothing makes sense anymore.

After speaking with Liddy yesterday, I crashed. Literally felt everything falling in on me. Before I knew it, I was rocking in my mum's arms. For hours, the tears fell.

"It's okay. It's okay."

"Why, Mum? Why me?"

"I don't know, Cam. I wish I could take your place."

But she can't, and it isn't okay. It'll never be okay again.

Standing on the doorstep today, she'd hugged me tightly, not wanting to let go. There was nothing left to say, nothing we *could* say. She doesn't know why this has happened or how to stop it. And now, I just feel empty, like the guard in front of me. It's as if I've dried up inside and am letting the world carry my nightmare fate forwards, like a journey on a train that I know is heading for a collision.

We turn into a small car park and pull up. The large gates clang as they automatically close behind us. The man sitting next to me leans over to open the door. He smells of disinfectant or some sort of strong carbolic soap.

"Please get out."

He waits for me to move before stepping out himself. His movements appear deliberately slow, or maybe it's just me. Perhaps I've acquired microscopic bug-eyes and am able to see every last detail. They say when you're afraid, your brain does weird things. Now is one of those times. Every action is unnatural, taking a long time to happen. He grabs my bag. The door slams. The car moves towards a parking bay. The engine is switched off. And still, I'm standing in the same spot.

"This way."

His monotone voice wakes me up. I follow him around the back of a tall, grey building to a metallic door. Above it is a logo – the outline of a multi-coloured phoenix – and the word 'Regen'.

He presses his hand against a security pad and a door swings back to reveal a white hall. There is a reception desk, behind which sits a lady. From a distance, she looks normal. It's only when she speaks that I notice her hollow eyes and realise she's another one of them.

"Name?"

"Camelia Chadwick."

She hands me a wide-topped, glass vial as she taps something onto a screen. "Spit into this."

I frown, but do as she says, then hand it back.

She places a stopper in it and hands it to the guard. "Room 462."

And that's it. No explanation, no reassurance. She doesn't need to. I'm a nobody, a deformity to be purged from society. My teeth clamp down on the soft flesh inside my cheek and I relish the pain. The more pain, the better. Soon I'll feel nothing. I look at the door we came through and wonder if I can escape, but there's no way out. I just need to get through this.

My mind flicks back to this morning. My mum had been flipping the last pancake onto a pile when she'd reached for her pills. She has this hereditary condition which makes her blood clot and normally she takes the medicine as soon as she gets out of bed, but this morning she'd forgotten.

My favourite breakfast is pancakes and chocolate spread, with strawberries on the side. We always have it at the weekend. But this morning wasn't a weekend and watching her was like a death knell, like she knew I was already lost. In the end, neither of us could eat, so we'd just pretended, biting the ends of the strawberries.

"You'll be back in a couple of days." She was neither convincing nor confident.

"I know."

I'd looked away at a mark on the yellow walls, wondering vaguely what it was.

"They're not going to take you. I won't let them." She'd grabbed my hand, squeezing tightly. "I'll work something out, I promise."

I'd pulled my hand away. "Work out what, Mum? What can you do?"

She'd flinched at my tone, her eyes watering. I'd regretted my outburst instantly. My condition would affect her, too; she'd have to go through the tests.

At least she's normal. She won't have to live her life segregated in a camp.

"Sorry, but what? What exactly can be done? Nothing!" I'd started screeching. "That doctor said I have less than six months and then I'm gone. They'll wipe my identity, wipe my memory and send me to the Golem compound. Isn't that what happens? Well, isn't it?"

She'd got up, sniffing, and left the room, muttering something about, "Should have contacted them sooner."

I'd felt my face heat with guilt, but then realised it didn't matter. Soon, my mum, Liddy, school, all of them would be gone. That was exactly when my insides went cold and dark, like a solar eclipse masking the sun, and the thought occurred to me.

I may as well take on my role as Golem, now.

The guard is leading me to a large, metallic lift. The doors close and a blurred image watches me. Distorted by the reflective surface, all I can see are my dark eyes, glowing out of a pale face. I turn away, disinterested, no longer caring. This is how I'll be, a blur; nothing of my former self.

CHAPTER FOUR

They've moved me to a one-bed room and told me to wait. It's typical of any hospital, really. White walls, windows to the left, a metal-framed bed plonked against the wall, a couple of chairs, a side cabinet with a plastic water jug and glass, and a cupboard to the right. There's also a small *en suite*, with white towels and a green robe hooked on the back of the door. Some other previous occupant must have left it behind. I shudder, wondering what happened to them.

A man in a blue cotton outfit walks in and sits down on one of the chairs. He's tall with dark hair and brings with him the smell of citrus aftershave.

"Miss Chadwick, I'm Dr Peter Schultz and will be administering your tests. May I call you Camelia?"

Balancing on the edge of the bed, my legs dangling, I shrug my shoulders in response. "Does it matter?"

"Well, we do like to keep things informal at such a difficult time; try to help you relax." He smiles but there is a sadness in his gaze, as if he knows this is the worst day of my life.

I glare back but find I can't keep it up. I'm drawn to his pupils. They grow bigger and bigger until his irises are only a thin circular outline. For a second my mind clouds over, as if I'm being dragged down into a deep sleep. I wonder what's wrong with me and shake it off, waving my hand as if I'm swatting a fly away.

"Relax?" After a morning of trying to suppress my emotions, this one word has my stomach tensing. Taking a deep breath, I jump off the bed and move towards the darkened window. No one can see in, and I can't see out. "How's that supposed to work, then?" I spit.

"Strange!"

I whip around to look at him. He's frowning.

"What's strange?"

"Normally, people find my words" – he hesitates, as if searching for the right words – "comforting."

"Comforting? No one's spoken to me since I arrived two hours ago. Why am I here?"

"Your test results showed some anomalies."

"I know I have HGS. I know I'm a Golem." I stride to the bathroom door, fold my arms across my chest and turn to face him. "Isn't that enough?"

"It's not the end of your life."

"Isn't it?"

He fiddles with the pen in his hand and looks down at his notes.

"You're going to take me away anyway when I'm sixteen, so why more tests now?"

My heart beats loudly, my ears pound and I take a second deep breath, trying to calm down, but his words provoked me. My jaw tightens; my voice becomes raspy and threatening when he doesn't respond.

"Oh, so you mean I have a choice. Well, if that's how it is, I think I'll pack up now." I sneer and laugh, a short, juddery explosion.

The calm façade I've been so careful to control was cracking up in front of this ridiculous man, like underground lava forcing its way to the surface. He frowns as I spit out my words.

"My choices are rather limited, wouldn't you say? A guard, receptionist or manual worker, with no emotions, no life, no family, or – lucky me! – go to the compound and work till I die."

He stares back, his face neutral and I begin to wonder if he's half Golem, too.

"'Golem' isn't a word we use here. The term is 'ungendered'."

I scoff at his words. "My body has stopped growing and you're all calm, thinking just because you call it 'ungendered' everything's suddenly okay." I open the bathroom door and walk in. "Excuse me if I don't feel reassured."

Slamming the door shut, I lean across the sink, breathing heavily as I turn on the tap and splash cold water across my hot face. I watch my reflection in the mirror. Water dribbles down my chin. My dark hair is damp, my fringe sticking to my forehead. I push it aside and stare, looking for the person who is me – hazel, almond-shaped eyes, small nose and wide cheeks. I touch the dimple in my chin as if somehow that makes me more real, but I'm not who I thought I was. Not anymore. Not ever.

"Camelia, are you okay?" The doctor is tapping on the door. "I know this has been a shock, but could you please come out?"

Picking up a soft hand towel, I mop up the drips on my chin and return to the room, trying to stifle the anger curdling in my stomach.

Don't feel anything. Shut down!

Returning to the bed, I pretend normal. He continues as though everything is.

"The tests will be completed by tomorrow and then you can return home. Nothing will happen yet."

"Five months left to be me, then."

For a second, a flicker of confusion crosses his eyes, but it passes.

"We'll start with blood, then skin, hair, urine, bone marrow, an EEG, a CT scan, various X-rays, and—"

"What for? None of it matters."

"Of course it matters. Just because you're one of the ungendered doesn't mean you're not part of the human race."

"Then why will I be segregated, sent to a compound?"

"It's the law. Genetics need to be protected, or we'll never survive as a race."

Having heard the words in lessons, I understand their meaning, but they no longer make sense.

"How am I going to affect anyone? It isn't a disease, is it? And that guard is allowed out. Why's that, then?"

I stifle a sob, pinching my arm to cause pain. He looks at me, frowning again and for a second, I think he might actually answer the question.

"Perhaps I should let you settle in and come back later."

"No," I snap at him, as if he's to blame for everything. "If I only have five months to live, I want to go home as soon as possible."

He hesitates, pulling up a chair and sitting down opposite me.

"As you know, you have a differentiation in your chromosomes."

"What's that, exactly? How can I have started the Change but then stopped? No one's telling me anything."

"We do get people who don't go through the Change, but there are few recorded cases of those who begin and then stop. Some sort of protein throwback from the past that may have been awoken when our predecessors sought to utilise junk DNA. We aren't permitted to tell you everything at this stage, and research is still very new, so checking these things is important to make sure we can proceed without complications. We don't want people to suffer unnecessarily."

"Suffer? Suffer!"

This man has a way of speaking that makes me just lose it. I think of Joe, of what they'll do to Liddy and how they could easily take away my memories. I might not remember my mum after they've finished.

That's when something inside me explodes. Shaking, I storm towards him. My arms outstretched, fingers taut, I focus in on the pulse of his neck, wanting to squeeze tight, wanting his eyes to bulge, to turn his life into nothing. Rage roars through my head like a waterfall shattering a smooth lake. I can't control it; I don't want to. The world around me narrows and I fly forwards, going for the kill.

"I hate you. Hate you all!"

Within a flash, he darts away. How he moves so quickly to the door, I don't know, but I fling his chair against the wall, smashing a mirror. Somehow, it makes me feel better, stronger. I move to the bedside table and yank at the lamp, throwing it against the window blinds. I look around for something else. Not much left but the bed. I reach for the mattress and tip it onto the floor. It feels as light as a feather. Adrenaline burns through me, its heat warming my cold veins.

"Please calm down. Nothing will come of this."

"Nothing?"

I move towards this man who's responsible for changing my life. How dare he speak to me as if everything is normal?

"You take everything from me and expect me to be calm?" Spitting out the words, my breath is heavy. A crazy laugh snorts through my nose. "I'm damaged, am I? You think I'm damaged?"

His eyes flick behind him and, just as I turn to see what's happening, I feel the prick of a needle in my neck. Freezing liquid darts into my muscles, numbing my shoulders and arms, zooming through my body and into my legs. I feel myself falling. Someone catches me under my arms and lays me down on the floor. An unknown female face appears above mine.

"Your actions are unacceptable."

I try to move my arms, pull my legs up. Nothing works. She's still staring at me.

"Until you leave, you'll remain paralysed from the neck down. Once the tests are completed, you'll be allowed to move again. Just because your genes are faulty, you think you can attack the doctors who are trying to help you. Your behaviour is improper, and now you'll face the consequences."

"No, wait. I'm sorry." I feel tears dripping down my cheeks. "I don't know what happened. I didn't mean to—"

But she's walking away from my view. My apology means nothing. I hear someone else moving in the room. Things being picked up. Then, like a doll, I'm dragged onto the bed, a pillow placed under my head, a cotton blanket thrown across my body. Dr Schultz appears, his eyes sad again.

"I'm sorry, but for now you have to accept this. A nurse will be in shortly to prepare you."

"Wait! Wait..."

Looking up at the white ceiling, I scream until my voice is hoarse, but no one comes.

"I don't understand," I whimper to myself. My plan was to keep calm, get through it and go home. I just don't get what happened.

I make an effort to slow my breathing, calm my mind, but still feel panicky. My chest must be rising, but I have no sense of it, no sense of my arms or legs, as if there's nothing below my neck. I can't even look down to make sure my body is there. A dizziness courses through my brain, numbing my thoughts, heating up my face.

"I'm alive. I am alive."

I say it over and over, louder and louder, screaming at the ceiling, as if somehow the words will help, but at the back of my mind, a tiny voice whispers, *For now...*

"Now, then," a female voice fills the air, "are you going to behave?"

An ultra-pale, thin face with dark eyes peers over me. I grit my teeth, determined to control myself. I hear someone else in the room, and flick my eyes towards the noise, but can't see who it is.

"We're here to help you prepare for the tests."

She shakes out a white gown in front of me.

"Normally, the patient would dress themselves in this, but as you're restricted, we're going to get you sorted."

She smiles as if I'm an invalid who doesn't quite understand what's going on. A man appears to my right. He must notice the look in my eyes.

"No need to be embarrassed. I'm a nurse, seen a lot of nakedness in my time."

He grins to reassure me.

Not helping!

"No, really, just un-paralyse me and I'll do it myself. I'll behave, I promise."

"I'm sorry, we tried Dr Schultz's method, and it didn't work. Now we do it the hard way."

The pounding noise in my ears gets louder as the man heaves me into a sitting position and the woman begins lifting my top over my head. I feel my face get hotter and hotter, embarrassed at the thought of them seeing my faulty body, and yet I was incapable of fighting back. I wear a padded bra, even though I have little to fill it. It just makes me feel a bit more normal. As she learns over and unclips it, tears fill my eyes.

"I want to call my mum. She should be here."

The female nurse smiles again as she pushes my arms through the sleeves and fastens the back of the gown. The man holds my neck and head as he lays me down on the pillow.

"You can't have any metal on you, so I'm just going to unclip your earrings."

I hear the noise of my shoes and socks being taken off, then my jeans and underwear. Closing my eyes, I give up, knowing I can't stop them doing whatever they want. I focus on the pounding in my ears to dissolve the room around me. At least the noise in my head tells me my heart still beats, the blood still flows through my veins and, independent of what they do, I'm still here.

The day fades in and out. I'm lifted on and off trollies and rolled into machines. I hear voices explaining injections, scans, X-rays and other stuff, but don't take any notice. They don't require my co-operation. My body doesn't belong to me, is nothing more than a mannequin they jab and prod, so I shut down and ignore everyone, closing my eyes, pretending they don't exist. The last jab mercifully puts me to sleep for the night. At least tomorrow I'll wake up knowing I can go home.

Someone's whispering. Too sleepy, I ignore it, but he's persistent.

"Camelia, wake up."

A hand grabs my chin, moves my head around, and then I feel a sharp slap across my cheek.

"Wake up!"

The shock startles me, but fighting the drugs is hard. Someone lifts each eyelid and shines a light across my rolled-back eyes.

"The sedatives are strong, but you need to listen."

He slaps me again and I breathe in, gradually becoming aware of the danger. There's a man in my room. I'm alone and unable to do anything. I fight the drug, open my eyes wide and begin a scream, but his hand smothers my mouth.

"No, don't scream."

And suddenly, I'm wide awake, my breathing heavy. A face looms over me. Dark eyes, a sweaty smell. Around him, the room is pitch-black. He leans forward and I feel his warm breath against my left ear as he speaks.

"It's Dr Schultz and I'm here to help you, but if you scream, we'll both be in trouble. Please, give me a chance to explain."

I gulp in air and turn my head towards him as much as I can. My neck and shoulders tingle, as do my fingers and toes – a welcome numbness. Realising his face is close, he pulls back a little.

"What's going on?"

"The tests are finished," he's whispering, "and tomorrow they'll let you go."

"Why are you here?"

"The cell abnormalities show not only a halted growth syndrome, but also that you are receptive to the AP protein. They're looking for people like you."

My brain feels dull. "Huh?"

His eyes flick towards the door and then he leans in closer again. His hot breath tickles my cheek.

"I know this isn't clear, but it is serious. Your condition means the plan has changed. Tomorrow you'll go home, but they'll pick you up in two days."

"But I'm supposed to have five months."

"Not with your results."

I'm having difficulty keeping my eyes open. Concentrating on what he's saying is almost impossible.

"I don't understand." My words slur.

"I can't explain everything tonight, there's no time. If I'm caught, my cover will be blown."

"What cover?" More confusion as I think about my favourite woollen blanket at home.

"In your jacket pocket is a telephone number and a codeword. Call the number and they'll tell you the rest. Don't use your phone or your mother's. They'll be watching."

"What? Who?"

"Just follow the instructions – it may save your life."

His scent is a mixture of antiseptic and faintly gone-off eggs.

"My life's in danger?"

"Yes, and remember, you only have a couple of days. I can't do any more. Make the call."

I feel him move. The door opens and a hallway light shines through for a second, before he quietly leaves and shuts the door behind him.

I stare up at the dark ceiling.

What a weird dream!

I want to remember it, understand its meaning, but it fades into sludge as the drugs take control and my mind slips back into a dreamless sleep.

CHAPTER FIVE

"Time to wake up."

Light floods into the room from a barred window on the right. My eyes droop and my head feels too heavy to lift. My desert-dry tongue is stuck to the roof of my mouth.

"You'll feel some numbness, but within an hour the paralysis will have worn off completely."

It's the same nurse from yesterday, but a different room. She leans over me, lifting my back and propping me up with a couple of pillows. It's only then I notice two drips attached to my body, one a clear liquid dripping towards me, the other a dark yellow, going out. She notices me staring.

"They'll both be removed once you can get up, and Dr Schultz will be in to check on you shortly. After that, you can get dressed and go home."

She looks at me, expecting some sort of answer, so I nod my understanding.

"Good."

She moves to the end of the bed, unveils my feet, and begins prodding me with a wooden stick. "Can you feel this?"

"It tingles." My voice is hoarse, my brain fuzzy.

"Good." She runs the stick along my arm. "And this?"

"Yes," I mumble, and wince.

With the tingling come sharp pains, starting in my arms and then scattering across my body, as if a sudden lightning storm is flashing through me.

"You should expect slight pain and aches as the paralysis leaves you. We can give you something for it."

"No, I'm fine."

She looks at me, probably checking to see if I'm sane.

"No more drugs."

"As you wish."

After a few more checks, she heads for the door. "You're recovering well and should be back to normal by this afternoon." She smiles. "I'll order the car for 2:00 p.m."

"One minute... what time is it now?"

She looks at her watch. "Nine." *I'll be glad to see the back of this one.*

"What?"

"Nine."

"No, what did you say after that?"

She frowns. "Nothing."

"Yes, you did. You said you'd be glad to see the back of me."

She stares at me for a second and tuts. "You lot are just freaks." With that, she leaves me.

I stare around the room. She's not wrong, I guess. Everyone will think of me as a freak. The kids at school will talk about me for a while. *Cam, the freak!* I can hear their voices in my head. *Hope I didn't catch anything! D'ya think she's a zombie now?* Even with all their horrid comments, I'd still rather be there than here.

The bright light coming in from the window sends grey lines across the floor. Next to me is a small bedside table. I look down at my body. My arms and hands have a smattering of plasters and bandages. Yesterday is a blur, but the scars remain.

The two bags hooked up to me can only be liquid food and waste. I frown in distaste at the yellow one, wondering how that is removed. Then I notice my feet under the blanket and focus hard on wiggling my toes. All I get for my effort is a flash of pain down my right leg. Sighing, I flop my head back against the pillow and follow the spidery crack from the bathroom doorframe up towards the ceiling. The magnolia walls bounce back at me, making me dizzy, and so I close my eyes and drift.

"Camelia... Come on, Camelia, wake up."

As if I'm snorkelling in deep water and someone is calling to me from the shoreline, the words take time to reach my brain. Eventually, I drag myself upwards and resurface. Dr Schultz sits in front of me.

"Ah, there you are," he smiles.

His eyes crinkle, setting off a memory, something important, something to do with the doctor, but I can't hold on to it. Frowning, I try to focus, but the thought is gone.

"Do you know who I am?"

"Yes." My voice is barely audible, so I speak again, louder this time. "Dr Schultz."

"Good. Now, could you try moving your left hand for me, please?"

I give the mental order and turn my head, expecting nothing, so when my hand lifts off the bed, I can't help smiling. "It moved."

"That's a good sign. Try your other hand."

He sits with me for half an hour, testing my increasing functions and measuring pain levels. Gradually, a sense of my body returns. I'm no longer a floating head. Although my limbs throb, I'm relieved. Eventually, I'm unhooked from the food and urine bags and told to sip a sweet and salty liquid. It oils the back of my rusty throat. Within seconds, I need the loo.

"Get her a bedpan, Nurse."

"No." I look at Dr Schultz. "I want to get up."

He looks as if he's not sure about it.

"I feel a lot stronger." *And need to get out of here.*

"Okay, but the nurse will help you."

Again, I hear the woman's voice.

Freak! She needs to be taken away from the public.

I look at the doctor. He doesn't react, just looks down at his stupid clipboard, flicking sheets. I wonder if I should mention the drugs are making me hallucinate voices – well, that bitch of a nurse's voice, anyway – but I know if I do, they'll keep me in longer. Maybe going mad isn't such a bad thing; the crazy might cope better than the sane.

Still, I try to behave normally. With her arm under me and across my back, my feet touch the floor for the first time. Grimacing, I lean on her heavily as I slide them across the cold tiles, slithering more than walking, until we eventually reach the bathroom. She sits me on the toilet, and then, to give me some privacy, stands outside the bathroom with the door slightly ajar. I don't even feel embarrassed; I'm way past that now. I just want to go home.

Seeing my mum rush out of the door and open the gate brings tears to my eyes.

"Mum!"

She throws her arms wide and pulls me to her. Her flowery smell comforts me and I breathe deeply.

"Are you okay?"

Still weak, I stand awkwardly with my arms dangling. The guard who brought me back climbs out of the other side of the car and walks around.

"Mrs Chadwick."

She stands back, looking at me, clutching my shoulders.

"You're so pale. What have they done to you?" Her eyes glisten with concern.

"Think I need to sit down."

"Sorry, let's get you in."

Half holding me up, she guides me forwards. The guard follows.

"Mrs Chadwick." His voice is deeper this time, more forceful.

She glances over my shoulder.

"I have her bag and instructions from the doctor."

"Give me a second and I'll come back."

We make it to the living room. The familiar smell of lemon polish fighting the dust fills my nostrils as I sink into the sofa. My mum lifts my legs up and gently pushes my head into a soft cushion, before covering me with a blanket.

"Rest, Cam. I'll be back in a minute."

Feeling safe at last, I close my eyes and let the world dissolve around me. I hear my mum come back in and feel sorry for her having a daughter like me. They'll make a show of taking me away; cameras and TV; the DC protecting the public and maintaining law. She'll be shunned. Might even lose her job and have to move. She'll be so alone; no one to walk in the local park with.

The thought reminds me of the last time we'd gone. I relive it almost as if I am there, half dreaming, half awake. We'd taken stale bread for the ducks, like we did when I was a kid, but they hadn't been interested in our offerings so, arm in arm, we'd decided to circle the lake a few times. Content in our own silent bubble, we didn't notice at first when a few of the kids from school passed by. They'd smirked and made comments about the 'zombie *lurgy*'. My mum had turned suddenly and exploded at them, swore she'd bash their heads together and knock sense into them if they didn't shut up. She'd half chased them away. They'd laughed at first, but then scarpered, not sure if she meant to act out her threats; a crazy mother protecting her crazy daughter. I'd giggled at the time, but now I just feel an aching in my chest. Salty tears slip down my cheeks. I wipe them away, sniff, and turn over, my face to the back of the sofa.

I hear my mum in the kitchen. The kettle's being switched on and paper is crumpled. She cries out as if she's in pain, walks back and forth, makes a drink and then calls someone, whispering her words, her tone frantic. I know something's going on and, if I focus, I could probably figure it out. My mum and I have always been close – often I know what she's going to say before she says it – but I let it all fade into background noise. I can't cope with more, not now. Maybe later I'll ask, but it's easier to just let the pain and worry go. Gladly, I let my nightmare world slip away, welcoming the bliss of thought-free sleep.

CHAPTER SIX

I wake with a start, sitting up suddenly and looking around. A lamp shines on my mum, who's asleep in the armchair, her head tipped to the side. I hear ticking and look at the wall clock. It's 2:20 a.m. My eyes flick to the drawn curtains. It's dark and quiet.

Realising I need the toilet and a drink (my mouth tastes so bad), I push myself up and stand for a second and test my weight, before leaving the room and heading first for the downstairs toilet and then to the kitchen. Mentally I check my movements. Though my body's still weak, my head's clearer.

Thank God!

Switching on a small lamp, I grab a glass from the cupboard and fill it with tap water before plonking myself down on a stool at the breakfast bar. In front of me, I notice an envelope with the phoenix logo on it. Underneath is my mum's name, Sonia Chadwick. Gulping back the tepid water, I stare at the envelope as if it is some live thing stalking me, readying itself to pounce. Instead, I pounce first, pulling out the letter and screwing up my eyes in the low light to read the words.

Dear Mrs Chadwick,

Your daughter, Camelia Chadwick, has now taken all required tests following notification of a potential ungendered condition, with abnormalities. The diagnosis was reconfirmed. Furthermore, abnormalities in her brain affecting cell development, which likely caused Halted Growth Syndrome were also discovered. Both will be further investigated once she is incarcerated. All details of the investigation will be kept strictly confidential. The Commission appreciates your support and understanding in this matter.

We are deeply sorry for your upcoming loss, but in line with constitutional law on purifying genetics, your child will be taken for reconditioning and isolation from the general public on 20th December at 9:15 p.m.

At the first read, I go too fast, afraid; on the second, I slow down, trying to grasp every word. Still, 'abnormalities in my magnetic field and number of chromosomes' doesn't mean much, but 20ᵗʰ December does – my birthday, only five months away. The date is set.

My hands fumble as I fold the letter and shove it back into the envelope. Involuntary shivering begins in my spine and ends up in my limbs. My teeth chatter as my head sinks lower and lower. Resting my cheek on the cold surface of the table, I let the tears leak. The world around me falls still as if it's all working in slow motion. From this angle, I see the tall fridge-freezer, with magnetic stickers on it – all the places I wanted to visit when I got older: waterfalls and mountains, cities and monuments. They dissolve through my tears. Unable to bear looking, I turn my head and face the plain, tiled wall.

"Cam?"

My mum's voice sounds strangely slurred, but it arouses me from my apathetic state. I sit up quickly, wiping my eyes. The shivering has lessened.

"Here, Mum."

Slipping off the stool, I head for the living room, glass in hand. She's at the doorway.

"How are you feeling? Do you need anything? Hot chocolate?" Her face is lined, worn out. I hold up the water to show I have all I need.

"Just thirsty."

She grabs me, squeezing tightly. "Oh, Cam..."

I'm not sure I can hold back the tears, so I gently push her away.

"Think I'll go to bed."

"Good idea. Do you need help getting up the stairs?"

"No. I'm okay, Mum, really."

"Right, then. I'll just switch everything off and follow you up."

"'kay."

Her eyes watch me for a second, judging whether I need support. I know she wants to hold onto me, squeeze me tight and never let me go, but her instinct not to frighten me battles with other emotions. She hesitates and I can tell she's hiding something, something important that's just beyond my reach. If I could concentrate, I might be able to figure it out, but I'm too weary, and the moment is lost as she turns towards the living room.

Climbing the stairs, I pull myself up by the banister. My body's so weary, for a second I consider just sitting down, but then my mum would worry, and I don't want her fussing. When I reach my room, I flip on the lamp and flop backwards onto the bed, my legs half on, half off. Only then do I notice I'm in the same clothes I wore when I left the clinic. Out of habit, I stuff my hand in my right pocket, looking for my phone. It isn't there. Checking the left side, I find a scrunched-up piece of paper. I unravel it and notice the phoenix immediately – a sheet of notepaper from the clinic, but I don't remember putting it in my pocket. Turning on my stomach, I crawl to the lamp to read the writing.

You have 2 days.
Call: 00923 57867924
Code: CH23 IO957
Don't use your phone.

I sit up, my forehead wrinkling. I feel I should know what this is. My stomach curdles with a creeping fear I can't explain. There is a knock on the door – my mum's outside.

"Cam?"

Quickly pushing the note under my pillow, I call out, "Come in."

She enters with a mug. "Thought you could do with a hot chocolate. Help you sleep." She places it on my bedside table, along with a couple of biscuits.

"Thanks."

With nothing else to say, the walls rebound in silence. She stands in front of me, hovering, wanting so badly to do something, anything to help me feel better.

"I'm okay. You look shattered. Go to bed."

It sounds dismissive and I cringe, but her sadness is killing me. It's as if she's crying on the inside and I can't bear watching it. She nods, still not saying the things she wants to say.

"Mum, do you know where my phone is?"

"Yes, it was in your bag. I put it in your drawer." She points to my bedside table.

"But I think it needs charging."

"Thanks."

She stares again, making me feel like a sick animal that needs observation.

"Really, Mum, I'm fine."

I don't mean to snap, but I need her to leave. As an afterthought, I add, "We can talk tomorrow."

She takes the hint, nods again and shuts the door behind her. Immediately, I grab the note and stare at it, trying to figure it out. Sighing, I reach for my phone and text Liddy.

You awake, Lid?

I wait for a response, but when none comes, I put the phone down and begin shrugging out of my jacket and looking for pyjamas. I hear a *ping* and dash back to my phone.

Am now.

Liddy's still typing, and I want to see what she says before I respond.

You wanna talk?

No.

What did ya wake me for, then?

Dunno.

He sends a sad face.

When did ya get back?

This afternoon.

What was the clinic like? Any cute doctors?

I know he's trying to cheer me up.

Dr Schultz wasn't bad, for a creep.

Huh! What did he do?

Nothing!

Come on... details?

I don't want to think about the clinic, or the letter. I begin to regret texting Liddy, when I hear a *ping* again.

Y'know, dark's my type. No slug on his lip, though.

He still doesn't get he's a boy. Guess it won't matter soon. My stomach sinks.

Deep voice or squeaky?

I play the game. When he's gone, I'll miss this.

Deep. Dark hair. Your type.

Ooh... no night-time visits?

Yuk!

LOL

And then, the room folds in on itself. I'm back in the clinic, it's pitch-black. His breath against my cheek.

Your life's in danger. Two days. The code.

My heart's pounding, my hands and forehead sweaty.

Call the number. They're coming for you.

Dizziness swarms through me. I tip forward, thrusting my head between my knees, forcing air between my gritted teeth. The phone falls to the rug, the pinging an endless echo in my ears – Liddy going crazy.

It can't be true. Must be a dream. The letter said I had until December. I scramble to drag the note out from under the pillow. Before my eyes, the evidence looms in black and white It happened, it really happened!

You have 2 days.
Call: 00923 57867924
Code: CH23 IO957
Don't use your phone.

I gasp and cling onto my pillow in a tight ball, squashing my face into it.

Maybe he was lying. *Why would he?*

The pillow is hot and steamy. Only when the craving for air becomes desperate, I uncurl and pull away from my soft anchor. The silent room comes back into focus, and I lie flat on my back, staring up at the ceiling. All that time wanting to move at the clinic and now I just want to remain rigid, as if somehow it will make it all go away. Why would the clinic tell my mum one thing, and the doctor tell me another?

Who do I trust?

I turn on my side and notice my phone is dead. Stretching to pick it up, I plug it into the charger by my bed. The screen flashes up again with a zillion messages from Liddy, the last of which is angry:

What's wrong with you? Just don't bother, then.

I click the dial button against his name and let it ring until it goes to voice message. Then I redial and wait. Several voicemails later, he picks up.

"What do you want?"

"Can you come here?"

"What, now?"

"N-need to show you something." I stammer, my voice low.

"Cam, you okay?"

"No."

"I'll be there in five."

"I'll be at the back door."

"'kay."

The phone goes dead, and I get up. I'm relieved Liddy only lives around the corner. He'll be here soon. I walk back and forth a couple of times and look at my watch. About thirty seconds have passed. Needing something to do, I decide I might as well change into my pyjamas and brush my teeth. I scrub hard, the stinging mint replacing the foul taste in my mouth. Picking up the scattered clothing, I dump it in a corner behind the door before creeping out into the hallway. Outside my mum's door, I stop and listen. There's a slight snoring, even and low, but she's a light sleeper, so I tiptoe down the stairs. By the time I reach the backdoor, Liddy's standing outside. I quickly unlock it and let him in, finger to my lips to shush the question on his lips. He nods, understanding the need to be quiet.

As we pass the kitchen bar, I notice the letter's still there and pick it up, along with half a packet of biscuits. Liddy follows, saying nothing until we reach my room.

"So, what's up?"

"Keep your voice low. My mum will wake up."

He sits on my bed, reaching for the biscuits. Liddy's addicted to anything sweet. He's already stuffed half of one in his mouth when I hand the letter to him.

"Read this."

Cramming in the rest of the biscuit inside his cheeks like a hamster storing food, he wipes his hand on his jeans and takes the letter.

"It's your mother's."

"Yes, from the clinic." I walk across to my desk and sit in the chair.

He seems to only glance at it before looking up, tears in his eyes. "Oh, Cam, on your birthday. How could they?" He drops the letter and rushes over to me, his arms hugging me tight. "It's just not fair. Why do they do this to us?"

"Liddy, stop, there's more." I hold his shoulders and push him back. "Something happened. I thought it was a dream, but I think it actually happened."

"What?"

He's sniffing, so I pass a box of tissues, waiting for him to calm down.

"There was this doctor."

"The dark one?" He half smiles.

"Yes, but that's not the point." I push back my fringe. "He said I'm in danger, that they're coming for me in two days."

"But the letter—"

"I know, I know, but he said I had some anomaly, something about my cells... I can't remember much, was sedated, but he said I had to escape. I don't know what to do."

Liddy flops on the floor. "Are you sure it wasn't a dream?"

"I wouldn't have believed it either, didn't even think of it until you started talking about 'night visits' and then it all came back to me. I found this in my pocket."

I hand the note to Liddy. His dark blue eyes squint, furrows form across his forehead.

"Is this real?" I don't get a chance to answer. "Well, obviously the note is, but I mean—"

"The doctor said some other stuff, something about they would explain it all when I called. I don't know what to do. What do you think?"

"Well, they could be some creepy, kidnapping, slave group."

"Not helping."

He looks away for a second, before turning back. "Call them. What have you got to lose? It's not as if you're going to meet up or anything, is it?"

There's some sense to what he's saying, but the slave bit was something that hadn't crossed my mind and I hesitate.

"Here," he passes me his phone, "do it now. If no one answers, at least you did something, and if something happens, I'm here."

"I can use my own phone." I move over to my bed, but he grabs my leg.

"Did you not read the instructions?"

"What?"

"It said don't use your phone."

"Oh yes, of course. Are you sure?"

"Course I'm sure! If it's a slave trade or a hoax, I'm gone by Tuesday and who knows when I'm back." He turns away, so I can't see his face. "They don't allow phones where I'm going."

With all my own troubles, I'd somehow forgotten his. Kneeling behind Liddy, I throw my arms around him and hold tight. He grasps my hand as I mumble into his neck.

"There must be something you can do, Liddy. Start conforming a bit. Show you're making progress."

He spins around, scorn on his face. "Not you, too." His anger turns to sadness. "Why doesn't anyone understand? I *am* right. This is me."

"Sorry."

He shrugs. "Make the call, Cam. I'm tired."

I nod, take the note from him and dial the number.

"Don't tell them your name."

"'kay."

Liddy presses speaker phone and we both listen to the ring tone, unsure what to expect. I look up and shrug. What were we thinking? It's the middle of the night. Liddy raises his eyebrows and leans over to cut it off just as a gruff voice speaks:

"Yes?"

I stare at the phone as if it's a hot coal I want to pass on. My eyes flash at Liddy and I mouth, "You speak."

He shakes his head and points at the code on the paper.

"Is anyone there?"

Feeling my face heat up, I swallow and stutter my answer. "Erm, code CH23 IO957."

The voice on the other end is deep. "You're from the doctor?"

"Er... yeah! Who are you?"

"He didn't explain?" He sounds surprised.

I shrug my shoulders. "No, he didn't tell me anything."

The man responds quickly. "How many days do you have?"

"I don't know. The doctor said two."

A few seconds of silence pass. My eyebrows lift. I want to know what Liddy thinks. He indicates for me to keep going, his hand spiralling through the air several times.

"Meet me at Abby's Coffeeshop on Wellington Street tomorrow, 10:00 a.m. sharp."

I glance up at Liddy and then back at the phone. "Wait, who are you?"

"No more dialogue. You want to be safe, meet me there."

"Where's Wellington Street?"

But the phone goes dead. Liddy and I stare at each other, his black pupils widen. "Well?"

"Well, what?" I stand, walk over to my window and turn around, hands on my hips. "Are you coming with me?"

Liddy straightens up. "You're going to meet some creep? You don't even know what he looks like."

I hesitate, swallow hard and stare at my pale face in my mirror. My response is definite. "What have I got to lose?"

"'kay. I'm coming, too."

CHAPTER SEVEN

"You look pale, Cam."

My mum's sitting opposite me at the breakfast bar, drinking coffee. She leans in to grasp my hand.

"I'm fine."

Her eyes narrow, showing worry lines at the corners. "It's Sunday" – her lips form an anxious smile – "how about we go out for lunch?"

"Can't. Liddy, I mean Lou and I are meeting up soon."

"Oh, well, I'll meet you both later then at that vegan place you like."

She attempts a solid smile, but the sadness inside her vibrates across the table like a dark cloud, navigating its way into my chest, causing a stabbing pain. I lean back on my stool and fake a casual mood.

"Y'know, it's his last day. They take him away tomorrow."

"Yes, he rang. The therapy's a good thing. Will help him a lot."

I know she's lying; I just don't know why.

"Help him? Mum, you didn't see Joe."

"Who?"

"Joe... Joanna. When he came back, he wasn't the same. And he'd lost his memory."

"It only affects some in that way. Lou will be fine. He's strong."

Another lie! She's not even blinking. She's just staring straight at me, as if willing me to understand some unspoken thought.

"What's going on, Mum?"

We've always been honest with each other. How can she talk about Lid like this? He's been like her second child; here more than his house until recently, when his dad forbade it.

She looks towards the window. I see her swallow hard. There are tears in her eyes.

"I have you to think of. I can't help Lou right now."

"But what if it were me and I forgot you?"

"To be honest, Cam, I'd rather you forgot me than go away for ever."

She touches the scar on her neck, a nervous gesture, one I've seen many times. Instinctively reaching over the table, I grab her hand and hold her fingers tightly. I want to reassure her, tell her everything will be okay, but the words are empty, untrue.

"I won't be going back to school, Mum. We can spend lots of time together."

I know what I'm saying might be a lie, but she nods, her face pale, eyes defeated.

"I wanted to talk to you, Cam. I think we should go on a trip, just you and me – maybe go walking in the Peaks."

"What about your work?"

"I'm going to take early bereavement leave. Would you like that?"

They call it bereavement leave, as if there's been a death in the family. An image flashes into my mind. I'm running in the street, knocking at every door and screaming, 'I'm not dead!' In reality, I just suck in my cheeks and hold my stomach tense, as if readying myself for the next punch in a boxing match.

"That'd be great."

I could promise her anything, especially if they're coming for me in two days. Nothing will make any difference. A lie is the least of my problems.

She smiles, relief in her eyes. "Really? I'll book it, then. We can go as early as tomorrow night, if you like."

"Er, yeah. Okay."

She's hiding something. I can tell, and she knows I know. We're just too close not to sense when one of us is lying. She probably knows I'm hiding stuff, too.

"What are you not telling me?"

Tears come to my mum's eyes again. She wipes under her lashes with a tissue. "I'm sorry, Cam. I can't talk about it right now. When we go away, I'll tell you everything."

The kitchen, so bright, so yellow, with wide windows, suddenly feels claustrophobic, as if the air is dense with humidity. Taking a deep breath, I stand.

"Fine. I'd better go, or I'll be late."

"Okay, have fun."

At the door, I turn for a second. She sits, her hands around a cold mug, her body rigid, as she stares down at the worktop. My chest feels tight, and I have the urge to rush back, to somehow hug the pain away for her. But I can't.

There's nothing I can do.

In the hall, I pull on my jacket, grab my phone and throw it in my canvas bag. Slinging it across my shoulder, I head out. I'm a bit early, but Liddy won't mind. We found Wellington Street online but will have to look for Abby's as it wasn't listed. Shouldn't be too hard if it exists. If it doesn't, we'll just turn around and come home, I suppose.

Liddy's early, too. He's already leaning against the red post box on the corner of my street – our designated meeting place since his father kicked me out. I get out my phone and pull up the map and directions as we head across the street. I'm staring at the screen as he speaks.

"I brought something."

"What?"

"Just in case."

As we reach a junction, I glance up to check for cars. Liddy grabs my arm to stop me crossing.

"Look."

I stare down into his open rucksack and gasp at the serrated breadknife.

"What's that for?"

"Well, we don't know who we're meeting." He zips up his bag and throws it over his back. "Think of it as insurance."

I grin. "Really? Which boxset have you been watching?"

"I'm serious, Cam, and you should be, too. I thought about it last night, when I got back. This could be a trap."

We cross the road and turn right on the path. The map's indicating that Wellington Street is a couple of turns away.

"I know." I stop again and take in Liddy's expression for the first time. His eyes have narrowed, his forehead creased. "Do you want to turn back?"

"God, no! I'd rather walk to a death of my own choosing than be dragged away and altered until I can't remember who, or even *what*, I am."

I wrap my arms around him and squeeze tightly. His hair smells of coconut oil. "Me, too."

We arrive at a bus stop with orange plastic seats. Without speaking, we both flip a couple open and sit.

"We're close." He picks at his manicured nails.

"I know." I tap his hand. "Don't do that. They'll split."

"You're giving me nail advice?" He holds the tips of my fingers. My nails are all different lengths, some cracked. "I could do yours, y'know."

"Nah, too much trouble."

He drops the offending object, tutting at my lack of interest.

"So, here's what I think. Whatever happens today" – he stands and walks over to the post as if reading the timetable, before glancing back at me – "we don't separate."

"Agreed."

He turns around, hands on his hips. "We don't get into any vans."

"Goes without saying."

"And we don't give away our names or addresses."

"Of course."

I glance down the road. In the distance, I see the bus rambling towards us.

"What if they have guns? Force us into a car?"

I'm starting to feel a bit sick. Then I have a thought. "Ooh, I know – let's turn on tracking."

His eyes light up. "Good idea."

At fourteen, we're allowed phones. Both of us found out our parents had installed tracking devices on them and so had immediately disabled the software. My mum was upset, but finally agreed. Liddy's parents weren't too bothered. The tracking regulation for minors is optional. Within seconds, both our phones *ping*, informing us the software is enabled.

I pull my bag over my shoulder and across my chest. "It's nearly ten."

"A last adventure, then."

My eyes blur with tears I immediately blink away. We used to talk about adventures when we were kids; what we would do when we were grown up, that sort of stuff.

Once, we went on a history trip to a genetics museum. The teacher led us around, telling us of the dangers of gene manipulation; how irradicating faulty genes in foetuses led to 'gene perfection' becoming a saleable item. There were pictures of the babies born with preferred traits and genders. That's how all this started. That's why we're here now. At the time, Lid and I had giggled and sat at the back of the bus, swapping made-up creepy tales of strange foetuses born with tails and glowing eyes. Little did we know we'd be the odd ones out, in an adventure so much bigger than anything we ever dreamt of.

"Y'know, Lid, my mum told me that in her grandmother's time, people were different."

"When the Change happened before birth?"

"Yeah, that, but also people would march against the government if they disagreed with stuff. Get them to change the law."

Liddy sits next to me. "Imagine that today. You know what I would want changing?"

"You, me... *this*!" I throw out my arms in frustration, but Liddy understands.

He smirks. "My dad would still be a prat."

I look down the street. The bus is a minute away.

"Probably, but if we'd lived a hundred years ago, we wouldn't be doing what we're doing right now. We'd be in school."

Liddy finishes my sentence. "Moaning about something else."

We smile at each other, but I sense the turmoil between us. A mixture of shock and grief, hopelessness and fear, all combine to make a confusing, emotional mush.

"What we're doing is probably against some law." I shudder at the thought of being caught.

"So, I guess we're secret protestors, then!" He grabs my shoulder. "Cam, it couldn't be much worse if they caught us. What are they gonna do? Drag us away? They're already doing that."

We take deep breaths and then hug each other; a last chance to change our minds, though we know we won't.

I'd felt calm to start with, but now my pulse pounds in my ears. I look up at Liddy. His lips form a tight line as he grabs my hand and squeezes my fingers.

"Okay, first right, second left."

I nod as we stand and walk away; I sense we're crossing a line. A tingling feeling runs down my spine. There's no turning back. Whatever happens now, this will always be the point I remember: the blue bus pulling up, the pungent smell of rubber tyres on a hot road, the sound of automatic doors opening – all of it will forever be part of this memory; a crossroad in our lives.

I fortify myself with the thought that each step we take is like a long-ago protest. We're defying the law, defying those who would see us taken away and, instead, making our own decisions and choices. Whatever becomes of us, whatever the consequences, it will be because *we* chose it.

CHAPTER EIGHT

The red-brick buildings around us are tall and old. There are a couple of businesses – a stationery shop, an office equipment store – but the further we go, the more shopfronts are boarded up with 'for sale' or 'to let' signs. Liddy grins as he stares through a cracked window.

"Perfect place for my parlour."

"Oh right. Pooches and their mums?"

"No way. Too smelly." He flicks back his hair and looks at me. "A special shop for girls like me."

Knowing it will upset him if I say anything to the contrary, I ignore the 'girl' reference.

"And what would you sell?"

"Hair, make-up, manicures, massages. Maybe even clothes – large sizes."

"And you think people would come?"

"Oh, definitely."

"Yeah, they'd be dressed in security uniforms and drag you away."

There's a sadness in his eyes and I regret the jibe instantly.

"A girl can have dreams. Besides, they're already planning to drag me away."

"Me, too," I mumble as we turn onto Wellington Street and look down the short road.

"It's a dead end."

"Got that!" We stop and scan the area.

"And deserted."

"Yep!"

There is a smell of decay, of dead things. "We're in one of those zombie films. Everyone knows we shouldn't go down the street, and yet we're stupid enough to keep going."

"Cheery thought!"

I giggle at Liddy's comment and watch as he digs out the knife.

"Told you we needed insurance."

I notice my heart pounding a little harder. "Can we make another rule?"

"Sure. Go for it."

"Don't let the other guy grab the knife."

"Perfect."

We both snort as we make our way down the middle of the narrow road. No cars, people or anything. The road has a huge number of cracks and potholes. We circle past a drain without a cover. It stinks of rot and damp. On passing it, we fall into step with each other, our elbows touching.

Liddy starts singing a song in a deep, grating voice. "Don't speak with strangers. Creep away from the dangers. Yeah, yeah…"

"What's that?"

He looks over at me, his lips curling, a wildness in his eyes. "Don't speak with strangers who smile."

I stop, laughing as he plays an air guitar, using the metal of the knife as a fretboard. "You're mad. Serves you right if you cut yourself."

We're walking slowly, half expecting someone to jump out of one of the deserted buildings.

"AGRA."

"Who?"

"Brilliant rock band."

"One of your ancient, dead ones. Why would I know them?"

"You don't know anyone."

"I do."

He tuts. "You need real music in your life."

I tut back and point to a dusty signboard. "There, see – Abby's Coffeeshop."

"It's boarded up."

We walk up to it and peer through cracks in the plywood.

"Can't see anything."

I push the door, knowing it won't open. There isn't even a handle.

Liddy sighs. "And I was looking forward to a coffee." After a second, he adds, "Let's go, Cam. This doesn't feel right."

"D'ya mean the ghost street or the pounding in my chest?"

He has an odd, half-grin on his face. His eyes flit up and down the road. "See that roof?"

I follow the direction of his upwards-pointing knife. All I see are red tiles, a broken chimney, and a backdrop of grey sky. "See what?"

"That's where the camera is."

"What camera?"

"The Watcher's up there monitoring us, and because I brought our insurance" – he waves the knife at me – "he's too scared to show his face."

Watchers are what we call government spies; people who inform on neighbours. I've always thought Liddy's dad might be one.

"Right!" My laugh is clipped. "You're stupid."

"Nah, just cool." He waves the knife around in front of him, dancing from one foot to another, leering at the non-existent camera. "Ya want some?"

I giggle and reach for my phone. "Smile, superhero!"

With a manic look in his eyes, Liddy lifts the knife under his chin and sneers. I click the shot and am about to show him when I hear a voice from behind us.

"Who are you?"

Startled, we both turn. A man – or maybe a woman, it's hard to tell at first – stands in the doorway. He's tall, wears a baggy black hoodie, which covers most of his forehead, sunglasses and a neck scarf across his mouth. Liddy holds the knife high.

"Is that a threat?"

Definitely a man; his voice is low and gruff.

"Depends."

He ignores Liddy and looks at me. "Why are you outside my door?" He crosses his arms and leans against the wooden doorframe.

"Er, sorry, didn't know anyone lived here. Was supposed to be meeting someone."

Liddy backs up. I follow.

"We'll go now."

The person clears his throat. "Wait." I glance back. "Code."

"Eh?"

"Code."

I heard him the first time, but my mind has gone blank. Liddy digs his knuckles in my side and points to my pocket. I pull out the piece of notepaper and pose it as a question. "CH23 IO957?"

The man nods. "There are two of you."

Liddy splutters. "I'm the insurance."

"Well," he directs his words at me, "you and your insurance had better come in." There's a hint of mirth in his tone.

After he disappears behind the door, Liddy grabs my arm. "Well?"

I shrug. "Guess it's what we came for."

The man pops his head through the doorway. "Don't worry, it's just me. I'll stay on the other side of the room and leave the door open."

I nod as he disappears again.

"Stay here, Liddy." Before he has a chance to protest, I explain, "I'll check the place out. If he's telling the truth, I'll call you in. If not, make a run for it and call the police."

He glances at me, looks down the street and then comes to a decision. "Okay, but take the knife, just in case."

I take it from him, the heavy handle dangling from my hand.

"No, hold it up and don't be afraid to use it."

Holding the knife high, I step forwards and peer around the door. A bulb hanging on a thin strand of wire provides a dim light. The man is standing in the far corner, leaning against the wall, his arms still crossed. At the back is a dusty counter with empty shelving above it. In a corner is a rickety table with three upturned crates and a three-legged chair.

"Only me here."

Next to him is another door.

"Where does that lead to?"

"There's an upstairs and a back alley." He seems to read my mind. "If I bolt the top and bottom, no one can come in this way." He pushes the bolts in place and rattles the door handle to show it's secure. I look over my shoulder.

"Safe to come in."

Liddy storms past me and takes the knife. We both lean on the wall close to the open doorway.

The man begins. "Being careful is good. We all have to be cautious about who we trust."

Liddy interrupts. "Who's 'we'?"

"We are an organisation set up to help people who are different."

"Different now?"

He looks at me. "As Schultz gave you the code, I assume you're the one they want."

Frowning, I rub the side of my temple. A dull throb in my ears is expanding into a full-on thudding in my body.

"The letter said December."

"Your sixteenth birthday?"

"Yes."

He has barely moved, just a subtle eyebrow raise. "But Schultz noticed something?"

"That's what he said."

Liddy nudges me in the shoulder. "Who's this Schultz?"

"He was the doctor who helped me at the clinic, remember?"

"Oh, that one. What's he got to do with this?"

The man responds, "He's on our side. Helps people like your friend here."

Liddy's jostling from one foot to the other. "Whose side is that?"

The man keeps his voice low, speaking slowly. "I know you're afraid, but this is how it works. When we get a referral, we explain what will happen and your choices. No names, no way of finding us. After that, it's up to you."

Although I understand his words, they make little to no sense. He continues anyway.

"You have an anomaly. I don't know what exactly, but it's chromosome related. It means you're not like the majority. It's usually spotted when they do the ungendered tests, but sometimes it comes about with specific triggers." He takes a breath. "Sound familiar?"

I nod, staring at the corner of the room and stuffing my hands in my pockets. Liddy shuffles closer to me.

"They allow you to go home, but within two days you'll disappear with no trace. They'll say you're a runner, scare your family into silence, and no one will ever come looking."

I think of my mum alone and frightened, being threatened by the authorities. There have been runners before. On TV they show how they're caught and gaoled, how their families are punished. Liddy's breathing hitches before he lets out a long blast of air through his clenched teeth.

"Isn't running wrong?"

I know Liddy's testing him. Maybe he's a Watcher and we've been set up.

He shakes his head. "Why did you come at all, if that's how you feel?" He points a finger at me. "In your case, they wouldn't even take you to an ungendered compound. They're too interested in finding out more about your genetics, why you're different. There are these places where they do experiments."

My legs begin to tremble. Tears flood my eyes. Embarrassed, I close the lids and wrap my arms tight around my body. Liddy's fist closes around my arm, and he holds me up as if he thinks I'm going to faint, but I'm not. I swallow hard and stand upright.

"How do we know you're telling the truth?"

"You don't, but I have proof." He pulls out his phone. "Close the door a little."

When we don't, he explains further. "I have a clip to project. Proof. But you won't be able to see it in the light."

I edge to the door and push it with my foot, though I still leave enough room to make a run for it. He tilts his phone at an angle until a light hits the far wall. A still picture appears of a white building with high walls and security guards at the gate.

"This is one of their facilities." He swipes across his phone. "This clip was taken in secret by Schultz on one of his trips there."

The clip is shaky, but a corridor of doors appears. Then a voice speaks.

"Dr Schultz?"

A hand reaches out and another one grabs it, though the faces are not in the shot. The camera must be hidden in a pocket or bag.

"Glad you could make it. We have an interesting case."

"One of the ungendered?"

I recognise Schultz's voice.

"With the abomination cells and an expanded brain network."

"Like all the others. Any other differences?"

"Not as yet, but the manifestations are repeating the same pattern. We found her recently, hiding in some woods."

They move to a door. Before it opens, I hear a scanner device beeping twice before light floods the camera and a room comes into focus. Two people sit inside, small notepads in front of them and some sort of machine to the left. They stare at something I can't see.

"Would you like to sit?"

"Prefer to stand if you don't mind. Long drive," Schultz answers.

"Of course. So, this is the subject."

The camera seems to jostle for a second before becoming clear again. Both Liddy and I gasp at the same time. The whole back wall of the room is glass. Beyond it is another white-painted room and in that room is a person, perhaps a girl, though from her body, she looks like we do before the Change, but she's taller than I am and older. Her hair is black coils, her skin shiny with perspiration. I notice her arms are manacled to a wall to restrict her movement. Her head rests on her knees.

"This is subject 4-9-7."

"Is it asleep?"

"No, but it's been with us a week, and is stronger than most. It's defied all our usual tests. Watch."

He presses a switch and speaks.

"Subject 4-9-7, please get up."

Slowly the girl looks up. Even with the shaky clip, the anger in her dark eyes is clear. Then she rests her head on her knees again.

"This is your only warning, Victoria. I won't repeat myself." He presses the switch, turning off the microphone so she can't hear. "It disobeys every time." His voice sounds happy. "Test two please, McCartney."

"Yes, sir."

One of the people in the room is doing something on his tablet.

Schultz speaks. "Which test is this?"

"M&E vibrational field. One of its abilities is the detection and manipulation of it."

"Magnetic and electrical?"

"All indications lean towards both, but we obviously need to do further tests. Watch what happens next."

There's a spark in the room, like static. Then a second spark and, as if it's a trigger, there are sudden bursts of cataclysmic flashes that bounce across the room. The girl stands, her arms stretched out, her back arched, a silent scream emanating from her mouth. Electricity seems to pour from her fingers, her eyes, her ears, her whole body, as if she's some sort of thermal-energy battery, blasting out heat and light. Holding my breath, I watch the torture, terrified, disgusted and yet unable to turn away. The clip abruptly stops, and the room goes dark. I hear my own heavy breathing, my heart pounding in my chest and lean back against the wall. Liddy voices my thoughts.

"Why were they doing that to her?"

"They weren't doing it to her. She was doing it. They just provided the trigger."

"Trigger?" I have no idea what he's talking about.

"In this case, a spark. In other tests, they use different things."

"And you think this is where they'll take me?" My voice has risen to a slight screech. I try to lower it, to be calmer.

"If Schultz is right about you, then yes. They'll want to know which triggers you react to."

"But why? What for?"

"'Purify genes and save the human race' is the official version, but that's rubbish, just a cover story. They're building a new race. They're building power."

"Building power for what?" My voice wavers. None of this makes sense. "How do we know this is real?"

"You don't. But something I do know is that you know nothing. The world isn't what you think it is. I am certain though that whatever they found in your recent tests, the anomalies were enough for them to send you to a facility like this."

"That can't be true. I'm not like her. I can't create static stuff."

"Schultz must think differently." His voice is unemotional, stating facts.

He waits for us to react, to be convinced, to say something, but only the silence of the decrepit coffeeshop bounces between us.

Eventually, Liddy does offer up a question. "What happened to the girl?"

"We got her out. Very recently."

At least that's something.

"Got her out to where, exactly?"

"A safe place." He waves his hand. "Don't even ask me the location, I'm not about to tell you. After all, you could be working for the enemy."

Liddy pipes up with another question. "Who's *your* enemy?"

He hesitates. "Again, there's only a limited amount of information I'm prepared to give you. I'm here to get you out, like that girl you saw, but it's your choice."

Glaring at him, as if he's to blame, I spit out my words. "And that choice would be?"

"Leave tonight. We'll take you in, hide you. Show you how to live outside the boundaries. You'll be protected from the facility and the tests."

Liddy's calm bursts. "Tonight? But that's impossible!"

"I don't think your friend has a choice."

I can't help snapping at him. "I thought you said I had a choice."

He sighs. "Yes, I'm sorry, you do. I can't force you to leave, and I'm only the messenger. But honestly, Schultz is in deep. He would never have risked sending you here if he thought you had any chance at a normal life." He uncrosses his arms and stops leaning on the wall as if readying himself to leave. "Here's the thing – the tests could be wrong. Schultz could be wrong. I could be telling lies, but does it matter? They'll still come for you in two days, and this will be your fate. You'll lose your family and all rights to a normal life."

There's a brief silence. I hear a scratching sound above us, some rodent scuttling along the floorboards.

Liddy speaks. "So, where's this hiding place?"

"I told you, it's safe, a sanctuary for her kind."

"My kind? There are others?" My brows raise high in surprise.

"Yes, there are others who are different, but the authorities are rounding them up faster than we can find them."

Liddy takes a step forward, flinging out his hands. "There are lots of people who are different." I know he's thinking about himself. "Why her? And why would you help someone you don't even know?"

He pushes back his hood a little, blond hair escapes. "You're right. There are many people who are different, and we believe we have a right to be different. The Diversity Commission, the facility, the testing, even the way people react to the ungendered and the Change." He shakes his head. "All of it is wrong."

"But the Change is normal."

"The Change is normal, but judging how a person decides to live is wrong. We want to stop that. Besides, the Commission have other agendas that people don't know about."

"How? What?"

It seems he's surprised by his own passion and struggles to master his response, stuttering a little. "L-look, I've already said too much. I have to go. It's dangerous to hang around here."

There's still one burning question in me.

"What about my mum? They'll punish her."

"No, they won't. Just leave a note saying you're running away and not to worry, that you'll be in touch soon."

Liddy interrupts. "I've seen it online, families getting punished for kids running away."

"It's propaganda, a lie to deter people running." He turns back to me. "Your mother will be watched for a while, have her phones tapped, but they'll focus on looking for you."

"Does that mean I won't be able to contact her?"

"Yes, until things have quietened. For your sake and hers."

Two days ago, I was at school, everything was semi-normal. Now, my life's threatened, and the one option I have is to go into hiding with a man I just met. I slide down the wall and bend my knees, like the girl in the clip.

"What happens to them?" I point to the wall as if the clip is still playing. He understands. His response is cold, but beneath it is anger. It's as if I can see the rage burning off him like volcanic ash rising from lava.

"They're tested until they're used up, till they can no longer think for themselves, till they become their soldier-slaves in a battle for ultimate power... or die, fighting back."

I have a thousand burning questions about this 'ultimate power', 'soldier-slaves' and a war I know nothing about. My brain feels as if it's about to explode.

The man moves towards the backdoor. "Okay, enough. If you decide to come, you'll know more. We'll wait until midnight, but then we're gone. Please shut the door behind you."

With that he slips back the bolts on the backdoor and leaves. I hear him lock it before walking away. Still, I sit, my mind unable to fathom what I've just heard.

It can't be true.

The Diversity Commission is controlling, yes, but it upholds the Holistic Law. It couldn't get away with this stuff without us knowing. But a big part of me knows that they could.

Liddy bends down near me, touching my knee. I hear his quiet breathing as I speak. "Do you believe what he said? Do you think it's true? That stuff about the girl, powers, soldiers? It doesn't make sense."

"Why would he bother making it up?"

"I don't know, but I'm not like that girl. I'm not."

"I know."

I begin shivering. Liddy rubs my limbs. "Come on, Cam. Let's get out of here."

I nod and force myself up. The grit under my shoes crunches as I stretch. Liddy guides me through the door into the daylight, his comforting hand on my shoulder. Drizzles of rain splash against the hard tarmac. Standing in the alcove of the shop, I wait while Liddy grips part of the boarding to pull the door shut. He steps up next to me. We stand there, watching the rain get heavier. I look up at the sky.

"Do you think it'll stop; all go away if we wait a while?"

He glances at me. "I don't think we have a while, Cam. I think we need to make a dash for it, get out while we can."

"Do you?"

"Yes."

"I don't think I can do this alone, Lid."

"What makes you think you're alone?"

I turn to look up at him. "So, you think it's all true?"

He frowns. "I don't know what's true, anymore. I just know both of us are gonna be taken away. We might as well make our own choices and go together, wherever that is, or wherever we end up."

A shiver runs through me. The thought of leaving everything behind is absurd. I can't get it out of my mind that we'll be hunted as runners.

Liddy steps forward and reaches out for my hand. I grab it and step out from the protection of the alcove into the torrential rainfall. For a nanosecond, I stand there, the water running into my eyes, until I feel Liddy yank my arm and we both begin running.

CHAPTER NINE

I open the front door and traipse into our narrow hallway, hanging my wet coat on the wall hook and slumping on the bottom step of the stairs to untie my trainers. The bottoms of my jeans are soaked, and my hair is damp. The plan is to run upstairs and get a hot shower, be alone for a while to think things through.

"Cam, is that you?" My mum enters from the kitchen, a worry frown on her forehead.

"Yes."

"What have you been up to? I expected you back ages ago."

"Went downtown and back to Liddy's, I mean, Lou's for a while."

I'd never told her about Liddy's dad stopping me going round, so she doesn't question it. We'd actually spent a lot of time in a coffeeshop, making plans and trying to work through what could go wrong.

She nods. "I need to tell you something, Cam."

I know, she's been hiding something for a while.

She pulls me into a hug. "Gosh, you're soaking wet." She steps back but holds my hands in front of her. "I love you." Her eyes water. "I always will. Whatever anyone says or whatever you decide, my love won't change." She's referring to the Golem thing, I know.

"Er, thanks. I love you too, Mum, but I'd rather die than become like one of those who have no memories or emotions." I'm thinking of the clinic security guard.

"Don't say that, Cam. I'll do everything I can to protect you."

I don't know what to say. She can't really do anything, but I don't want to upset her. I'll be gone soon. My chest hitches. One way or another, this may be one of the last conversations I have with my mum.

"Can we not do this right now? I want to get a shower and get changed."

She gives that thin-lipped smile, agreeing, but not agreeing. "Are you hungry?"

"Nah, ate at Li... Lou's."

I move towards the stairs. If I stay much longer, I'll confess everything to her: the meeting, the stranger, Dr Schultz, running away.

"Okay. Do you want to watch that old Viking programme?"

We're in the middle of a boxset – ancient, but watchable. I'll probably never see the end. An image flashes through my mind of my mum alone on the sofa. I swallow hard and look away as I dash up the stairs. "Yeah, sure."

My hair now wrapped in a towel, I slip into my pyjamas and sit on the end of my bed, staring at my reflection in the mirror. My desperate, hazel eyes look greener in this light. My mind pleads for another solution, but it's all decided now. Liddy and I spent hours thinking through all the things that could go wrong, what we would do and how to protect ourselves. Then, we made endless lists of what to take, narrowing it down to essentials and nothing more than one rucksack. We even emptied our bank accounts. Not that there's much between us, but at least we can get on a bus, should it all go horribly wrong. Liddy's read so many spy novels, his imagination was wild.

"We need to hide an extra phone or at least a sim card, just in case they take ours off us."

"You think they'd do that?"

"Secret organisations won't want to be traced. Besides which, we can't let the authorities trace us either."

"You're right. What about our money?"

"Good thinking. We'll need to hide that, too."

"If they're as bad as that, they'll find whatever we have."

His eyes light up as if he's had an eureka moment. "My dad has a small magic box with a secret compartment. We could use that."

"Magic box?"

"Yeah, he used to show it to us when we were kids. It's impossible to find the compartment unless you know the trick to open it."

Now, I turn my head upside down and scrub my scalp hard, before throwing the towel on the floor and reaching for my comb. Waving the hairdryer around for a few minutes, allowing the heat to warm my head, I eventually lose patience and tie my damp hair back.

From my wardrobe, I pull out my old rucksack and shake the dust off it. In it, I pack a pair of jeans, four long-sleeved tops, a pullover, pyjamas, underclothes, toiletries and a towel. That's it, that's all we agreed, but it seems so little of my life here. My eyes catch the small photo hung in a frame on the wall. It's been there for ever and shows my mum, my late Aunt Lucy and me laughing on a sunny day, the sea behind us. I'm about four, my mum must be in her early twenties. I don't take after her much. I inherited my aunt's looks, even my mum agrees. Lucy used to visit us every year on my birthday until I was ten, then she passed away. We'd go somewhere exciting each time. I still remember the words she used, "A special day," she'd say. As for who my dad really is, I'm unsure. My mum never talks about him and there aren't any images...

Reaching for the photo, I take it down, slip it out of the frame and carefully place it down the side of my bag. Finally, I sit at my desk to write the letter. I was going to do it on my laptop and print it off, but then thought it might be more convincing to the authorities if I write it by hand. Ripping a sheet of paper from my school notebook, I pick up a pen.

Dear Mum,

And then I stop. How can I do this to her? Tears fill my eyes and sadness aches in my chest as I imagine her reaction in the morning. Still, I force my hand to write the words Liddy and I agreed upon.

I'm sorry. Please forgive me, but I have to leave. This is not your fault, it's mine. I'm too afraid to be taken, to be a Golem, and so I'm running. Please don't try to contact me. I won't answer my phone.
And sorry about the trip. Would have been great.
I love you, Mum.
Cam xx

Folding the sheet with trembling fingers, I place it on top of my laptop and write 'Mum' on it. Sighing, I just sit there and stare at it, as if by thought alone I can make this whole mess go away.

"Cam, are you ready?" My mum's calling up the stairs.

"Yeah, coming."

At least I can spend the last few hours with her. It's now 6:30 p.m. – only four hours before meeting Liddy at the top of the street. Hiding my rucksack in the wardrobe, just in case my mum comes in, I switch off the lamp and go down to join her.

CHAPTER TEN

I listen, my ears pricked for any movement. The night-time noises lend themselves to the jitters: creaking floorboards, a flap of wings on the roof, a barking fox stalking the street, a distant car. It's been an hour since we went to bed and I'm sure my mum's sleeping but, just in case, I creep around. Pulling my clothes on top of my pyjamas, I sling the rucksack over my shoulder and grab my most comfortable trainers. The hinges on my door squeak if I open them too wide, so I slip out the smallest of spaces and tiptoe down the stairs, stopping a couple of times when a floorboard moans. Sitting on the bottom step, I tug my trainers on and grab my jacket, before heading to the front door.

Taking one last look up the stairs, I swallow the lump in my throat.

Bye, Mum.

I close the front door behind me.

Liddy's already on the corner and walks towards me. His eyes flick around and he's rubbing his hands together.

"You're late."

"Only five minutes."

No one's around but we're still whispering. Every so often, there are curfews. It's against the law to break them. There isn't one tonight, but it still feels frightening to be out so late. Not all the streetlamps work, and the light shining down from those that do is orange, giving everything a weird glow.

"Did you switch off tracking?"

"Yes."

"Good." I pull his arm back as he strides ahead. "Are you sure, Liddy?"

"Sure about what? Running away, meeting up with some unknown organisation, being on the run?"

"I guess."

He stops; his pupils wide, making his eyes dark and intense. "There are two things

I'm sure about. One, I'm not having the same therapy Joanna had, and two, if there's a chance that facility testing thing is real, I'm not letting them take you. Everything else, we'll deal with."

His certainty makes me feel better. I breathe deeply. "You're right."

"We stick together."

"Definitely."

"Well, then, let's go meet our creepy rescuers."

I grin. "Creepy is the new norm."

He snorts as we turn the corner and make our way down a back alley. Even the route was planned so we couldn't be picked up on the main streets or seen by cameras.

For a while, we walk along in silence, passing the bus stop we sat at earlier and entering the run-down street with all the windows boarded up. The lamps in this area aren't working at all and both Liddy and I stop at the corner. A shiver runs down my spine, curdling its way into my stomach; I am on edge, as if every cell is tingling. I pull my phone from my pocket and turn on the torch. Its light is bright enough to see what's in front of us, but nothing more.

"Liddy, let's go along the edge."

"'kay."

"What if no one's there?"

"We go home."

I grit my teeth, my lips forming a thin line. "Do you have the knife?"

"Yep." He pulls it from a side pocket. It glints in the torchlight as we pass a bundle of rags in an alcove. The rags grunt, startling me and I step on Liddy's foot.

"Hey!"

"No drugs, no money. Please don't hurt me," a voice gurgles from under the rags.

I glance at Liddy and back at the man, swinging the light into his face. A head of curly hair appears followed by a dirty face, covered in whiskers. He protects his eyes.

"We're not here for you."

He grunts and hides under an old blanket as we move away. My chest booms and I feel like one of those old cartoon characters, with a heart trying to force its way through its ribcage, stretching its skin in an effort to escape.

We've just reached Abby's when a van careens up the street, so quickly we hardly have time to step back. A flush of adrenalin shoots through my veins, prickling my skin and heating my face. Liddy pushes me against the doorway as the van skids to a halt in front of us. Two people, covered in black from head to toe, jump out.

"Run!" Liddy yanks my arm, twisting me in the opposite direction, but before we even have a chance to escape, they block our way, some sort of gun pointed at us.

"Drop the knife!"

I hear the clang of metal on the ground. One of them kicks it aside, before picking it up. The other one keeps the gun aimed at us.

"Any more weapons?" The voice is male, deep and demanding.

"No."

"Good." They lower their weapons. "Now, we need the code."

I feel like I need to give my head a good shake to wake myself up. "What?"

"The code."

Liddy nudges me and mouths, "Go ahead."

"CH23 IO957."

"Which one of you?" The one speaking is female. She's about a head taller than me and her back is straight, as if she's holding herself tense.

As I speak, my breath condenses and drifts into the cold air. "Which one, what?"

"Which one of you is coming?" She's sharp, perhaps annoyed. "We were told there was one pickup."

Liddy steps back, dragging me with him. "Who are you? Where's the other guy? The one we met."

The woman's tone becomes exasperated. "There's no time for questions. Which of you was given the code?"

Both she and the man scour the street, their heads flicking one way and then the other. I follow their gaze, wondering what they expect to happen.

"Time to go. Whichever one of you is coming, get in the van."

My heart's pounding as I grab Liddy's hand, hoping he understands not to say anything. "We're both coming."

The female turns her head to me. "I know you're afraid, but our orders are for one person."

Liddy looks at me. "You should go."

"No! No way. We'll make a run for it on our own."

The man growls at his partner. "This is taking too long."

A noise in another street distracts them. They pull their guns to their hips and face the sound.

"Look, let's just forget this. You get in your van, and we'll leave."

A siren blasts out. It's close, somewhere in an adjacent street, a police car coming our way. I squeeze Liddy's hand tighter as my stomach tenses.

"Did you tell anyone about your meeting?" The man has turned his gun in our direction.

Liddy spits out his response. "Of course not." He looks at me. "Cam, we need to go. If they catch us here..."

I nod, but unsure if Liddy can see me in the dark, I yank his hand. "Yeah, let's go."

As the police car turns the corner, the siren pierces the night, and the flashing orange light blinds me. Liddy's pulling at my arm, urging me to move, but there's no way we'll make it. I hear the clicking of guns being engaged. As if they are in a war movie, the soldiers in front of us raise their weapons to their faces. They're going to shoot the police!

The female screams orders. "Go for the tyres!"

I hear a powerful boom, a shockwave ricocheting through my ears, before a bright flash and clattering of metal bullets against the car down the street. The smell of sulphur hits the back of my throat, and I begin coughing.

One of my arms is being pulled forwards. I cling onto Liddy to assure myself he's following.

"Quick, both of you. Get in."

We're pushed into the back of the van. The other two jump in and slam the doors shut as the van speeds away. I'm still coughing as the interior lights come on, a red glow. Before we can ask any questions, the man leans over.

"Right, hand over your phones."

We do as he says, having half expected it. He takes out the sim cards and smashes them with the heel of his gun. Then, he does the same to the phones. Liddy looks at me with a 'told you so' expression, but there's fear in his eyes.

The woman is looking through a peephole in one of the back doors. "Good hit. We lost them." She's breathing heavily. I watch her chest rise and fall.

"For now. How long do you think we have?"

"Ten minutes, tops." She turns and faces us all, inspecting Liddy and I as she answers the man's query. He glances back and forth, waiting for his orders.

"The rendezvous?"

"Change of plan. Get him on the transmitter."

He nods and pulls out some sort of device. Liddy and I watch as he twists a couple of knobs, before putting a plug in his ear.

"This is SR1. Plan A aborted. Police on tail. Over."

A hissing static noise is heard and then a crackly voice responds. Their communication is fast and to the point.

"SR1 this is TB. Move to plan B."

"Plan B confirmed. Over."

"Check for implants. Over."

"Will do. Over and out."

The woman tuts and swears under her breath before looking up. "Tell Byron."

He nods and crawls towards us. I scrunch over to Liddy as he leans in and slides back a connecting window to the driver up front.

"Plan B."

A gruff voice responds. "Thought so. How long?"

"Give us five minutes."

"Will do."

I never thought you could smell fear, but inside the small confines of the van, I can taste the tang of sweat pulsating through our skins. Pulling my knees up, I wrap my hands around my legs. Whatever was supposed to happen has gone wrong. I feel the pressure of Liddy's hand on my shoulder and glance over. He's deathly pale, his hair falling loose around his face. No jokes, no sarcastic comments, just silent fear.

"Right, you two, before we reach our next destination, we need to do a scan."

They still wear their masks, made of some sort of black stretchy material, impossible to see what they look like. The female is smaller than the male, but definitely the one in charge.

"A scan?"

The van swerves around a corner and I lean into Liddy for balance.

"Someone knew about this meeting. Either you were followed, or they implanted one of you."

"Implanted?"

She pulls out her bag and reaches inside. "Which one of you was at the clinic recently?"

There's no point in denying it now. "I was."

"It's possible they implanted you with a tracker." She lets it sink in. "So, if you wouldn't mind—"

She has what looks like a large, black phone sitting in her palm. It has a screen lit up with green numbers and a bar. The thought that something might be inside me and that it's my fault all this happened sinks like a heavy weight in the pit of my stomach. "Okay. What do you want me to do?"

"Lie flat on your back and keep still."

I pull my rucksack off my shoulder and shuffle over. The man moves to the right as I extend my feet to the end of the van.

Liddy is watching. "What are you doing?"

She scoffs at him. "This isn't the part to worry about."

On her hands and knees, she moves the scanner across my body, starting at my head and moving down to my feet. The machine beeps with a slightly elevated pulse.

"Flip over."

In the confines of the van, twisting around is awkward. I use my hands as leverage to stop my face hitting the cold, metallic base of the van. This time she begins at my feet. As she reaches the bottom of my spine, the beeping increases and by the time she's leaning over my shoulder, it's a screeching, high-pitched tone. I glance over my shoulder.

"Is that it?"

"Yes."

My heart hammers. Heat floods my face. It's my fault we were pursued. They must have known we'd gone to Abby's earlier, as well.

"Tracker." She looks at her comrade, her body taut, her tone of voice full of dread. "Why didn't Schultz warn us?"

"Maybe he didn't know."

"Send TB a message. Schultz's cover could be blown. He needs to get out, immediately."

Liddy asks the question I have in my head: "What now?"

I roll over and sit up. She looks at me as if she's judging how much I can take.

"This happened once before, and I gave the same choice."

But I know the choice, or at least one of them. My voice is harsh, angry. I spit out the words, "Get it out."

Liddy gasps and is about to argue.

"Think, Liddy. If they put a tracker in me, then they were watching, and coming no matter where we ran. The facility, the torture, maybe it's all true."

He nods, rubbing away a frown on his forehead. "I just don't get it, Cam. What do they want? Why are they doing this?"

"Does it matter? We can't go back, and we have nowhere else to go."

He puts his arm around me, as the woman scuttles over carrying a small first-aid kit. From it, she takes a finger splint, a swab and a bandage. She stares at me as if judging my resolve.

"This will hurt, but you can't scream." She hands over the splint. "Bite down on this. It's not much, but it might help." She glances at Liddy. "Hold this." She hands him a torch and then gives her next orders. "Take off your jacket and top. I need to reach your left shoulder."

Instantly, my face heats up. The thought of stripping in front of everyone, of them seeing my stupid body... But she's already behind me, tugging off my coat.

"We have to be quick. They can still locate us."

I pull my long-sleeved top off. Underneath, I'm still wearing my pyjamas. Slipping out my left arm, I half undress, while at the same time clutching the front, trying to cover my chest. She doesn't comment but the space in the van seems to contract, getting smaller as my whole body burns with embarrassment.

"You... Liddy, is it?"

"Yes."

"Blood bother you?"

"No."

"Good, sit here and keep that torch steady."

I feel the cold swab on my back and Liddy gasping. I half turn to find out what's happening and see the glint of a knife. My heart thuds.

"Right, I'll count to three. Remember, don't scream."

"'kay."

"One..."

I tighten my stomach and bite down on the wood in my mouth, preparing mentally, telling myself I can do this, focusing, waiting for the next number. So I don't immediately react when an unexpected searing pain rips through my back. Within seconds, the message hits my brain and the agony storms through my body. A gurgling sound escapes my throat as I try to block out the fire, but it's all-consuming. Survival kicks in and I pull away but find the man's holding my shoulders. My eyes flash a threatening look, but he's strong. I can't move. Liddy grabs my hand, and I lace our fingers, clinging on and squeezing my eyes shut. My head droops and tears fall as the smell of rust reaches my nostrils and salty saliva fills my mouth. Gulping, knowing I'm going to be sick, I spit out the wood and heave a deep breath in, but the sickness rises and, unable to stop it or warn anyone, I spew liquid vomit. That's when the shuddering begins.

The woman maintains control, throwing out orders. "Keep her still."

Arms grab me, and I find my hot face on the cool, van floor. My mind fades in and out. Pain, no pain, pain, no pain. With relief, I let myself fade further, caring only that the torture goes away.

CHAPTER ELEVEN

I'm holding a pneumatic drill, splitting concrete. The tremors from the drill pound through my body. My arms feel weak, my chest is in pain and my back burns in the hot sun. Why am I doing this job? I haven't received my gender assignment yet. I should be in school.

Confused, I try to hold onto the drill, to keep it steady, but it flips out of control and falls onto me. I step back, afraid I'm going to be torn apart, but a wall blocks my escape. The drill has a face, evil eyes, a manic grin. It stalks towards me, and I begin screaming.

"Wake up."

Someone's smothering my mouth.

"Cam, wake up."

I claw at the hand, heaving breaths.

"Cam, stop."

My eyes flash open. Dark hair falls around my cheeks, blue eyes close to mine – afraid, glistening. There's a throbbing in my back, pain shooting through my shoulder.

"You're dreaming."

"Huh?"

And then Liddy's face comes into focus. "Lid?"

His thin-lipped smile shows relief as he leans back on his heels. "How are you feeling?"

"Dunno. Things hurt. What happened?"

"You fainted."

"I did?"

"Not before you decorated our friend in vomit." He's grinning.

"Eh?" I try to sit up, groaning as more pain shoots through my chest.

Liddy places a hand on my shoulder. "Don't move yet. The tracker was embedded. Took Happy over there twenty minutes to dig it out, along with half your flesh." He frowns as he glares over at someone beyond my range of sight.

"Who? What?" My brain's foggy but I know Liddy's banter is his way of coping.

"Here, sip this." He crosses his legs and leans forward, gently placing a hand under my head. "It's hydration salts and some sort of antibiotic."

Grateful for the cool liquid slipping down my parched throat, I listen as he fills in the gaps.

"In case it's a bit of a blur, I'll summarise for you." He has a weird look on his face as if he's about to tell one of his tall stories. "We ran away, met with Happy and Beefy, who shot the police car to bits. All your fault, by the way!" He goes for a grin again, but it doesn't reach his eyes. "Then we found and dug out a slither of a tracking device embedded in your flesh. After lots of blood and gore – and sick and fainting, on your part – we ended up here." He raises his shoulders and flaps his hands. "Tah-dah!"

I stare at him, the cogs in my brain taking a second longer to process everything he's saying. He looks deflated even though he tries to make fun of it all.

"Right, yeah." I strain my neck to look around. The room is dim, but there are three people talking quietly to each other in the corner. "Where's here?"

"Dunno. Some sort of warehouse, I think."

"Are we safe?"

He shrugs. "From what I can make out, the driver's gone and we're in hiding."

I groan. "Can you help me sit up? My back's killing me."

"Think you're supposed to stay still. That doctor you mentioned stitched you up."

"Schultz's here?"

"Turned up about four hours ago."

I lean on my elbow. "What time is it?"

He checks his watch. "7:15."

I struggle to push myself up. He sighs and supports my lower back and shoulders.

"Lean against me. The stitches might tear."

I lean into him, my right arm resting against his side. "Thanks, Lid."

We sit in silence for a while, staring around the small warehouse. On the left are some grimy, old pallets. There is a room further along with a fluorescent light and a square hatch. Beyond the antiseptic smell emanating from my own body, there's a dusty, dank stink, as if water has pooled somewhere and gone bad.

"Morning or night, Lid?"

"Morning."

I try to look up at him. A spasm of pain shoots down my back. "Ouch!"

"You all right?"

I struggle to find a smart answer but can only come up with something we said as kids. "Half-left, actually." Grunting again, I shift my position. "Got any painkillers, little girl?" I say it as if I'm some grimy street druggy, looking for her next fix, but Liddy takes it differently.

"Now you see me as a girl. What happened to accepting myself for what I am?"

His voice is shrill. I look up at him. He has dark bags under his eyes.

He wipes his hand across his face and sighs. "Sorry, didn't mean for that to come out the way it did."

"It's okay."

Before we can say any more, our rescuers come over. Schultz is the only one without a covered face, but he looks rough, dark rings around his eyes and a shadow on his chin. He's wearing jeans and a sweatshirt under a blue jacket.

"How are you feeling, Miss Chadwick?"

"Cam. My name's Cam."

He smiles, his dark eyes kind and reassuring. "Cam it is. Please call me Peter, or Schultz if you prefer. So, do you think I can look at the dressing on your back?"

"Yeah, right. Thanks, by the way" I look around at the others watching. He seems to understand.

"Why don't you all leave Cam and me to do our work?"

The two masked superheroes walk further away, but Liddy holds onto me. "I'm staying."

"No, Lid. It's okay."

He looks offended, but Schultz helps me out.

"Could you make some toast and coffee? Before we give Cam more painkillers, she'll need to eat something."

Liddy stares into Schultz's eyes as if transfixed. Lid is always saying he likes tall, dark and handsome, even though he'd get into heaps of trouble if anyone but me heard him.

"Lid, I'm a bit hungry and could do with a coffee."

He has difficulty looking away from Schultz, but eventually responds. "Are you sure?"

I know he's talking about being left alone. "Yes."

He gently lowers me and allows Schultz to take his place. I watch Liddy stride away and enter the room with the fluorescent light. There's some clattering and I hear a kettle being switched on, before my attention is drawn to the doctor. Again, it's as if he can read my mind.

"You can ask questions while I check the stitches and re-dress the bandage but keep them short."

There's a thin mattress on the floor I hadn't noticed before. I carefully remove my jacket and top. Then, still in my pyjamas, I lie down on my stomach, trying not to sound like a baby, but the yelp still escapes, so I bite down on my bottom lip to control the outbursts.

"I'm going to lift up your top and roll it back to just below your shoulders."

I nod and feel the cool air touch my warm back. His hands carefully prod around the injury.

"Any sharp pain?"

Taking a deep breath, I answer, "Feels tingly and numb."

"Good. The anaesthetic is working. Once I've checked the stitches and cleaned the wound again, I'll inject some more. We'll need to be on the move soon, so try not to jerk or make any sudden movements."

"On the move where?"

"To a safe place."

"And where's that?"

He's putting something cool on my back. It smells like calamine lotion and reminds me of when I had chickenpox as a kid.

"As a new referral, you'll be taken to Base One." Before I ask my next question, he fills me in. "There are several bases. This one's fairly close by. We should get there before dark."

I hear a flicking sound and glance over my shoulder. He's tapping a syringe, preparing an injection. "Hold still. You shouldn't feel anything." There's a slight pinprick against my skin then he rolls my top down and helps me sit up.

"Your injury is clean and should heal well. There'll be a bit of a scar, but nothing much."

I turn around and carefully pull my sweatshirt and jacket back on, trying not to jerk my left side. He's storing the needle in a box. He stops what he's doing, looks at me and then across at the two who rescued us.

"Look, you have less than one minute to ask questions, otherwise they'll get suspicious and come over. And I won't answer anything that puts us in danger. Agreed?"

"Okay. So, how are we getting there?"

"Driving, then a plane or boat, depending on how safe it is."

My mind rocks. "We're leaving the country?"

"Not quite." He makes a show of packing up the rest of his kit.

"Anything else you can't tell me?"

He's quiet for a few seconds as he picks up a small box with yellow writing. He begins tapping it across his palm, hesitating. "There are usually two plans to get kids like you out."

"Two? Why?"

He raises his hand. "Before you ask, I don't know anything about the second plan, and I can't tell you much more." I open my mouth. "No more questions. Wait till we get there. If we're caught, the more you know, the riskier it is for us. We can't chance the Diversity Commission finding us."

"I don't get it. Are they the enemy, then? Aren't they supposed to be the good guys who stopped humankind from becoming extinct?"

"I know this is confusing." He sighs. "You were shown the clip of the facility?"

"Yes. You were there. You watched that girl suffer."

"I was. I worked for one of the testing clinics, but I was a mole. It was lucky you came to my clinic. We may not have found you, otherwise."

"You help people like me?"

"You were my last case." He pulls out a strip of pills from the box he's holding. "Have something to eat and then take two of these. If necessary, you can take up to two, every four hours, and have all of that drink. It contains antibiotics." With that he stands up and I think he's going to leave, but he turns back. "We leave within an hour. There's a bathroom to the left, but don't take a shower."

"Er, thanks."

"You're welcome."

"No, I mean, thanks for everything – for rescuing me, too."

"I should thank you. We wouldn't have known my cover had been blown if you hadn't come in." He shakes his head. "I only just got out in time."

I don't know what to say about that. Everything is just bizarre; I can't get a grasp on what is real and what isn't.

He smiles, before moving towards the man and woman who pushed us into the van. His back is broad, his limbs long. In my peripheral vision, I notice Liddy coming over, a tray in his hands. He places the tray on the floor and sits on the mattress next to me.

Staring in the same direction as I am, he clears his throat. "Well, what did the doc say? Did he tell you anything?"

"Nothing much about them."

"What, then?"

As I repeat the conversation, his eyes widen. "I don't get it, Cam. It's as if everything we've ever been told…"

"I know."

He grunts but is still staring in the direction of the three strangers who saved us.

"At least we know the journey involves driving and maybe a boat or plane, though not out of the country. Your guess is as good as mine."

"Mmm…"

Seeing him stare at Schultz with admiration, I'm about to laugh and make a joke about Liddy behaving like a girl but hesitate. It would hurt him. Not for the first time, I wonder what it must be like to be Liddy – a male body and a female brain. How difficult is that, and how the hell did it happen?

Could it be we both have something wrong with us?

"Why do you think they want to help us?"

Liddy turns back to me. "I think it's you they want to help. I just happened to get in the way."

"I don't know. We're both odd, Lid, but at least they treat us like normal people."

"If you call ignoring us and whispering in the corner treating us 'normal'." He picks at a nail and, seeing me frown, explains. "It broke dragging you out of the van."

"Sorry about that." I rest my hand on his, stopping him from splitting his nails further. "Did you get any sleep?"

"Was watching *Sleeping Beauty*. Long film, that one."

I smile. "I'm so glad you're here. Don't know what I'd do without you."

"I do, you'd starve. Now, eat some toast."

CHAPTER TWELVE

"Time to move. Do you need help?" Schultz squats in front of me. Liddy is sitting near, cross-legged.

"Thanks, I'm fine." Pushing myself up, leaning right to compensate for the pain, I manage to get to my knees without groaning. Both of them stand, hovering, as if waiting to catch me if I fall. "Really, I'm okay." Sitting back on my heels, I lever myself up into a standing position. My brow has speckles of perspiration on it and my head spins for a few seconds, but it passes quickly.

"Good, let's move, then. The others are already outside." Schultz strides towards the exit and we follow.

"Where's my rucksack?" I ask Liddy but Schultz responds.

"Stowed in the car."

I wobble a little but stay upright. Liddy links his arm through mine.

"Let's cuddle." His eyes narrow with that look that says, *I'm not taking no for an answer.* As we walk towards the back of the building, I'm glad for his strong arm.

Schultz begins to explain the plan. "We're going to split up. Jenny—"

"Who's Jenny?"

"She's the female operative leader who picked you up. David is the communications specialist."

Liddy's surprise is the same as mine.

"Now we're on a first-name basis?"

"Yes. Our plans have changed, and you need to know their names."

"Why?"

"They're looking for at least four people, two of which are you, and they know what you look like. Travelling together is dangerous, so we'll separate and meet at the rendezvous point."

We've reached a door. Schultz opens it wide, letting us both walk through before flicking off a light switch and locking up. It's warm and humid, the sun blanketed with clouds.

"We have three vehicles. David will take Liddy. Jenny goes with Cam, and I'll travel alone."

"No way!" Liddy explodes before I have a chance. "We're not separating."

He sighs. "This is the best chance we have. Your faces have been splattered across national news."

"What?" I think of my mum. I imagine her pale face, her hands clinging to a cold mug of coffee. My chest tightens. "Why would they?"

"Because they want you back."

"Why? This is crazy."

Two small cars pull up in front of us, the first is blue and the second silver. A woman with short, red hair leans out of the first car. I don't recognise her, but when she speaks, I know it's Jenny.

"Let's get going. Schultz, the bike's in the back."

"Thanks."

A young man, early twenties, with black hair and dark skin winds down the silver car's side window. "Liddy, let's get going." He thumbs to his back as if hitching a lift. I recognise his voice from the van and realise this must be David Schultz was talking about.

Liddy clings onto my arm, both of us unsure what to do. Jenny watches us, then glances at Schultz. "You get moving. I'll sort this."

Schultz presses my shoulder. "I know it's hard to trust us but try. This is the best way." He disappears around the corner. Jenny opens the car door and swings her legs out, leaning her elbows on her knees.

"Life is full of choices." She looks up, her piercing blue eyes holding each of us for a second, before staring down at the grey tarmac. "The day I ran, I thought I'd die. I thought my family would perish; I thought I was being selfish. I was petrified." She glances at David. "But I chose my future and now I decide who I am and what will happen to me. Not the Commission, not the authorities, no one but me." Her tone of voice is almost comforting, as if she's empathising with our situation, but I know this story is leading somewhere and wait for the hook that snares the fish.

"Yesterday, you both made the choice to run. Today, you have another, possibly fatal, decision to make. Get in the car assigned and let's get out of here, or we're going to drive away and leave you both. I won't risk all our lives or our community for the sake of either of you."

I flinch at her words, instinctively holding my breath. There's truth to what she's saying, and the plan is logical, but... I look up at Liddy.

"No, Cam. Don't even think about it. We stick together, remember?" He tightens his grip on my arm. David's watching us and then he voices my concern, as if reading my mind.

"I promise to keep him safe and to bring him to the rendezvous point."

Liddy explodes. "No... No! What if they just drop us off somewhere and leave us to be taken in?" His eyes are glistening, and I know he's thinking of himself, that he was just the insurance, the friend – not really wanted.

"They won't, Lid."

"Why not?"

"Because we know too much. We know their faces, this place, Schultz."

"Yeah, all good reasons just to kill us, then."

We hear an engine revving. A motorbike swings around the corner. Jenny gets back in the car as Schultz stops in front of us and pushes his visor up.

"Are you ready?"

On impulse, I make a request. "Under one condition."

"Condition?"

"You stay with David and make sure Liddy makes it."

Schultz glances at Liddy – watching him cling to me, tears in his eyes – and then back at me. "I give you my word."

Schultz saved my life. He told me the truth. I know that's not much to go on, to risk our lives with, but it's all I have. He turns to Liddy.

"Liddy, relax. We have no choice but to separate."

Liddy stares into Schultz's eyes, almost besotted. His pupils dilate and I know something's amiss. Schultz has some sort of charm offensive going on again. "You'll be safe, I promise you."

And just like that, we dismiss our rules about not getting in strangers' cars and sticking together. Climbing into Jenny's vehicle, I look over my shoulder to see Liddy pulling on the seatbelt. I'm sure I've hurt him, betrayed his trust. I swallow the lump in my throat and face forwards to watch the grey road on this grey day as we turn right, separating from the others.

"There's a bag at your feet. Pull out the wig and glasses and put them on. There's also a green top. Switch it with your top. If we're stopped, it won't help much, but it might work if they're not too close."

My shoulder aches as I manoeuvre out of my top and pull on a musty-smelling, dark green sweatshirt, at least two sizes too big, and roll up the sleeves. The wig is a short, dark blonde affair and I pull it on like a hat. Flipping down the sun visor, I find a mirror and stare at my face for a second. Olive skin, green-flecked hazel eyes, small nose and high cheekbones, but the wig makes me look older, somehow. More like my aunt. For a second, I feel happy. Maybe this is what I'll look like when I grow up. But then I remember I won't grow up, and I can't bear to look. Covering my face with my hands, I rub my eyes until they feel dry and sore.

What the hell am I doing? I don't know these people, don't know where we're going, and what if they dump Liddy somewhere?

Panic rumbles in my stomach, bubbling up to the back of my throat like bad indigestion, but I swallow hard, making sure my face shows no further emotion. Instinct tells me Jenny wouldn't sympathise. After all, if everything they say is true, she's risking her life to rescue us.

Forcing doubt out of my mind, I tug the wig into place and shove my own hair under it, the roughness and physical pain distracting my thoughts. Once the dark glasses are in place, I flip back the visor, slouch and stare out of the front window. Cars whiz by, and I notice we're on a motorway.

"Where are we?"

"Heading south, towards the coast."

"Are you going to tell me any details?"

"No."

"'Right."

As we exit onto the inner lane, I notice my ghostly face reflected in the windscreen. My breath hitches and I blink rapidly to stop the tears falling, pinching my arms until the pain gives my body other things to think about. I figure the best thing to do is block out the world, and so I close my eyes and mind to stupid thoughts. At this point in time, I think I might welcome some sort of drug to help me sleep till we get wherever we're going. Another stupid thought! I need to be wide awake to know where we are, or in case it all goes horribly wrong.

"Shit!"

I open my eyes at Jenny's outburst. "What's up?"

"Roadblock."

"What?"

"They've moved quickly."

I look out of the window. Cars are slowing down and being herded into one lane.

"It's just roadworks."

"If that makes you feel better."

"What do you mean?"

"Grab the blanket from the back, cover yourself and curl in a ball. Pretend to sleep."

I stare at her for a second, wondering if she's a bit mad.

"Do it!"

Her sharpness makes me flinch. I glare at her but then stretch around the seat and grab the blanket. It's rough, one that might be used for dogs, but I shake it out as Jenny continues to give instructions.

"Listen carefully. I'm Jenny Parsons, your mother. We're going home to Carlton."

"Great! Where in Carlton do we live, then?"

"14 Garden Street."

"Right, and what's my name?"

"Caroline, and you're thirteen."

"I am. What about IDs?"

"I have a licence; you don't have anything."

We're moving slower now. I can hear horns, some distant music and engines rumbling to a halt. A dog is barking somewhere, and a kid is crying. I squelch myself up into a ball.

"Push the chair back."

Releasing the lever, the seat tilts, almost flattening out. I lie with my cheek against the rough seat cover. It smells of sweaty bodies, greasy food and grime. Saliva hits my mouth and for a second, I think I'm going to puke, but the sickly feeling passes.

"What about school?"

"What?" She glances over at me, her forehead lined.

"Well, if I'm thirteen, I'd be at school."

She's silent, thinking for a minute. "Get a tissue from my bag at the back." I dive around the seat and scramble for her green bag, at the same time noticing my backpack is there. "While you're there, give me my wallet." I do as she asks. She slips the wallet in the side pocket of the door as I reach for tissues. "Good, now stuff one in your cheek."

"Why?"

"Dentist. That's where we've just come from. You've had a tooth out and you're sleeping off the anaesthetic." She glances at me. "Think you can do this?"

"Sure we need all this for roadworks?"

"Trust me, this is not roadworks."

"Fine," I sigh, and bunch up the tissue before stuffing it in my left cheek.

"Now wrap yourself up and pretend to be sleeping. Oh, and take off the glasses."

"Oh-*kay*!" I dump the glasses on the floor, convinced this is stupid and she's overreacting. No one would go to all this trouble just for Liddy and me.

After half an hour, I'm hot and stuffy, the blanket is itchy and we're still inching forwards. I want to get up, but she won't let me, although she does at least keep up a bit of a commentary.

"Your school is St Anne's."

"Right." I open my eyes and look across at her. She's lithe and muscular. Her jawline is sharp and tense.

"It's a secondary school in Carlton."

"How do you know so much about it?"

"I lived there as a child."

I don't respond. It's the first bit of information she's given about herself. It must be weird passing so close to her hometown. I wonder if her family are still there.

"What's my name?" She's drilling me.

"Er, Jenny. Jenny Parsons."

"Our address?"

"14 Gardens Street."

"Garden."

"'kay."

"And what about your school?"

"St Anne's."

"Age?"

"Thirteen. Surely they'll never believe that?"

"As long as we stick to the story." She leans to the side. "There are drones. Keep your head down and eyes closed, and no talking from now on."

I snap my eyes shut and rely on my ears to understand what is happening. A few seconds later, I hear her low voice.

"We're about to pass through. They're stopping every car. Remember, you're drowsy from the dentist."

I wipe the prickly sweat off my forehead with the blanket. The tissue in my cheek has dried up my mouth and I'm desperate for a drink. Surely, the roadblock can't be for us. The car halts, the window is wound down.

"What's wrong, Officer?"

"Good morning." The voice is someone weary. "I'm sorry to delay your journey, but I'm afraid a couple of runaways have attacked police officers. They're dangerous and armed."

My heart's pounding in my ears. I grip the blanket closer to my chin.

She was right.

"Good gracious." Jenny has changed her accent to sound posh. I feel her stroke my back. "Are we safe?"

"We're doing our best, madam. Now, just a couple of questions."

"Certainly."

"Can I see your driving licence, please?"

"Here."

I want to peek, but daren't open my eyes. I'm trying to steady my breathing, thinking about what I might look like as a sleeping thirteen-year-old.

"Mrs Parsons?"

"Yes."

"And may I ask who this is with you?"

"My daughter, Caroline."

"Is she sick?"

"A tooth was taken out this morning, poor girl. Knocked her out." I feel her stroking my back again. "She'll be fine after a good night's sleep."

"And where are you heading?"

"Carlton."

"Your address?"

"14 Garden Street."

He doesn't respond for a few seconds, but I can hear the pinging of a tablet as he checks information. Jenny still has her hand on my back.

"Is everything okay, Officer?"

"Yeah, we just need to do facial recognition checks."

"I've never heard of that before."

My heart is thudding, my stomach writhing. It takes all my control not to jump up and run.

"It's just like having your photo taken. Nothing to worry about. But you'll have to wake your daughter, I'm afraid."

"But she's underage. I'm sorry, I can't permit you to take her photo."

"How old is she?"

"Thirteen."

I know he's looking at me.

"She looks older."

"She's tall for her age. Our family has always reached the Change younger than most." Jenny's voice is strained, less charming than before. "Look, Officer, she's had a tooth out. Why don't you just take my photo?"

His voice becomes demanding. "Let's just get this over with, Mrs Parsons. We're holding up the traffic."

I lie still, my head throbbing, my mouth devoid of any spit due to the tissue wedged in my cheek. Knowing she'll have to do as he says, I begin thinking about how we'll escape. Somewhere she might have guns, but the traffic is backed up. How will we get out of here?

A hand strokes my shoulder. "Caroline, baby, wake up."

I do nothing, prolonging the inevitable, imagining myself being dragged away.

"Come on, honey. You can go back to sleep, soon."

Jenny leans in and whispers in my ear, "Play for time. Schultz will be here, soon."

Having no idea what Schultz has to do with it, I groan a little. "Uh..."

How would I feel if I had my tooth out?

I stick my tongue in my cheek. "Shleep."

"Yes, I know, but we just need to take your photo."

"Why?"

"Come on, darling." I feel her leaning away. "Are you sure we need to do this?"

"Yes." The officer sounds annoyed. "Look, I can try to take the photo of her asleep. I'll come around the other side."

Jenny whispers again. "Whatever happens, don't let him get a full image. Eyes closed!”

I squint. Her eyes flash towards the side window, her brow furrowed. A wave of real sickness passes through me, and I scrunch the blanket up, pulling it higher as the door next to me swings open and warm air whooshes in.

“Could you remove the blanket from her face, please?”

Jenny gently and very slowly removes my clinging fingers. The officer is tutting. I hear a scratchy radio voice.

“Four-zero-five-nine. What’s holding you up?”

“Sick child. Nearly done.”

“Hurry up.”

“Yes, sir.”

Jenny speaks. “Is this okay?”

I murmur again, trying to reach out for the blankets as if I’m in some sort of a nightmare – which I am. “Mum…” It’s peculiar to say Mum to a stranger and even odder to hear her reply.

“It’s okay, baby. Just a quick click.” She’s grabbing my hands as if trying to pry them away from the blanket.

I crumple up my face, playing the game. Coffee-scented breath reaches my nostrils. A body leans over me and the sound of clicking reaches my ears, probably a scanner.

The officer speaks. “Right, let’s check it.”

A motorbike rides up and stops beside us. The officer raises his voice. “Hey, you, get back in the queue. Just because you’re on a bike, it doesn’t mean—”

Schultz’s voice is calm and soothing. “Thank you, Officer.”

“Thank you for what?”

“For doing your job so well.”

“Eh?”

“Did he take the photo?”

Jenny responds, “Yes.”

“So, Officer” – his voice has a silky edge to it – “I want you to relax.”

“Eh?”

“Relax.” His voice is deep and cavernous. “Could you do something for me?”

“Yes, sir.”

“Please delete any photos you took of this car and its passengers.”

“Er…”

I can't help but open my eyes and look up. Jenny presses me down, but I see Schultz staring at the officer, who's got that same immobile look as...

My brain's trying to remember something, but I'm so intrigued at what's happening, I push it aside.

"Yes, that's right, just delete the registration plate." The officer is clicking something on his screen. "And the photo. Very good. Now, I want you to do something else." Schultz's voice is hypnotising.

Then it hits me... But no. No one's that good, surely?

"See that silver car, back there? Registration FD05 NJC."

"Yes, sir."

"You're going to let them pass with no check. You'll also let this car and me pass."

"Yes, sir."

"Very good." I can almost sense him smiling. "And then you'll forget everything about us – the car, our faces, registration. Everything. Please confirm that."

"I will forget everything about you, this car and the one with the plate number FD05 NJC."

"Thank you, Officer. Are we free to go?"

"Yes, sir."

Our engine immediately ignites and we pull out.

I turn to Jenny. "What was that?"

"Shh! Stay down. We still have a barrier to get through."

"So, Schultz's a hypnotist, or what?" My words come out funny as I still have the tissue in my mouth.

"Quiet!"

Through the vibration of the seat, I feel the engine changing gears and speeding up. I'm so hot, I throw the blanket on the floor and then kick off my trainers and socks.

"Keep still."

"Fine."

We slow down again, and I hear a woman's voice outside: "Keep moving."

Jenny's knuckles grip the steering wheel as she nods at the person beyond my vision and then speeds up. After a few minutes, she glances my way.

"We're through but keep your head below the dashboard. There are cameras and drones on these roads."

My mind flips through the police scene again. I think of my mum. Somehow, I have to get a message to her soon, tell her I'm okay.

"Why are we—" Realising I can now remove the tissue, I pull it out of my mouth and drop it on the floor before finishing my sentence. "Why are we being blamed for attacking the police?"

"People will inform on you if they think you're dangerous." She glances at me. "To be honest, we've never had this much trouble, but the Commission are getting desperate. Schultz tells us they're closer to their goal, which is why they're bringing in kids like you."

"Golems?"

"Something like that."

"And you lot, who are you, and why get me away from them?"

She stares at the road, frowning. "There were two plans put into action to get you out. One with us and one I know nothing about, so you must be important to our leaders, too."

"I don't get it."

"Once we get to the base, I'm sure we'll find out."

I'm about to ask what that means when I hear a beep from her phone attached to a device on the windscreen. She looks at it and sighs.

"Good, they're through."

"Liddy?"

"Yes."

I stretch my legs out, touching the mats, feeling my body relax a little.

"How far behind us are they?"

"Five or six cars. Schultz's travelling between us."

That reminds me. "So, he's some sort of hypnotist, then?"

"That's one of his talents." Her face screws up a little before going back to neutral.

"He's pretty good at it."

"It doesn't work on everyone. He took a risk back there. We could have handled it without him."

I can tell by her tone she doesn't approve, although I'm not sure how she thinks we could have handled it if my face had been scanned properly. How exactly would we have got away?

Only then do I remember the day at the clinic. He'd told me to relax, too, but it hadn't worked. He'd done the same with Liddy. That's why Liddy didn't fight to be with me.

"But the police... What if it hadn't worked?"

"We'd all be locked up by now." She says it with little emotion, but her jaw is tight, her arms stiff. She rolls her shoulders and cracks her neck from side to side, hands gripping the steering wheel.

It occurs to me how much danger they're putting themselves in for Liddy and me. I can't figure out why they would do that. Whatever her reason, I'm grateful. Without them, we'd both be in facilities, both having our brains fried. The clip of the girl screaming flashes through my mind and I shudder as my imagination transfers my own face to that of the girl's. Would they really have done that to me? I decide, there and then, that this secret community Jenny and Schultz have must be better than the alternative.

Last week, I was laughing at Liddy trying to stretch her hair (she wants it to grow longer) and now, well, the world has turned crazy. I'm a Golem; Liddy's condemned; secret meetings, safe houses; two plans to get me out and some sort of rebel group shooting at the police.

What the heck is going on?

CHAPTER THIRTEEN

I'm falling in and out of sleep. The combination of drugs, the hum of the engine, the sticky heat inside the car and the throb of wheels pounding the road have the effect of a sleeping potion, creating a half-awake, half-asleep nightmare. Every so often, I jerk, as if fighting quicksand, and come up for a breath, only to be sucked down again. At some point, I hear Jenny talking to someone. Her voice draws me back to reality and I open my eyes. The car has stopped, a door is open and a cool breeze dances over my hot cheeks.

Hearing other voices, I push myself up. Jenny is with David and Schultz. Liddy is sitting on a low wall behind them, his shoulders bent, head down and black hair dangling. Opening the door, I slip out and move towards him. He looks up and grins.

"Hey, Blondie!"

For a second, I wonder what he means, but then remember the wig and pull it off my head. As I sit close to Liddy, we touch shoulders playfully and Liddy teases me. "With everything going on, you slept?"

"What? No. Only a bit."

Schultz walks over. "How's your back?"

"Throbbing a bit."

"Take some more painkillers. It should ease it a little. Once we get there, it will be checked out properly."

"Thanks."

He passes me a bottle of water. "Here, drink this. You look a little flushed. Are you hot?"

I gulp half of it down before wiping my mouth on the grotty jumper sleeve. "I think it's just from the car, but thanks."

His job done, Schultz moves a short distance away and I turn to Liddy. "What time is it?"

"2:30 p.m."

"Can't be." I realise I've totally lost track of time. "What day is it?"

"Tuesday."

"No..."

Jenny and David are at the silver car getting something out of the boot. I search the area for any landmarks I might recognise. We're sitting on an old wall with broken stones and aged moss; there's a worn lane around a wooded area in front of us; birds chirp from high in a canopy of branches burdened with summer leaves; there's a scent of sweet wildflowers and pine needles. Any other day, I'd have gone exploring.

"Where are we?"

Liddy frowns. "Don't bother asking. They're not telling."

Schultz overhears. "It's for your own safety... and ours." But his mind is on something else and, after a few seconds, he stands by Jenny and David. They all have their heads down, muttering. Liddy and I watch them, but I give up trying to hear anything.

"If you were awake, Lid, why didn't you see anything?"

"Because I was forced to lie flat," he sneers. "What with all the cameras and drones."

"Me, too."

"Yeah, right. As if..."

He has a point. There can't have been drones all the way. I watch as they take something out of the back of the car.

"What do you think they're doing?"

"It's that communication device they used in the van."

"It is?"

"They said the ports and airports are being watched."

My eyes flick to Liddy, but I'm more interested in the trio and the new gadget they're standing over. "What... who?"

He leans over to pull some biscuits from his backpack. "You hungry?" Untwisting the half-eaten packet, he offers it to me. They're his favourite chocolate oat cookies. I smile and take one, nibbling at it. The sweetness tingles my saliva glands.

"So?"

He smirks, pointing at my jumper as he chomps down half a biscuit in one go. "Green isn't your colour."

"Liddy..." My voice is strained.

"You think I have the answers because I was awake?" He swallows the other half of the biscuit. "David, the mute over there, told me nothing."

"Then what's this about the airports and stuff?"

"I heard them going on about it when we stopped."

"Well, I'm not sitting here. I'm gonna find out."

Liddy pulls on my arm as I get to my feet. I glance back.

"Be careful of Schultz."

"Why?"

"As much as he's my type, there's something about him I just don't" – he looks sideways, before muttering – "trust."

I shove my hands in my pockets and lean forward so he can hear me when I whisper back. "He's fine as long as you don't look into his eyes."

It's Liddy's turn to frown and look confused. "What do you mean?"

I sit down again, moving my head close to his. "Remember back at the hideout, when you didn't want us to separate?"

"Yeah. Well, I didn't want to. We just didn't have a choice."

"I think Schultz hypnotised you."

"What? How do you know that?" I can almost see the cogs in his mind turning. "He—"

"He uses the word 'relax'. I heard him with the police officer. That was the only reason we all got through."

"But that's not right." He stands, glaring at the group by the car. "Didn't you stop him?"

"Sorry. Only figured it out later."

We both stare in his direction.

"Don't worry. I'll watch out for you, Lid."

"What?"

I look at him, feeling good about myself, for once. Liddy's always been physically stronger, even more so since he became a boy. "It doesn't work on me."

He shifts to the side a little. "And how would you know?"

"He tried at the clinic. It didn't work."

Liddy's jaw tightens, his fists clench. But then, his stern mouth breaks into a wry smile. "Let's find out what's going on."

I nod as we stride over. "Just in case, keep your eyes down."

David has earplugs in and is bent over the communication device. Up closer, I can see it has old-fashioned dials and knobs. He's twisting them and clicking switches. I know they're afraid of tracking and stuff, but surely they have mobiles that block signals? Still, that's not the most important question.

"Got it. Over and out."

He switches the machine off and packs it away in a small toolbox. Jenny's giving out orders. She stands with her hands on her hips, legs slightly apart.

"David, clear the area of any signs, hide the vehicles and make your own way via the usual route. Schultz, you're with me. We'll take the long way round."

Both nod as she turns to us. "As you probably heard, we can't go via a plane or ferry but have just confirmed an alternative route."

"Where are we?"

Liddy looks away as he speaks, trying to avoid eye contact with Schultz. It makes him look anxious. Jenny's voice is clipped in response.

"About two hours from base camp."

I stare at her as if, somehow, I can force her to give us more details. "And where's this base camp?"

"About two hours from here." Jenny's mouth is stern, her blue eyes cool. David leans against the car boot, sighing, exasperated.

He intercedes. "Look, we can't answer your questions, not on the mainland, so you may as well stop asking. Once we're at the base and safe, you'll get answers. For now, you'll have to trust us."

Schultz rolls his eyes and moves towards his motorbike, grabbing a backpack from one of the panels on the side. "We're on foot for a while, so you'll need your bags."

With that, David and Jenny walk away.

Liddy leans in to whisper in my ear, "Well, that went well."

I cross my arms and kick the car tyre.

"Yep, that'll fix it."

I frown at Liddy. "Fix what?"

He squeezes my right shoulder; he's grinning but his eyes are sympathetic. "Come on, let's get our stuff."

My mouth purses. "We don't know what we're getting into. What if we don't like this base camp? Can we just leave?"

"If we're walking, we'll know where we're going and can figure out our way back."

"Mm... good point, Robin." A reference to another old show Liddy likes to watch.

He smirks at me. "Hey, I'm Batman, you're the sidekick."

I manage a smile. "At least they aren't separating us again."

Carefully dragging the scabby sweatshirt over my head, I stomp towards the blue car to retrieve my jacket and bag, but once there, I sit inside, staring out the windscreen, and sigh. The events of the last few days are like some sort of unbelievable story. Who would blindly follow people they don't know? People who claim the Commission are killing those who are different.

What have they really shown us? A clip from a clinic.

My mind whirls. Not long ago, I was grateful for their help, but now I'm doubting again. I rub my temples and take a deep breath. My shoulder throbs but the sharp pain has lessened. Must be the drugs. And that reminds me: a chip! A tracking device in my shoulder. Is that the norm? Do the Commission do it as standard, in case the 'abnormals' run? My brain feels numb. I no longer know what the truth is, and sorting through it all only makes me feel crazier.

I hear a high-pitched beep from Jenny's phone. She must have left it on the dashboard by accident. For a second, I stare at it, but it takes only a millisecond more before I grab it. Desperate, I press the key to unlock it, but there's no way I could guess the password; useless to even try. There are some notifications though, and I pull them down to sneak a look. One is the weather, twelve degrees in Lymington.

Lymington, where's that?

"What are you doing?" Jenny is by my side door.

"Er... your phone beeped."

She puts out her hand and I pass it over. "Did you use it?"

"What? How could I?"

She looks down at her phone and knows I have seen our location. Her face hardens. "Get your bag. We're moving."

Jenny's up front, Liddy and I are in the middle and Schultz brings up the rear. We're trekking through thick woods, keeping away from the main path. I hear a dog barking and someone calling, "Jojo!" Jenny moves in the opposite direction, skirting a wild bramble bush. A creeping thorn snags at my jeans, pricking my skin as I pull away, but my mind is on other things. I'm trying to keep track of where we're going, which is pretty much impossible. Even if I were some sort of amazing navigator, I have no compass or map, and the sun is blocked by clouds and the thick covering of overhanging branches, so we could be going in any direction. The one clue I have is the name of the town. When we get to wherever we're going, I'll look up Lymington and find a wood close by. At least then, if we decide to leave, I'll know which way we entered their base. Satisfied with the plan, I pull out the half-filled bottle of water and gulp a couple of mouthfuls before pushing it back into my side pocket.

Liddy stops and I almost crash into him. Jenny has halted and is pulling us into a circle. She whispers instructions.

"We're close to a large, open field. On the other side is a narrow river, with an old hut. We're heading for the hut." She waits for us to nod our understanding. "There's a farmhouse not far to the left, so we're going to crawl through the wheat. Any questions?"

Schultz speaks. I notice Liddy staring in the opposite direction, biting his lip. "Should we go in twos?"

"No, let's just move. If we separate, make for the hut." She shifts the bag on her shoulder. "Keep low, no speaking."

She reaches the edge of the woods first and peeks out. "Jesus, how much more can go wrong on this bleeding mission?"

I step forward to lean out, but she holds me back. I notice the tendons standing out on her neck as she grips my arm. Her eyes narrow at something. On looking through the thinning trees, I understand why she cursed, and take a deep breath myself. The wheat is almost harvested, shorn like a stubbly haircut – an early crop. But out there is a combine harvester finishing off the far side, directly in the way of our escape route. The engine is purring, but the driver is standing next to it, speaking with two officers. My body becomes rigid. I don't even dare rub my clammy palms down my jeans in case my movement attracts attention.

Liddy stands to my right; Schultz is on Jenny's left side.

"How could they know?"

I offer up an explanation. "Maybe it's nothing to do with us."

Jenny throws an 'are you that naïve?' expression at me, before responding in a more conciliatory tone. "Whatever they're here for, we can't take any chances."

Liddy pushes his hair behind his ears, his voice a hoarse whisper. "What does that mean?"

"It means we take no risks. We wait until no one's around before crossing the field." She crouches low, staring ahead.

Liddy and I sit, pulling off our bags and leaning against a tree. I shuffle sideways a little to avoid pressing against my left side. The humidity in the woods is sticky. A fly buzzes around my face, and I waft it away. After about ten minutes, Schultz gets up, disappearing into the woods. I wonder what he's doing, but it isn't long before he's back.

Liddy grins at my silent query and mouths, "Toilet," standing up himself.

Jenny looks around. "Where you going?"

"Looking for the bathroom."

She stares at him, then at Schultz, who has just put his bag down.

He sighs. "I'll go with him."

Then, like a little kid, I realise I need the toilet, too. "I'm coming."

Jenny's rolling her eyes. "Just stay low and keep quiet."

On our return, Jenny's pacing. Hands on hips, taut body, she leans slightly forward. When she turns to face us, she's biting her lip. "Get your bags. We're moving out now."

"What?" Schultz walks over to her. "I thought we were waiting."

"We were, but the police have driven away and the man's disappeared into the farmhouse." Jenny picks up her bag and slings it across her shoulder.

"Wait, Jenny, wouldn't it be better to wait till dark?" Schultz sounds worried.

"Maybe, but I'm not very good with boats in the dark." Her voice is full of strained sarcasm, her eyes steely and cold. "Are you?"

"Guess not." He shrugs and picks up his bag.

Liddy and I glance at each other. I mouth, "A river?" He raises his eyebrows as if to say, 'I guess so!'.

Before striding out, Jenny gives her final orders. Her pale face is sweaty, her left cheek has a streak of dirt across it. She has us all squatting near the edge of the field, pointing out her plan.

"We skirt the field and then turn left at the bottom, towards the hut. There's no one around so we should make it unseen but, just in case, we're a family, hiking."

We all nod. Seems simple enough.

In unison, we step out, staying in the shadows of the trees. Liddy is close behind me; Schultz brings up the rear. The pounding in my ears blocks out all other noises, as if I'm in a silent world. Speed-walking towards the end of the field, I glance over my shoulder, checking on the house. From this angle, I can't see it, so I assume we can't be seen at the moment, but once we turn, we'll be in full view.

At the corner of the field, Jenny stops and stoops. Waving her hand at us, her instructions are clear: "Everyone down. We crawl from here."

There's a flat border along the side of the field that has yet to be harvested. The wheat to my left is about 4ft high. Just ahead, about 6ft in, is the silent, red combine harvester. Keeping my head down, I resist the urge to peek above the parapet and, instead, push myself hard, cutting my palms on the dry grass. The pain is like a paper cut, but I grit my teeth and ignore it as I focus on keeping up with Jenny, who streams ahead.

Just as we're passing the combine harvester, its engine blasts out and it begins moving down the field. From my position, I can see the man high up in his seat. He only has to turn his head to notice the four of us hiding.

No way would he think we are out on a family hike.

Jenny stops. "Get down!" She flattens to her stomach. We copy her. I press my cheek into the scratchy stalks and jar my back. Pain shoots through my shoulder and a low moan escapes my throat, but the engine is loud, and no one could have heard me beyond our group. Jenny scowls at me.

Schultz mouths, "Okay?" I nod and keep my head down. The clunking of metal chopping and clearing rings in my ears. Dust scatters and flies across us. Closing my eyes tight, I turn my face in the opposite direction, hold my breath, and bite on a loose piece of flesh in my mouth. The taste of blood, salty and sickening, hits my tongue.

I feel a tap on my shoulder and look up. Jenny is crouching. She pulls out a hat to cover her red hair. Schultz and Liddy are next to her, and I squat beside Liddy. The tractor is behind us, moving towards the end of the field.

"We're going to make a run for it." She peeps over the wheat. "There's no one around, so it's a good time. We need to be at the hut before he turns." She looks directly at me. "No noise."

We all nod like soldiers about to climb out of the trenches.

"Let's go."

She's so fast, for a second I'm left behind, but Liddy prods me. "Come on!"

I leap up and charge forwards. Schultz is a couple of sprints ahead already and Liddy strides out in front of me. All of them have long legs. Before I know it, I'm at least a metre behind. My heart thuds in my chest and sweat trickles down the side of my face. When Liddy slows down and grabs my arm, I'm already flagging – a cramp in my side. He yanks me to keep up. A sharp pain rips through my back, and I yelp. My throat is dry and hoarse, my tongue sticks to the upper palate. Still, I keep my head down, and push myself harder, determined not to be left behind.

"Hey, you two, what are you up to?"

The voice is a woman's. Just beyond the hut, a dumpy lady with short, curly hair waves at us. She's wearing khaki pants and a white, stretchy top – both look a size too small. With her is a brown, shaggy dog. Liddy and I stop as she closes the gap between us. The hut is a few strides to our right. Schultz and Jenny are poking their heads out from behind, watching us with worried faces.

"This is Mr Jenson's land. What are you doing here?" Breathing heavily, we just stare at her. "Well?"

Her dog is sniffing around our feet. "Jojo, come here." The dog returns to his owner and she bends down to put him on a lead. He whines and barks a little, but she shushes him, stroking his shiny coat. I realise she's still waiting for an answer.

"We're in training."

"Training?"

Liddy's face is sweaty, his hair plastered around his cheeks.

"For a marathon." I lean on my knees, breathing, trying to look innocent.

"Yeah. Raising money for an animal charity."

She hesitates, not sure if we're telling the truth. Her dog begins barking and straining at the leash. "Shush Jojo. Well, you shouldn't be running across Jenson's fields."

I begin to make excuses in my head, but Liddy speaks first.

"Sorry, we didn't know it wasn't allowed. We haven't cut across the crops or anything."

She narrows her eyes. "Don't I know you from somewhere?"

"Huh? Don't think so." I lick my lips but find I don't even have enough saliva to moisten them.

Out of the corner of my eye, I see Jenny's face getting redder. She's looking behind me, pointing. The harvester is turning. We have to get out of here quickly.

"I suppose you could ask permission. Mr Jenson's here." She flicks her hand in the direction of the harvester. "Surprised he didn't see you."

"It's okay, we won't do it again." I pull on Liddy's sleeve and together we jog past her as if continuing our run. Jojo's barking madly.

The woman's shushing him. "What's wrong with you? Don't be silly."

Once we are a short distance away, I look back. She's turned around to check up on us and is rubbing her chin, trying to figure out a puzzle. Then, her face shows shock and, as she pulls a phone out of her pocket, I know she remembers where she's seen us – on television.

Jenny darts out, grabs the phone and covers the woman's mouth. The woman struggles but Schultz steps forwards. He touches her forehead.

"Relax. Stay quiet. Hear the soft beat of your heart."

Her face suddenly has no expression, even though Jojo's straining on his lead.

"Calm your dog. Stop him barking."

She bends down, soothing and stroking, but he's wild, froth forming at his mouth. From nowhere, her fist rises, and she slaps him hard across his muzzle. He whines and lowers his trembling body, but the barking stops.

By this time, Liddy and I are back with them. Jenny pulls us aside. "Come with me."

As we walk away, I hear Schultz doing his thing. "You will go home, have a cup of tea and forget you saw any of us. Would you confirm that for me please?"

"Yes, I will go home, have a cup of tea and forget I saw any of you."

"Good. Now, off you go."

Without another word, she walks away, and Schultz joins us behind the hut.

Liddy glares at him. "Don't ever do that to me again."

Schultz drops his chin to his chest, takes a deep breath and then looks up and nods. "It isn't something I do lightly."

It doesn't satisfy Liddy, but Jenny waves us forward and we trek across a muddy bank, towards a small river with long reeds. The air is damp, and the stink of slimy rot permeates my nostrils. A long-ago memory flashes into my mind: a place with frogs, where we caught tadpoles with a net and squealed at the creepy-crawlies. But as I struggle with the slimy bank, the memory fades just as quickly as it appeared.

"Here. Schultz, I need your help."

Schultz pushes past Liddy and me. Only when Jenny steps aside do I notice the corner of a green dinghy, hidden in the reeds, upside down. My first thought is that we won't fit, but as they pull it out and turn it upright, I see I'm wrong.

Liddy stands next to me. I lean in close, glad for his presence. He places his arm around my waist and squeezes for a second, before moving forward to help Schultz drag the boat onto the shallow water. Jenny retrieves two wooden oars and puts them in the boat. Schultz is holding onto a rope tied to the dinghy.

"Let's get out of here."

Jenny, no longer her aloof self, curses again. "Damn, will I be glad to get home." She looks up at Liddy and me as she straddles her feet between the shore and the dinghy, trying to stop it swaying. "I don't know what's with you two, but you'd better be worth it."

Sitting in the boat, watching as Schultz and Jenny each take an oar, I wonder where *home* is. I visualise our tiny, two-up, two-down house, my mum's face at the door, smiling, and our cosy kitchen chats. I picture my bedroom, an unmade bed, the curtains closed, my school uniform draped across the chair. For ever the same, a never changing image in my mind. Tears come to my eyes, but I blink them away. Liddy's sitting at the front of the dinghy to balance the weight. He waves and smiles a sarcastic grin. I can almost hear his thoughts.

"Lovely day for a river picnic, darling."

I raise my eyebrows, wondering if he can read my face as well as I can read his. "Certainly. Would you like another strawberry?"

CHAPTER FOURTEEN

Other than the quiet splash of oars and bird song, the journey along the narrow river is peaceful. Trees overhang the water, their roots clinging to the bank in a fantastically warped fashion. They remind me of an old man's bony fingers digging into the earth. In other circumstances, I'd have laid my head back and closed my eyes, but my mind is racing as I attempt to track the route and form a map in my head.

From Lymington, we went through a wood, Jenson's fields and onto a river, which must be a tributary. We're just entering a wider stretch of sea, so somewhere off the coast, maybe.

Waves crash against the dinghy, jostling it around. One smacks into the side, splashing salty water in my face and leaving my left arm soaked. I gasp and cling to the rubber handles as we hit a rough patch. Jenny and Schultz pull harder on the oars to control our direction. Peering ahead, I see a sudden thick mist drifting towards us.

"We have to go back." I point beyond Liddy, who flicks his head around.

Jenny's voice is strained as she heaves on the oar again. "We'll be there, soon."

"But the fog?"

"We're going through it."

"Through it?" Liddy shouts from behind them. "Are you mad?" He starts to crawl towards them, wobbling the boat.

Schultz snaps at him. "Keep still. The fog won't last long. We'll come out of it within minutes."

Liddy sits back as we enter the thick, wet blanket. Eerily, the dense clouds block the noise of the cawing seabirds as if we've just switched them off. The thick air tightens my chest, but worse, the stench of rotting fish causes me to gag and splutter as if I'm about to be sick.

Where is that coming from?

Shuddering, I swipe the back of my hand across my brow, but everything seems tainted with the stinky mist. Even my eyes begin to sting, as if the air is trying to infiltrate my insides.

Liddy begins coughing; it's chesty, like an old man who smokes too much. Part of me holds on to the fact that Jenny wouldn't do anything to risk her own life, but a voice in my head screeches that we're all going to die in this fog. I lower my head, squelch my eyes shut and wrap my arms around my stomach.

A hand touches my arm, and I flinch.

"We're through." Schultz is leaning forward. He smiles to reassure me. He and Jenny have pulled the oars on board and we're drifting on what appears to be an open sea. The fog, the smell, the wetness has all gone. I glance behind me with wonder. It's still there, circling us, a wall of thick clouds sitting just above the water. I can't see through it, or over the top. It's weird and unnatural.

Liddy calls over to me. "You okay?"

I nod and force a tight smile. He looks rather green himself.

"Look." He points behind him and over his shoulder. A small speedboat is heading our way, the drumming of its engine quietening as it slows and settles beside us. A tall man in grey shorts and navy T-shirt grins and hails Jenny.

"Been a difficult one?"

"Hell, yes. Let's get out of here."

She throws him the dinghy rope and he drags us towards him. The waves are choppy, and we are tossed around a bit, but he manages to tie the rope to a rail. Finding my balance, I grab his hand and carefully step over the gap to reach his boat.

"Thanks."

"No probs. Captain Smith, at your service." He grins, but I just stare, not sure what's going on. "You can sit over there."

He directs me to a wooden bench. After the dinghy, it feels as if I'm stepping on solid ground and I plonk myself down, grateful for the rescue. As Liddy sits beside me, I look around. The mist still floats behind us, but then I notice it forms a circle. In the centre of it, no more than a quarter of a mile from us, is a rock protruding from the sea. Liddy follows my eyes.

"A castle with a moat, then."

"What?"

His face is pale, his hair dangles around his cheeks. Under his eyes are traces of black mascara, making him look like he hasn't slept for weeks. He gestures towards the rock and the mist. "A castle... Moat..."

"Oh, yeah, right. It's odd."

He puts his arm around me and pulls me in close. I'm grateful for his warmth.

"We're still alive."

"We are."

"And we're still together."

I look up at him. He's trying to make me feel better. I feel obliged to help him out. "Bet your cookies are wet."

He grins. "Y'know how I love to dunk." I can't help grinning back and our eyes meet, his wary and uncertain. Mine probably look the same.

"I'm so glad you're here, Lid."

"Me too. Wouldn't have missed this for the world."

I giggle, though it comes out almost hysterical.

Schultz sits opposite us. He's leaning over the boat, looking towards the rock. Jenny stands with the captain, who switches on the engine and begins turning the boat around. The dinghy bobs up and down behind us as we aim for the rock.

"Schultz, is the base that rock thing?"

He turns to face me, a strange look in his eyes. "It is."

Liddy looks over Schultz's shoulder. "But that's impossible. It's too small for a pigeon to live on."

An impossible fantasy book I read a couple of years ago pops into my mind. "Is it underground?"

Liddy glances at me, and then looks away, trying to avoid any eye contact with Schultz.

"Some of it is. You'll see in a few minutes."

The captain's swinging us to the left as if we're heading away from the rock. The waves batter against the boat and rock it, tipping Liddy and me low. Gripping the rungs and planting my feet hard to stop me sliding off the bench, I fight with flapping hair as it slaps across my face.

"Are we going out to sea?" I address the question to Schultz, but he doesn't need to answer, as the captain swings around and brings the boat into a straight line, before veering out again as if making a letter S.

I notice several anchored buoys indicating dangerous underwater currents, with arrows to proceed away from the rock. My head turns as we pass by. Wondering why we're not heeding them, I don't immediately look up until Liddy nudges me. His eyes are wide, and his mouth has fallen open. He's pointing towards the rock. Only, the rock has disappeared. In its place is a larger island with a circular port and a long, wooden jetty. Several boats and yachts of different sizes are docked. Beyond that are buildings. They look like warehouses or shops, and there are people, at least twenty, milling around. My heart begins beating in my chest as we close in. I hear Schultz chuckling in the background.

"Liddy, can you see it? How is it possible?"

"So, I'm not dreaming?"

"Not unless we're in the same nightmare."

As the captain slows the engine, steering the boat towards a docking bay, Jenny sits down next to Schultz, facing us. "I know this is a lot to take in."

A torrent of questions follow, from both Liddy and me:

"Is it real?"

"What happened to the rock?"

She smiles – the first time I've ever seen her relax. "The rock is the illusion. This is Base One."

"But how?"

"Magnetic field and projection, military grade."

Still unbelievable.

"You project an image into thin air?"

"Not quite. Just beyond the magnetic field is a reflective wall."

"A wall in the sea?"

"Our security is the most advanced cloaking system available. Not many have the expertise to set this up. Those that do, work for us."

Liddy pushes his hair off his face and grasps it at the back of his neck, as if he's about to tie it up. "But surely anyone could just... I dunno, accidentally crash into it?"

She looks his way, her green eyes bright. "The danger signs keep people away, but social media is great, too. Every so often, we put up a fake story about someone drowning or a ship sinking in the area. Other than that, the magnetic field affects compasses, which is cause enough for ships to veer towards land."

"How come we're not affected, then?"

"Well, the entrance is a corridor with specific coordinates. Our equipment navigates through it."

I gawp at her, wanting to ask a million questions, but I am lost as to which one to ask.

Liddy engages his brain first. "But from the air? Satellites, that sort of stuff?"

"Obviously, we scramble the images satellites pick up."

Obviously!

"To the general public, we're a small, privately-owned rock, bought in memory of a family disaster many years ago. For anyone who digs further, they hit the security protocols of a top-secret military base. Our influence is at top level. Enough to keep people away."

Schultz has been quiet, but now clears his throat. "On the very rare occasion someone manages to find us, we have the ability to deal with it."

Liddy can't help himself. "You hypnotise them to forget."

Schultz smiles, his demeanour humble. "My talent is comparatively minor, but yes, that's a possibility."

I wonder what the other possibilities are as we reach the landing area. A broad, blond man catches the mooring rope and drags us closer to the pontoon, tying the boat to a thick post. The captain leaps onshore, grasping the man's hand and grinning.

"Newcomers?"

"Yep."

"Tarsiers."

They both laugh, Jenny and Schultz grin, but as I don't get the in-joke, which I assume is at our expense, I ignore it.

"Liddy, this is—"

Liddy completes my sentence, "Amazing technology!" His eyes are wide and shining. He stands up to get a clearer look. Amazing wasn't my first thought.

If people can't get in, how do we get out?

Schultz is trying to reassure us. "You're both safe now. No one will find you here."

Jenny's authoritative tone is back. "Get your bags and let's check you in."

I get up, hitching my backpack across my right shoulder. "Check us in where?"

She's following Schultz off the boat and glances back to answer me. "Procedure. Everyone entering the base for the first time is checked in. After that, it's automatic."

The shops and cafes are to our right. They are brightly painted and could be on any high street. I notice some people sitting at tables, drinking coffee. They watch us as we are led left along the pontoon towards larger, warehouse-looking buildings built out of grey cement blocks.

I become aware of seagulls crying overhead, the smell of salt and the sound of crashing waves. They remind me of a school trip we went on once. We visited a working port and saw huge ships. There was a museum with a wooden warship, hundreds of years old. It had sunk in the defence of our coastline from an invasion. Years later, they'd literally lifted it out of the sea.

A few people stare, but most just pass us by, busy doing whatever they're doing. I glance up. Grey clouds still cover the sky, but the light is different. I lift my wrist, only to remember I left my watch behind. "What time is it, Lid?"

"Er…" His eyes flash down. As a lefty, he wears his watch on his right wrist. "5:45 p.m." He looks over at me. "You okay?"

"Don't know. You?"

He shrugs and we plod along in silence for a few seconds before he offers up his thoughts. "At least we don't have the police on our tails."

"Mm…"

After everything that's happened, I should feel better, but I'm having trouble keeping things straight in my mind. My shoulders sag, the pain in my back's throbbing again. I wonder if I should take another painkiller, but I don't much want to be sleepier than I already feel.

"Are you scared?"

"Not scared, not really. But weirded out, I think."

I lean over, lowering my voice. "Do you trust them, Lid?"

His eyebrows raise. "The only people I trust are you and me. We stick together."

I nod in agreement.

He looks down at me for a second, his eyes serious before giving me a lopsided smile. "I'm hungry."

"Yeah. Me too." Dragging out my water bottle, I tip the remaining contents into my mouth and squash the plastic between my fists.

"Wonder Woman." He's trying to distract me.

"You watch way too many old TV series." I don't really feel like playing this particular game and am glad when Jenny interrupts it.

She's opening a door and guiding us through. We enter a brightly lit room with two sofas and a coffee table on one side, an empty desk on the other. A lady, dressed in a black suit with a purple blouse, enters from a corridor on the right. She looks about fifty and has her blonde hair tied up, though straggly bits frame her face. She smiles and greets us, a clipboard in her hands, as if she's on the street doing market research.

"Welcome to reception at Base One. My name's Ruth Bracken." She shakes our hands formally. "Shall we sit, and I'll explain how the check-in procedure works?"

In the corner is a cupboard with a drinks machine. Jenny strolls over to it, much friendlier now. "Coffee, anyone?"

Schultz nods, but both Liddy and I respond at the same time.

"Please, with milk."

"Milk for me and very sweet, if you don't mind." Liddy must be having a sugar dip.

Ruth points to one of the cupboards. "There are sandwiches in the fridge, if anyone's hungry."

Liddy jumps up, opening the bottom door to reveal a small, white fridge. From it, he brings out two plates covered in plastic wrap. As he places them on the table, I see delicate, triangular and rectangular finger sandwiches. Liddy dives in as Jenny brings the coffees, and Ruth continues speaking.

"I'm here today to take you through processing."

Liddy's stuffing his mouth with something that looks like ham. I'm trying to find a meatless option.

"Processing will take about one hour and then you'll be taken through to the reception area."

Having found cheese and tomato, I look up. "Reception area?"

"We keep all new associates at reception for two days to check for viruses, etcetera."

Liddy lifts his hand to cover his mouth, intent on chewing and talking at the same time. "We're not sick."

"Most people aren't. It's just a precaution in the first forty-eight hours."

Schultz intervenes. "Your back needs checking, anyway."

I nod. The cheese, tomato and mayonnaise is somehow the best sandwich I've ever had. My taste buds run wild, tingling in appreciation. The aroma of the coffee is delicious, the taste a perfect balance of bitter and something deeper, almost liquorice. I realise the thought is my mum's, not mine. My throat tightens as I gulp the hot liquid.

Ruth continues. "Whilst at reception, you won't be able to enter the city, but after that you'll be assigned quarters in our main training facility."

I look at Jenny, who somehow reads my mind.

"Every new associate takes training. Once you pass, assuming you want to stay, you become a citizen and take on a role."

My question pops out just before Liddy's. "A citizen of what?"

"We have to pass training? What if we fail? Do you just kick us out?"

Ruth smiles. She has a wide mouth, but it suits her. "Training is about accepting who we are, our rules, our way of life. Not all associates agree or want to stay. We do not force anyone. You're free to leave."

"And my citizen question?"

"You'll learn more in training, but we do not give allegiance to any nation you know. We are an independent country, made up of several states – our bases."

"A country?"

"Each state is named after its founder, but our country is called Libertas." Ruth looks down at her notes, ticking a box as if she has a list to get through.

Liddy and I widen our eyes at each other, our eyebrows rising in unison.

"I know this is a lot to take in, but before we start, I just need you to fill in these forms. After which, there are showers and fresh clothing down the corridor."

The forms are short – name, address, age, gender, allergies and food preferences, and reason for coming to Base One – that's it. From the corner of my eye, I notice Liddy tick the female box. Although the three of them are watching us, no one comments.

Jenny stands up. "Well, we need to report in, Ruth. I think they're in good hands, now."

Ruth nods. "A little harder getting here than expected?"

"Yes, but we were prepared."

Schultz looks over at Ruth. "Remember, the clinic at reception needs to check her back."

"And both of you remember to get checked out, as well." She speaks to them like a schoolteacher.

Both Liddy and I get to our feet. "You're leaving?"

"Yes, our job's done, but we'll see you around. Not a huge island, you know." Schultz grins.

It seems to me there is a lot of grinning and smiling going on. I can't tell if it is real or fake. Are they doing it for our benefit or are they just glad to be safe? I glance from one to the other and then at Liddy, who is more interested in eating, and sits down again.

"Right. Thanks, then."

Jenny turns to go, but Schultz reaches over and places his hand on my shoulder. "You'll soon get used to things here and feel like one of us." He must see something in my expression – forlorn, alone, rejected. I'm not sure what he sees or how I feel. Everything has happened so fast. He glances towards Liddy.

"And you have Liddyana, a friend, which is more than most do when they first arrive."

It's strange to hear Liddy's full name, but Schultz is right. He nods at my silence, which he takes as some sort of acquiescence, and steps past me to follow Jenny out of the door.

Ruth claps her hands like a nursery-school teacher. "Right then, shower time."

I hear Schultz's voice as he walks away. "It should be okay to shower, but avoid wetting the bandage, if possible."

I get up to walk in the direction she's pointing. Everything feels odd, as if my joints are out of place. They're behaving like this is all normal. Just have a cup of coffee, a sandwich and a shower. Go along with their procedures on this hidden island that no one can enter. I don't know what to do, what to think. Yes, they saved us, but what are we getting into? Who are they?

As I reach the showers, my body shudders, there's a fluttering in my stomach and my chest tightens. I should feel safe, but I don't.

CHAPTER FIFTEEN

The hot water gushes, massaging my body. I'm holding the shower head at an angle, trying to avoid the bandage. The shower gel has the clean, citrus smell of aloe vera and the shampoo stings my eyes, but beyond that, I'd happily stay under for longer, blocking out the world and everyone in it. I need time to process, to be away from people, but they're waiting, and my back stings a bit. So, I turn off the tap and tuck the towel around me.

Wiping the condensation off the mirror, I stare at the stranger in front of me. She stretches her mouth wide, sticks out her tongue and frowns. Although my life has turned upside down, I haven't changed. My brown hair hangs around my pale, high cheekbones, and my chest is still flat, but I feel different. What I thought and felt just a few days ago is now a muddle of emotions. Ridges form on my forehead and, for a second, my mum's expression is plastered on my face. Sadness and guilt flow from my stomach to heat my face. She'll be out of her mind. If she knew I was safe, would she be glad we ran? I hear her voice in my head: *'Don't worry about me.'*

That's exactly what she'd say. Or would she? Am I just putting her words in my head to make me feel better? I rub my body dry and am about to turn my head upside down to scrub at my hair, when I remember my stitches. Instead, I towel dry my scalp whilst staring at myself in the mirror, then tie my hair back before opening the long cupboard for clean clothes. Ours were soaked on the journey. The cupboard is full of navy jogging pants, grey hoodies and even underwear. Finding the extra small of everything, I get dressed quickly. The sleeves and legs are still too long, so I take a second to roll them up before pulling out a small toiletry bag. Inside is a travel toothbrush and toothpaste, a comb, some tissues and nail clippers.

Standing outside the shower room, I stop, as if on the brink of a precipice. I can still hear Liddy's shower. He loves long hot baths and showers. Beyond that, there's the slight hum of electric lights.

Part of me wants to step off, freefall into this new life, accept there are good people wanting to help us. I take a deep breath to lighten my heavy chest. It doesn't work very well. Looking behind me, I wonder if I should wait for Liddy. Seconds pass. I can't just stand here. Taking another deep breath, I suck in my cheeks and force myself to step out into the corridor and this strange, new world.

Ruth chats as we wait for Liddy to finish. I wish Liddy would hurry. I fidget with the toggle on my hoodie.

"So, it was Schultz who found you?"

"Found me?"

"At the clinic."

"I guess."

"And Liddy's your friend?"

"Yes… since we were little." I stare towards the corridor.

He won't be my best friend if he doesn't hurry up.

"Do you know much about your test results?"

"No, just that there's something different about my growth genes, and that I'm" – I stutter the words – "a G-Golem." Looking up from under my damp fringe to see if she cringes, I'm surprised when she smiles.

"There are no Golems here, Cam. May I call you Cam?"

I nod. "What do you call people with HGS, then?"

"People!" Her face is stern, but her green eyes sparkle. "Humans." She continues with her synonyms, as one side of her mouth rises. "Let's see… individuals, friends oh, and normal."

"Normal?" I notice my fingers twisting the hem of my top and force myself to stop. "I can't see how that works, when the majority are Gendered."

"You're right, 'normal' is the wrong word. Us minorities are exceptional. You'll discover so much more here than you ever thought possible." Her eyes are bright and she's smiling. "Don't let anyone tell you how to think, Cam. Your life is as valuable as anyone else's. I hope you'll discover how truly exceptional you are, during your stay here."

I stare at her for a few seconds. She's being absolutely sincere; no sarcasm or irony. *I bet she's a teacher.*

I don't know how to respond, so eventually I just break eye contact and look at a picture on the wall. It's a print of Monet's *Water Lilies*, with stunning hues of blues, greens and purples. My favourite colours.

"Do you like impressionist art?"

"I like Monet."

"Me too. I have a book—"

A door slams, interrupting our conversation. To my relief, Liddy appears, wearing the same clothes as I am. Two short, French plaits hang behind his ears, and I notice he's made an effort with his face, which means he brought make-up – not on our list of things to bring. I can't help but grin.

"Looking good."

"Thanks." He glances at Ruth, wanting to know how she reacts. At home, his father would send him back to the bathroom to wash it off.

Ruth watches us both and then smiles. "You come from a different world, one which battles our natural evolution."

Yep, definitely teacher material.

"That means?"

She looks at Liddy, her face serene. "You try to shock me. A boy who thinks himself a girl, who wears make-up, who still uses his first name." She picks up her coffee and takes a sip. "But you're in our world now and you have many things to unlearn. In our world, we oppose the Diversity Commission. We oppose the clinics, compounds and orphanages; the testing of young people; the Foetus Deficiency Therapy, and the whole process of body and mind-meddling."

Interrupting, I push my damp hair behind my ears. Obviously, I know about the clinics and compounds, and I'd vaguely heard about orphanages being set up for unfortunate kids, but the Foetus Deficiency Therapy is new to me. "Foetus deficiency? Body and mind-meddling? What are you talking about?"

She glances at me, then Liddy, and then back at me. "Liddy didn't tell you?"

I look at Liddy; his neck and face are turning a deep red. "What didn't you tell me? What's going on?"

He stretches his arms out in front of him, interlocking his fingers. "Y'know. When they took me away for a couple of months."

"After your coming-out party?"

"Yeah."

"The place that helps you adjust to your physical gender?"

"Sort of."

'Sort of' doesn't make sense. He went away and when he came back, he was a boy.

That's how it works for boys. But Liddy's grunting, which I know means he doesn't want to talk about it right now. Something else must have happened and he didn't tell me. His eyes plead.

"Later?"

"'kay." My stomach flutters and I grit my teeth. *What was so awful that Liddy couldn't tell me?*

Ruth clears her throat to gain our attention. "You'll have plenty of time to talk at the reception centre.

"What happens next, then?"

"Forty-eight hours of relaxing. There's a games and entertainment room, books, a TV. After your trip in, it will give you time to adjust. One of the clinicians, probably Gabby, will come in to take blood for testing today."

"Testing what?"

"Oh, just the usual: viral, bacterial, genetic, protein levels, drugs, vitamins, minerals – that sort of thing. Then there are the physical and mental tests, which won't start until tomorrow. The scans take place on day two – all prep work for your training. Nothing to worry about. Once everything's done, it helps us to establish a baseline from which to build."

She waits for us to respond, but what can we say? I already know the answer to my next question: "Do we have to do the tests?"

"Yes, part of check-in."

I look up at the Monet as she continues speaking.

"I won't see you again until you've finished, but after that, I shall be your guardian while you're on this base."

Liddy spits out his response. "Guardian?"

Ruth remains calm, her hands resting on the clipboard. "All associates under eighteen are assigned a guardian; adults entering for the first time have a sponsor. A guardian's role is to ensure things run smoothly, that you adapt well. Any problems or questions, you come to me." She waits, smiling, as if expecting a torrent of questions.

Liddy slumps back against the sofa, I lean forward, elbows on my knees. "How many people like us come here?"

"We have new intakes about four times a year, but the Diversity Commission have tightened up in the last few months, so we only have you two and three more we managed to get out a couple of days ago. You'll be joining them in training."

"So, there's five of us."

"At the first stage of training, yes. Others are at different levels."

Liddy sits up. "This base, is that what it is, then? A training camp?"

"It's one of its focuses; others are research, communications and planning. We also run missions from here across the Western Hemisphere."

"Missions?"

"Well, getting people out is an example."

I sense there are more to these 'missions' than she's willing to say, but I have another question. "Do you know why the Diversity Commission is so against us, or why they wanted to take me away?"

"Until the tests are done, we won't know for sure. Dr Schultz probably has a better idea, but my guess is that your brain reacted to the AP protein and so developed differently to others with HGS. This development is incompatible with their gene purification goal."

"What's the AP protein?"

"People who go through the Change normally, don't have it. Those with HGS can be sensitive to it. It's probably better we know for sure before we discuss it further, Cam."

Liddy stares at me; a wry smile cuts across his face. "Always knew you were peculiar." He turns to Ruth. "Has everyone here got this AP protein, then?"

"No, some choose to be here. They believe in our way of life."

"What about you?"

Her eyes light up, as if Liddy has chosen a subject that brings her great joy. "You and I are similar, Liddy. I was just like you at your age, though in those days we had to hide it. The Diversity Commission hadn't gained the power it has nowadays, and my parents had connections to get me away."

I respond a little too abruptly. "You mean you're male, not female?"

"Remember, I told you that the first part of your programme is to unlearn. I'm *human*. How I choose to present myself to the world is my concern."

Her conviction is absolute and, for a few long seconds, there is silence in the room. Under his make-up, Liddy first turns a shade of white and then flushes a deep maroon. He flexes his fingers and swallows hard as we all just stare at each other, like some odd comedy spoof. I can see his mind working, almost hear him speak. His silent voice is hopeful but cautious. *How come? How do you get to live this life? Can I?*

She looks and behaves so much like a female, I can't help but wonder if she has male bits underneath. I dispel the thought but do notice she has a tiny Adam's apple – unnoticeable unless you look for it. She's been altered in some way. I don't know how to feel about that.

"So" – she stands up – "should I take you through?"

Both Liddy and I grab our bags and walk around the coffee table to join her in the reception entrance.

"Oh, if you give me your clothes, I'll get them cleaned and sent back to you."

"Er, thanks." Liddy bends over and begins untying his duffel bag. "I just have a couple of things I want to take with me." He pulls out a large toiletry bag, a purple make-up bag and the puzzle box, which I'd totally forgotten about. I wonder if it's waterproof and whether the sim card is still usable. Finding my toiletries and the photograph, which I slip into my pocket, I hand my backpack over.

"What's that?" Ruth's pointing to the box.

Liddy's response is one he's already thought about. His voice drops a level. "It's a puzzle box my grandmother gave me. She died when I was young. We were close."

I'm impressed with his acting skills. Ruth just nods as she slings a bag over each shoulder. "Okay, anything else you need over the next couple of days, just tell one of the clinicians. They'll get in touch with me."

"Thanks."

She leads us through another door and down a long corridor with white walls. To the right is a lift. She places her hand on a pad, the lift beeps and the doors slide open. Liddy follows her in.

"It's a scanner?"

"Yes. Does that worry you?"

She makes me feel guilty, after everything they've done. I shrug and join them, slipping in just before the door closes. I see my face reflected in the metal doors. It looks blurred and elongated as if I'm a wax figurine melting in the hot sun.

Ruth presses a pad with 'minus one' on it. The lift begins its descent.

"I know you've been through a lot. It's hard to trust people, to know what's right. But we're here to help you."

As she's staring at me, I force a thin-lipped smile to acknowledge her words. I don't know how to respond. I don't know what these people want. Surely, we can't just arrive here and just... well, *live*? What about the cost? Do we have to work, or something? What I do know is that Liddy and I can't leave without Ruth's scanner-hand.

The lift halts and the doors open. She indicates for us to go ahead, like a bellboy inviting us to view a room. I rock back and forth on my toes a couple of times before stepping out. Once outside, a short turning to the right leads us to an open space that sparkles with refracted light. Looking up, I notice the high ceiling is made of arched glass panels and beyond that is the sky. The clouds have cleared, and the evening sun throws an orange haze on us. It's like being in an enclosed courtyard.

Liddy exclaims first. "Wow."

"The design brings in maximum light, and the panels reap solar energy," Ruth responds in a matter-of-fact tone, as she places our bags on the floor and then leads us to the right.

Only then do I notice sofas, chairs, a dining table, bean bags, and a massive TV screen.

"Behind the partition is a small kitchen with a kettle, toaster, snacks and drinks. You're expected to sort yourself out for breakfast, but all other meals will be provided." She looks at us for confirmation that we understand before continuing. "If you come with me, I'll show you your rooms."

We pass a large shelf holding books and board games. Taking another corner, we find ourselves in a hallway. Several doors line the corridor, each with a number.

"Rooms one to three are taken, but all others are empty, so you have a choice, though they're all the same inside."

I glance at Liddy and stalk to the furthest room, wanting to be away from whoever else is already here. "I'll take number ten."

With Liddy at my shoulder, I open the door and we both peer inside. The light is dim, but the queen-sized bed takes up most of the room, along with a small built-in wardrobe. Against the middle wall is a desk and chair. There's also a bedside cabinet with a lamp on it. Nothing fancy, but at least there's an *en suite*. The door to the bathroom is open. I switch on the light. Inside is a white shower, bath, basin and toilet.

Liddy peers over my shoulder. "Guess tonight's activity will be a long soak, then." He grins, but it doesn't reach his tired eyes.

"I might do the same."

"Nah, you and baths don't work. You haven't learnt the art of water relaxation, yet. Besides which" – he points to my back – "stitches!""

We hear Ruth's voice outside: "Good evening, Gabby."

"Hello, Ruth. How's the tour going?" A broad woman with dark skin and black, frizzy hair held back with a band stands in the hallway. She looks at us through red-rimmed glasses.

"Hi, you two. My name's Gabrielle, but you can call me Gabby." She's wearing blue scrubs as if she's just come from surgery. Stepping towards us, she reaches out her hand. "And you must be Liddyana Mitchell?"

"Liddy." He shakes her hand and steps back.

"And Camellia Chadwick, how are you doing?" Her grin is wide and reveals a mouth of straight, white teeth.

"Fine, and Cam will do."

"Good to meet you both. I'll be one of the team looking after you for the next two days." She turns to Ruth. "Any allergies I should know about?"

"No, but Cam doesn't eat meat or poultry."

Gabby looks back at me. "Fish, eggs, cheese okay?"

"No fish, thanks."

"No problem. Now, if you'd like to get settled, I'll be back soon to take your bloods. After that, you're free to relax for the rest of the evening."

As Gabby walks away, Ruth pulls us together, holding my right shoulder and Liddy's left. "I'd tell you not to worry, but I can see by your faces it won't do any good."

I frown, staring over her shoulder. The hallway has spotlights set in a central line on the ceiling.

"Remember, I'll be back in two days and, until then, you can contact me through Gabby or one of the other staff." Ruth has a habit of waiting for a response before finishing her message. Neither Lid nor I say anything, so she continues. "Okay, any questions before I leave?"

One pops into my head; not sure why I didn't think of it before. "When can I contact my mum?"

She drops her hands; her voice lowers. "Once we're sure it's safe, we'll initiate a drop."

"Drop?"

"We'll make contact with both your families through untraceable sources. Right now," she hesitates, "they're being watched. We're watching the Watchers. Once we find a route in, we'll let them know you're well."

Liddy snorts. "Don't bother with my family. I don't want my dad to know anything. I'd prefer it if he thinks I'm dead."

"As you wish, Liddy."

"Good."

Thinking of my mum all alone, a lump forms in my throat. I imagine her pacing our small front room, wondering if I'm alive. At least she'll know I'm with Liddy.

"I'll leave you to it, then. I'll send your clothes through tomorrow afternoon."

With that she turns and exits the corridor. I hear Liddy's deep breath as it whistles through his clenched teeth and look up at him. He feels me staring and meets my eyes.

"On the one hand, this seems an impossible dream. A place I can be myself, Cam. A place where people don't judge you or try to change what you are. Hey, a place I could set up that salon." His lopsided grin is soured by the pain in his eyes. He's tapping his thigh with his fingers, as if drumming out a tune only he can hear. I feel a wave of anxiety emanating from him, hope and fear jumbled together. "But what if it's all just too good to be true?"

"I can't figure out the catch. Why would they do this?"

"The Diversity Commission?"

"Yeah, that. But all this, too?" I throw my arms wide. "Think of how much it must cost to run this place, and they say this is just *one* base."

"I don't know, Cam."

We saunter over to the sofa, passing a dining table on the way. "How can the whole world live by the rules and this one little group, whoever they are, hide in plain sight?"

Liddy flops down. "And just rescue people."

I join him, crossing my legs under me. There is a large TV screen on the wall and a remote thrown on the coffee table in front of us. "Maybe they don't just do that."

"And maybe the whole world doesn't live like us, Cam. Have you thought of that? What do you know about other countries, really?"

He's right. I shake my head and lean forward, my elbows on my knees. "They must want something, though."

"Maybe they just want a different life – like me."

"Maybe, but—"

"But what?"

I sigh. "Don't know."

"Well, until you figure it out, I'm going to raid the kitchen. Coming?"

I smile. "Sure. Bound to be some cookies in there."

"Better be." Liddy chuckles and heads out towards the kitchen. I watch him as he opens and slams cupboard doors, searching for snacks. My thoughts return to what Ruth said about 'meddling with minds and bodies'. Normally, we share everything, but Liddy's keeping something from me, something they did when he went away.

My whole body feels taut, my jaw aches, my back throbs. Rolling my shoulders, I surprise myself by standing up and jumping up and down for a couple of seconds before a pain shoots down my back. Feeling as if my mind is flitting in all sorts of different directions, I decide the only thing to do is follow Liddy, who's already opening a packet of something.

Perhaps a whole lot of sugar will help me think more clearly.

CHAPTER SIXTEEN

I'm lounging on the sofa with Liddy, halfway through my hot chocolate, when Gabby comes in. Trailing her are two boys and a girl wearing the same clothes as us.

"This is Victoria, Taor and Jonathon."

The first thing I notice about Victoria is her beautiful ebony skin, black eyes, and how her hair spirals around her face. She looks vaguely familiar, but I can't think where from. The younger boy, Taor, is tall and skinny. He looks young, maybe only fourteen. When he plonks himself down, his legs protrude in front of him like some stick insect.

Jonathon glares around at us. He has translucent blue eyes that seem to look startled all the time. He's the first to speak. "Welcome to paradise."

Unexpectedly, he has a sing-song Irish accent, which I love, but when he grins, I can't tell if he's being sarcastic or just trying to be funny. Liddy introduces us.

"I'm Liddy and this is Cam."

Jonathon sneers. "So, are you a girl or boy?"

Gabby interrupts. "Now, now, you know that doesn't count, here."

He grunts, sits in the armchair and picks up the remote control, switching on the TV.

"Football, anyone?"

Victoria tuts and storms off towards the kitchen. Taor seems shy, awkward – not sure whether to get up or stay.

Gabby touches Liddy's shoulder. "Could you two come with me, please?"

Liddy's face is taut, his eyebrows join at the centre to form an angry monobrow. He springs up and shoves his face into Jonathon's. "I'm a girl. You got a problem with that?"

Jonathon pushes himself into the back of the sofa and mocks Liddy, his hands in the air, feigning innocence. "No, but you obviously do."

Liddy holds his stare for a second more before backing off. I glare at Jonathon as we both pass him and follow Gabby to a small office behind the kitchen.

As Gabby takes four vials of blood from each of us, she tries to calm him down. "Don't let him wind you up."

"I'm not."

"They'll have finished and will move out tomorrow, but you'll be training with them."

"Oh, goody."

"Keep that temper in check. In such a small community, we can't have discord."

Liddy grunts, but nods as Gabby jabs him. When the last needle goes in my arm, I look away. Liddy's still frowning and slumped in a chair.

"We don't even know them, Liddy."

"Know his sort, though. Remember Brian, at school? He was a bully."

"Yeah, but maybe this Jonathon kid was just curious."

"Curious is fine. Attitude is something else."

Gabby glances at Liddy as she finishes labelling the vials. "Everyone we pick up has their own story, and not everyone has had it easy. Give them a chance."

Liddy's knee is jiggling up and down. "Whatever."

Gabby has begun checking my back. "There'll be a scar, but other than that, it's healing nicely." She cleans the wound with some antiseptic and sticks a fresh bandage on. It stings a little but, miraculously, the pain is already fading.

"Be careful in showers until the stitches dissolve naturally."

"Okay, thanks."

"You can go now. Dinner will arrive soon, but I'd recommend an early night. Long day tomorrow."

I don't move. Her comment bothers me. The memory of the clinic is still raw. "What exactly are these tests we're having?"

Liddy looks up. "Yeah. Tests don't seem very welcoming."

Gabby frowns. "I know my assurances not to worry won't work, but the tests aren't intrusive like the ones you may have had at the DC's clinics. The blood tests will check for viruses and infections mainly, but we also look at your DNA and protein levels. The rest are about your physical, mental and emotional health. That means things like a treadmill, IQ tests on a computer and brain scans. You've had EEGs and MRIs before, haven't you?"

I bite the inside of my mouth and look away. I can feel Liddy staring at me.

"And once we've done them, we're free?"

"Liddy, you're freer now than you've ever been. You just don't know it, yet."

We both nod and get up to go, but before we leave, Gabby has a warning. "This is a small island. It's better to have friends."

Liddy's chin hangs low as we walk back. I pull him to a halt. "So, I'm to call you a *she*, now?"

"I've always been a she."

"What about the Change?"

"Of all people, Cam, I thought you'd understand." He stamps his foot, flashing angry eyes at me, before stalking off, leaving me standing in the corridor. I feel guilty for upsetting him. It took ages for me to think of Liddy as a boy and now he wants me to switch back.

For a second, I think about what Ruth said, about people being human, not labelled as one thing or another. In a way, it makes perfect sense. Humans are humans, but what about the biological stuff? I stand there making fists, like some surly child. To me, Liddy is Liddy, always has been and always will be. Does it matter which pronoun he – no, *she* – chooses to use? The louder voice in my head says, no, of course not, but there's a tiny bit of me that finds it hard to be 100% on board.

We sit around the dinner table. Jonathon and Liddy sit opposite each other, Taor to the side and Victoria next to me. Liddy has gone all out with the make-up. She even has false eyelashes on tonight. It's as if he – I mean, she (*I must remember!*) – feels she needs to prove her gender with how she looks. My body slumps, remembering our earlier conversation. Have I let her down? I poke around at my food.

They're eating some sort of beef stew with chips. I have a spicy lentil pie, which is tasty, if a bit dry. I glance at Liddy. He... I mean, *she* is stuffing a large piece of meat into her mouth and glaring at Jonathon. I can almost see the icy daggers flying from his... *her* eyes into Jonathon's heart. Jonathon's smirking, enjoying the animosity.

I take a sip of water and ask the first question that pops into my mind. "So, where are you all from?"

Victoria speaks first. She has a broad accent. Again, she reminds me of someone, but I can't place where I've seen her before. "Bradford, and call me Vicky."

Taor mumbles, looking down at his plate. "The Lakes."

I smile and nod, swallowing a chip.

Vicky speaks next. "Where are you two from?"

"Lincolnshire."

"Both of you?"

"Known each other since primary school."

"Cool." Jonathon leers. "Does that mean you're girlfriend and girlfriend, then?"

Liddy jumps up, his chair falls backwards as he bounds towards Jonathon, dragging him to his feet and pushing him against the wall. "You got something you need to get off your chest, just spit it out."

He pushes him into the wall harder. Jonathon meets Liddy's gaze, as if this is a friendly encounter at a bus stop. Taor jumps up and pulls at Liddy's shoulder, but he... *she* shrugs him off. Vicky scowls but continues eating.

"Hey, just asking, like," Jonathon continues. "Want to be clear on this whole girl/boy thing. Don't want to offend."

Moving to Liddy's side, I pull on his (*her, her, her... gotta remember!*) arm, but she's strong. "Let's go. He isn't worth it."

Liddy's breathing hard, but on glancing at me, her face squelches up, confused. "You're right." She shoves Jonathon to the side and storms out of the room.

Vicky stands in front of him. "You're an idiot, Jon. We all have our problems."

"Yeah, he – oh, sorry. I mean, *she* – just hasn't learnt to control that testosterone yet." He rolls his eyes at Vicky. "Still, you're not the angel you pretend to be either, are you? Should I tell them your secrets, too?"

Vicky looks as if she's about to punch him in the stomach. Heck, I want to slap him myself, but she just storms off.

I flare my nostrils and scowl. "You find this funny?"

"Hey, little girl – or are you gonna be a boy? – you gotta find your entertainment where you can." He sticks out his chin. "Come on, take a punch."

And I would so like to smack him, but instead, I follow Vicky's example and walk away.

"Lid?" I knock again. "Come on, Liddy, let me in."

I hear the door unlock from inside and turn the handle. Liddy's lying on her side on the bed, looking towards the wall. I walk over and sit on the edge. Under his...

her eyes are streaks of mascara, her face is flushed, and she's hunched over. My chest tightens as I kneel in front of her and wave a packet of chocolate biscuits.

"The rest of your dinner." I smile and push back her hair. Her skin is warm.

He... *she* sniffs, dabbing her nose with a tissue and then turns her face to the pillow. Putting the biscuits on the bedside table, I put my arms around her and squeeze.

"Why did you let him get to you?"

She rolls onto her back and stares up at the ceiling. "You don't understand."

I sit on the edge of the bed, grabbing her hand. "Help me understand, then."

Pushing herself up, she looks at me. I know she's thinking about whether to tell me something. "When you look in the mirror, what do you see?"

Her question wasn't what I expected. "Er, brown, scraggly hair; hazel eyes."

"Yes, but more than that. Do you see a girl or boy?"

"I'm nothing, Lid. I'm a Golem."

He sighs, (no, *she* sighs), as if I'm exasperating her. "Okay. What do you most hate about yourself?"

"I'm small." I hesitate, not prepared for this conversation, but Liddy's trying to tell me something. "I... *Me*. I haven't grown up properly. Haven't been through the Change. My body's wrong." Tears come to my eyes, but I blink them away.

"And how's your body wrong?"

I look down at my flat chest, thinking about HGS, and know it isn't my fault, but can't bring myself to say any more. Liddy doesn't force it out of me.

"Y'see, when I look at me, my body's wrong, too, even though I went through the Change. It doesn't match with what I think it should be. Sure, I put on eyeliner and mascara, but I try not to look down at the rest of my skin." She sniffs and wipes her nose. "When they told me I was definitely going to be a boy, I didn't believe them."

I go for a smile, to encourage him... *her* to go on. Liddy has never told me this stuff before. She's stuttering and staring across the room, trying to explain.

"The clinic wasn't just for adjustment; they *were* the adjustment. They told me it wasn't my fault I had Foetal Deficiency Syndrome."

"What's that?"

"Well, they said people like me don't receive enough foetal chromosomes to ensure the Change is complete. The brain's deprived of the right chemical hormones when the Change starts, so while my body thinks its male, my mind works more like a female's."

"Never heard of it. Is that true?" I'm shocked. "Didn't even know there were male and female brains."

"Not something they teach at school and, to be honest, I don't know how true it is." She looks down, picking at her nails. "Anyway, they tried to fix it by injecting me with chemicals that physically speed up the Change. The pain was mind-numbing. Some of them even had surgery. Imagine closing up down below and growing extensions that weren't there a couple of weeks before."

I don't know what to say. Tears roll down her cheeks as she stares at the door, reliving moments I cannot even begin to imagine. I stroke her hand.

"Changing from what you are now to what I am, requires physical developments that can otherwise take years."

"But why?"

"Why what?"

"Why do they do it?"

"Girls don't have to. Their change is less intrusive – nature takes its allotted course. You just grow proper ovaries and stuff on the inside. But for those changing to boys…"

She doesn't have to fill in any more details. I know what gender change is about. I just didn't know what happened at the clinics. My heart beats a little faster than usual. Liddy's clinging to my hand now as if she's falling off a cliff and I'm the only one who can save her.

"And it isn't just the physical side and learning to cope with stuff like going to the toilet." She sneers with disgust. "They have this 'visual reinforcement' treatment if you don't react to their version of 'normalisation'." She shudders and takes a deep breath. "After feeding you drugs, they hook you to a machine and flash male and female images at you to get you to feel you're somehow wrong. When you see a female body with your own face, you get an electric shock to your brain and the drugs make you throw up… to reject it." She gulps and tears run down her cheeks. "Some of them came back as zombies, night after night, fighting the process."

"Like Jo."

"Yes, just like her."

I pass Liddy a tissue and she wipes her face.

"So, I pretended, just to get out of there. I went along with everything. Let them cut my hair, my nails; wore boys' clothes. When it came to the mental assessment, I told them what I knew they wanted to hear. They were pleased with my progress and said after a few months, everything would become more natural."

My fingers are beginning to go numb, but I don't let go of her hand. At last, she turns to face me, staring into my eyes, as if willing me to understand what it's like, fearful of rejection.

"When I look in the mirror, I hate myself, hate the way I look. Sometimes, I'm so angry. Other times, I can barely breathe, as if I'm trapped in a box, clawing my way out. I see my Change as a disfigurement of what I was, and every day's a battle not to give up, to remember who I am."

My chest aches and I swallow a lump in my throat. She's been hiding this from me all this time. Didn't she know it wouldn't make a difference?

"When I meet people like that twat Jonathon, who thinks this is funny, I can't keep the anger in anymore." She pushes herself up suddenly and leans her head against the wall, closing her eyes and taking a deep breath.

"Oh, Lid...?"

"I know it's hard for people to get it. Hell, it would be easier just to be my body's gender, but my brain refuses. It's not me."

"I understand."

She gazes at me. "Do you, Cam? Do you, really?"

"I think I do. I know it's not the same, but when I look in the mirror, I hate the way I look, that I have no real gender. But I think, in my head, I'm a girl. Not a *girly* girl, like you." This brings a smile to her face. "But still a girl."

She grasps both my hands. Tears of relief fill her eyes. "This place is a chance for me, Cam, to live my life how I want to. In the normal world, I couldn't do that, ever. My body would rule my gender. People would hate me for how I want to live."

"Y'mean, you want to be like Ruth."

She nods, her eyes bright and I know I can't let her go through this alone.

"So, we make a go of it – this new life?"

"Just two flat-chested girls, doing what they can to save the universe."

We both chuckle.

"But please, no nail polish."

She smiles. "Come here, girlfriend."

Gladly, I allow her long arms to encircle me.

CHAPTER SEVENTEEN

I'm lying on my back, half awake, half asleep. I know it must be morning, but I'm not quite ready to jump out of bed and face whatever it is we have to do today. I don't want any tests. My stomach feels as if a stone has been dumped into it. That's when I hear a quiet tapping.

"Yes?"

Liddy pops her head around the door. "Room service." She grins. "Brought you coffee and toast."

Smiling, I sit up, rubbing my eyes. "Er, thanks."

She strides in, sits on the side of the bed and hands me a steaming mug, placing a plate of toast on the bedside table.

"You're already dressed." She's wearing the same clothes as yesterday but has a French plait hanging down her back. It's short but reminds me of how she used to wear her hair before she became a boy.

"Been up a while."

"Any sign of the creep?"

One half of her mouth curls up. "You'd be totally proud of me. I ignored him and, best of all, they've already been shipped out. We have the place to ourselves."

"Good."

"Anyway, Gabby asked me to wake you. We're to start at 8:00 a.m."

"Oh, right." I sit up and sip at the scalding, strong coffee. Just how I like it.

Liddy stands. "Be in the games room."

"'kay."

Watching her leave the room, I remember what she told me about the clinic yesterday and feel sadness creep into my chest. *How could the Diversity Commission be so cruel? How could her parents allow it? Maybe they don't know.*

But I know many parents who would allow it. Even if they disagreed, they'd be too scared not to.

There's this history book at school that says how 'gene perfection' got us into this mess in the first place. Anything deviating from the Two-Gender System and the Holistic Law is a threat to humankind. They'll go to any lengths to prevent what happened in the past. I wonder about it sometimes. If people hadn't messed around with genes, tried to have the perfect, disease-free baby, would Baby X have been born? Would the Change still take place in the womb, as it used to? It would have been so much easier to be born with a physical sex than to go through it at puberty.

Liddy's father flashes into my mind. How angry he would be now if he knew what was happening. I pick up a piece of toast, attacking it with the hunger of a starving lion that hasn't eaten for weeks, and smile.

"This measures your heart rate." Zoe, a clinician, is sticking a small suction pad on my chest. "The electrode net measures brain function."

She is wearing green scrubs and white plimsolls; her dark hair is tied back in a ponytail. Leo, her assistant, is a tall man with blond hair and a long nose. He's getting Liddy ready. I stare over at her, and she raises her eyebrows. We both sit on hospital beds covered in white sheets, wearing identical shorts and vests, as if we're about to go to the gym.

"During all tests, we'll monitor both brain activity and heart rate, so I'm afraid you have to wear the electrodes all day."

I nod as she lifts the net over my head and clips it under my chin.

"There are twenty-six mini electrodes on the net. They'll measure all activity in your brain stimulated by various actions and decisions you make during the course of the day."

I pull at the strap digging under my chin. She notices.

"Bit tight, I know. Let me see..." She adjusts the strap. "Better?"

"A little."

"Good, you're ready to go."

Zoe reminds me of a bird, chirping away in the garden early in the morning, as if daylight is a magical moment. "You both ready?" When we nod, she chirps back, "Great! Come with me."

I jump off the bed and follow Liddy out of the door and down a corridor. Leo stays behind. Before we even get into the next room, I groan. Through the glass doors, there are two running machines, exercise bikes and a weight machine.

Liddy chuckles. "Your favourite, Cam."

I half punch her in the arm. Zoe pushes open the door and holds it as we walk through.

"Not everyone likes exercise, so we get it over with first."

"Great... exhausted before noon."

Liddy laughs at me. "Will you need a nap before lunch?"

"Shut up!"

Zoe interrupts. "Remember, we're creating a baseline to measure your current levels of fitness. This is not a competition."

We start with a ten-minute fast walk, which isn't too bad, but then she wants to test our resistance levels and adjusts the machine to imitate a sloping hill. It hurts the backs of my calves, but I still manage to keep up with Liddy.

"Well done, both of you. Have a quick rest. There's water in the small fridge over there if you want some, but only sips please."

Liddy brings me a bottle as Zoe taps on her digital notepad, bringing up the results. Leaning against the wall, I untwist the cap, expecting her to give us some indication of how things are going.

"So, everything okay?"

"Perfect." Her teeth glow white and I wonder which toothpaste she uses. Probably not appropriate to ask, but whatever it is, it's doing a really good job.

"We'll move on to jogging and running. I'll be setting you different paces this time."

"Ugh, I'm useless at running." My shoulders slump.

Two hours later, I'm sweating and every muscle aches. After the jogging and running, we had half an hour on the bikes, an hour testing which weights we could lift and a flexibility exercise. At least I had an excuse with the weights – my shoulder wound prevented me from lifting too much. The only thing I could do better than Liddy was touch my toes and bend my legs in awkward positions.

Zoe doesn't have to give us the results – I already know how unfit I am.

She points to the mats. "Time to relax."

"Relax?"

"Yes. Monitoring your brain during relaxation and sleep is important."

"Right."

We lie on the mats and cover ourselves with the light blankets Zoe supplies. As she dims the lights, I glance over at Liddy.

"See, forced naps."

"Ha! As if you need to be forced."

Then we hear a soothing voice with soft background music. "Take a deep breath. Fill your lungs and allow your ribcage to rise."

I stifle a giggle, but it comes out as a snort. Liddy pokes me in my arm, her eyebrows arched, one a little above the other, like a cartoon character. I grin and am about to poke her back when Zoe switches off the recording.

"I know this is unfamiliar but think of it as another test."

We both lean up on our elbows.

"Just listen to the words and the music. That's all I ask."

"'kay."

"Right."

She taps her screen and, as the recording starts again, the lights are dimmed and I close my eyes, trying to focus.

"Feel the whole of your body fill with oxygen, your arms, your legs..."

"Wake up, sleepy."

"Hey!"

Liddy's pushing me. For a minute, I don't know where I am. I splay my fingers, feeling a soft mat beneath them. Then it all comes back to me. "I didn't sleep."

"Yeah, you did. You were snoring." I stifle a yawn as Liddy waggles her fingers in front of my eyes and speaks in a deep, hypnotic tone. "Sleep... time to sleep."

This time, I do punch her arm, but she just snorts and throws her head back, amused at my reaction.

"Whatever you're thinking, remember I'm bigger and stronger." She ruffles my hair like I'm a child, rattling me further.

I push her arm away. "Stop it, Liddy."

"Oh, come on. I'm only having a laugh."

We're following Zoe out of the glass doors and down the corridor.

"At me."

Crinkles appear above the bridge of her nose. "What's wrong with you?"

"Nothing... just, I dunno. Stop teasing. I'm not in the mood."

"Er, sorry."

I don't respond. I'm not sure why I'm irritated.

"The next tests look at personality traits, character, IQ and emotional wellbeing."

Liddy and I are sitting at screens, a keyboard in front of us and a headset around our necks.

"The first will take about an hour, but there is no set time, so you can relax." Zoe's leaning against a desk at the end of the room. "There are a hundred and twenty questions, but all are multiple choice. All you need to do is choose the answer that most closely feels like you."

Liddy swings her chair around. "I've done stuff like this before and find it difficult."

"In some questions, there's an 'I don't know', or 'none of the above' option, but we encourage you to try to choose a different response, even if it isn't exact."

"Any chance of a coffee?"

"Sorry, but at this stage, caffeine would affect your brain and alter the measurements."

Liddy groans.

"Right, I'll be here, if you have any questions." Zoe points to the seat behind the desk. "To get started, just click the start button."

Obviously!

Skimming the page, I read the first five questions. I have a sudden urge to click neutral on everything, just to make it difficult to evaluate me. But, in the end, I just answer whatever first pops into my head.

In the afternoon, we have two tests. The first is an IQ test.

Liddy sneers. "You know IQ tests are not reliable?"

Leo is administering this one and responds. "We don't take this as a stand-alone result – it's part of an overall picture, so we know what to build on."

"And they don't measure emotional intelligence."

"We know that, Liddy. It's just mental agility we're looking at in this one. Are you nervous about it?"

"Just don't like them; they don't give you enough time to think through the questions." Liddy's slumped in a chair.

Leo looks at me, his head tilted to the side. "Have you ever done one?"

"No, but I like logic puzzles."

He nods. "There are seven sections to this test: verbal, mathematical, spatial reasoning, visual skills, classification, logic and pattern recognition."

Liddy slumps further down her seat, her knees far off the edge.

"You have ninety minutes to complete this test. We ask you to do as much as possible. However, if you don't know an answer, don't linger. The best thing is to try to eliminate the wrong answers and make an educated guess."

Liddy grumbles. "I'll be guessing a lot, then."

"You'll be okay, Lid."

She's picking at the hem of her hoodie, but glances across the room at me. "No, I won't. I get rubbish scores on these things."

I hadn't realised how serious Liddy was taking all this, but then I remember she wants to make a new life for herself.

I turn back to Leo. "Does it really matter what score we get?"

"No. This is not like school. You aren't going to be put in different sets or judged on the results. This is to help create a baseline for your training, remember?"

"But we get judged on our training, whether we pass or fail. That's what Ruth said."

"True, but 99% of the time people pass, and training helps us allot work placements. Everyone supports our states by contributing their best work. You may not be a brilliant scientist, but an excellent trainer. Why would we force you to study science, if your skills lie elsewhere?"

It seems to make sense, but Liddy snorts as I turn to the screen and click the button to begin.

Two hours later, we're both placed in separate rooms. Leo stays with Liddy and Zoe sits with me. Images are flashed on the screen, and I have to verbally answer two questions: What's the first word that comes into your head? How does it make you feel?

The first image is a black blob that looks a bit like something a little kid would make when she first picks up a paintbrush. It reminds me of the time I spent with my mum when I was three or four. We used to have these fun, 'anything you want' days. I would make a list, and we'd do everything on it. I loved painting and Play-Doh, but I remember the day always started with chocolate pancakes. A lump forms in my throat – one of happiness and sadness at the same time.

Zoe interrupts my thoughts. "So, what's the first word that comes to mind?"

"Splodge."

"Splodge?"

"As in paint. Am I supposed to see something else?"

"No, that's fine." She's tapping on her screen again. "And how does it make you feel?"

"Happy and sad."

She looks up, her eyebrows raised. "Would you care to explain the contradiction?"

I hesitate, but then tell her my memory and clarify the emotions that come with it. "Happy because it was a good time. Those days were special. Just me and my mum. Sad, because I may never see my mum—" I can't even finish the sentence. My vision blurs and I blink hard to remove the tears. Zoe squeezes my shoulder. I try to smile but am glad when she moves on to the next splodge, which is green and looks like a tree with expanding roots. My response is instant.

"Tree. Happy."

"Why?"

"I love the countryside, mountains and trees. Stuff like that."

She nods, tapping away, and we go through another twenty or so splodges, but then something changes. For a nanosecond, I think it's a detailed picture of an Edwardian carriage clock, with a black, ornate face and French numbering. I hear it ticking and chiming three o'clock, but then it disappears and we're back to a gold, square-ish shape, which reminds me of the clock, anyway.

"Clock. Surprise."

"Why?"

My brow furrows. "I…" My face heats, I'm wondering if I'm seeing things. "Just thought I saw more detail this time. Must be getting tired."

"Sometimes our brains fill in what isn't there." Zoe's eyes widen, betraying some sort of excitement, but her voice is neutral. "It's normal."

Another image flashes up. This time, a rabbit. I see its whiskers, a twitching nose, blue eyes and white fur. It looks at me, and I know it's happy as it hops across the screen. Just as quickly, it changes into a static white blob.

I turn to look at Zoe. "Is this part of the test?"

"What do you mean?" The corner of her mouth twitches and she looks down at her screen a little too swiftly.

"Well, flashing up clips before the blobs. What do you call that? Subliminal stuff?"

"You're seeing clips?"

"Yes. Didn't you see the rabbit? It was there for at least five seconds."

"No, but the images look different to everyone. So, you saw a rabbit?

"I saw an actual rabbit hopping across the screen before it became a blob – which now looks like a rabbit, of course. This is weird."

She stares at me, not explaining what's going on, before pressing something on her notepad screen. "Shall we do a couple more?"

"Fine." This time I just see a shape and wonder if I'm going mad. I answer in a monotone voice. "Book. Happy. I like reading."

"Next."

"Supermarket. Hate. Don't like shopping." My stomach sinks. Did I actually see the moving images?

"Next."

It happens again. I hear chatting and laughter, the movement of feet. My pulse beats against the side of my temple, as I focus on the static image that follows. "Crowds of people going into a theatre. Happy. I like the theatre, when I get the chance to go."

She's tapping away, and the next nanosecond clip hits the screen. A row of cows in a slaughterhouse on their way to death, shrieking and snorting, terrified, trying desperately to escape. I can even smell the blood. Disgusted, I look away. "How could you? That's horrible."

"What did you see?" Her brow creases.

"Cows being slaughtered, crying out. They know they're going to their deaths."

"You heard them as well?"

"What?" I wonder if she thinks I'm mad. My heart is hammering in my chest. Salty saliva floods my mouth, and I clutch my stomach and lean forward. A sharp pain shoots through the back of my head as I cradle my hot face with my hands.

"Camelia, what's wrong?"

"I feel sick."

I hear her move, hear water sloshing, but don't open my eyes. Her hands grab mine and place a cool glass in it. "Drink this."

Turning away from the screen, I squint enough to lift the glass to my lips and sip the water, swallowing hard. My face is burning, and I roll the glass over my cheeks.

Zoe moves again, bringing back a wet cloth. "Here, use this." She takes the glass and I cover my face with the flannel. It relieves the heat and the sickness. Eventually, I come back to my senses. She's watching me, concern in her eyes.

"I'm okay."

"Are you sure?"

"Yes, but I can't do any more of this test."

"There weren't many more, and I think we have enough for the assessment."

I nod. My brain hurts. My stomach's sick and I feel weak. I need to lie down.

"Cam, can I just ask you to look at the screen?"

Her voice is gentle, but insistent. I turn around again, squinting, ready to look away, but all I see is a row of upright shapes. To me, they still look like cows in a slaughterhouse.

CHAPTER EIGHTEEN

Gabby follows me into my bedroom. I sit on the edge of the bed, head in my hands. The room is swirling, and my head is banging like a drum. I feel as if I might vomit any minute. At least I'm no longer wearing the net or the electrodes on my chest.

"Hard first day?"

"Not really, just the last test."

"Zoe asked me to bring some medicine for your head and stomach."

I squint at Gabby. Specks of light flash before my eyes and a streak of pain hits the side of my head. I groan.

"Something for pain and sickness."

"Anything to take it away." Not wanting to disturb my head or stomach, I place my hands on the bed and stiffen my arms, trying to keep myself upright.

"Do you mind an injection? It will work faster."

"Okay."

She taps the syringe. "I need your arm and can't roll that sleeve up far enough."

Keeping my head as still as possible, I pull the top off. Underneath I'm wearing a vest, so at least I'm covered up – though, to be honest, I just want the pain to go away; I don't care what I look like at the moment.

I feel a jab and the heaviness of a vein being filled. Gabby's putting something around my shoulders.

"The medicine will knock you out for a while, but it works fast."

"Thanks." I know I'm mumbling, but my brain's fogging up.

"Your clothes came back. Let me help you undress." She's lifting my arms into the sleeves of my pyjama jacket.

"It's okay—" My words slur. "Do it 'self." But she's moving around, pulling my shoes, socks and jogging pants off. I don't have the strength to stop her.

"I think you can sleep as you are."

I feel her kind arms direct me to a pillow. My head sinks into its softness. A duvet is wrapped around me and hands tuck me in as if I am a child. The last thing I hear is the swishing of the door against the thick carpet and the quiet click as it closes.

I wake up with a start, as if someone I know is in my room, and lean over to switch on the lamp. For a second, I'm still in my dreams and don't know where I am, or who's supposed to be here. It slowly fades and I notice the open bathroom door, which makes me realise I need the loo. On returning, I see a plate with a sandwich and cookies, along with a box of juice, on my beside table. On top is a note in Liddy's flowing handwriting: 'Eat up!'

My stomach growls as I crawl back under the covers and pick up the plate. Peeling back the clingfilm, I seize the cheese and tomato panini. It's cold, but I don't care and take a huge bite, swallowing before I've chewed enough. The lump hits my empty stomach and I sigh with relief. Opening the juice, I guzzle it and begin to wonder how long I've slept. From the stillness, it has to be the middle of the night. Then I realise I no longer feel ill – no headache or sickness. In fact, I feel good; wide awake, even.

Taking another bite, I glance around the room. My clothes are folded neatly on a chair. Next to it is the desk, on which is a large book that wasn't there before. Getting up again, sandwich still in hand, I walk over and stare down at it. It's a coffee table book and on its cover is Monet's *Water Lilies*. The book is entitled *Impressionism*. It takes me a second to realise Ruth must have sent it.

Thoughtful! I hope she can help Liddy.

My skinny legs are bare, and I shiver. Putting my food on the desk, I pull on my pyjama bottoms and grab the blanket at the end of the bed. As an afterthought, I pull on a pair of socks. Clasping the book under my arm, I balance the juice on the plate, along with the sandwich and cookies, and head for the TV room. At the very least, I might be able to find out the time.

Even though it's dark, the moonlight through the arched glass ceiling allows me to see the sofas and coffee table. It must be a cloudless night. Walking over, I plonk the plate and book down and lower myself into a seat, pulling up my legs and wrapping the blanket around me. I pick up the remote control to switch on the TV, but before I do, I hear a voice. At first, it's a whisper, but it gets louder, and I turn around, expecting someone to walk into the room, but it's eerily empty. My face flushes as I wonder if I'm hallucinating again, but then I hear a mumble and another voice, but not so clear. The first person speaks again. I can't really tell if it's a man or a woman.

"You brought me down here at this time... for this? Couldn't it wait until tomorrow?"

Curious, I get up and, leaving the blanket behind, take a step in the direction of the voice. I know I shouldn't eavesdrop, but I have a sudden overwhelming desire to know what they're talking about.

"You haven't even finished the tests. It might be a discrepancy."

It's odd. Such deep, hypnotic tones, but so clear, as if the person's standing next to me. I wonder if it's Dr Schultz, but no, it doesn't sound like him. Someone else's saying something, but I can't decipher it. I turn the corner that leads to the lab Leo was in. My heart's pounding, my palms sweaty. I wipe them down my pyjamas, unable to control my feeling of being on edge. I might be spying on people, but they're talking about us behind our backs. I'm sure of it.

"But, Tom, we just want to get ahead on this."

So, Zoe's talking to a man.

"Okay, fine, you have my permission to compare our genes. Where do I sign?"

But it's more than pure curiosity, it's that voice. I begin to feel as if I know the person, as if I've met whoever it is before. I'm convinced that if I open the door at the end of the corridor, I'll find a long-lost friend or relative. I feel happy, excited. I know it's illogical. Maybe I'm dreaming, still. I shrug, unbothered. What's the worst that could happen?

"Can I go? Wait, there's someone—"

Standing outside the door, I feel like I am being drawn by a powerful magnet, as if I will dash through, straight into the arms of my friend inside. My head tells me I'm stupid, but my body can't resist the pull. Trembling, I reach for the handle, but before I can open it, it's flung back.

In front of me is a tall person with hazel eyes and short, dark hair. I can't tell if it's a man or woman, but it must be this 'Tom'. His eyes meet mine and the shock is reflected back. I can't turn away, can't move. It's as if we're locked together, unable to escape each other's space. My breathing is irregular, my body burns and my skin tingles. I want to reach out and touch him, to see if he's real. There's a voice behind him, but the language is slurred, like a song that's been slowed down so much it's become incomprehensible. I lift my arm and watch as he does the same, a mirror image. Between our reaching fingers, the air sizzles like rising heat on a desert runway. I hear his voice, though his lips don't move.

"Who are you? How are you doing this?"

I feel his mind in mine as our fingers get closer. I should be afraid, but I'm not. This stranger is so known, so much a part of me. How can I be afraid of myself? My chest aches, my body aches, I need to be connected to him, and he doesn't resist. He wants it, too. I feel him craving me. His mind is clearer, his thoughts more analytical. Mine are a jumble of emotions. It seems to take an eternity, but our fingers eventually grasp each other. I take a deep breath and hold it in as the world around me goes crazy.

Like flashing images on a computer screen, I view his childhood – his parents and siblings, a lake and a fishing rod, friends at school, swimming in a pool, an ice cream on a sunny day, his tests, a clinic, an escape – and, at the same time, he sees me. And I see him seeing me, as he watches my life flash before his eyes: my mum, the death of a father I don't remember, school, Liddy, the day of my test – my whole story splashed across his mind in a few seconds.

I have a sense of falling, deeper and deeper, as if a part of me is searching for something, as if I'm rushing through a powerful waterfall. It crashes down on my body. I gasp, barely able to breathe.

The noise blocks out everything around me. There are no walls, no rooms, no one and nothing but him and me charging recklessly, abandoning ourselves in pursuit of the one thing that draws us together: a bond so strong, so deep, it takes away our being –who and where we are – as if we are nothing and everything, broken and whole; as if all our particles dissolve into a flood of pure light. Within the light is the glow of twisted chemical strands, rotating in a double helix, a nucleus spinning on an axis. The cells circle around, presenting the essence of our true selves as they crash together in an almighty explosion.

I'm thrown against the far wall, banging my shoulder into the edge of a doorway. My breath is forced out in a gurgle, my eyes close. The world is spinning, tipping gravity on its side. I try to hold on, to stay awake. I want to understand what all this is about, but the light fades into a pinhole and disappears into darkness.

I hear a voice.

"What's going on, Tom?"

Someone's lifting me up and placing me on a bed. I know it's him. He smells of rain-sprinkled trees.

"Tom?" Zoe's voice sounds fearful.

"How long was it between me opening the door and her collapse?"

I feel them staring down at me. It's almost as if I can see their confused expressions.

"Seconds, perhaps two or three. Why? What happened?"

"She's definitely an Apex or she wouldn't be a Processor."

What's he talking about?

"How do you know?"

"Her brain's fast. Even hard for me to keep up."

"You're not making sense."

Zoe's right. He isn't making sense.

"Look, it doesn't make sense to me, either. Somehow, this untrained associate was able to connect with me, to process thought at speed."

"Like you."

"Yes, but it was more than that."

I'm coming round, enough to know to keep still, to listen to the conversation. I want answers, too. I hear Tom chuckle.

"Why are you amused?"

"Nothing..."

I wonder if he knows I'm awake.

"So, tell me what happened."

"Cam connected with me."

I like the way he says my name; I like that he thinks we have a connection. I don't know why, but it feels right.

"On a vibrational, cellular level, Zoe."

She gasps.

That sounds bad. Is there something wrong with me?

"But—"

"Yes, I know. Totally dangerous and not something I've ever done before. But she was so fast, I wasn't expecting it. I tried to slow her down, control it, but I don't even think she knew what she was doing."

"Are you okay?"

"Yeah, just a bit shocked."

"And Cam?"

I hear a chair grate as if he's leaning against it.

"She's strong. Had I been someone else, I think they'd have come out of it worse."

"How could it manifest so quickly?"

"Something triggered it, I guess."

"Could it have been the tests?"

"Possibly. The Diversity Commission uses technology to ignite a reaction, but I get the sense this response is a combination of the tests and meeting me."

Meeting him? Tests? Triggering?

I'm trying to stay still so I can understand more, but I feel my toes curling and my jaw tightening.

"Like mini sparks causing a major explosion?"

"Something like that. It's different for everyone."

I sense him close, and I instinctively want to reach out and touch him again.

No, no. Not until you're trained.

It takes me a second to realise his voice is in my head and then I panic.

I'm losing it.

A numbness creeps across my brain and a sickness rolls through my stomach. I just need to go back to sleep. This is all some sort of weird nightmare. They're still talking as if everything they've said is perfectly normal.

"Look, Tom, I know you have plans, but I'm not sure we—"

"Yes, yes. I'll stay and work with her myself. I'm curious to see who and what she is."

His voice is in my head again.

You're not losing it. Take a deep breath!

"I'll even take time out to train her, if my boss permits it."

"You will?"

"She needs to learn control, fast. She could hurt someone – unintentionally, of course"

I wouldn't hurt anyone.

His voice comes back at me, and I realise he's having two conversations at the same time.

I know. Calm down.

I respond in my head. *Calm down! How can you say that?* But no, that's telepathy. I must be going mad. *No, no, no! It's just a dream. This isn't real. This isn't real.*

"Those gene comparisons you wanted to do – I think you'll find we're of a similar make-up. I'm wondering how close the proteins in our junk DNA are."

My mind swims in confusion. My heart's banging in my chest.

"Bonding at cellular level." He sighs.

"Surely, that's impossible? There would be some sort of meltdown."

He takes a deep breath, and the room goes silent for a second. "When I first came here, my tutor told me about it. But it's never happened to me before."

They're obviously speaking English, but the words don't make sense. I squint, the light above me blinding. Spots float in front of my eyes, my head screams in agony. "What's going on?" My voice is hoarse and whispery.

Zoe leans over me. Her face is pale, her eyes dark. "How are you feeling?"

"I didn't do anything."

Tom smiles at me but doesn't come too close. I still feel a strong pull towards him, but it isn't so demanding.

"Bet you need some painkillers."

I try to nod but groan instead. Movement of any kind sends waves of sickness through my body. I gag, gulping back bile and closing my eyes.

"You'll feel better in the morning."

A sharp jab in my shoulder causes me to flinch. My mind begins fading again. I fight to stay awake. Now that I accept that I wasn't dreaming, I want to get some answers to the zillion questions I have, but the drug takes effect. His voice calms me.

"Rest. I'll still be here tomorrow. You can ask me then." The last thing I hear is his voice. "With your permission, Cam, I'm going to cloud your thoughts a little. It's a lot to take in and you aren't prepared. If you remember all this when you wake up, any small amount of panic could be dangerous for others around you. I can remove the cloud easily enough when you're ready."

I don't get a chance to ask what he means. Zoe answers for me. "Go ahead, Tom."

CHAPTER NINETEEN

"Cam? Cam, are you okay?" Liddy's sitting on the side of my bed, a frown on her face. "You look so pale. Still got a headache?"

"Don't know." I push myself up, groaning. I have a nasty taste in my mouth, as if I didn't brush my teeth last night. "God, what happened? Feel like I lost a boxing match."

She grins, softly placing her hand over mine. "After the last test yesterday, you got some sort of migraine. Gabby put you to bed."

I rub my forehead as if it might help somehow, and glance around the room. The lamp light is on low, but it still makes me squint.

"Don't you remember? Must have been spending too much time on the screens."

"Maybe…" I feel as if there's a black hole in my head where memories have fallen through.

"Did you eat my ever-so-nutritional snack?" She points to my bedside table.

"Oh, yeah. Some, I think. Thanks." I massage my temples. "What day is it, Lid?"

"Thursday, I think."

"Right."

"What is it?" Liddy's speaking in a low voice, like a caring parent looking after a sick child. She huffs and wraps her arm around me. "What's wrong? Tell Aunty Lid."

I can't help but grin and sniff at the same time. "I don't know. I feel sad… No reason. Like I've lost something, or someone." My head slips to her chest.

"You're homesick, that's all."

When she starts stroking my head, I just feel plain silly and pull back, wanting to speak properly, but my head clashes with Liddy's chin.

"Ouch!"

"Sorry! You okay?"

"Yeah." She's rubbing her jaw.

I swing my legs out of bed. "This is stupid."

Liddy grins, such a familiar half-smile. "Sure is."

"I'm not doing this. All these headaches and tiredness. Not on!" My voice is determined.

"Good."

"A hot shower will fix things. Why don't you make coffee, and I'll join you outside?"

She softly punches me in the arm. "That's my girl."

I cringe. "Oh, please!"

Laughing, she walks out the door as I enter the bathroom.

"Twenty minutes."

"'kay."

Having showered and dressed, I feel a bit better, though my brain still feels foggy. I enter the open area to see Liddy's set up the dining table as if we're in a hotel — well, a budget one, at least. There are cups, saucers, plates and bowls, cutlery and an assortment of cereal, toast, jam, muffins, milk and coffee.

"Voilà."

"Ha! You've missed your calling."

"What's that, then? Cheerer-upper to miserable, sick friend who keeps collapsing on me?"

I smile. "Thanks, Lid. Sorry. Don't know what came over me."

She waves her hand, dismissing my apology. "Well, we're living in the basement of a dungeon at the moment, with no method of escape, being tested by weird scientists to see if we can join their club."

"You've given this some thought, then?"

"Had a bit of time on my hands last night. My bestie was napping again."

I sit down. I'm aware Liddy's making an effort and so laugh at her comment, though my jaw is tight and my stomach aches. Liddy has known me almost all my life and is a master at reading my moods.

"It will pass, Cam."

"You sound like my mum."

"You look like your mum."

"I don't look like her at all."

"And your mum's cute."

"Yuck!"

"Not for me, but for oldies."

I almost remind her that my mum grew up normal, but I bite the inside of my cheek, not wanting to ruin the mood with my cry-baby misery, so I just go along with it. "So, you saying I'm cute?"

"Sure, you are. D'ya think I'd hang around with an ugly?"

I roll my eyes at Liddy, but she's leaning over to reach for the pot of coffee and doesn't notice. She pours me the thick, black liquid. It smells delicious.

"Percolated?"

"Yeah, found the machine last night."

"Mmm, wonderful." Adding milk, I cradle the wide mug. "Tastes even better."

With satisfied *ahs*, we're content to be quiet. It's easy in Liddy's company – comfortable and homey.

Liddy puts her cup down and reaches for toast. "What are you dreaming about?"

"I was just thinking" – a short laugh bursts from my throat – "that when you set up your poodle parlour, you should serve your dog clients coffee and high tea, with scones and cakes."

She snorts and feigns exasperation. "You're calling my future clients 'dogs'? Though, actually, that's not a bad idea. A coffeeshop attached to the parlour..." She licks an imaginary pencil and pretends to write on a non-existent notepad. "Note to self: don't invite Cam to parlour opening. She won't bring poo bags."

I burst out laughing and choke at the same time, splattering coffee down my chin. Picking up a tea towel, I first wipe my chin and then bat Liddy with it. Liddy jumps up and runs to the kitchen for another cloth. Twisting it around, she begins whipping at me. Giggling, I step around the table, but she follows as if we're in a sword fight, leaping backwards and forwards to avoid the thrust of a foil.

We're laughing so much, that both of us bend over, stitches in our sides. I lean against a wall. "Stop, please stop."

"Do you concede?"

An unknown voice ripples through the air. "Concede what?"

We both look up. Standing with Zoe is a tall boy of about seventeen with short, black hair, high cheekbones, and a clean-shaven jaw. He has a familiar face, and I wonder if I know him from somewhere. Zoe looks pale. She has dark lines under her eyes as if she hasn't slept well, and her hair, although tied back, is not as neat as yesterday.

Liddy speaks first. "Morning, Zoe. Want some coffee? Apparently, I need practice serving people."

I laugh again, but it's more of a short burst. The boy's staring at me strangely and I'm unable to glance away. I feel a flutter in my stomach and a lightness, as if all the loneliness of the morning has vanished, like a hot sun drying a damp path.

He breaks eye contact to speak to Zoe. It's almost a whisper. "She has no memory of it. I may have gone a bit too far with the clouding."

Liddy straightens up, pushing back her shoulders. Her tone is abrupt. "No memory of what? Who are you?"

"Hi. Sorry." A hand with slender fingers stretches out to Liddy. "I'm Tom Beresford."

Zoe continues. "Tom came to us three years ago. We rescued him from the Diversity Commission Clinic before he'd undergone too many tests."

Tom pulls a face and, somehow, I understand he'd had more tests than Zoe's telling.

"Tom, this is Liddyana Mitchell and Camelia Chadwick. They've just joined us."

As this is a formal introduction, Liddy leans over to shake hands. My head still feels a bit heavy, but laughing with Liddy has made me feel better. Stepping forwards, I'm about to do the formal handshaking bit, when Zoe and Tom step back.

Tom speaks first. "Sorry, Cam, but would you mind keeping your distance?"

I halt in my tracks, and like some sort of comedy sketch, I glance at Liddy with a 'what's going on?' expression. We both cut to Tom and Zoe and then look back at each other, shrugging our shoulders and waiting for one of us to figure it out.

Zoe moves to the sofas and armchairs, speaking like a school counsellor. "I think we should all sit down. There's something we need to discuss."

Tom follows her and I feel a peculiar urge to step in his shadow, but instead I force myself to go in the opposite direction, grabbing my coffee and muffin on the way. Liddy and I seat ourselves opposite them. I notice the Monet book on the coffee table and wonder how it got there.

"What's going on, Zoe?" My mind flicks back to the blood tests from yesterday. "Have I got a disease, or something?"

"No, no, of course not, but I've been up all night doing some comparisons. You have an anomaly" – she pushes her hair behind her ears as if suddenly aware she's a bit untidy – "which of course you knew and we expected." She uncrosses her legs and crosses them again. "And I haven't got all the results – gene-testing takes time – but what I have got" – she looks at Tom and then at me – "suggests you have a similar dynamic mutation in your brain structure to Tom, which is part of the reason he's here."

I look at Tom. "Is that a bad thing? Heck, does it mean we're related, or something?"

Maybe that's why I feel like I know him.

"It isn't a bad thing and no, it doesn't necessarily mean you're closely related."

Liddy interrupts. "So, what are you saying?"

"This is going to come as a bit of a shock, but Tom has... *talents.*"

Tom takes over; his voice is matter-of-fact. "You won't have heard about this. The Diversity Commission keep it a massive secret, so the best way to tell you is to just spit it out. In our world, there are three types of humans: those who fully transition to a male or female biological sex during the Change, those that have HGS and for ever remain genderless and then, there are those like us, Cam."

"Us?"

"Yes. The third type."

Liddy and I glance at each other. We both shrug and raise our eyebrows like some silly comic imitations of each other.

Zoe takes over, speaking low and calm as if she believes we might go into shock. She might be right!

"We've been researching it longer than the Diversity Commission, so we know those who have HGS also produce a unique AP protein in their brains. If they are sensitive to this protein, it kickstarts the Apriori Pex Cells and the development of something we call the E-Mag Network. Think of this network as creating new pathways and structures in your brain. This is why you and Tom, as well as others like you, are different. This is why you can develop talents.

The room goes silent as everyone stares at me, expecting some sort of reaction. My mind goes blank. This doesn't make sense.

Liddy leans forward, elbows on knees. "Is this something to do with the genetic 'purification' stuff Ruth was talking about?"

Tom intervenes. "It's a dynamic mutation that may have been due to our wonderful ancestors who messed with junk genes when they tried to design the perfect human. Not that I'm complaining."

Zoe jumps in. "Obviously, you know the history of junk DNA?" Both Liddy and I nod. We learn it early on at school. "Well, the Diversity Commission look for the type of irregularities you and Tom have."

Tom is watching me; his eyes seem to delve into my mind. I look away, feeling my face heat up.

"Your tests would have shown your reaction to the AP protein and highlighted your different brain structure, which is why they wanted you taken away so quickly. They are just as keen to be ahead in all this as we are."

I splutter the first things that pop into my mind. "Ahead of what? Am I ill?"

Tom smiles. "Not at all. In fact, you're extraordinary. You're an Apriori Pex."

"A what?"

"An Apex. The first indication would have been that you started the Change and then it stopped."

His hazel eyes seem to pierce my soul. My cheeks flush again with heat and I feel dumbfounded. I lean my elbows on my knees, my face in my hands, trying to hide my embarrassment.

He chuckles at Zoe, who looks annoyed with him. Liddy's clenching and unclenching her right fist, as if she has cramp in her fingers. I feel this uncomfortable electricity bouncing between Liddy and Tom.

"This is just unreal." Liddy's eyes are wide. "How could it be hidden from society?"

Tom smiles. He has a kind smile, one that says I can trust him. "They have control of the media, Liddy. They have control of everything, in fact." He turns to me. "People like us, Cam, don't go through the Change. Our energy diverts to the development of a new type of brain. I can show you."

I can tell he wants to say more but Zoe snaps a warning. "No, Tom, that is not the best way of explaining."

"Why? They know the facts. Cam needs to see it for herself."

"No." Zoe holds her palm up to stop him. "Give them time to take this in. It isn't new to you, but to them, this is vastly different from everything they know." Zoe is determined to close the conversation down and Tom acquiesces, even though I can tell he desperately wants to show us something.

Zoe leans forward. "Normally, after we finish the tests, you'd get a class about who we are and what our purpose is. We'd introduce you to everything slowly. But after what happened last night, I'm going to give you a brief outline. Do you think you can manage more information today?"

Realising I have an ache in my chest from holding my breath, I breathe out. "What happened last night?"

"Let me give you a brief overview first. It might help to have some background about us, about how it all started."

Liddy and I look at each other and shrug. The earth has just reversed its rotation, and I feel as if I'm spinning in the wrong direction.

Liddy grasps my hand. "Isn't this what we ran away for, to get away from the Commission, to live the life we decide?"

"Sure!"

"Then we need answers."

"Okay, Lid."

"And remember, we are in this together, Cam. No matter what."

I hold her hand tighter and then turn back to Zoe. "Go ahead."

CHAPTER TWENTY

I'm sitting cross-legged on the sofa. Liddy is next to me, her legs sprawled out in front of her. Tom and Zoe face us in the armchairs. Zoe looks worn out. The lines around her eyes are more defined than yesterday.

"Our operations started after the last world war with…" She hesitates and looks at Tom. He briefly shakes his head. "A British family. This family owned the island we're on now. Two cousins in the family were in the early cohorts that were born from genetically modified embryos, before we knew how dangerous it was."

"What? That's years ago now."

"Yes, almost a hundred since they did the first trials." She pushes a piece of straggling hair behind her ear. "So, Thomas was one of the children modified. When he turned seventeen, he was fit and healthy and was sent for military training. By eighteen, he was fighting in Europe. He spent four years in a prisoner of war camp. During that time, he was experimented upon. The enemy at that time wanted to understand what was happening to these so-called perfect human beings. On returning, Thomas was damaged. He claimed he could hear and see things others couldn't."

She waits for us to take in the information. I wonder why she thinks this is important to tell us now. I glance at Tom. He's rubbing his hands together and looking away. This is not a story he likes to hear. Liddy's reading my mind, as usual.

"Never heard this stuff before. What's it got to do with us?"

"You wouldn't have, and this has everything to do with why we are here today." She sips from a mug – cold coffee. "Anyway, doctors believed Thomas should spend the rest of his life in a home for those adversely affected by the war, but his parents didn't give up on him. After everything he went through to survive, and the suffering he'd endured, they believed he needed solitude and a peaceful place to recuperate. So, they set up this island to protect their son and others like him. This was the beginning for us." She picks up her coffee and sips it. "That's when our research and development lab was set up to find out what had affected Thomas so badly. Other veterans who'd been placed in institutes were also offered sanctuary on this island."

Tom rolls his shoulders and leans back. I can't help thinking I know him from somewhere. Zoe glances as him, as if expecting him to contribute. He raises his brows in mock-childlike innocence.

"After many years of research, his parents discovered junk DNA and the AP Protein were connected, and that dynamic mutations were taking place. It is possible the war experiments awoke it, although this isn't certain. It could just as easily be environmental or social factors. The DNA may have mutated without interference, but whatever it was, it changed Thomas and others like him, for ever.

"Essentially, what I'm trying to tell you, Cam, is that you, and those like you, are taking a different evolutionary path." She breathes in, as if she's coming to her point. "We were at least ten years ahead of the Diversity Commission in our research into the brain's function as it changes. Now they know about it, they actively search for it using blood tests, EEGs, MRIs. When your brain is scanned, it is like every connection is firing all at once."

I know Liddy feels the same as I do: as if someone has punched me in my gut on the way to altering my whole sense of what is real. She's so quiet, it makes me uncomfortable.

"So, again, I'm some sort of freak?"

Tom's response is both defensive and explosive. "No, as I said, you're – *we* – are extraordinary."

My stomach churns. Having someone who is similar to me, someone who is obviously happy with what he is, makes me feel less of the oddity I have always felt.

Suddenly, the girl from the lab comes to mind; there's something about her that's bothering me, but I can't figure it out. "We were shown a clip of a girl being tested. The guy we met said it was her causing the electrical storm."

"One of the possible manifestations of the mutation."

"One?"

"It isn't an exact science. These genes continue to change through generations and vary in what they do, adapting and evolving, depending upon a person's will and control. Think about them as a language that some people can understand and speak, whilst others can't even hear it. For example, Tom uses vibrations to process information quickly, as fast as a computer. Some people have even mimicked stem cells and repaired damage to their own bodies. Tom can also connect to people in ways normal humans can't."

She watches our reactions as if she expects us to implode or something. When we don't, she continues. "We're not even sure what his final abilities will be – he's still developing them."

"So, what you're saying is, my inherited junk DNA has mutated and somehow generated a protein that woke up some cells, that then adapted into something else to have weird powers?" I hear my long-winded, almost reasonable question, but my mind is freaking out.

"In essence, yes. These cells could have lain dormant from a now extinct generation of Homo sapiens, or it could be the result of a convergence of gene species as we evolved from sea creatures to humans. It could even be from aliens for all we know, but it's there."

"Well, that clarifies it!" I don't mean to be sarcastic, but it is just so absurd.

Liddy has leant forward. "But not everyone is affected?"

"No, not everyone. As Tom said, there are three types of humans: the Gendered, the ungendered and those who develop and react to the AP protein."

I sigh and lean back. Tom has been quiet for a while.

"Think of it as the diverting of energy from the growth of the body, to produce the Apriori Pex Cells, which in turn reconfigure the brain to work in fundamentally different ways."

"Different, how?"

"Zoe said we read a different language. That language is vibrations."

We're all quiet, staring away from each other, before Zoe continues.

"It isn't just us. We have friends from America, Europe, Africa and Australasia – five bases around the world representing the states named after their original founders, but our purpose was slowly redefined. You know the history, how the Diversity Commission grew and extended its global influence in terms of genetic purity, puberty change, the Holistic Law and the Two-Gender system – so I won't go into that. Our primary goal now is still to escape persecution and build our own way of life, but also to find a way to stop the Commission's control and current direction."

Liddy has slung her arm across the back of the sofa. She's staring at Zoe, concentration causing her brow to furrow. "How?"

"We do many things, which you'll learn more about later. Let's just say, beyond our research, we also infiltrate and decapitate." She half-smiles at her own words. "There are now five families who head our leadership committee. We've been at the forefront of genetic testing for years, and the most recent technical advances have made it possible for us to understand much more than the average scientist."

"Isn't genetic testing forbidden?"

"You don't think anyone has really stopped, do you? It's now a race of who gets there first."

Tom's steepled his fingers. Liddy stares at me and I can tell she's trying to process everything. She copes in her usual way.

"You do realise we've just walked onto the set of a sci-fi film?"

I suck in my cheeks and raise my eyebrows. "You're the one who wanted to give this a go and make a new life."

Zoe's voice is quiet and low. "I know this is a lot to take in."

I watch her for a second. She's worried about something. "And you just help people like us for free? No catch?"

"Eventually, you'll take your place in our society and work. You can't just be trainees for ever, nor can you do nothing."

Liddy interrupts. "So, who decides what we do?"

Zoe pushes her hair behind her ear and tries to go for that reassuring, kind-eyes smile again. "It's a joint decision between you, your guardian and your trainers."

Tom's eyebrows join as he frowns and gazes at a spot just over my shoulder. "When they rescued me, I was a mess. They found me because, like you" – he points to me – "I was classified as a Golem."

Zoe exclaims, her voice at a higher pitch. "We don't recognise those terms, Tom. They're prejudiced and insulting."

"Yes, but they're terms Liddy and Cam understand. I'm trying to make this easier."

She nods her agreement to go along with him, for now.

The words spill out of my mouth. "You're a Golem like me, so you didn't go through the Change? I... I thought you were a boy."

"Zoe's right. Golem is the wrong word, Cam. Apex is how we describe people like us. As for being a boy, without any biological sex defining me, it's what I choose to be; what my mind tells me I am."

Liddy glances at me, her eyes wide. "And I choose to be a girl, like Cam."

This type of conversation is new to me and expressing it aloud feels awkward, but Liddy is so up for it. Her eyebrows rise as she nods, encouraging me to confirm what she's saying.

"It's more about what I feel… or rather what I think I am, or would have been had I gone through the Change." Tom's response makes me feel somewhat less of an oddity. "I would have been classified as a male had I completed the Change. Like you, the process started but halted after a few months."

Liddy turns towards me, her manner cautious. "Cam, are you the same as before the Change? I mean, *below* and stuff?"

It's a question Lid has never asked. Her cheeks flush and I feel my neck and face heating up, too. I nod, flex my fingers and then, conscious everyone is watching me, I push my hands between my knees. Lid smiles at me.

"I wish I was still like you."

"I wish I was like you. At least I'd know what I was meant to be."

Tom leans forward, elbows on his knees. "Cam, your situation is slightly different. There are many people who reject the way you think. It doesn't matter that you lived your life as a girl for most of your life. The biological Change is the defining factor for them."

Liddy's lip curls as she stammers her next question at Tom. "There are rumours that there's still treatment, y'know, that changes you physically, that 'fixes' you. There was talk of it at the clinic I went to."

"If you want to go that way, it is something you'd have to discuss with your counsellor," Tom continues. "Right now, I'm happy with how I am." He hesitates a second before starting his next sentence, unsure about sharing it. "I actually believe there's no such thing as being born in the wrong body. I was born this way, and I don't need fixing. To me, it's both the Commission's indoctrination and fabrication – nothing but a myth to control people." He takes a deep breath. "I am not wrong nor broken, and neither are you, Liddy."

Liddy nods and slumps back. "That's easy for you to say. I wouldn't mind being a Golem or an Apex at all. At least it's closer to what I feel I should be."

The room's silent for a few long seconds. I glance up at the dark clouds where a dim light shines through the ceiling, and then back at Liddy. I feel an aching sadness for her. She'd rather be one of the ungendered than have a proper gender, and now she's thinking about changing herself physically. Is that why she wants to stay? I remember the meeting with my mum and the doctor telling us that if we'd come sooner, they might have been able to help physically or with hormone treatment, but he said we'd left it too late. Surely, any treatment now would be painful and confusing? I want to drag Liddy away to have a chat, to understand better. I sit up straighter.

"I think I need time. This is all so much... madness."

I move to stand up, but Zoe holds up her hand. "Just a few more minutes and we'll let you go. I'm sure you two have a lot to talk about." She sits up straight as if her back is sore. "All this brings us back to last night, Cam, and how similar to Tom you are."

They're watching me, expecting a response. All I can manage is a stutter. "Y-you mean, like this brain change thing and reading vibrations – what does that actually mean?"

They look at each other as if they're preparing to blow something up and this is the last chance to change their minds.

Tom frowns. "I can show you, but it involves me waking up a memory in your mind."

"What?" I notice the book on the table again and, standing, pick it up, clutching it to my chest, before marching over to the dining table and sitting with my back to them. I'm not sure what I'm intending to do. I think of Dr Schultz and hypnotism. "I don't want anyone meddling with my head."

Liddy agrees with me. "No, no one's touching her."

Tom's about to say something, but Zoe presses his shoulder, and he stops. "Last night, you woke up and left your room."

Surprised, I face Zoe. "I did?"

Maybe that's why the book is here.

"You found Tom and me talking in the lab."

"I don't remember." A numb tingling sensation runs down my spine, and spots of light flash before my eyes. I shiver, wondering if I'm going to get a headache again. My hand drifts towards the breakfast table and I begin breaking a piece of toast into bits, throwing them on a plate.

"We have security footage, if you'd like to see it."

They have cameras in here?

"You were in some sort of trance, like a dream state. When you met Tom, you had a cellular connection, which is when he was able to assess your genetic make-up."

It's as if they're speaking a gobbledygook language like Lid and I did when we were kids.

Tom pleads with me. "I've never had such a strong connection with anyone. All I want to do is help you remember last night. I won't do anything else. I promise."

"What does it involve?"

"It won't take more than a second and I won't even come near you. You'll feel a sudden dullness, but then it will be gone and your memory of last night should return."

Liddy's lips are thin, tight lines, her eyes angry. "Like Schultz's hypnotism?"

"No, nothing like that."

"And how would we know?" Liddy's glaring at Tom.

"I just wouldn't—"

I interrupt. "I want to talk to Liddy alone before I decide anything. This has all been... well, a lot."

Liddy nods and gets up. Her eyes narrow. I can feel waves of anxiety streaming from her body, as if they are heat and I'm standing next to a fire. "Come on, Cam. Let's go to my room."

CHAPTER TWENTY-ONE

We're in Liddy's room. Other than the fact that the bedspread is a deep teal colour, the room is identical to mine, except it is tidier. The curtains are drawn, the bed is made, and nothing hangs off the chair. Liddy leans on the door for a second before stalking over and perching on the edge of her bed. I'm sitting on the chair by the desk. I notice the puzzle box and pick it up, tossing it around in my hands.

"Did you check it?"

"The sim? Yeah, but haven't had a chance to try it."

I nod, replace it on the desk and stare at the wall. "What do you think, Lid?"

"I think this is one crazy place."

"Yes, but do you believe all the stuff they said, about the brain, the protein, the new cells and talents?"

She jumps up, walks over to the door and faces me, hands on her hips. "Part of me thinks it's just one big, fat lie, but I can't get why they'd lie to us – although, I guess if you're going to lie, you might as well go big."

"It makes my brain ache. I just don't know what to think. How could they get away with it for so long?" Absentmindedly, I pick up the box again and roll it around in my hands.

Liddy sits on the end of the bed and reaches out to touch my shoulder. "That's easy. We have a controlling government, Cam, telling us what to think and what to do. That's what that purity line is all about. You know this."

"Yeah, I know."

"That's why we ran away, why we're here. We don't fit in there."

"And do we fit in here?"

"We might. But I think there's one thing you have to be careful of, and that's Tom. There's something about him I don't like."

"What do you mean?"

"He's just a bit too keen to get into your head. Did you see him? Almost begging!"

She picks up a nailfile and begins filing a split nail. "And this connection, what's a 'cellular connection', anyway?"

I shrug. "Something to do with cells?"

"What's with the book, by the way?" She picks it up and flicks through, glancing at the pictures.

"Oh, Ruth sent it, I think. When we were waiting for you in reception, we discussed impressionism. She said she had a book."

"Nice of her."

"It was in my room yesterday. This morning it was outside."

Her mouth forms a thin line. "So was your plate and half-eaten sandwich."

"So, you think what they're saying is true?"

"You could have just been sleepwalking."

I take a deep breath. "I don't sleepwalk."

"Maybe it's everything that's happened. Stress can do peculiar things."

"And they said they had everything on camera."

Lid looks around the room. "Do you think they have cameras in here, or in the bathrooms?" When I don't respond, she continues. "Okay, let's just say, for now, it's all true. Then what?"

"I don't know. What if I turn out like that girl we saw at Abby's?"

"You won't."

I look into her concerned eyes. Liddy's always been there, always supported me and I feel safe with her around, no matter what.

"Maybe we should speak with Ruth about what's going on and about what Tom wants to do, before you decide anything. She's our guardian, after all."

"I think that's a good idea. Although Ruth is one of them, she seems to understand."

Liddy's face brightens. I know what Liddy really means is Ruth understands *her* but still, another opinion can't hurt and it gives me time to think about it.

"So, we're agreed. I'll ask Ruth to come over. Everything can wait until we see her. You don't have to let anyone do anything, Cam. And don't let anyone in your head. Promise me."

"I promise."

"Good."

"And what about me losing my memory?"

"Sometimes we block things out for protection."

I roll my eyes. "Liddy the psychiatrist."

"No, I'm just saying. You don't need some hypnotic trick. It'll come back when you're ready."

"Probably, but all that stuff about 'cell mutation' and 'talents'. God, that's got to be out of a comic book."

"Superhero stuff, you mean?" She waggles her fingers and hums a weird sci-fi tune.

I grin and push her shoulder. "You're the weirdo around here."

"And proud of it."

The long conversation with Zoe and Tom was meant to reassure us, but Liddy knows how to make me feel better just by being herself.

There's a knock at the door. Liddy answers it, allowing Zoe to step in and speak.

"This has all been a shock for both of you. We were a little too keen. Totally our fault. I explained too much, too soon. I'm truly sorry." She glances around the room. "This is why we usually take a slower pace. Tests, then training. It's just... well, never mind, we would never force anything on you."

Liddy's voice is determined. "We'd like to talk to Ruth."

"Of course, I'm sure she'll want to talk to you, too."

"And Cam doesn't want Tom around."

I frown at Liddy. "That's not exactly what I said."

Her lips pucker at my contradiction. Zoe reaches for the door handle as if she's about to leave, but she hesitates and turns to face me.

"There may be other ways to recover your memory, Cam, without Tom intervening." Her forehead wrinkles as if she's thinking about something. "No matter. We can talk about it later."

Halfway out the door, she leans back in. "For the moment, let's just continue with the tests as scheduled. When you're ready, we'll do the MRI scan. In the meantime, I'll give Ruth a call."

I nod. "Thank you."

Once she's gone, Liddy grins. "Good. Glad that's sorted."

I glare at her. She raises her hands in feigned innocence. "What's that look for?"

From feeling grateful for having her around, I now feel cross and want to snap at Liddy. I don't know why and so bite the inside of my cheek instead. "Nothing. I'm going to brush my teeth."

Only when I'm alone in the quiet of my bathroom, staring at the mirror, do I figure out why I'm irritated. Somehow, Liddy pushed me into a decision. Yes, I didn't want Tom doing whatever he was going to do, but I didn't want him to walk away. He seemed genuine enough. Sadness rises to the back of my throat, and I feel tears brimming. Confused, I slap my cheek – not hard, but enough to stop the blubbering. That's just pathetic.

You don't even know him.

The person in the mirror just looks at me for a second, before she – they, whatever I am – picks up their toothbrush and scrub hard to wash away the morning's grime.

I'm wearing a thin, blue gown that falls just below my knees. Gabby's leading me into a room with a large body-scanner, from which protrudes a bed. The tiles are cold on my bare feet, and I stand there, lifting first one foot and then the other.

"Have you had an MRI before?" Gabby holds a clipboard.

"At the clinic."

"Any problems with claustrophobia, or other adverse reactions?"

"Don't think so." I look over her shoulder at the large glass window. Leo and Zoe are sitting behind a bank of computer screens. Liddy's in the games room. We'd tossed a coin to see who went first.

"Okay, good. We're going to do a full brain and body scan, so it will take around ninety minutes. At the beginning, we'll ask you to look at images on a screen on the inside of the cabin, and afterwards, you can close your eyes and relax."

I nod.

"Jump up, then." She says it as if I'm a little kid, having a fun day. "These ear plugs will help with the noise." She hands me some squashy yellow things, which I push into my ears. "Now, lie flat. Your head needs to be positioned exactly here." She points to a circle marked out on the bed. "And your hands at your sides, please." She walks around the side of the bed and places a button with a long, white lead next to my right hand.

"You'll have to keep still during the whole exam so, if you feel you need a break, or get panicky at any point, press this and we'll bring you out immediately."

"Okay." I hear the door close, after which the bed slides into the tunnel. I take a deep breath and close my eyes. Soft piano music is played and then there's a voice, Zoe's this time.

"We're going to start now, so please try to stay still."

The loud banging noise isn't unexpected, but still makes me flinch when it starts. The thudding vibrates through the whole of my body. I try to pick out the background music, but it can't compete with the noise of the machine. I then try counting backwards from fifty, with the idea of boring myself to sleep.

By the time I reach thirty, my thoughts have wandered back to Tom and the weird conversation earlier. I rack my brain, trying to force the memory of waking up in the middle of the night back into my head. I think of the book. I must have taken it outside. I imagine myself getting up, walking down the corridor with the book in my hand and sitting on the sofa. In my head, I even make myself a hot chocolate and flick through the artwork. It's the sort of thing I would do, but was it real? A voice disturbs my thoughts.

"Cam, can you open your eyes, please? We're going to show you some images."

An image is projected onto the inside of the tunnel, just above my head. Staring at it, I realise it is one of those splodges of paint again. "Didn't we do this yesterday?" I'm not sure if they can hear me.

"It's similar, but we are measuring your brain patterns. No need to speak for this one."

"Okay." My stomach curdles. Yesterday, this gave me a pounding headache. The image changes. It's red this time and reminds me of blood. Someone has cut their arm. The next is green and shoots up like long grass in a spring meadow. I can almost smell the early morning dew. It's replaced by a clip of a man in jeans and a top. He's standing in the middle of a busy city street; hands waving, a big grin on his face. He's calling someone from afar. It disappears and is replaced by a blue splodge, which reminds me totally of the man. I take a deep breath, trying to stay calm. "This is the same as yesterday."

The chunking of the machine stops for a minute; the tinkling sound of the soft music is still playing.

Zoe's voice comes over the speakers. "Sorry?"

"I'm seeing clips again."

"That's fine. We want to monitor your brain's response. Are you all right with this?"

"Not sure."

"Why don't we try a couple, see how it goes?"

"Fine!" I take a deep breath. The scanner has a strange smell, a cross between a hot engine and disinfectant.

The machine starts up again and several clips appear, followed by the still image. A blue sky, five jet planes moving across it, plumes of coloured smoke trail behind; crowds below cheering on a warm summer day. The next is a sheer cliff face, mountaineers climbing, ropes dangling around them as they dig in their picks, their faces grimace as they struggle to get the next foothold.

Each of the clips tells a story and I begin to get lost in people and their lives: a woman asleep on a heavy rug in a lamplit room, a fire burning at her back. Smoke curdles up the chimney as a cat stalks over and snuggles in under her arm; a toddler on a swing, face aglow with winter sun, screaming, 'Higher, Daddy!' I sigh. So nice to have had a father, pushing you on a swing.

"Everything okay?"

"Yes."

"Cam, I'd like to show you a three-second clip of our security camera last night. It's not much, but it might help with your memory and it's less intrusive. This is your choice, though, and we don't have to do it."

I take a deep breath and squish my eyelids tight, before responding. "Is this what you meant when you said another way to bring my memory back?"

"We thought it worth a try."

"Okay." My stomach churns. I'm not sure what to expect.

"Here it is, then."

An office in dim light. There's a lamp on, somewhere. I see outlines of furniture and a computer screen lit up. It's here in the training facility, one of the offices. There's someone in the doorway. I see the back of his head and short, dark hair. Beyond him is a girl in pyjamas. I start in surprise as I recognise my own face. My eyes look bright, excited. The boy looks back for a second, saying something to a person behind him, and I see Tom's visage. He reaches towards me. Our hands touch. There is an explosion of light, and the clip stops.

"That's it?"

"Yes. Do you remember anything?"

"No." I snap at her, though it's not her fault. Something's wrong with me. Why did I forget this?

Maybe I was sleepwalking. I don't get it.

A sudden, sharp pain rips through my head. In my mind, I'm back in the corridor with Tom. I relive the incident from the previous night with a different perspective. An intensity grips at my stomach. It's thrilling, but also frightening. We're somehow connected. I don't understand how or why I know that. It's as if we're... I don't know. I can't explain it. I reach up to grab my temples, but the tunnel is in the way. A ripple of panic shoots across my chest and my breathing changes, my heartbeat becoming a thudding noise in my ears.

Get me out!

I can't find the button, can't reach it. My legs kick out, my knees hitting metal. Pains grip my chest; my hands claw against the top of my white coffin. Squeezing my eyes, I see spots of light flashing on the back of my eyelids, like neurons sparking one after the other. An explosive crashing noise drowns out a scream and a desperate plea. "Get me out!"

The bed slips out from the tunnel in ultra slow motion. My reactions are sluggish, and I wonder what's wrong with me. Three people stare through the glass panel, their mouths moving, but their words are slurred, making it impossible to understand what they're saying. There is a reflection in the glass; it looks like the girl from the clip, the one they were testing, the one that had electricity shooting out of her, but it isn't her. The face is mine. How can that be? I don't understand.

I squint to see the reflection better. It is me, but I look all wrong. My hair is spread out, as if static is pulling at the roots. Lightning shards emanate from my body. I sit there, barely moving, a cry of agony paused on my face, my eyes wide, my fingers splayed. I give my brain the order to move my arm, but all I feel are tingles down my neck and shoulders, as if the message isn't getting there. My mind is panicking, shrieking at my body to move, but nothing happens.

What's wrong with me? Am I having a stroke? Surely, I'm too young!

A movement to the left of me. The door inches open. It seems to take for ever. Maybe this is what a stroke feels like? Maybe half my brain isn't working but then, how can I think so clearly? How can I see what I'm seeing?

The tip of a shoe, an ankle, followed by a body and a face creep around the door. All impossibly slow. I try to move, jump off the bed, tell people there's something odd going on, but nothing's reacting the way it should. No one hears me. I don't even hear my own voice – only a thudding in my head, like an old grandfather clock that has broken down and only ticks every twenty seconds or so. It crosses my mind that this could be one of those clips they've been showing me. Perhaps I'm still in the tunnel, but it feels too real and yet not real at all.

I look towards the panelled glass again. Zoe's now standing, her finger points towards the door. She's saying something. I squint, trying to make out what she's saying.

Why aren't they helping me?

Many seconds pass before I'm able to turn my head. When I manage it, Tom is standing in the corner, his hands are stretched out in front of him, as if he's warning me of something, but I can't hear clearly. His words sound like an old record with the speed turned to its lowest. My mum has an antique one, with heavy vinyl that squeaks when played.

"Cam?" Tom's voice echoes in my head, but his lips don't move, his body stays rigid.

"Tom, help me. I can't move."

"I'm here to help, but you need to stay calm."

"What?"

"You're in shock and spiking."

"Spiking?"

"You're panicking."

"Wouldn't you?"

"Ouch! Yes, perhaps we shouldn't have shown you the clip. Sorry, but you're okay. Just take it easy."

"I can't move."

"You can, you are. Please, I can help— Ouch!"

"What's wrong with you?"

"Nothing. I'm fine. Let's sort you out."

"Sort me out?"

"Get you back to normal."

"Yes, but why—"

"You're triggering. It happened to me when I was a bit younger than you."

"Am I ill? Going mad?"

"No, neither. You've accessed the vibrational realm and are manifesting talents."

"I don't know what that means, and I'm not doing anything."

"Of course not!" There is humour in the words. "How do you think we're speaking with each other, Cam?"

"What?"

"We can't speak normally in Processor mode. I'm using telepathy to reach you."

"Impossible."

"Ow... ow... ow! No... not... impossible." His shrieks of pain continue for a few seconds, but I hold onto his voice, afraid to let go, afraid this madness will drive me to a place I can't return from.

"I can't move."

"You can. It's just to do with speed. Try to slow down."

"Slow down? I told you I can't move."

His hands are now lowered and he's slumping against the wall. Before I can repeat myself, he has a question.

"So, your mum had an antique record player, then?"

"Yes, how do you know?"

"Tell me about it."

"Why?"

"I'm interested. I like old things."

"But—"

Unbidden, the record player comes to the forefront of my mind. A box – red and white, with a small, gold clasp to lock it. I imagine a younger version of me, chubby fingers reaching out to run my hands over the bumpy surface and fiddle with the clasp. My mum shows me how to open it and inside is a turntable covered in green felt.

Tom's voice enters the memory. "Tell me how it works."

"You place records on the metal spindle thing in the middle. Then the arm comes across to balance it." I close my eyes, seeing my mum showing me. She selects the speed.

"Keep talking."

Opening my eyes, I glance over. Tom's sitting on the floor. I notice his mouth twitch.

"Well, she – my mum – would choose a record. A larger one meant it was an album. She'd let me select the speed of thirty-three. A smaller one was forty-five."

"I've never seen one. Was it big?"

I move my arms wide; they seem a little slow but are almost responding at a normal rate. "About *this* big."

"And how did you get it to play?"

"There's this other part with a needle, called" – I watch as my hand creeps to my head, scratching it like a little kid at school as I try to remember the name – "a stylus, I think. Anyway, you lift it onto the corner of the record and pull the switch back to start the turntable spinning."

"But how can you hear music from it? Does it have speakers or something?"

My mouth opens and real speech comes out. There's a distant quality to it, like on an aeroplane when your ears get blocked. "Not sure. Something to do with vibration, I think."

Tom looks up, grinning. "Feeling better?"

Remembering I have ear plugs in, I reach up to take them out. Tom spoke aloud. He sounds abrupt and noisy. I move my legs to hang off the bed. They weigh heavy, but normal.

"I don't know what I feel."

The thudding in my ears has returned to a normal heartbeat. Zoe, Gabby and Leo are staring at me through the glass, their eyes wide. Zoe uncrosses her arms and moves towards the side door. As she enters, she glances first at me and then Tom.

"What happened?"

I stare at them both, wanting an answer as badly as Zoe.

Tom stands. "Uncontrolled Processor. Telepathy. Possibly other stuff." He looks at me. "Try not to be afraid. It's always confusing, at first. I've been through this, and you'll be okay. Trust me."

I shiver and rub my arms. "I don't get it." The words don't really explain how I feel, but Tom seems to understand anyway.

"Everything – from the tiniest atoms, to sound, to the universe itself – vibrates. Because of the way your brain is wired, you're one of few who are able to access these vibrations and manipulate them—"

Zoe interrupts. "Is she safe?"

"Yes. I'll leave you to it. I'll be in one of the offices, if you need me."

"Thank you."

He's about to leave and I have an uncontrollable urge to stop him. "Tom?"

"Yes?"

I feel silly and blurt out the first thing that pops into my head. "I don't know what you did but thank you."

He's rubbing his hands across his face. "You're welcome." He's about to turn again, when I think of something that's bothered me for a while.

"Do I know you from somewhere? I mean, other than last night."

He somehow manages to smile and frown at the same time. "Until last night, we'd never met, but we have a connection, a bond. Something we don't see much of around here."

"We do?"

"Can't you feel it?"

Lifting my chin, I lock eyes with him. At first, there's nothing. Just a person. Then I feel a tentative pull, as if my body is being yanked towards him, as if we are magnetic poles drawn together to become one. I take a deep breath and look away. Like a stretched elastic band snapping back into place, my sense of preservation returns me to my own self. I notice my pale face in the glass panel – my hair's askew and I'm biting my lip.

Tom grins, but his eyes are heavy. "Yep. Scary, isn't it?"

Yes, but... I don't know how to finish my thought. "Are you..." I want him to stay, but don't know how to ask.

Somehow, he understands. "I need to figure this out as much as you do, Cam. So, yes, I'll stick around, and I'll help, if you want me to."

He leaves and a shudder runs down my spine, but I feel better.

Damn, Liddy's going to be so annoyed.

CHAPTER TWENTY-TWO

"I'm not normal, am I?"

"Define 'normal'."

"That's not an answer."

Zoe and I are sitting on tatty, maroon armchairs. They're the leather type with indented buttons creating a diamond pattern. Her office is comfortable, but tiny. To the left is a desk with a laptop and neatly piled papers and files. There's a pane of glass, but it just looks out onto the corridor. I wish we could open a window and get some fresh air. I take a deep breath and let it out slowly, trying to calm my mind.

What's happening to me?

Why do I feel so connected to a person I've never met? And did we really speak using telepathy? I slump, feeling exhausted, as if I've been running a marathon. My limbs are still trembling, and my knee jiggles up and down. I watch it for a minute, before lifting my legs and crossing them under me.

"Don't be embarrassed to eat more, if you want to. You used a lot of energy and your body's craving carbohydrates."

A plate of half-eaten buttery crumpets sits on the coffee table between us. The huge pile of blackberries she brought in are already demolished. I can't resist and lift a third crumpet to my mouth, looking at her as I take a huge bite. Since our meeting this morning, she's changed her clothes, applied some make-up and tied her hair back. There are dark lines under her eyes still, but she looks better.

"If you mean 'normal' as in Liddy or me, then no."

I swallow a lump of half-chewed dough before speaking. In the outside world, Liddy wouldn't be classed as normal. "But neither of you suddenly turn into a freak of nature, with lightning shooting out of your body?"

Zoe watches me for a few seconds before speaking again. "Cam, not all ungendered or those with HGS end up with talents. In 'normal' people neuroplasticity is generally fixed by the time the Change takes place. In Apex's it seems it is constantly evolving.

So, when I say, you're not like Liddy or me, it is not something to be ashamed of. What's happening to you now is your normal and it is a gift. You just need to learn control."

"It doesn't feel much like a gift right now." My voice is at a higher pitch than normal. I take another deep breath and sigh. "If you know I need to learn control, why did you risk putting me in that scanner?"

"We weren't sure what would trigger you, but it is better this happened in a controlled environment. If it had happened around others—"

"You must have known something would happen."

"Well, yesterday the images were an indicator, but it seems the biggest trigger was Tom. Has anything like this happened before?"

I cringe a little, now remembering the strange 'Tom connection' of the night before. "I don't think so. Never stuff like that." I wonder, though, at the telepathy. Sometimes, it felt as if I could read my mum's mind – and Liddy's, come to think of it – but I just thought we were close, that all people could do that.

"Today, it must have been the clips you saw or perhaps the security footage."

"But why? I don't get it."

"I'm sorry, I didn't expect such a volatile reaction." She looks down at her hands. "It must have been frightening for you."

I swallow my last mouthful of food. A sickness rises from my stomach to the back of my throat as a realisation occurs. "You were experimenting just to see what would happen?"

She picks up her clipboard and pen. "Not exactly."

I can tell she's *not exactly* being truthful, but there's a more pressing question. My voice is shaky as I ask: "So, what have you discovered?"

"You're a Processor, like Tom."

"And that is?"

She crosses her legs and settles back in the chair. She looks down at her clipboard before continuing. "A Processor is someone who can speed up information; use their brain a bit like a computer. According to Tom, when you're doing it, people around you appear to slow down."

I think back to the MRI room, how I thought I'd had a stroke. "Your voices were slurred."

"That's not the only proof, of course. We also have the MRI scans, which showed your brain's physical spiking – lighting up a myriad of different pathways."

I must look confused, as she feels the urge to illustrate her statement.

"Think of your neurons as a million twinkling Christmas lights – all connected. Now imagine them all exploding so fast, you can't even see which shatters first. In Processor mode, your brain works at speed. Uncontrolled, it blasts outwards. Hence, the electrical storm." She hesitates for a second, wanting to know how I'm coping with her explanation. "That's why you can see those clips before the static images – which, by the way, are a nanosecond long. Most people don't even notice them because they haven't developed the additional neural pathways."

I nod, trying to keep my face blank, even though the pounding in my ears gets louder and I feel my face heating up. "Anything else?"

"You'll have noticed the telepathy, of course."

I frown. The weird sickness in my stomach has reached the back of my head and is trying to crawl into my brain. I shake it off, grabbing the glass of water from the table and holding on to it.

"Some people are able to use telepathy, but it's most often one-sided and not as useful. I tried to develop it once, but don't have the cells to manipulate vibrations." She looks away for a minute, as if embarrassed, but then faces me. "You and Tom have dual telepathy, meaning you're able to speak to each other."

I think back to the MRI room. When I couldn't understand anyone, his voice was clear. He was able to reach me when others couldn't. I don't know what to say. My mind's going in a million different directions. "Explain 'manipulating vibrations' to me again."

She crosses and then uncrosses her legs. "Every living thing has a resonance because every living thing is made up of electrons, vibrating. Humans give off low frequency vibrations, but most can't hear or sense it, whereas many animals can." Her fingers rap the board on her knee. She notices and stops. "So, elephants for example. Did you know their low frequency calls travel further along the ground than through the air? They can detect seismic waves using their trunks and the skin on their feet. They can tell danger's coming from miles away."

I nod, which she takes as an indication to continue.

"Insects use vibration to warn of danger, as do mole rats, spiders and frogs. With people like Tom and yourself, your heritage allows you to hear, see and even manipulate those vibrations. In essence, that's what you and Tom can do that most other people can't – sense and use vibrations in a different way to what we think of as 'normal'."

I nod again as if we're having a chitchat over coffee. "Can Tom do other stuff?"

"What do you mean?"

"Can he manipulate minds, like Dr Schultz? Force you to forget things?"

"Tom would never do that. He's signed our oath of no harm. There are those that would, of course."

Somehow the glass is back on the table. I don't remember putting it there, and now I'm biting my fingernail. I don't remember doing that, either. I pull it away from my mouth but can't help picking at it. Liddy would be appalled. When she was younger, her father would slap her fingers when he caught her biting her nails.

"Right." I say it like it's a matter of fact, when inside my head there is this crazy woman, hands over her ears, rocking back and forth.

I slowly lean forward, pick up a juice box and stick the straw in it. Looking up from under my dangling hair as I take a long sip, I try to sound casual. "So, what's next?"

"Well, no more tests for now, just until we're certain they won't have adverse effects."

"Good."

She considers me like a scientist examining a lab specimen. "I must say, you're taking this remarkably well."

I stare a little too long into her eyes. She glances away nervously, and I get the impression she's not as comfortable around me as she's making out.

"What choice do I have?"

A thin-lipped smile and a nod is all the response I get. "I'll have to report the incident to Head Office, but I want to wait a while, see if we can determine a little more."

And I'm her lab specimen again. "How exactly are we going to determine that? No more scans."

"Of course not, and we don't need to do them. Tomorrow, you and Liddy will move out of reception to work with the other associates. There'll be some classes you can do together, but if you're willing to work with Tom alone, he could show you faster how to control what we know you already have, as well as potentially stretch your boundaries."

"And that means?"

"Ah, yes. Well, the structure of your brainwaves is rare. Tom is the only other person we know of with the same configuration. He is the most qualified to teach you how to learn and use vibrations."

I frown and replace the empty juice box on the table.

"Yours are so similar to Tom's, you could be related from some distant past."

I push past that bit of information. I want her to keep talking and she seems to be on a roll. Her eyes are bright with the excitement of sharing knowledge.

"We have to stay ahead of the Diversity Commission. You and Tom are helping us do that, but they are moving quickly."

"The Diversity Commission?"

She hardly needs the prompts to continue. "Well, this is all a relatively new science, but the Commission see it as an advantage. Their agenda is highly classified but imagine what they could do with someone like you or Tom on their side."

"Why would they need us on their side? They already control everything."

"They don't. We are a growing movement, and they know there will come a time..." She hesitates. "Some people with talents do agree to join them. Others are forced."

I couldn't imagine ever agreeing to work with them or to hurt people like Liddy. I redirect her. "How many different talents are there?"

"We've discovered four or five that recur." She uses her fingers to count them off. "Telepathy is a big one, though only a few are dual. Controlling the earth's natural forces, such as electricity—"

I feel my facial muscles tightening. I wrap my arms around my centre and lean forward. She purses her lips and clasps her hands.

"Perhaps we should leave it there for today. I wanted to settle your mind, to explain a bit, let you know we're on your side. But now you need rest. Liddy won't finish her tests until four and Ruth will come for dinner around six, so you won't be disturbed."

"Oh, Liddy!" When I tell her what happened with Tom, and him being in my head again, she won't be happy.

"I'll tell her you're in your room but won't tell her what happened." She stands up. "I'll leave that to you."

Escaping and being alone to think things through sounds like a good idea. I nod and stand up. My feet tingle with numbness from sitting cross-legged for so long. She follows me to the door and opens it.

"There's one thing I want you to consider, Cam." Her hand squeezes my shoulder, and I turn to look up at her worried face. "Tom's keen to work with you, to understand your connection with him and to help you develop. It would mean training with him alone, away from Liddy. I know how close you two are."

She leaves the statement unfinished, but I understand what she means: Liddy will be upset.

"I'll think about it."

CHAPTER TWENTY-THREE

Trudging down the corridor to my room, I know what my answer will be. The idea of working with Tom creates a warm sensation in my chest. There's something about the link we have that makes me crave more – a need to be close to him.

In front of my bathroom mirror, I brush my teeth for the second time today. Thinking about Tom brings a red heat into my face. I press my cheek with the tips of my fingers, watching the skin pale and then turn maroon again. I try to laugh it off, but the flush only deepens through my ears and down my chest.

This is stupid! You don't even know him. And think of Liddy.

I scowl at my reflection and snap, "Get some perspective, girl!"

That's what Liddy would say. Yanking down the bottom of my eyelids, I groan at the sore, red blood vessels. I splash my face with cool water and kick off my shoes, before falling on the bed and wrapping the duvet around me. As I close my eyes, I mutter to the air, "Very tired."

In response, I hear Tom's voice in my head. "Sleep, Cam. I'll catch you later."

It should worry me that he can walk into my thoughts at any time, but I smile instead. "How long have you been there?"

"Just reached out."

"You'll have to teach me how."

"Later. Gonna leave you now."

"Right. Later."

I wake with a start, and gasp. Hot and stuffy, I kick the duvet off and roll onto my side, trying to find a cool spot on the bed. I'm about to drift off again when I hear his voice.

"Still sleepy?"

"Tom?"

"Who else?"

"Well, there are others with telepathy."

"True, but it doesn't quite work like that. People aren't permitted to just enter your head. You have to agree to it."

"That's good to know."

He's tentative, as if he's jumping in and out of the conversation from a distant point. Maybe that's what telepathy feels like.

"Well, except for those without heritage."

"Heritage?"

"Term we use around here for Apexes."

"So, what you're saying is that we can enter most people's heads, except for those with this heritage thing?" Even in my head, my voice sounds screechy. His, on the other hand, has an amused tone.

"Only because those with heritage know how to protect themselves from invaders. But, yeah, I guess that sums it up."

I push my hair out of my face. I can't quite bring myself to open my eyes yet. "Are you kidding? Tom, that's most of the human race."

"Hey, we have rules. We don't just dig around. It's dangerous."

I roll over again, wondering why we can speak to each other so easily and others can't.

"It turns out our junk DNA strands and Apex Cells are very similar, almost identical, in fact."

I cringe. "You can hear my thoughts, not just what I'm saying?"

"When you're in Responsive mode."

This is a whole different thing. I have private things I don't want him to know. "'Responsive mode' is?"

"When you're allowing me to."

I crouch into a ball and cling to my knees, trying not to think of my red face in the mirror just a few hours ago. Of course, my whole body responds and heats up. He doesn't say anything, and I wonder if he knows how embarrassed I'm feeling. "But I didn't agree to anything."

"Same here, but you're in my head, too. Was that *bond* thing that started it, I think."

"What exactly is that bond thing?"

"That's one of the things I'd like to explore. If you're willing to train with me, we can find out together."

Liddy comes to mind. I know he sees it. It's almost as if I can see him raising his eyebrows, but he doesn't comment. I change the subject. "How do you find me, to speak like this?"

"You have a signature vibration. Everyone does, but yours is easy."

"I'm easy?"

I hear him chuckle. "Look, I can teach you everything I know, all about vibrations, how we access them, how to be careful around others so we don't hurt people."

Hearing all this is so bizarre! I remember this morning and the pain he was in.

"Yep, that's you spiking and me being the beneficiary."

"Sorry."

"No problem. First lesson: stay calm like you are now and no one gets hurt. That means no sudden jerks in emotion. Second lesson: gain permission from the person before entering their minds."

I'm about to ask how, but he jumps in. "Will teach you, later."

"Okay. Anything else?"

"You have to sense a vibration to use it. Everyone is different, but once you know it, you can recognise it, like a person's face. It's unique to them. I can show you the information to find me, if you want."

"Will it hurt?" My whole body tightens, readying itself for some sort of torture.

"No, and it'll take less than a second."

"Okay." I grit my teeth, expecting pain anyway. Instead, I feel a surge of warmth, as if I have chocolate overload, and then sense, rather than hear, a low humming, like the rumble of an earthquake far away, or how we measured infrasound at school. And I know it's his frequency lodging itself in my mind and becoming familiar.

"Done!"

"That was weird."

"Hey, we're all weird. They haven't figured out where this heritage even comes from yet. We could be aliens, for all they know."

"Or, we could just have genes from Neanderthals. Or elephants."

He laughs. "Wouldn't mind a trunk."

"So, I can find you now?"

"Needs some practice, but I'm close, so shouldn't be hard. Just focus on the vibration. Right, I have to go. Work to do, and you're about to get a visitor."

"I am?"

"I think Liddy's on her way."

"You can see her?" I picture him sitting outside my door.

He laughs. "So, you think I'm a creepy stalker, then?"

"No..."

"She's just finished her tests."

"Oh, right. Is it four already?" I'm shocked. I must have been asleep all afternoon.

There's a quiet tapping at my door, and suddenly I feel guilty at the thought of explaining all this to Liddy.

"Glad you're handling it."

"Stop reading my mind."

"Sorry! Next lesson is how to block people like me reading your thoughts when using telepathy."

"Good idea."

"So, you agree to training with me?"

"This was a show and tell, wasn't it?" I sigh, realising he planned the conversation to persuade me I needed him.

"A bit."

"Wasn't necessary, you know."

"I know."

"Of course you do."

"'Bye."

And he's gone.

Liddy's head peers around the door. For a second, she looks over at me and I can tell her eyes are adjusting to the dark. She whispers as she slips into the room and closes the door quietly. "You awake?"

I roll over and turn on the lamp. "Yeah, come in. There's something I want to talk to you about."

She sits next to me on the bed, legs stretched out in front of her. "Zoe said you weren't well again."

"The MRI scan brought on another episode."

"Another?"

"It also made me remember my walkabout last night."

She takes a deep breath. "So, you know what happened, then?"

I tell her everything, including the discussion with Zoe and Tom – although I avoid the recent telepathy bit, letting her think it was all face-to-face meetings. She sits quietly, letting me talk. At first, she's relaxed, but by the time I've finished, she's pacing the room, hands on hips.

"What was the point in asking Ruth to come in, then?"

"Sorry?"

"Well, I thought we'd decided to discuss Tom and this thing he wants to do with you, together. Apparently, that's no longer the case. You and Tom have already decided, without me."

I stare at her, aghast. "Of all the things I've said about the training, how things work here, our future life, my weird heritage or inability to handle these stupid triggers and reactions, you pick on that?" I knew she would; I'd just hoped the other stuff would distract her.

"I thought we were in this together."

I clasp my hands around my knees. "We are. All our training will be together, with the exception of Tom. I have to learn how to control this thing, Lid. I could hurt people."

"They must have other trainers. That's what they do here, isn't it?" She's stopped the pacing but is now glaring at me.

"You don't get it. None of them were able to bring me back. They aren't Processors and can't use telepathy."

"How do you know none of the trainers can do that? Have you met them?"

"No."

"Have you asked Zoe?" I shrug. "So, there may be others?"

"What have you got against Tom?"

"Why are you in such a hurry to trust him? How do you know he hasn't manipulated your mind to agree with him?"

"There are rules—"

"We've been here two days, Cam. We have no idea what they really do, and we only understand what they've told us. We don't even know if we're staying."

"I thought you wanted to give this place a go, make a life?"

She runs her hand across her face. "I just think we need to stick together and be careful what we decide, until we know the facts."

Her logic is sound, and I agree with everything she's saying, but feel I have to defend myself. "I've done nothing wrong." My voice is a pitch higher. "I'm just trying to figure all this out."

"And I'm just asking we figure this out together." She's still pacing. I wish she would sit down but she just stops and stares at me, waiting for a response. My insides tighten. I know that's what we've always done. Any crisis has always been a discussion together, talking it through, weighing up the odds. Eventually, she crosses over to me and sits on the edge of the bed, leaning forward.

"Remember, this is *us* in this together. There have to be other options."

Fiddling with the edge of the duvet, I stammer my response. "B-but, Lid, this is what I want. It's what I *need*... I can't go about *exploding*."

Her eyes water. "So, what am I now, then? The sidekick in a novel about Cam, the witch, who suddenly discovers she's got magical powers? The one who gets killed off when no longer needed?" She sniffs. "I have wants and needs, too, Cam. I'm real."

"Lid, don't say that." I reach out for her, but she jumps up and looms over me. My stomach clenches tighter and a pain shoots through it, as if someone's punched me in my centre.

"You don't see it, but I do." She's blinking rapidly. "He's already manipulated you, changed how you think. You're no longer the Cam who walked in here two days ago. When she comes back, let me know."

Without waiting for a response, she storms out, slamming the door. The pain grows and I cradle my stomach, my forehead touching my knees. A deep, guttural sound escapes my throat, and I heave, tears flooding down my cheeks. I'm crying for my mum, for Liddy, for everything that's happened, but mostly just for me; for the guilt I feel, knowing my mum is suffering, knowing my best friend is hurting, and knowing I won't change my mind about Tom, even to make Liddy feel better.

I don't hear the door open or feel him sit next to me. Tentatively, he places his arm around my shoulder, wanting to comfort me, but not sure if I'll hurt him. I feel a tingle run down my back as he strokes it, but nothing painful. He's close enough for me to smell soap, like he's just washed his hands.

"Quiet, now. It'll be all right." His voice is soft and soothing in my ear. "Liddy will get over it."

Just being with him calms me. The shuddering begins to ebb, and I start to feel a bit embarrassed. Tom gently turns me around and places his hands on my shoulders, but I can't meet his eyes.

"Liddy doesn't understand. She can't."

I sniff like a child without a hanky.

"I came here to speak face to face. I want you to know, I didn't force this decision through some sort of mind-manipulation. It was your choice, and you can change your mind, if you want to."

I'm fiddling with the duvet cover again. There's a bit of loose cotton. I wrap it around my finger and snap it, before lifting my head. "I don't want to."

He smiles. "Good. Would you like me to join you for dinner tonight?"

"Perhaps not."

"I understand. Will you be okay?"

"Yes. Ruth's coming. She'll help, I'm sure."

He nods and gets up. "Later, then."

"Later."

CHAPTER TWENTY-FOUR

I strut around, packing up my few things and then plonk myself down on the edge of the bed, head in my hands. Ruth came over yesterday, but Liddy wouldn't come out of her room. In the end, Ruth had to speak to us separately. I don't know what was said between them, but we're leaving reception and moving into our accommodation on the training campus. Surely, Liddy can't ignore me for ever.

I trudge out to the main seating area with my backpack slung across my shoulder. The room is dark. I look at the glass panelling above us. Storm clouds. I could almost believe Liddy's controlling the weather to suit her mood. She's playing a game on the large TV, hitting the remote control as if it offends her. Throwing my bag on the floor, I plonk myself next to her and nudge her shoulder.

"Come on, Lid."

Her jaw becomes stiff, the muscles tightening as she grits her teeth. Turning to face her, I try a different approach.

"Wanna steal some cookies to take with us?" Her face is expressionless. "Liddy, why are you doing this? I don't get it."

She shuts down the game and switches off the TV, before standing up and looking around. "What's that squeaking noise? Sounds like some little, flat-chested kid."

I get up, fingers clenched together. "That's not fair."

"There it goes again. A little kid, whining. Glad it's nothing to do with me." With that she strides away, leaving me with tears of anger and frustration.

I shout after her, "Fine. If that's how you want it, then that's" – I stammer as I hear a door slam in the bedroom corridor – "it, then."

We're sitting in a classroom, preparing to watch a short introductory video. The chairs are the kind with flip-back desks. Liddy's at the back – the furthest from me she can possibly be. Vicky, Taor and Jonathon are in the room with us. Some of their induction training was delayed so we could start it together. Ruth stands in the corner.

"Your first morning will be spent learning about what we do and touring the island. We always begin with the welcome video from one of our leaders." She has a remote control with which she dims the lights. A film flashes up on the whiteboard. A tall, dark-skinned man with thick, black hair speaks.

"Welcome to Base One." His accent is different. Maybe Australian. "My name is Peter Abimbola, and I am one of the leaders of our community."

The picture spans outwards to show him standing next to a 3D graphic of the island. "You are here." He smiles, pointing to a block named 'Training'. "To the back of you is our science and research departments and behind that are our staff quarters."

I lean in, paying attention to what looks like footage from a drone. The staff quarters take up the whole length of the island and beyond them is a private staff beach – or, at least, that's how it's labelled.

"We have the office and admin block to the right. This is where you'll get your assignments, should you choose to stay with us. Below it is the mission ops, which is out of bounds for trainees." He smiles, his teeth straight and white.

I wonder what sort of missions require such secrecy. They already told us they rescue people, that they oppose the Diversity Commission's regime, but what else do they actually do?

"The clinic's attached to admin. Hopefully, you won't need to use that during your training." He grins again, as if we're all thrilled at his comments.

I glance around. Vicky's leaning on her arms, looking bored; Jonathon's knee is bouncing up and down; Taor's legs protrude, and Liddy's slouching, but none of us are smiling.

"As you can see, here's the guest housing."

The film is swerving to the right of the island, but I'm just able make out a garden space with a children's play area in the centre and I wonder if there are kids here. Liddy's earlier comment comes to mind.

How could she call me a flat-chested kid? She knows how much— I pinch my arm. The pain helps me to refocus.

"We are fully self-efficient." He says it with pride. "We have our own helipad and small runway, water treatment centre, solar energy, and a food production unit.

There's also a crèche, a meeting hall and cinema."

Angling towards the bottom of the island, I see a supermarket, a coffeeshop, a clothes shop and a bicycle hire facility. The picture then veers back to the quayside warehouses and the reception building. Finally, it reaches the training facility again. To its right is another beachfront, labelled 'For Trainees'.

Peter's now sitting down in what looks like the very room we are in. He's wearing casual clothes. "We know how traumatic your last few days have been, but I want to reassure you our sole purpose is to help you develop a new life, away from those who would harm you. You are safe here." He pauses, staring intently, as if he's in the room, weighing up our reactions.

"Our mission has always been to protect those who need help and to challenge those in our society who bring about injustice, inequality and suffering. You may think the whole world believes gene purification is a good thing, but this is not true.

"The human race has always evolved. Although our founder's original goal was protecting freedom, of late, we, as a community, have also evolved. If we don't, we'll be destroyed, our way of life will be gone. So, we match strength with strength and, until such time as we can live peaceably, part of our remit is to infiltrate and destroy on a global level the Diversity Commission and those who support them. Anyone who tells us how we should be and how we should live our lives are our targets."

Although he slipped it in subtly, their enemy is obviously the Diversity Commission – or, at least, it is one of them. I'm not sure how I feel about that. On the one hand, I agree with him – everyone should be free to live their own lives how they choose to. On the other, the DC brought peace when there was chaos. Yes, they have made mistakes; yes, they have stuff wrong – like with what they planned to do to Liddy and me – but to destroy a huge group of people? What exactly does 'destroy' mean? Seize power? How do you do that without people dying?

I already feel uncomfortable. Maybe I should discuss it with Tom. I feel my stomach twist. Tom was the first name that came to mind, not Liddy.

Peter's voice deepens with passionate belief. "We want everyone to be free to choose who they are, to be comfortable with their bodies, with the commonality that we are all human, irrespective of our differences. We all share this planet, and we all deserve respect."

He stops and I imagine an audience cheering him on, though our room is silent. I glance back at Liddy. She's sitting upright now. His words have got her attention. I knew they would. This world is her chance to live as she wants. She notices me staring but avoids eye contact.

Peter begins speaking again. "You are the lucky few who have escaped a society that rejects the evolution of humankind. We recognise people like you are special. You are our future. You will be the creators of our brave, new world – one that rejects the Diversity Commission and everything it stands for. We are the Libertas Diversity Resistance League – DRL or just the League, for short. And your heritage is our future."

He leans forward and I know this is the punchline: "Will you join us in fighting against the evil that is the Diversity Commission?"

The film ends and the lights are bright again. Ruth has an ironic smile on her face. I'm not sure what it means, but it passes as she addresses us. "Anyone have any questions so far?"

Jonathon sneers. "Is he for real?"

Ruth is ultra patient. "Peter is dedicated to our mission. And yes, Jon, he's for real."

I can't understand why Jon is so nasty. After all, he was rescued. Taor slithers down his chair, his shoulders low, his legs spread out for miles in front of him.

"Any other questions?"

Liddy grates her throat. "Erm, when he said to 'infiltrate and destroy on a global level', what exactly does that mean?"

It's as if Liddy read my mind. Ruth throws it back at us.

"What do you think it means?"

Vicky responds. She's twirling one of her hair spirals. "You have like this huge army, or something, all over the world that blows people up, like the Diversity Commission?"

Ruth smiles. "Well, not quite, but something like that. The Diversity Commission spreads lies and false rumours. In many countries, they now control through fear, although a few manage differently, but all of them demonise those we deem 'normal'. The evolution of humans is to be who we truly are, not controlled through experimentation or mind-meddling." She glances a Liddy for just a second. "The Diversity Commission weeds out those who are different, either through forced change or by creating workers unable to think for themselves."

I think of the Golems I've met, the blank-faced cleaners I've seen and ignored on the street. They just seemed a normal part of life. I question whether any of them were actually Apexes like me. Now I understand better what I am and why I'm the way I am, I despise how I so easily accepted what the government and media told us; heck, what the teachers told us, what *my mum* said.

"Their second – and hidden – motivation is to find people with different heritage: DNA that can work towards their cause."

I feel my face heating up, praying she doesn't use me as an example. Instinctively, I glance at Liddy. Her eyes are dark, her face a mask.

"Those who can manipulate vibrations can utilise power. Imagine an army of people like that, under their control. DC are committed to finding people at increasingly younger ages, taking them into state-run institutions and orphanages to educate them into their beliefs. So, our second motive is to stop them at all costs and by any means."

Jonathon slaps his knee. "Hey, that's you, Vicky. Though your heritage's hardly hidden."

Vicky sneers at him. "You have no idea what you're talking about, Jon."

"Oh, I think I do. Spent a lot of time cleaning that hallway outside your room, y'know."

I glance from Vicky to Jon.

They know each other! What does he mean by 'cleaning outside her room'?

Ruth ignores the snide comment, glancing around, waiting for any other questions, but no one says anything. I'm just about to point out that her answer to Liddy's question wasn't clear, when she changes the topic. I frown. Another question for Tom.

"We're going to discuss your schedule for the next four weeks. Later, we'll take a walking tour, and I'll sign you up for tokens."

Taor sits up. "Tokens?"

"We use them in place of cash. As trainees, you get a personal access card with thirty-two tokens a month placed in it. You can spend them at any of the shops on the island."

Taor grins. "Cool."

Jon mimics him. "*Cool!* Could be worth nothing."

Taor turns bright red, his shoulders slump. Liddy looks like she's about to snap at Jon.

Ruth intervenes. "That's enough."

But Jon is on a roll. He turns around to sneer at Liddy. "And why are you sulking in the corner? Got issues with girlhood?"

In my mind, I imagine Liddy jumping up and attacking Jon. But she doesn't and, for the first time ever, I can't read her face. That I don't know what she's thinking makes me sad. I blink back tears. It isn't Jon's teasing that upsets me, it's Liddy's non-reaction.

Ruth's screwing up her eyes, her hands clasped in front of her. "Although you all made a choice to come here, and we agreed to take you in, we can, if we decide you do not fit in with our way of thinking, ask you to leave." She looks at Jon. "Not only that, but we'll also wipe your memory of everything you know about us."

Jon throws his hands up, feigning innocence.

"We do not make jokes at the expense of others. Do you understand?"

"Yes, ma'am."

"You can call me Ruth."

I put my hand up as if I'm in class. "You can wipe memories?"

Her eyes twinkle and I can't tell if she's telling the truth. "Only in extreme cases."

I put it on my list of questions to ask Tom. He'll know.

Before Ruth leaves, she asks Jon to go with her.

Vicky jeers. "In trouble, boy. I feel a memory wipe coming up!"

Ruth shakes her head and tuts again. "I'll see you all outside in five minutes."

CHAPTER TWENTY-FIVE

We've been given the afternoon off, providing we read the brightly coloured material handed out at the end of the induction class. It's a history of the leading five families and the formation of League. I'm sitting alone in the corner of the canteen. There are others in groups of twos and threes, but none I know. Some glance over, but I look away, not wanting to talk to anyone.

If Liddy were here, she'd be laughing with me over our schedule. My mornings are about to become my worst nightmare. Between 7:00 and 9:00 a.m., we have swimming, exercise classes and the gym. 9:00 a.m. to 12 noon is spent in typical school classes such as maths, English, history and science. I somehow didn't think we'd have to continue studying but, apparently, they want to assess our levels to evaluate what we have an aptitude for to prepare us for 'real world jobs'. In the afternoon, we have self-defence and one other elective sport. Ruth took me aside and told me I'd be working with Tom from 2:00 to 4:00 p.m. every day, so at least I escape the elective bit.

I flop my head in my hands and close my eyes. Although it isn't a particularly hot day, the sun is now shining through the wall of glass windows to my right and warms my cheek. I hear a low humming noise, as if there is a pneumatic drill underground and, just as I'm trying to figure out what it is, Tom pops up in my mind.

"Did you feel me coming?"

My face heats up at the thought of him being in my head again, hearing my thoughts.

"That was you?"

"Yes. I made it a bit louder than normal."

"You did?"

"That's how you're supposed to announce yourself before hopping into someone's mind. It's a courtesy for those with the heritage and gives them a chance to refuse or block."

"What about the rest of the population?"

"They wouldn't be able to pick up the vibration. In most cases, they don't even know you're there."

"You've done that?" He knows I'm talking about going into someone's mind without their permission.

"Only as necessary, and if it's part of my work."

"What work?"

"Can't stay long. Was just confirming our session at 2:00 p.m. today. I'll meet you at the coffeeshop. Do you know where it is?"

He hasn't answered my question. And just to make sure he knows, I think it again. *You avoided my question about your work.* He still doesn't respond. I shrug and sigh. "I have a map."

"Later, then." And he's gone, like a conjurer disappearing behind a curtain. I feel like the amazed audience, in awe of this magical being.

Lifting my head, I see Taor standing in front of me. He has his hands tucked in his jeans' pockets; his shoulders high.

"Sorry, were you having a good dream?" He smiles tentatively.

"Er, no. I..." I can't tell him I have a date with Tom. *No, not a date. Where did that come from?*

I sit up straighter. "Is everything okay?"

"Yeah, just wondered if you wanted to come for a walk or something, but" – he looks away, a muscle twitching in his cheek – "I can see you're tired."

Taor's limbs are out of proportion – all gangly, as if his body hasn't caught up yet. His nose is slightly too long, his eyes wide and his dark blond hair looks as if he hacksawed it only yesterday.

"Where's the rest of them?"

"Oh, they all went to the bicycle shop."

"What? Liddy too?" My eyebrows raise in surprise. *Why would she go off with Jon?*

"Look, I should go." He turns, but I call him back.

"No, wait. Have you seen the beach yet?"

"No."

"We could take a walk there, if you like. I have to be back by 1:30 p.m., though." I notice his watch. "What time is it?"

"12:50 p.m."

"Okay, let's go, then."

The training room is built on two levels. The ground floor has the gym, pool, basketball court and workout rooms, a couple of classrooms, a communal games/ TV room, the canteen and, at the back, junior accommodation. On the first floor is senior accommodation. We walk down the corridor between the canteen and junior accommodation to reach the exit. Stepping outside, I stop and breathe in the air, stretching my arms out behind my back as if I'm a bird about to take off. Taor watches me, his eyes curious. I shrug and smile. He says nothing and I like that about him.

The path we take leads onto a narrow cycle road. We cross over it onto a grassy bank. Taor's quiet, shy.

"So, is Taor your real name?"

"Nah, it's Taorin. Taorin Courtney."

"That Jon's a moron."

"He's not that bad."

"You know him?" We're walking down a slope. I thrust my fists in my hoodie pockets.

"We ran away from a foster home, lived on the streets for a couple of years before being picked up by the Diversity Commission."

I stop and stare at him. His green eyes are sad. I'm not sure what to say. This story of him and Jon doesn't fit with my picture of them.

"I know he behaves stupidly sometimes, but it's all show. Without him, I wouldn't have survived."

"Right. How come you're here?"

"They were doing baseline tests on 'normal' humans," he stammers. "To compare with others, like you. Some people from here rescued us, although their target was Vicky, I think. Jon forced them to bring us. Said he'd scream the place down if they didn't."

"So, you knew Vicky before you came here?"

"Not much. They kept us in separate cells. Jon and I shared." He looks distanced, reliving something.

A picture of a small room with a bunk bed comes into my mind. Jon's pacing, his eyes are wild and he's pushing the hair off his forehead.

"The tests did something to him."

"Eh?"

"To Jon. They made him mad, angry... different."

I don't know what to say. He and Jon are just normal boys.

I look out to the dark sea. The waves are noisy as they crash forward and recede. The familiar, humid smell of salt and the sound of screeching seagulls above us attack my senses, reminding me of home. My breath catches as my mum comes to mind: our walks along the beach on blustery autumn days, the hot chocolate to warm our freezing fingers, and then picking up fish and chips on the way back.

We continue in silence towards the sandy beach. It's more of a small cove, with rocks on either side. We could walk up and down it twice within twenty minutes.

"You and Liddy are friends?"

"Yes, best friends." I turn to lead us down the small cove. "We've known each other since we were four. She lived ten minutes away from my house."

"You had an argument or something?"

I kick a pebble. "Not really. We just disagreed on something."

He doesn't pry, which I'm glad of. "How old are you, Taor?"

"Fifteen in October. You?"

"Sixteen in December."

"You don't look it."

"No." I glance at him, but he isn't being unkind. "I'm one of the Gol—" – I stop myself saying the word "Golem', determined not to use it anymore. I also don't feel comfortable saying Apex yet – "oddities. I never developed a proper gender."

"Oh. And Liddy?"

I smile, missing my friend. "Liddy's a whole gender to herself."

By the time we've walked back up the beach, I've decided Taor is a nice person – shy and reserved, but kind.

"Right, I have a class to go to."

"We don't have classes this afternoon."

"I do. See you later."

"Yeah, okay."

Tom's already sitting at an outside table, an empty coffee cup in front of him. He's leaning over, reading some documents. I stand and watch him for a moment, watch how he turns the pages. He could be sitting in any café, anywhere in the world, but he's here with me.

The air around me seems to cool, and I shiver. That's when he looks up as I approach and smiles.

"Hello, Little Miss Noisy."

I grin as I sit down opposite. "You think I'm heavy-footed?"

He taps the side of his head. "Only in here. Once you attune yourself to a person's vibration, it's like rumbling thunder as you approach."

"You've attuned yourself to me?" I can't help being delighted.

"Excuse me, but you forced it on me."

"I didn't!" He shoots me an ironic look. "I did? But how?"

"That's what we're here to find out. First things first: coffee? Cappuccino? Or something fizzy?"

I look towards the entrance of the coffee shop. It has a fancy espresso bar with hanging lights. Several people sit at cast-iron tables; no one I recognise.

"Mocha?"

"Coming up."

He moves towards the bar, his slim-fitting jeans and dark green top accentuating his sinewy muscles and height. He glances back and I wonder if he's reading my mind. My face heats up and look away, busying myself with examining the bobbing boats. There's at least five, one of which is a larger yacht.

When he returns, I'm drumming my fingers on the tabletop, but I stop as he places two cups down.

"Coffee's excellent here."

Sipping the hot, chocolatey-bitterness, I have to agree. I look up at him over the rim of my mug. His eyes are hazel with green flecks like mine, his dark hair is windswept, and his face is without blemish. I begin to feel myself slip into a dreamy state and want to reach out and touch him. He snaps his fingers in front of my face.

"Wake up! Not doing any practising here."

I frown, embarrassed, not sure what he means about practising, and again turn my eyes to the harbour. "We had this introductory class today."

He points to the reading material on the table. "You got all the bumf, then?"

"Yeah, but there's stuff I don't get."

"What?"

"Well, can they kick us off the island and wipe our memories if we don't pass?"

He guffaws, leaning the chair back on two legs, before slamming it down and folding his arms across the table. "Ruth been giving you a lecture?"

"Well, I like Ruth—"

"Ruth's okay. She'll be a good guardian and help Liddy."

I sigh, glancing away. He notices.

"You and Liddy will make up, don't worry."

I pull one of those false smiles, wanting to move on. "So, the memory-wipe thing?"

"Certainly, they can or, rather, some people can. Would they do it? Have they done it in the past to trainees? Not sure. Do they do it if someone is a threat? Absolutely."

"Hmm. And the missions? What are they about?"

"If I told you, I'd have to kill you." His leans forward, his eyes unblinking and I feel my heart take an extra beat. Then he bursts out laughing. "Jeez, you take everything so seriously."

I go for a grin but am uncomfortable with his comment.

"Come on, drink up. We're going somewhere."

"Where?"

"A place to practise."

A girl of about seventeen or eighteen walks up. She has a sway about her, almost model-like. She flicks long blonde hair behind one ear and smiles. She has perfect white teeth, startling blue eyes and the sort of facial features you only see in magazines.

"Hi, Tom! Is this the new kid you're working with?"

I hate the way she calls me a kid and take an instant dislike to her.

"It is."

She puts her arm around his back and squeezes, pulling him in for a quick peck on the lips.

"Cam, this is Amy. Amy, Cam."

I hear the ensuing conversation as if from a distance. "Nice to meet you, Cam." Her hand extends and I shake it, mumbling hello. "Are you coming over tonight?" She's talking to Tom; I'm no longer relevant.

"Yeah, sometime after 7:00 p.m."

I stand there, my heart pounding, my fists clenched, nails digging into my palms. Most of all, I just feel stupid and want to run away and find Liddy. Of course, he has a girlfriend.

What was I thinking? Just because we have this 'bond' thing.

Then an even worse thought pops into my head: *God, can he hear me?*

My chest aches, making me angry with myself. I hear a buzzing in my ears and shake my head. *I have to get away.* I begin walking towards the quayside, first lengthening my stride and then running full pelt, swinging my arms out wide, until all I can hear is my thudding pulse and rasping breath. As I reach the water, I slow down and turn towards the jetty.

I hear the humming before his voice enters my head. Catching up to me, both his file and my homework under his arm, he stops in front of me, blocking my path.

"I'm sorry. I intended telling you today."

I frown and skirt around him. "About Amy? I'm confused."

"Amy, yes, but more about how intense our bond is, and how to understand the feelings that come with it." He slows his pace to keep up with my short legs.

"Stop reading my mind and stop the telepathy stuff."

"Sorry." He speaks out lout. "You're angry."

"I'm... not angry with you." My feet keep me moving, passing the moored boats. When I come to the end of the jetty, I halt, my arms crossed and stare out at the sea. I feel betrayed, frustrated and silly all at the same time.

Am I so naïve? Tom would never like me. Amy is properly formed, beautiful, her skin perfect. I'm just an oddity.

He's there, next to me. Silently waiting for me to say something. I feel his presence, our connection. Part of me wants to tell him to go, but a stronger part can't bear him to leave. I sit on the end of the jetty, my child-like legs and size-three feet dangling off the edge. The water is deep below, but the waves are peaceful. The ebb and flow of the current quietens the buzzing in my head. It's a clear, warm afternoon. I close my eyes and tilt my head back, enjoying the sun and the salty aroma.

Coming out of my reverie, I squint into the distance and spot land. "Is that Lymington, over there?"

"Yes." *How does she know?*

I hear the thoughts that follow his speech as clearly as if he says it aloud.

"I know, because I saw the sat nav on Jenny's phone."

"Now who's reading minds?" he thinks.

"You haven't taught me how not to yet," I reply, silently.

When he speaks, it's to answer my comment about Jenny's phone. I'm glad he doesn't bring up Amy again, or my immature stalking off. I feel ridiculous enough already.

"Ah, of course, it was Jenny and David who picked you up."

"And Dr Schultz who found me."

"Yes, I read the report. He was lucky to escape."

I glance to the side, watching a man on a bicycle as he speeds towards the warehouses.

"He was one of our insiders, feeding information to us on their progress with heritage kids, but they found out about him. If he'd stayed, he'd have been tortured for information."

"Heritage kids?"

"Imagine an army of DC people with talents like us, trained to wage war. Now imagine them reaching this island and what would happen."

"But that doesn't make sense. Why would anyone want to use their talents to wage war?"

He stops and looks at me. "Cam, you only need one person with mind-manipulation on your side to convince others to join you, to get you to believe you are on the right side. And remember, they find these kids young. All they know is that they're not pure, that they have the capacity to pollute humankind and destroy them. Given a choice to be hidden away and die, or help the nation defend itself, what would you do?"

"I don't know."

We sit in silence for a while.

"And Dr Schultz, there are others like him?"

"Yes. Some are paid, some volunteer."

Pleased he's not reading my thoughts, I wonder if he'll answer my next question. "And their job is?"

"To keep track of the Diversity Commission's progress, their decisions, who they've taken and what they're doing."

"Simple as that."

"None of it's simple. The Commission know people like you disappear. They also know we have hidden bases and have sent spies in before. But so far, we've managed to weed them out and, well, either convert their way of thinking, or send them back with false information."

"Mind manipulation."

"It protects us."

"Right."

"And now it protects you."

I look out at the mainland again. Last week I was just another schoolgirl, studying for exams. Liddy was talking to me, and extra genes and halted growth weren't even on my radar.

A sudden thought overrides my self-pity. "How come I can see through the barrier?"

"What? Oh, you mean the one surrounding the island? It's a bit like two-way glass, I guess. It stops people coming in."

"And if I wanted to leave, how would I know which way to go?"

"There are coordinates, which most of us use."

"Most of us?"

He has an impish grin. "It's a vibration, so I can sense it. The opening in the corridor has a different frequency, more natural, like" – he squints over the open sea – "like normal humans hearing a wave hit a cliff, I suppose."

"Do you always hear frequencies?"

"It isn't *hearing*, as such. More like aligning or identifying different vibrational levels. It takes practice, but once I've picked up a frequency, I can remember it. It doesn't mean I switch it on all the time. That would be chaos. And just because I can sense a frequency, it doesn't mean I can use it."

I decide, right then and there, that I need to work hard. Being able to get off this island if I want to will make me feel better, stronger, more in control. I push back my shoulders. I may not be ready to embrace everything, but I am ready to understand more. The conviction lasts for about three seconds before I slump and sigh, gripping the edge of the jetty.

Who am I kidding? What makes me think I can do this? Be something like Tom?

Other doubts creep in. *Do I want to be like him? And if I become this other 'thing', who will I be then?*

What if Liddy is right? What if I'm not me anymore?

CHAPTER TWENTY-SEVEN

I pull my knees against my chest, wrapping my arms around my legs. Uncertainty plagues me. I watch the waves glisten for a second as the sun and clouds battle it out for dominance. Breathing in the salty air, I wonder if Tom's picked up on my inner ramblings and change the subject.

"So, you're aligned to my frequency?"

"Yes. You're aligned to me, too. You possibly feel it as a deeper connection at the moment."

Amy comes to my mind, and I can't help but wonder how he feels her connection. He touches my shoulder to comfort me, and I lift my eyes. If I'm going to train with him, I have to get over being embarrassed, so it might as well be now. Besides, there's a depth to him, a kindness I like. The awkwardness begins to fade, and I wonder if he's playing with my mind.

Would I know?

"Things will become normal soon. I remember when I first came—"

A low vibration tingles through my body. It's soft and appealing and I focus my mind on it. The longing to reach out and be with him returns and I lift my hand to touch his.

"No, Cam. No." His voice is firm inside my head.

My breath hitches. I feel a sense of flying towards him, as if I'm entering through his eye sockets and delving into his mind, his very being, but I also feel him latching on to me. At first, he struggles to unbind himself, to be free; he's strong, pulling back like a catapult with a stone in it, ready to be launched forward. But then he lets go and I hear his voice:

"Slowly, Cam. Calm. See what I see."

A picture forms in my head. I know Tom's placed it there. Watching it unveil itself, I don't at first understand, but then it becomes clearer. We're sitting on the jetty. There's a silver glow around us with flashing blue and yellow lights. The lights vibrate, producing two independent humming sounds. Intuitively, I know they represent us – we each have our own unique identification. As the lights mingle, turning a beautiful shade of emerald, so do the vibrations. The tone changes to a deep purring, as if we are a two-piece orchestra, melding our tunes.

What am I seeing?

"You're seeing our bond."

I watch it, amazed. A sense of lightness enters my body, as if I'm floating in zero-gravity. "It's for real?"

"Very real. Everyone has it, though humans don't see or hear the same as we do."

"I'm human."

He doesn't respond directly, but I hear his thoughts.

With a few differences.

Seconds pass and the world around me seems to fade into insignificance in comparison. I can no longer even hear the waves or the screeching seagulls – it's as if nothing else is important. The bond feels so strong, so real, more fully me than I am when alone, without Tom.

"This is why you feel the longing."

"Do you feel it?" I know he does but I need him to confirm I'm not imagining the whole thing.

"Yes, it's because our vibrations are completely in tune."

His response assures me but the wonder of it remains. I feel as if I could reach up and run my fingers through it, as if it's a solid mass. "And you've felt it, before?"

"A little, but not as strong as this. It was more like telepathy, plus some. Our bond's definitely something we need to understand—" He hesitates, gulping. I can tell he's trying to sound confident but he's also in awe. Part of me, though, is disappointed he's had this experience with someone before.

"My trainer."

"Your trainer?"

"Yes. Because of our connection, she taught me quickly. It might have taken me years otherwise."

It's hard to think of questions with such a stunning Veronese-green bouncing between us. I watch it shimmering and sparkling as if it is alive.

"So, this 'bond' thing happens a lot?"

"No, it's rare. I haven't heard of any cases as strong as ours." There's sadness in his thoughts. "Ivy, my trainer, died last year, trying to rescue some kids from a facility. We had a similar Apex Cell but nothing like our connection."

"Oh. I'm sorry."

He waves my sentiment away. "Everything about our DNA is almost identical. From the AP protein to the junk DNA it affected and the resulting Apex Cells. Even our E-Mag Network is similar."

I'm not sure how to respond. "E-Mag Network? Remind me again."

"How the synapses in our brain develop neural networks. A cauliflower lighting up every part of your brain." He grins at his useless analogy.

"Somehow, we're related?"

"Possibly, many generations ago, but it could also mean we just developed in a similar way. I can only think, on some level, there are different growth paths, and somehow we took the same one."

It's hard to grasp the complex concepts in this state, even though it seems they've been explained to me several times. I'm just not used to it. He understands my confusion immediately.

"Are you ready to let go, to come back?"

"Yes. How?"

"To keep in control or, in this case, to let go, you have to find an image. Mine is a catapult or an elastic band."

"I saw that."

"Think about pulling back."

A picture of a bow enters my mind. I'm heaving back the string, an arrow fixed between my fingers. The string is tight and hard to stretch, but I focus and bend it to my will. I hear him giggle.

"Don't shoot me! I only have a catapult."

His eyes come into focus again; they're shiny with excitement. Then the noise of the sea, birds and distant laughter slams into me. I take a deep breath, gripping his fingers to prevent myself falling forward. "Weird."

"You'll learn to manage that."

We sit quietly for a moment, but then he takes my hand and places it on the hard boards of the jetty. "Better we don't touch, at the moment."

"Is that why it happens?"

"It seems to make the connection more immediate. Although, with practice, I'm sure we could do it at distance. You did well.”

“What did I do?”

“You didn’t hurt me, for starters.”

“Huh!”

“You were also able to listen to instructions and control moving away. That will make training easier.”

Pride swells up inside of me, though I’m not sure what for.

He grins. “It also makes it safer to explore what we can do together. If you were totally out of control, it could be dangerous for both of us, as well as others. The faster you learn, the better.”

He’s gazing out at a distant ship. We watch as it skirts the shield around the island. “First, you have to find out which vibrations you can pick up and use.” He speaks as if this is a totally normal topic of conversation.

I feel like I’m wandering down a forest path. Patches of dazzling light leading me further in, seducing me into a sense of security. But, when I turn around, everything looks different and confusing. The world I knew is no longer the same place.

“I get it’s a lot to take in.”

“Mm. You said something about picking up vibrations and using them?”

“It sounds complicated but now you’re waking up, you’re actually doing some of it instinctively. We’re surrounded by vibrations that hold a natural power. Which ones you can sense will dictate what you can do. You can already use telepathy and mind processing.”

“I don’t even know how I do it. And ‘mind processing’ is what, exactly?”

He smiles kindly. “Did you notice how the sea barely moved whilst we were using telepathy. Now it’s lapping again.”

“You mean, we were in Processor mode? I didn’t—” I remember the MRI test and how I couldn’t understand why everyone was a statue. “Oh, yeah.” I want to try doing it again and tell myself to look around, to experience the world slowing down. But I know it’s because I crave our connection, as if I’m a drug addict who hasn’t had quite enough methadone to curb her longing for heroin.

“What else can you do?”

“I can use vibrations to confuse people, to get them to change their minds or walk away. There are also simple things, like moving objects or cracking glass. Some people can do that. We can actually develop any talent related to sensing vibrations, which is pretty much how the world works but most people can only manage one or two proficiently and so tend to focus."

"This is so..." 'Weird' comes to mind, but it doesn't really cover how I feel. "How come I didn't do anything before?"

"You might have but never noticed, or thought it normal. Left alone, your talents could have gradually emerged or even lain dormant. Either way, now you've been triggered, you'll need to learn how to use them. Are you tired?"

"No, not at all. I'm wide awake."

"Good. Wanna go practise in a safe place?"

"Sure."

We both stand. As we do, I notice he moves to distance himself from me. "Best we don't get too close, particularly when others are around. We don't yet know what will happen."

"Right." I stuff my hands in my hoodie pockets. He's still carrying both his file and my reading material. "What's this 'safe place', then?"

"A lined practice room. You'll see."

The wind is picking up and I pull a raggedy band out of my jeans pocket to tie my flapping hair back. As we walk up the wooden jetty, Tom on one side, me on the other, I feel the connection between us but no longer see it. It draws me in, and I feel more relaxed with its presence, less anxious, as if someone is soothing an aching muscle with a gentle massage.

I want to ask Tom if he's altering my state of mind in any way, keeping me calm. Perhaps he thinks I'm a danger to others if he doesn't interfere, but I daren't ask. If he is, I'd have to tell him to stop.

Obviously, can't have him mind-meddling!

On the other hand, it feels so good to have him nearby. Whatever he may or may not be doing, at the moment I'm happy not knowing.

CHAPTER TWENTY-EIGHT

We're walking along the quayside away from the coffeeshop, turning left towards the reception building Liddy and I first entered. Tom points for us to go towards the larger warehouses, a bit further down. A few people are milling around. None of them pay us any attention. One man is driving a forklift truck with boxes of produce on it. I spot some greens and something red underneath. We skirt to the left to avoid him.

"Do you think Liddy and I have similar vibrations? We get on so well." I glance at him sideways as we walk past another building. "Normally."

"Possibly. You can check, but you'd need to be careful. I knew this old couple once, when I was about five. They said they were soulmates and went everywhere together. I called them Mr and Mrs Silver. My mum told me not to call older people 'silver', that it was disrespectful." He glances at me to see if I understand.

"You weren't talking about their hair, I guess."

"Nope. After some time, I realised only I could see it. As I got older, I persuaded myself it wasn't there."

"Do you see it now?"

"I could if I want to. It's a vibration, after all, but it's distracting. Sometimes, I use it to read peoples' moods, without delving too deeply."

Does he do that with me?

There are three warehouses: the first much smaller than the others. They look sterile – blocks of cement painted white.

"What's in those?"

"Some storage. Mostly for indoor food production."

"Hydro pods?"

"Stacked layers."

"We went on a school trip once, to a local hydroponic farm. It was huge."

Liddy was with me, both of us ungendered at the time. I picture her with long plaits, wearing a pink dress she was fond of. Before puberty, we only have to wear gender uniforms at school. Otherwise, we can wear want we want. My chest aches thinking about Liddy. Why can't she understand I need to work with Tom?

We stop in front of the second warehouse. He passes his wrist across a security pad at the side of the door. It makes a whirring sound before clicking open.

"You have some kind of microchip in your skin?"

"If you choose to stay, you'll get limited access passes until you graduate."

"How long does that take?"

"Depends on what you train for. I'm still a trainee."

"A trainee what?"

"I hope to be a mission operative."

"What job is that?"

We enter a corridor. Lights automatically click on as Tom pulls the door shut, revealing magnolia walls and blue doors.

"I've booked room three. It's small, but the others are taken."

I notice he hasn't answered my question, yet again. "Right. Umm, how many people like us are here?"

"On the base?"

"Yes."

"Only about five or six. There used to be more, but some moved away for different jobs."

"Is Vicky like us?" I trail my fingers along the smooth surface of the wall.

"She has some differentiation."

"Who's training her?"

Tom glances at me and I wonder what he sees – not what I look like in the mirror, but how deep he goes.

Does he just know everything? Can he see beyond the conscious mind?

I grind my teeth, swallowing hard and suppressing a tremor rising from my chest.

"Sally. You haven't met her."

I nod. "And how many people are training... what do they call us?"

He barks a laugh. "Humans."

"You know what I mean."

"Those with weird genes? Apexes, Cam. You know what Apex means, don't you? Top of the mountain, highest point. Do you get it?" He's grinning as he says it, but his teasing only serves to irritate me. He notices and becomes serious again.

"Sorry, only Sally, full-time. After Ivy died, they were supposed to send another, but our numbers dropped."

Liddy was right, then. I did have a choice regarding trainers, but would I have chosen Sally over Tom? Amy enters my mind again. "Does your girlfriend have abilities?" I'm relieved my voice sounds normal.

"No, Amy is like Taor and Jon, but she grew up on a different island."

"She did?"

"Her parents are relations of one of our leading families." He rolls his shoulders, as if my question stresses him.

"Really! Who?"

"Do your homework. Look for the name Weber" – he waves the papers in front of me – "and you might be able to guess."

We stop in front of a blue door with the number three on it. He flips the sign to 'engaged', then waves his wrist across another security pad. Stepping into a windowless room, about 12ft across, I notice the walls, ceiling and floor are padded with a soft, white material.

Should I be wearing a straitjacket?

He chuckles as he throws the papers and files on the floor, along with his bag. I look across at him as he sits against a far wall, his knees bent.

"You're reading my mind again."

"Hard to resist when you throw your thoughts at me."

I slump down against the opposite wall, cross my legs and stare at him. His dark hair's sticking up from the wind. I know he's spying again when he swipes his hand across his head to flatten the wayward strands.

"How do I stop it? And how do I block people?"

"We start with words or images. After practising for a while, it will become part of you, like breathing or walking."

I lean my elbows on my knees. "Right, and the padded walls?"

"Just in case the training's explosive." He laughs out loud at something I don't get. "Also, to stop interference from outside. No one can hear us in here and there are no distractions."

I shrug. "So, images or words?"

"Yes. I can show you."

His face is symmetrical – high cheekbones like me, a perfectly formed nose and a dimple in his chin. The only imperfection is a small scar on his right cheek. He raises an eyebrow, and I look away, trying to suppress my schoolgirl crush.

A tiny part of my brain tells me it's the bond drawing me to him and that I'm stupid even to feel this way. Every other cell in my body believes it's a lie. I've never been drawn to anyone like I am to Tom; never had such a physical reaction I can't control. Why would I? Everyone – except Liddy – hated me at school.

My face flushes warm. Just the thought of having these feelings overwhelms me, but the fact that he can probably read what I'm thinking makes my cheeks burn hotter. "So, how do I block people reading my mind?"

At least then I can stop him knowing what I'm thinking.

"The reason they asked me to train you is that with our connection, it will be more efficient. We learnt that with Ivy. She was a Processor, too. I can guide you and you can see how it is done for yourself."

"Makes sense, I suppose."

I hear the low humming again, recognising it as his vibration. I hold myself tight, resisting the urge to reach out – not just physically, but with my whole being and mind.

"Don't move." His voice is quiet. "Breathe slowly. Close your eyes, if you need to."

I bend my legs up and wrap my arms around my knees. Lowering my head, I close my eyes. His humming sends a silky shiver down my spine, delicious and painful at the same time. My body becomes taut as I fight off urges I shouldn't have. Then I hear him in my mind.

"Think of a place you feel safe in."

Immediately, my bedroom pops into my head. My blue curtains, the desk with my laptop, the orange lamp on the bedside table. Slowly, the image seems to expand, like a jigsaw with large pieces clicking together until suddenly I'm sitting against the foot of my bed. Tom's leaning against the closed door, looking around.

"Nice room."

I follow his eyes, inspecting the room. Parts of it appear and then disappear. "How are you doing this?"

"I'm not. It's your memory we're in. Brains are incredible things. They are really only synapses and chemicals that we learn to programme, but the conscious and unconscious mind controls them. We can train both to do amazing things, but we can also deceive it to believe we're sitting in your room. In this case, you're telling it something it already knows and recognises so it is relatively easy."

"Right, so this is all in my head?"

"Yes. Do you notice how, as you focus on one area, it becomes more visible, and the other bits lose detail?"

I look at my mirror. It solidifies. I flick my eyes to the right and the window materialises. In my peripheral vision, there's a shimmering where the dressing table was. "This is so weird."

"At first, but you get used to it. Remember, we're manipulating vibrations to work for us in a different way. The mind vibrates differently, depending on emotions. With this one, you are using a high-level frequency, a feeling of safety. When practising our talents, the feeling of safety is important."

I struggle to make sense of his words. I mean, I get what he's saying, but how can it be real?

"Again, a lot to take in, but this will become the norm very soon."

He's still leaning against the door. I'm gawping around the room. My bookshelf suddenly fills itself with school workbooks, and then fades as I notice my wardrobe appear. I jump up and walk over to the door. Tom moves out the way as I grasp the handle. It seems so solid. I look at my hand and then open the door, quickly moving onto the landing. My head spins as the carpet grows to include the banister and staircase. I look back and, for a moment, the wall has vanished. It reconfigures itself as I think about it, but I'm starting to feel dizzy.

Tom is in the doorway. "You won't find your mum."

"How did you—" But, of course, he's in my head. "None of this is real?"

"Sorry, no." He can even feel the enormous disappointment that fills me. "Remember, your physical body is sitting in the training room. We can go back there, if this is too disorientating."

I stalk back into my bedroom and sit down. "No, no, I want to be here." My chest rises as I plonk myself down, my back leaning against the foot of the bed.

How can I even feel the floor, the bed, my hands running through my hair?

"Let's just get on with it."

He's now sitting with his back to the door. "If you're ready, I'm going to try one thing. It's a shortcut to training your synapses. I'll be tricking your mind into believing you have learnt stuff you haven't. If it works, your training will move faster. This is actually how I started."

"Does it hurt?"

"It's uncomfortable but think of it like downloading information at speed onto a computer. Information you can then access, to learn from."

Whispering my response, I know he understands my consent to go ahead. A sudden jerk, as if someone is pulling me to the left, hits my body and a dizziness floods my brain, making me feel as if I'm falling forward. I fight the sensation, pulling myself up. My heart beats harder in my chest, my cheeks flush hot and my forehead becomes damp. Tom's strained voice sounds high-pitched.

"You have to accept it. Don't fight. I won't hurt you." I peer across at him. His body mirrors mine, only he's not looking up. "Focus, Cam."

Wiping the imaginary sweat off my imaginary forehead with the back of my imaginary hand, I close my eyes and allow him to show me what he needs to. He's flicking through images so fast I can hardly keep up. A black cloud; a wall; a castle; a barrier; a bear standing upright; a thick forest. My head begins to pound, but the images are fast and furious. A burner; a flood of water; an iron boulder; a shield; a line of medieval soldiers, dressed in red and bearing swords, all flashing before my eyes, one after the other.

I start to feel afraid, unable to control what's going on. It's those tests, all over again. I'm going to freak out like the girl in the glass panel who was me, but not me. Lightning flashes, snow fills my head; a tornado whirls. I'm trembling, losing myself to the storm in my head. I can't do this. Can't keep up.

Tom, stop. Stop... Stop! In my mind, I'm screaming, my hand outstretched, pushing him back. And then, I'm standing on the top of a mountain. There's a valley in front of me and he's far away, a speck on a peak in the distance, shouting silent words at me, jumping up and down, waving his arms. I feel like an invisible veil has been drawn between us. The wind crashes around my body and crushes my chest but, somehow, I remain upright.

Shocked, I open my eyes. I'm back in the white room and he's staring at me, a strange smile on his face. "A veil. I can see it, but not through it."

"What?"

"You've found your block."

"A veil?" My body aches. Relaxing my arms, I slump back against the wall. "Is this how we train? You bombard me, to see how I react?" The words come out resentful, but I don't mean it.

He frowns. "Sorry, we can try another way. It's just… Well, Ivy taught me that way and I wanted to see if it would work with you. Are you angry? I can't tell."

"Can't tell?"

"You've successfully blocked everything. Your mind and vibrations are completely closed to me."

"I did? How?"

"You have intuitive responses. It's a good thing."

I stretch my trembling legs, rubbing my knees.

"What do you see?" His eyes narrow with curiosity.

"Huh?"

"Well, all I can see is your veil."

"Oh. I'm on a mountain and there's a valley between us."

"Good, keep that image clear. That's how you block people from entering your mind. And it's strong, by the way." He's grinning, so I think I'm supposed to be happy, too. "Don't ever tell anyone what your block looks like."

"But I just told you."

His lip curls into a grin. "Hey, if you can't trust *your bond partner*, who can you trust?"

I like the way he refers to me as his 'bond partner'. A summer warmth spreads through my stomach and into my chest, as if the sun has just appeared from behind a cloud. Then I remind myself he has a girlfriend and, with that, the cloud returns, blocking the rays and causing an ache I find desperately silly.

I need to get over this thing with him.

I lower my voice and speak in what I hope is a calmer tone than what's going on in my mind. "So, what's your block?"

He stares back, unsure, quiet. I throw his own words back at him. "Hey, if you can't trust your bond partner, who can you trust?"

"It's just, you're untrained. Although you have a block, it might slip. Someone else could read your mind and find my block, without you or me ever knowing it. They could find backdoors to enter my mind, to even manipulate me, without me being aware."

"Now you're scaring me."

"Don't be scared. I'll protect you." He leans on his elbow. I consider what his protection will look like.

"So, you'll tell me your block when it's safe?"

His answer is on a totally different track. "We also learnt something else."

"What?" I stretch out, awareness of the exhaustion seeping through me.

"That you can take the 'downloading of information into your brain'. That means you'll learn much faster."

I don't say anything. The thought of going through that again sends shivers down my spine. I do notice he's changed the subject from his block.

"What are you thinking?"

I look up from under my fringe, pushing a stray piece of hair behind my ear. "You really can't read anything?"

"No. Feels odd."

Feels great!

My stomach rumbles. "I'm starving. Any food around here?"

He laughs, his head thrown back, revealing the line of his long slender neck. No bulging Adam's apple! I can't help thinking about him being like me – no proper gender. I'm tempted to dwell on that but stop myself. It's a path going nowhere.

"Until you get used to it, that block will draw energy. Let's go to the canteen. I think twenty minutes' training is enough for day one."

"Twenty minutes? Feels like ages."

"We were in Processer mode for some of it, remember."

"I need a watch." Pushing my weary body to a standing position, I look up at him. "How come you got so tall, if you're like me?"

We leave the room and retrace our route down the corridor. "When I came, I was shorter and narrower, more your shape. We have this special protein which promotes bone and muscle growth, though it tastes disgusting. They'll start you on it soon. You'll need strength, even more so with all the physical exercise. Weights helped as well, though."

"Right. I'd like to be taller."

"I get it."

And I know he does.

We're moving towards the training block. A few people turn their heads and say hello to him. One of them pulls him aside to have a whispered conversation. I wonder if I could read Tom's mind to find out what they're so serious about but I'm too tired and, besides, would I somehow have to dismantle the block to do it? He soon returns and we enter the canteen.

"Strange not hearing you in my head."

"Was I always there?"

"Ever since the first night."

"You heard every thought?"

"No, silly, you think I'm a pervert? I blocked out most of your ramblings, but your vibration and moods were ever-present, like a distant motorway."

"And now it's gone?"

"Very odd."

I grin, determined to keep up the veil for a while. It feels like protective armour, as if I am a knight surrounded by unpierceable steel. But I also feel a loneliness, an ache like I've lost something precious and don't know what it is. I glance up at him, wondering if he feels the same. His eyes are bright and shiny, almost excited.

Nope, just me, then! Damn, I need to get over him.

CHAPTER TWENTY-NINE

The canteen is a little more crowded than earlier. People I don't know; people who could have abilities and might read my mind, or even manipulate it. My jaw tightens as I bolster my veil, imagining everyone in the room as dark silhouettes standing on the distant mountain peak with Tom. The effort causes vertigo for a second and I stand still, splaying my fingers as if to catch myself before I fall.

Tom notices. "You okay?"

"Yeah..."

"Come on, you should eat."

We head for the buffet to load our plates. The fumes of delicious food cause my saliva glands to go into a salty overdrive. With a huge pile of penne covered in tomato sauce, I turn around to look for a seat. My inclination is to find one somewhere quiet, but I notice Liddy sitting alone in a corner, reading. Tom understands immediately.

"Go. You need to sort it out and I have papers to fill in."

"Thanks."

"These are yours I think." He hands me the papers and turns to go. At the last minute, he gives me a strange look. "You do know I could make everything between you and Liddy better in seconds."

"I don't think she'd—" I start and then I realise what he means. "Wait, you're talking about mind stuff?"

"Yes."

"No, I couldn't do that to her."

He nods. "I know. Just offering."

"Mind manipulation is one of the things she most dreads."

"No problem. See you tomorrow, then. Same time at the warehouse."

"Yes."

"If you need anything from me before then, you know how to find me."

"I don't, actually."

"Of course. I'm in the guest block. Room twelve. Or you could just call my name, seek me out with our bond."

"Wouldn't that mean bringing the veil down?"

"You could draw it back a little."

"I can? How?"

"Leave you to practise. Think of it as homework from me. Oh, and enjoy the swimming tomorrow morning." He's laughing as he turns. I groan inside. He must already know I'm worried about it.

Moving the plate to my other hand and stuffing the papers under my arm, I walk over to Liddy. Taking a deep breath, I reach her table and plonk my food down as I pull back the chair.

Without raising her head, she spits out her words. "Seat's taken."

I sit down and spear a piece of pasta, almost burning my mouth as I chew quickly and swallow. "We have to talk, Lid."

She grunts but continues studying the pages of a magazine in front of her.

"I spent all of twenty minutes training with him. That's all."

Another page turned.

"And there's only one other trainer. Vicky has her as a tutor."

No response.

"Liddy, please."

She stares down at me, her eyes half closed. "And how do you know he isn't in your mind now?"

"Because he can't get in."

She looks startled.

"I have a block, to stop people."

"What is it?"

At least I've got her full attention.

"An image."

"Of what?"

Tom's words float into my mind. Every instinct wants to share this with Liddy, but the warning about people finding out frightens me more. Liddy has no protection against others. Spearing two more pieces of pasta, I know I have to give some sort of answer. "A black cloud."

She frowns and I wonder if she knows I'm lying. "And he taught you this?"

"Yes."

"So, how do you know he isn't just manipulating you?" She tilts her head, but her eyes demand an answer.

"It's hard to explain."

"Try me. Never been hard to explain things to me before."

"I know the difference now, know what it feels like."

"So, after twenty minutes of training, you're an expert?"

"Lid…"

She sighs, exasperated. I pick at my pasta as the silence widens the gap between us. The tomato sauce suddenly reminds me of the image I saw in the MRI of the cows being slaughtered and screaming in fear. My stomach churns, my appetite gone.

I glace at Liddy from under my fringe. She's turning a page, avoiding my gaze, but at least she doesn't tell me to go away. I want to reach out to her, to know what she's thinking, to somehow say what she needs to hear for us to go back to the way we were. Instead, I'm clicking the fork prongs against the white plate, trying to calm myself.

At first, I think someone's using a power drill somewhere, but the sound I hear is closer and sends a wave of sadness through my bones. I glance at the top of Liddy's head – her hair parting is slightly crooked – and gasp. There are brown waves emanating from her body, shooting towards me. My instinct is to back away but instead I bite down on the inside of my cheek as I hear a voice in my head.

That dopey look she gives him. Soon, they'll be best friends.

And I know without a doubt these are Liddy's private thoughts, that I'm somehow peering into her mind without even knowing how I did it. I want to pull back, I don't want to intrude. Thinking of Tom's training, I pull the string on my bow and force myself to step away, but not before I hear more pained thoughts.

And she doesn't even see what's happening. Probably already fallen in love with him. Won't want me at all. I can't compete with that – with him.

My fork clatters on the table. Liddy looks up at my stricken face. Her concern looks like the old Liddy, for a second.

"You okay?"

"Er, yes. Just went a little dizzy."

"Finish your food, then."

I stare a little too long. Tears come to my eyes as I relive the pain I felt in Liddy. She's afraid. Of mind manipulation, yes, but more afraid she'll lose me as a friend, that she'll be alone. Doesn't she know that will never happen? My chest constricts and I spurt out the thing that has most been on my mind over the last couple of hours. "You know, Tom has a girlfriend."

She pales, then stands. The brown light around her turns yellow, then merges into red and orange in an instant. "Is that why you're so upset? Why you came back to me?"

But she's got it all wrong.

"No, Liddy! That's not it at all."

"Look, Cam, give me a bit of time. Things have changed. I just need some time."

I gaze at her back as she walks out of the canteen. Pushing my plate away, my stomach cramps up and misery engulfs my thoughts.

She got it so wrong, but it's my fault. I shouldn't have been in Liddy's head.

His thrumming melody is close, asking for permission. I must have dropped my veil.

"Fine."

"Yes, you dropped your veil."

"How?"

"When you saw her mood and allowed your emotions to take over. Controlling the veil, controlling everything you are, is about logic and cool headedness."

"But I created the veil with emotion."

"That's just the training."

"Right."

"Emotions can hurt others, Cam. Stepping into someone's mind is not about causing you hurt, but about not hurting them – especially those who don't even know you're there."

"Thanks." Somehow, all I feel is resentment. "Now, please go away."

"Eat and sleep."

"Yes, please go!"

CHAPTER THIRTY

Our assigned rooms aren't bad. The furniture is utilitarian – all corners and edges – but easy to clean, I guess. In the centre of the room against the far wall is a double bed with bedside cabinets. There is also a set of drawers with a square mirror, and a small cupboard with kettle and coffee supplies. The fitted wardrobe is to the left of the main entry, and the seating area in the corner has a couple of small armchairs and a coffee table.

The thing that most got my attention last night was the laptop on the desk. I immediately opened it up to check my email, but found it had no Internet access. The TV is similarly restricted with very few channels, none of which show local or regional news. Something to do with security protocols and tracing our location. Ruth told us we'll eventually have clearance and access but, for now, we just have to be patient.

As I close the door, I glance at the map of the training facility and exit routes on the back of it. It also has a list of rules about noise, curfews, cleaning your room and doing your own washing. There's a utility room down the corridor, somewhere to the right, with washing machines and stuff.

Throwing my homework on the desk and kicking off my trainers, I can't decide whether to read the history of this place first or take a shower. I miss Liddy; miss her jokes and laughter. She's right, everything's changed, but that doesn't change us. We're still best friends. Why can't she see that?

There's a sudden knock on the door and, although it startles me, I jump up, thinking it might be Liddy.

It's not. Vicky stands outside, holding a large, brown paper bag. She offers it to me. "Here, Ruth asked me to give you this."

"Oh right, thanks."

"'Sokay."

I reach over to take the bag, ready to close the door, but she leans in, looking over my shoulder.

"What you up to?"

"Not much, still have to do the homework."

"Can I come in?"

Surprised by her directness, I step back and let her pass. She smells flowery, like violets or something.

"My colours are blue. Think I like yours better."

I shrug, staring at the magnolia walls and maroon duvet. She saunters over to one of the armchairs and sits down.

"You have any juice?"

"Er, I think so." I pass her a box from the fridge and lean against the set of drawers, waiting to find out what she wants. Her long-sleeved T-shirt is a light green, her leggings emphasise slim legs, and her tight-laced, heavy boots remind me of something the army would use. She unwraps the straw and slowly takes a sip. As she looks up, she flicks back her spiral hair, pressing her lips together, trying for a friendly smile.

"So, what do you think?"

"About what?"

"All this." She flicks her hand around the room as if she's talking about the flat-pack furniture. I dumbly glance around, hearing her tut. "I see Liddy's the bright one."

I frown and cross my arms. "What do you want?"

She looks at the window, blinds half down, her ebony skin perfect in the late afternoon light. "Don't get me wrong, I'm glad they rescued me."

"What are you going on about?"

"The Diversity Commission. The League. All of it."

I plonk myself of the edge of my bed and watch as she strokes the arm of the chair with the tips of her fingers.

"The tests were excruciating, of course. Don't think I could have stood much more." She glances at me when I don't respond, weighing me up. "Pushing me to see how I react, testing me for telepathy, processing, psychokinesis and other stuff. Course, most of it was just painful." She hesitates again, as if her mind's in another place. The clinic, probably. I wonder why she's in my room, telling me this stuff.

"Not sure why they rescued me. There were others there much stronger. I could hear them screaming, begging for the tests to stop. And then, there were those that were just totally gone. We had this common room, like a residential home for oldies. We called them the 'dribblers' – the ones who no longer knew who they were. They pushed them too far. You have to be strong to survive there."

"Sounds bad. What happens to them after?" My words don't show the horror I feel. I could have ended up at a place like that.

"They slowly disappear." She drops her head to the side, stares blankly and sticks her tongue out as if she's been strangled. "You were lucky."

"How so?"

"Well, you never got picked up, did you?"

"I guess." Although being dragged away from home doesn't feel lucky, right now.

She sits up straighter and changes the topic. "Anyway, this history stuff. 'The five great families spreading justice and equality, building a new future for those of us evolving'."

"I haven't read it yet."

"You haven't memorised the leaders' names yet?" She counts them off on her fingers. "Beresfords, Dantes, Lins, Abimbolas and Webers. Saviours of the new race."

"Did you say 'Beresford' and 'Weber'?"

"Yes. Recognise them?"

I stalk to the fridge and bend down to find water. Hiding my face behind my dangling hair, I hear my pulse beating in my ears.

Tom and Amy. Both are related to the original families. Why didn't he tell me?

I want her gone; out of my room so I can think. I squat a little longer than necessary before standing and turning to face her. "Well, I'd better start reading, then."

She doesn't take the hint. I flex my hands and tighten them into balls. She watches me, smiles and slinks back into the chair, stretching out her legs.

"Have you wondered why they're doing it, and where all the money comes from?"

I have, but don't want to share anything with her. "Not had a chance to wonder about much, yet. Still have the reading to do." She ignores my second hint, so I go back to the edge of my bed, sipping water as I go.

"I get that the first family – one of the Beresford's, by the way – bought this island, and also that they wanted to protect their son. I even get that why they created a community of likeminded people. But that was years ago. I also understand why the Beresford's might want to protect their son who had been damaged in the war. But then there's this global stuff. What's that about?"

"Global?"

"Five islands on five different continents."

"Oh, yeah." I remember Zoe gave an overview.

"Yes, exactly. They're pretty powerful, too."

Scuttling further back, I cross my legs and lean against the headboard. She's obviously not going until she's said what she's come to say. I'm starting to wonder what that is.

"So, I got to thinking."

"You did?"

And she's off again. I examine her as she talks. We may be genetically similar, but she's nothing like me. Taller, to start with; dark eyes, hair and skin. Beautiful eyes. She also looks a couple of years older, though it's hard to tell. I do notice her chest is flat. Not even a false bra.

"At the clinic, they told me things. I didn't believe them at the time, thought they were making everything up. But now..."

"What did they say?"

"Y'know the 'enemies' in the last 'great war'?" She's doing that air quote thing, which I hate. "They wanted to weed out the weak, the diseased, leaving only the strong. They didn't have the knowledge the allies had in embryo modification; it wasn't shared till the end of the war as no one trusted them, so they experimented, trying to learn from those who were cohorts of the original biological technology. Atrocities!"

She's waiting for me to get something but, as I already know this stuff, it doesn't have the shock factor she seems to want. Tutting and flipping her hair, she continues.

"I was told the tests may have somehow triggered the accidental awakening of dormant cells, ones that could have been in us for ever, but not used, or something like that. Though, to be honest, there were other weirdo scientists who continued experiments after the war, so who knows what's true?" She rubs her head, trying to remember something. "Eventually, it was named something else 'The Epic... no not epic, Apex maybe. Yes, that's what they said, 'The Apex Agenda'." She's watching me again, waiting to see my reaction.

"Look, they told me all this." I push the pillow further up my back. "I don't know what happened to you, but we can't trust the Diversity Commission. They destroy people like us." I think about the guard who took me to the clinic. "You said it yourself. Seems to me, you're either with them, or not. And if not, it's a camp or you become one of the emotionless braindead in complete servitude." I remember what she said earlier. "Or, in our case, dribblers."

"I know, I know. And I didn't believe them. But reading this history stuff has got me thinking: the Apex Agenda must be true. The League have said the same thing, more or less. Maybe the DC was just trying to get things back to 'normal'."

"What, by getting rid of people like us?" I tut and flick my head in disgust.

"No, by fighting people like the League."

"The League doesn't fight them, they're protecting us. How can you even think that?" But even as I say it, bells are ringing in my head. Infiltrate and decapitate – those were the words used.

"Another thing, if this island was bought just after the war to protect one of the family's sons – the one who was in a prisoner of war camp – and he'd had his chromosomes messed about with, then that must have been why they set up the research and development unit. But why are they now honing our skills? I mean, what for, and what are these other missions?" Her voice is getting squeakier and she's prodding a rip in her leggings.

"Evolution, freedom, equality." The words from the introductory clip pop out of my mouth.

I hear her sigh. "Maybe you're right. Maybe their aim is a fairer society. But the Commission said something, and I can't let it go."

"What?"

"They said the League were building an army of elite citizens. Changing the natural evolution of mankind."

"That can't be true. They fight against the Commission, yes, but they're not building an army. We'd see it." Then something else occurs to me. "Wait, they know about this place?"

She's curling her hair around her fingers casually, but I get the impression I've caught her out on something. I'm not sure what and she's not about to tell me. I wish she'd just go.

"Well, they talked about 'the enemy', not specifically this island. But think about all the places that are off limits to us here. We don't really know what's going on."

My mind whirls, finding it hard to claw through the mire of lies and possibilities.

It feels like I'm standing on a high wall, looking down. On one side is a stormy sea and on the other a serene lake. When I blink, everything changes and the lake is crashing against the wall, as the sea laps gently against a sandy beach. It keeps switching, unbalancing me, as I consider which version is real and which is illusory.

"Look" – Vicky's staring at me – "all I'm saying is, we don't know everything that's going on. It's hard to know who to trust."

She sounds like Liddy, but I'm not about to join her club, or whatever it is she wants. She contemplates me for a few seconds before spitting out what she's really come to say.

"I've decided I'm going to find out for myself."

"You are? How?"

"I'm going to have a look at that research lab and maybe the mission ops building. Just poke about a bit." Her eyes shine, round and dark. "Before I can commit to anything, I want to know the whole truth. I've been told so many lies in the past." She lets the thought drift. I don't know what to say. "Don't worry, I won't implicate you, but if I find out anything, I'll share. How's that?"

"I, er—"

"Just promise me not to tell anyone else, for now. It'll be our secret."

"Look, I don't know if I want anything to do with this. In fact, why are you even sharing it with me?"

"There are things they're not telling us, Cam. We need to watch out for each other. You and I are the same."

"And the others?"

"Taor and Jon?"

"And Liddy."

"They're not like us. What could they do, anyway? We can at least keep a look out for them."

I can't afford to believe her conspiracy theories – not now, not with everything going on – and I'm definitely not promising her anything, but I do want her out of my room.

"So, you came here to warn me?"

"Nope. Just came to give you your bag. The rest of it spilled out." She shrugs, crinkling her eyes. "Thanks for the ear."

"That's okay"

She's about to get up, but then she leans back. "Do you know your talents yet?"

All this sharing on her part hasn't made me any more trusting. "Do you?"

"I can sense vibration at a distance and use it to detect stuff. Found out the hard way, at the clinic." She looks towards the door. "Think of me as your personal sonar detection unit. Metal objects particularly stand out, so anything coming this way by sea and I'll know about it."

"Right."

"Sally says I can develop it further, use it to magnetically affect equipment, even send boats or vehicles the wrong way."

"Sounds useful."

She snorts. "Very, if you need that sort of thing." Her intonation is conspiratorial again. "I'd like telepathy, so been practicing, but…"

I hear a humming, like a woodpecker tapping a tree. It's a new signature but it feels different to Tom. It's more like someone is trying to push their way into my head. I don't like it. "Is that you?"

Her face lights up. "You heard me?

"Far away."

"That's all I can do. Sally said I should keep practising, but I bet it's nothing like you and Tom. Liddy says you have a bond."

"She did?"

"Yeah, she was angry. Said you shouldn't trust so easily."

I cross my arms and sit up straight. "Liddy should keep her mouth shut."

"Hey, we're on the same side, remember. And Liddy's just worried."

I don't feel we're on the same side at all and I'm sure she knows it.

"So, what does it feel like with Tom, and what are your other talents?"

I'm desperate for her to go, and so get up, stretching. "Oh, I'm new to this stuff. A bit of processing I think, and obviously the telepathy."

At last, she takes the hint and stands. "Amazing! What does processing feel like?"

"Freaks me out."

She nods and walks towards the door. Just as I'm about to close it, she puts her hand out to stop me.

"Hey" – she bites her bottom lip – "is Liddy your girlfriend?"

I know she's asking if we're in some sort of relationship, but it strikes me as odd. I'm still not used to all this 'everyone's human' and 'we can be who we want to be' stuff. But then, Tom and Amy look happy. Flickering pictures of Liddy flash through my mind – that pink tutu she loved, her coming-out party as a boy, and now her change into a girl again. Vicky's waiting for an answer.

"Er, no." I stammer, remembering Liddy's thoughts earlier in the day: 'How can I compete with that?' Something like a fissure of electricity runs through my mind. *Surely, Liddy doesn't think of me as something more...* No, it can't be. She's always saying she likes tall, dark and handsome. *I'm not that. I could never be that.*

"No, no, I'm not her type. We're best friends."

"Good." She grins. "Just checking. Her eyes sparkle and she has a mischievous look about her. "Wouldn't want to break anything up."

She walks down the corridor, her back straight. At the corner, she turns and waves. I hear the woodpecker again. Nothing intrusive, but I wonder if she's telling me the whole truth about her abilities. I sense she's keeping secrets, but then, so am I.

Re-entering the room, I lean on the door to close it. The empty juice box sits on the table. The brown paper bag is plonked on my bed. Something doesn't feel right about Vicky, and not just about what she said or how she acted. I'm sure, had my veil not been up, she could have delved deeper into my mind.

And that last question about Liddy. Does she want to go out with her? The thought of them being together is strange, but why, I don't know. Physically, Liddy is a boy, and Vicky is more girl than boy, I suppose, so it could work.

In the larger world it would be banned. Gene-pure partners producing perfect children is fine, but ungendered or same-sex relationships were made unlawful way before I was born. The Holistic Law forbids any abnormals forming physical relationships. They are morally corrupt. But this island is different. I have to keep reminding myself gender isn't an issue. Maybe Liddy would like a girlfriend, although her preference has never been for girls.

I try to be selfless, but a picture of them arm-in-arm, going to classes, develops in my brain. I don't know how I feel about that. Maybe I should warn Liddy, tell her not to trust Vicky, that something isn't quite right. But Liddy wouldn't be so stupid as to trust someone we've just met.

The irony of the words doesn't escape me, the same words Liddy used about Tom.

I traipse back to my bed and look in the brown bag. A note sits on the top of some clothing. Tipping everything on the bed, I take in a full swimming costume, goggles, a swimming cap, gym clothes and trainers. "Jeez."

My hand hesitates as I reach for the note – that's Tom's word, not mine. *Need to get him out of my brain!*

The note is brief:

Cam,

As your guardian, we meet every two days, so could you pop over tonight at 7:30 p.m.? Will cook a bit of dinner. Meet you at the staff accommodation entrance. Press 38.

Thought you might need the clothes.

See you later,

Ruth

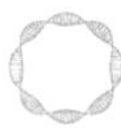

Just as I'm about to climb in the shower, the internal phone rings. It warbles like I imagine a tropical bird might. I wrap a large towel around me and scuttle over to the desk.

"Cam?"

"Liddy?" I can't help being happy to hear her voice. I sigh and sit down, desperately wanting things to be normal again.

"You going to Ruth's?" Her question is tentative.

"Yeah, you?"

"Yep. Thought we might walk together, if you're okay with that?"

My chest tightens with a flutter of hope. "'Course I am."

"See you outside your door at 07:00ish?"

I can't help grinning. "Okay." I think she's going to hang up.

"And, Cam?"

"Yes?"

"We're best friends still, aren't we?" She sounds quiet, awkward.

"You don't need to ask."

"Just that—"

"Yeah, I know."

I hear her breathing down the phone, waiting. Feeling a need to fill the gap and lighten the mood, I splutter out the first words that pop into my head. "Have so much to tell you. Plus, I think someone fancies you."

She doesn't immediately answer. Her normal retort would be snappy, funny even. She clears her throat, and I wonder if I've made a mistake telling her.

"So, you been arranging my love life behind my back, then?"

Her voice has an American twang, but I hear the strain as she tries to play the game. I wish now I hadn't said anything.

"Tell you later."

"'kay."

"'Bye."

Why did I bring that up right now? Bad timing!

I turn the shower on turbo and full heat to block out my idiocy. The water crashes down on my skull, burning away at the irritation I feel. Not with Liddy, I realise, but with myself. I can only stand the scalding for a few seconds before stepping back and reducing the heat. Reaching for the shampoo, I soap up my hair, return to the shower and begin scrubbing. Encircled by a wall of water, I close my eyes and allow the outside world to evaporate with the steam.

CHAPTER THIRTY-ONE

"So, what do you think?"

Liddy has her arms out as she twirls in front of my doorway. She's wearing tight black jeans, a frilled purple blouse that flows down to her thighs, suede ankle boots with high heels, and a multi-coloured woollen wrap. She's even got a false bra on, which I didn't even bother with as my top is baggy. Her black hair is shiny, hanging straight to her shoulders. She's clean-shaven and has gone to town on her face – green and gold eyeshadow, thick mascara, deep red blusher and pink lips.

I stare, stunned at the immediacy of her change – or rather the reversion back to her old self. A year ago, this was Liddy. She's waiting, watching my face and eyes for a reaction.

"Not too much for dinner, d'ya think?"

I know she's desperate for my approval. "Er, no. You look great." I glance down at my worn jeans, plain navy hoodie and old trainers. "Shows me up completely."

She grins, her tight shoulders slumping a little. "You never did have any dress sense. I wanted to make a good impression."

As we walk down the corridor and Liddy throws her wrap across her left shoulder, I notice the small, black clutch bag under her arm.

"Where did you get all this stuff?"

"Went shopping, today."

Without me?

"Hired a bike, too."

"Yeah, Taor said. About the bike, I mean."

"You spoke with him?"

"A bit." I shrug my shoulders. "Seems okay. He and Jon have had a bad time."

"I heard from Jon. You know, he came and apologised to me, said he had been wrong and wanted to start again."

"Very odd. Maybe Ruth had a word with him."

"Must have been a major word. He's changed a hundred-and-eighty degrees."

After Vicky's conversation, a seed of doubt creeps in. Would they use mind manipulation to get Jon to change his behaviour? Surely not. But Dr Schultz had used something on Liddy when we were escaping. I'd thought that necessary to get us moving, but what if they use it more casually? And how would we even know?

We stroll along a pathway at the side of the training facility. Streetlights with an orange glow are already on. Tiny shrubs around the edges of the walkway look grey and shrivelled, their leaves shivering on the end of tough stems. The wind's picking up, lashing my hair across my face. I pull it back and wrap a band around it (I always keep one on my wrist, just in case) and pull up my hood.

"There are a couple of clothes shops: one for work gear and the other for casual. I could help you choose some stuff, if you want."

"Maybe." I hate shopping, but she's trying to act normal, and I need to meet her halfway. "Did it cost much?"

"A quarter of my tokens for this outfit, including the boots and bag, so not a bad deal."

"Right." My fingers are chilly. I stuff them in the front pocket of my hoodie and pick up my pace a bit. Liddy keeps up without any effort. To our right is the small, grassy park with a few trees and bushes. There're also a couple of benches and a children's swing set. I can imagine children running around or playing catch. Then I wonder where the children are, whether they live in the permanent housing block. My forehead crinkles. I don't remember a school in the description of the island.

The swing creaks as the wind rocks it back and forth. Looking beyond it, I notice the forbidden mission ops building. Several windows glow. People must still be working. Vicky pops into my mind. I wonder how she will get into the building and what she'll find.

Liddy makes another effort to keep the conversation going. "They've got a film showing at the cinema. Not a real cinema, just a hall. But anyway, we could go see it? Something to do."

She's hesitant as if she's unsure whether to ask. I flick my eyes at her, navigating the awkwardness of the new us.

"Yeah, I'd like that. What's the film?"

"Never heard of it. Some action/adventure thing."

"Do they have popcorn?" I try for a little lightness in my voice.

"Better have."

We reach the two-storey science and research block on the left. All the buildings are built in a similar fashion – blocks of cement painted white – but in the subdued light, they seem daunting and eerie. The staff accommodation is not far ahead of us, and still Liddy and I have said nothing of consequence to fix our friendship.

Stopping, I glance up. A few stars and a crescent moon are just visible. She follows my eyes.

"Pretty."

"Yeah."

But I'm not paying much attention. Biting the inside of my cheek, I swallow hard and stammer the words that have been going round and round in my head. If I don't spit them out now, I know I never will. "I... I don't like this, Lid." I watch her watching me, her dark blue eyes wide. "Us, I mean. I want things to go back to what they were... before."

She flicks her hair back, looking over my shoulder. "I know. Me, too."

"Just because things have changed, it doesn't mean we have to."

"I don't think..." She's tapping her foot and clinging onto her shawl. "I think we'll get through this. I want to."

"Me, too."

We both force a smile before turning forward. I feel better for saying something, even if it was a bit lame. A gust of wind blasts across us and I shiver. Can't believe I came out without my jacket.

"Here." She's holding out half her wrap and I move closer, grateful for the warmth as it cradles us together. Moving forward is difficult, like people learning to dance for the first time. She steps on my toes.

"Ouch!"

"Sorry."

We stop again as she makes adjustments, handing me the corner of the wrap. "Hold on to the other side and I'll keep my big feet off your tiny *Cinderella* toes." She grins – a real Liddy grin this time, with playful eyes.

Giggling as we inch forward, the awkwardness of a few minutes ago almost disappears.

"So," I hear her mischievous sarcasm and wonder what's coming. "Who's this person who fancies me? Not that I'm surprised, with my good looks."

I playfully punch her in her side. "Vicky asked me if we were seeing each other."

"She did?" Her eyes widen. "What did you say?"

"Told her we were best friends."

She looks away, frowning. A lilting Irish accent sprouts out of her mouth. "That we are, that we are."

I laugh but am aware she's feeling awkward. To cover my own confusion, I go with the flow. "You should apply to be a leprechaun."

"What? Oh, you mean at that leprechaun school?"

The shawl has slipped across my mouth and nose, my breathing has warmed the bottom half of my face, but now I need some air. "You trying to kill me off?" I yank at the shawl and pull it lower.

"No, my dear, you're quite capable of doing that yourself."

We laugh, before returning to a few moments' silence. Liddy picks up where she left off. "So, Vicky thinks I'm cute?"

"Well, she didn't quite say that."

"Y'think she might be asking for someone else? Jon's more my type, though Vicky's kinda nice, too. What do you think?"

"I'm not sure about either of them. You and Jon friends now, are you?"

"No, but if he's making an effort, I'll go along. Both of them are a bit young for me, anyway. Saw a cutie in the canteen though. Sitting with your new friend."

"New friend?"

"Tom." Her voice is level. "Tom the bonder." She's trying to make a joke.

"Oh, Tom. Not sure if we're friends, as such."

"But the bond and stuff?"

"Turns out it might have been my fault." I kick at the gravel footpath. "It's hard to explain."

"If your best friend can't understand you, who can?"

We're close to the staff accommodation and so have slowed to a snail's pace. I can feel the tension as if it's vibrating off her. This is the crux of our problem, and she needs to know.

"Okay, so friends have stuff in common – you do things together, you know stuff about them, their likes and dislikes."

"Of course."

"Well, I don't know Tom. In fact, I know nothing about him." Saying this out loud makes me realise how true this is. "We aren't close like you and me, Lid. Our whole lives around the corner from each other. It's more of a 'cellular bond'."

"Cellular? And that means?"

"We're able to connect with our minds, speak really fast to each other. I know that sounds crazy, but that's what it is. And it's that connection that bonds us. Nothing else, no friendship – just this weird 'sameness'. Similar chromosomes that link us. A chemical thing. Nothing more." I'm rambling and my face heats up as guilt floods through me. I feel as if I'm betraying Tom in some way. "Because of our connection, he can train me faster, so I don't hurt anyone."

"You couldn't hurt anyone. Haven't they seen your muscles?"

"Lid, you don't know what it's like."

We've reached a set of dark glass doors, and a white security light goes on. To the right is a panel with tons of buttons on it, each with a number from one to forty-five. We stand there, staring at the panel. The wrap squashes us together but there is still a cavern of unspoken words separating us.

Liddy's voice is calmer. She's trying to be aloof, calm, but I know her better. "You'll have to tell me what it's like, then."

"I'd like that. We could have coffee tomorrow after classes."

"It's a date, as long as you promise to get some new clothes. You can't go around in your jeans and hoodie for ever."

I know she's right. "Sure, fine. You can advise me."

"Even better."

She releases me from our cocoon and presses number thirty-eight. There's no sound and we can't see through the doors, but after a few seconds we hear a buzzing and then Ruth's voice.

"Hi! I'm coming."

CHAPTER THIRTY-TWO

Ruth opens the door and ushers us into her second-floor apartment. Smells of homecooked food send my saliva glands into explosive appreciation and my stomach growls in agreement.

"Welcome, both of you." She smiles at Liddy. "Been shopping?"

Liddy grins back. "Do you like it?"

"You look wonderful. I'm so glad you're finding yourself."

Liddy's eyes sparkle at the acceptance and, for once, I perceive her as Ruth does – a young, determined person, knowing exactly who she is.

Unlike me!

Noticing Ruth's clothing, I realise how underdressed I am. She's wearing an expensive-looking flowery dress, pinched in at the waist; her blonde hair loose around her shoulders, make-up perfectly applied.

"Please, come in. Make yourselves at home."

She leads us through a small hallway into an open plan living and dining area. To our immediate right is a corner sofa with a coffee table in front of it and a large media screen on the wall. There are a couple of decorative prints, some ornaments and photos in a cabinet to the left, and a variety of lamps, creating a cosy, warm atmosphere.

We move to the huge glass and metallic dining table, already set up with three sets of plates, glasses and cutlery. Beyond that are patio doors and a lit balcony, through which I can see a couple of chairs and potted plants. Liddy folds her wrap over the back of one of the chairs.

"Have a seat, both of you. Dinner's ready." Ruth moves over to the kitchen area on the left and busies herself taking something out of the oven. "How did today go?"

Before we can answer, a tall, blond man walks in and kisses Ruth on the top of her head. She spins around, smiling. He puts his arm around her shoulder.

"These your new charges?"

Liddy and I stand beside the tall-backed dining chairs like children waiting to be told what to do. I glance at Liddy, and she raises an eyebrow. It's as if I can hear her thoughts:

Ruth has a partner! All things are possible here.

I check to make sure I'm not accidently probing Liddy's mind like I did before, but I'm not. I just know her well.

"This is Jake. He works at the research lab."

Jake moves towards us, arm outstretched.

I shake a large, soft hand. "Very nice to meet you, Jake."

"Hey, no need to be so formal. You must be Camelia."

"Cam."

"Okay, Cam it is." He looks at Liddy, reaching out with both hands and giving her reassuring nods and smiles. "And you're Liddy. Heard so much about you. I think you'll do well here."

Liddy's almost as tall as him and, as green eyes meet blue, an understanding passes between them.

Ruth comes up behind with the dish from the oven and places it on the table. "Stop embarrassing them, Jake."

"I'm not, am I?"

Liddy's response is enthusiastic. "Not at all."

He grins. "Well, I'm off. You girls have a good time." At the entryway, he blows a kiss to Ruth. "See you later, darling."

Ruth blushes, but her eyes sparkle as she sits down. Liddy pulls out a chair and I follow suit. Copying Ruth, we place napkins on our knees. As she serves what looks to be vegetarian lasagne, Liddy speaks.

"Jake didn't have to leave because of us, did he?"

"No, of course not. He had work to catch up on." She holds her hand out. "Pass your plate, Liddy, and Cam, help yourself to salad."

The lasagne is steaming, and I pick at the edges, trying to find a bit that won't burn my mouth. In the end, I satisfy myself with lemon-flavoured tomatoes and cucumbers until the pasta dish is edible. It's worth waiting for. The tomato sauce is slightly spicy and the cheese, strong and tangy. "Ruth, this is delicious. Please teach me how to make it."

"Of course. Glad you like it."

Liddy's shovelling so fast, her mouth is too full to comment, but she murmurs a few *mms* and *ahs*. I point out a blob of sauce on her chin, much to her horror, before helping myself to seconds. Dessert is banoffee pie, sticky and sweet, with fresh cream and a hint of coffee and chocolate flakes on top.

"You're a marvellous cook."

"Thank you, Liddy."

"Invite us over any time."

"I'll bear that in mind." She's smiling as she says it. "Anyone want this last bit?"

Liddy's hovering over the dish, holding a large cake slice. Ruth laughs. Liddy flushes with embarrassment at her eagerness. I think about teasing her, but decide not to push our only-just-glued-back-together friendship.

I sip water as Liddy finishes off the pie. Ruth gets up and begins clearing the table.

"Oh, I'll help."

"No, Cam. You're my guests tonight. Another time."

I drift over to the patio doors, with the glass in my hand, and stare. The balcony is wide enough for two seats, a small table, an outdoor heater and a few potted plants. I notice one is a fuchsia, one of my mum's favourites. Ruth said they remind her of her mother, who had a huge bush in her garden.

I wonder if my mum is all right, if she understands why I ran, if she knows it wasn't to hurt her. Maybe I should have told her something, anything, but it was all decided so quickly. I breathe in deeply and turn to find Liddy at my side.

"Penny for your thoughts?"

"Not that cheap," I smile. "Perhaps some gold and I'll tell you."

She laughs and pushes her hair behind her ears, wafting a sweet scent in my direction.

"What's that perfume you're wearing? It reminds me of some soap my mum had."

"Roses."

"Where did you get it?"

"Stole it from my mother's drawer."

"Thought we weren't bringing make-up and stuff?"

"You brought a photo."

"That's different."

She concedes with a cheeky shoulder shrug and moves over to the sofa. I follow and we both plonk ourselves down on soft corduroy material. Liddy's stroking it and leaning her head back.

"Could sleep here."

I grunt in agreement and, looking around, spot a print of Monet's *Bridge over a Pond of Water Lilies*. There's a small lamp above it, showcasing the colours wonderfully. To the left is an old-fashioned grandfather clock, which ticks away quietly.

"Coffee, tea, anyone? Or would you prefer a soft drink?"

Ruth pops her head around the corner of the kitchen. She's drying her hands on a teacloth. In the background, I hear the clunking of a dishwasher.

I lift up my glass. "Usually, I love coffee, but I think I'll stick with this. My stomach won't take any more."

Liddy agrees. "Not for me either, but thanks."

"Okay, I'll be with you in a sec."

Liddy nudges me, mimicking a little kid. "What ya' thinking?"

I smile, staring up at the black flat screen hanging on the wall. "Oh, y'know."

"Nope, I don't read minds."

"All this reminds me of my mum."

"It doesn't remind me of my family at all. Mum tried to cook but Dad always caused a fuss, nothing ever good enough. It was easier to have a sandwich in my bedroom."

"I know."

Liddy's family are more than a bit dysfunctional, mainly due to her dad being a bully.

Before we have a chance to say any more, Ruth sits down on the corner end of the sofa, facing us. "So, how have you both been getting on?"

"Okay."

"Fine."

She leans forward on her knees and tries a different approach. "This is all so new. There are bound to be difficulties."

After such a lovely dinner, I feel obliged to find her a problem to solve. "The classes are fine, just like school." *Although without all the staring and fear of being outed.* "But do we have to do so much fitness? Liddy's great at this stuff, but I'm rubbish. With my size and everything, I'll struggle to keep up."

"You'll get stronger, Cam. Everyone has to be able to defend themselves – it's part of the programme – but with your abilities, DC will come after you. The only way you can protect yourself is to become strong, mentally and physically."

It wasn't the response I wanted. I'd have preferred she conceded.

Yeah, like that was gonna happen.

"You've reminded me, though, I do have something which might help." She gets up and disappears around the corner again. We hear her dragging something out of a cupboard.

Liddy raises her eyebrows at me. I shrug as if to say, 'Don't ask me'. Upon returning, Ruth has a large paper bag, which she hands to me.

"This will build your bone strength and muscles."

I'm about to open it when the grandfather clock begins chiming and startles me. "It actually works?"

"Yes, Jake likes to fiddle with things. It was a wreck when we bought it, but now it's almost perfect. It has a mind of its own though and we never know when it's going to chime."

There's pride in her voice as we count it striking the hour. Already 9:00 p.m. The last two hours have whizzed by. I smile, enjoying the sound and the company.

Inside the bag are five sealed packets and one of those portable, protein shaker bottles.

I take a packet. "What is it?"

"Mainly protein, but it's formulated for people like you, with different chromosomes. Think of it as a supplement."

"Is this the stuff Tom told me about?"

"Probably."

I look up at Liddy. "Made him grow taller."

"How?"

Putting the protein back in the bag, we both look at Ruth, but she doesn't answer. I don't really care what's in it, as long as it helps me grow.

"You take two doses a day. A tablespoon in water or any kind of milk. Shake it well though, or it'll be lumpy."

I nod. "Thanks. Hope it works."

"It should."

"Now, Liddy" – Ruth turns to her – "I think it might be good if we had some sessions alone.”

“Why?”

“If I’m to guide you on your life here – your options as well as any potential changes you may want to make – it’s better done one-on-one.”

Liddy looks at Ruth and then at me for reassurance. Her eyes show excitement and apprehension. A few days ago, this discussion could never have taken place.

“This is what you’ve wanted since forever, isn’t it? To be a girl.” I’m trying to be supportive.

“I am a girl.”

“Yes, I know…” I don’t want to bring up the obvious physicality. “Well, you know what I mean.”

She presses her lips together and grips one hand in the other, before responding to Ruth. “Okay, yes. I’d like that. Thanks”

“Good, I’ll set that up.” Ruth is about to say something else when a phone beeps. Leaning over, she picks up a black mobile. She frowns and states, “Answer,” placing it to her ear. “I have guests. Is this—”

A shrill voice interrupts. Both Liddy and I can hear it clearly. “Put on the news, from the beginning.”

“Now?”

“Yes, now, and call me back immediately.”

“Will do.” With her phone on her lap, she raises her voice.
“TV on. Main news channel. Begin at start.”

For a second, I wonder what she’s doing, but then realise her TV has voice activation. The screen on the wall flicks to life, jumps to the channel and flashes, before settling on a black-haired man in a grey suit and blue tie, standing in front of a large screen.

“Good evening. Tonight, we have some breaking news. The Diversity Commission has issued a warning for these outlaws.”

The screen next to him flashes up five faces: two are covered with balaclavas, the remaining three make me gasp. Liddy, Dr Schultz and I stare back, last year’s school photos of Liddy and me. My stomach curdles, as if all the food is rolling around inside.

“Pause.”

The man is halted just as he’s about to say something else, our ghostly images fading. Ruth turns to us. "I'm sorry, but I think you should both leave."

"No way." Liddy voices my feelings exactly. "I want to see this."

We haven't been allowed television or phones. This is our first glimpse of outside life since we left it behind.

"We're not little kids. We have a right to know what's going on," I add to Liddy's comment.

Ruth is still weighing up the pros and cons, whether now is the right time to allow us access to the outside world.

"Don't you trust us?"

"Of course, I do. It's just… Well, fine. Let's just get on with it." She turns to the screen again. "Play," and the thing comes alive, our faces enlarged.

"These two are criminals. Their names are Camelia Chadwick and Lou Mitchell. Do not approach. They are armed and dangerous. Call the police on the number below."

A telephone number floats across the bottom of the screen in red and white as the shot cuts to the night we escaped. We're in the street outside Abby's Coffeeshop and the police car is blaring out its siren. The clip is from the police's viewpoint. The must have had some sort of dashcam. Liddy and I are climbing into the van; Jenny and David are shooting. One man falls. The scene pauses on our faces, before returning to the presenter.

"I repeat, do not approach either of these criminals." He takes a breath before his next line. "Just yesterday, we gained an exclusive interview with Lou's parents."

I grasp Liddy's hand as her dad appears on screen. Her mum sits beside him, her face pale and blank. Her dad is big, with a wide face and shoulders. He leans forward and spits out his words.

"We tried our best. He just wouldn't conform. We had him registered for therapy." Liddy's dad raises his voice. "And he just ran. Not caring about his poor mother or his siblings. What does he think he's doing?"

The presenter asks him if he has anything to say to his son. Liddy's dad turns to the camera.

"Lou, it's time to come home. You've had your bit of fun, but now you need to come back. We all know Cam's been a bad influence, what with her faulty genes, she's unnatural, but you're pure."

My hand's sweaty, but Liddy doesn't let go. Her dad sneers and spits out his words.

"He's always been an idiot, easily led astray."

He is turning red, and I recognise the emotion as barely controlled anger. I remember the time he threw Liddy's bike at her because she came back late. I was there, saw it clip Liddy on the head. She still has the scar.

"I want you to know" – his wide, unshaven face fills the camera – "if you're not home by Friday, you're no longer our son. Don't bother coming back."

Liddy jumps up and stalks around the back of the sofa, pointing at her dad. "Yeah, as if I'm ever coming back to you."

They zoom in on her mum. She now has tears dripping from eyes that have either been punched or not slept for days, probably the latter. Liddy tuts, but she's also frowning with concern. "She's stupid for staying with him so long. No wait, she's stupid for ever marrying him. Sixteen, she was. What did she ever see in him?"

I let the comments pass, knowing how manipulative her dad is; how he refused to let Liddy's mother work, or do anything much outside of the house. She relies on her dad's income to feed the kids. Liddy has two younger siblings.

"I'm well out of it, I'll tell you." Liddy walks over to the wall and leans on it as the presenter moves on.

"And in another twist, the Diversity Commission has given us exclusive permission to report further on Camelia's mother, who was taken in for questioning five days ago."

Now, it's my turn. I glance at Ruth. "Did you know?"

Liddy comes back to sit beside me as Ruth pauses the programme again. "Maybe you should both leave. I didn't realise this was coming out..." She hesitates. "I should have asked before putting the programme on."

"I want to see this. I have a right to see it." I gesture for her to restart.

She sighs but nods, and the screen shows my mum being dragged out of our house by DC security officers. The cameras follow her distraught face. Journalists are shouting out at her:

"Anything to say, Mrs Chadwick?"

"Is it true the police found air tickets in your house?"

"Were you planning to run away with your Golem child?"

I suck in a breath as if I'm about to leap into deep water, remembering my mum wanting to talk to me about our trip.

Had my mum been planning an escape for us? Was that what Jenny was talking about, when she said two plans?

Unable to do anything, I watch as she's dragged along, bushy microphones pushed in her face.

"Do you have anything to say?"

Her face is at a strange angle, giving her a distorted, unnatural look. She screams over the noise and bustle as she's hauled away. "My daughter's innocent!" Finding a camera, she pulls away from the guards and stares at it, as if looking straight at me. "Cam, don't worry about me. Stay away, stay safe." And then she's pushed into a black van parked on our curb.

A pain shoots into my chest, my breath catching. Tears roll down my cheeks and I turn to Liddy for comfort, thinking the reporter has finished, but his voice draws me back to the television.

"The Diversity Commission released the following footage five minutes ago. This is exclusive breaking news, ladies and gentlemen."

There is glee in his voice as the screen behind now portrays my mum prostrate on a white hospital bed. Eyes closed, tubes and wires attached to her body. An agonising groan slips out from somewhere deep inside me, as a man with blue surgeon's scrubs steps up beside her.

"Mrs Chadwick has had a heart attack and is in a coma. If her daughter's watching, we advise her to contact local police, and they'll bring her to her mother. There isn't much we can do, and Mrs Chadwick only has a few days left, at the most."

The presenter goes on about the importance of the work the Diversity Commission's doing, but I block it out, squeezing my eyes tight, clinging on to my sides. They've taken my mum in place of me. And now they're killing her. My mum's dying, I'm sure of it. I breathe deeper, trying to catch my breath, but my chest is an empty space. I heave as if I'm asthmatic and a noise like a wounded cat escapes my mouth, before turning into a loud sobbing. Liddy pulls me into her shoulder.

I can't think straight. I can't get the picture of my mum out of my head. She's dying with no one to comfort her, without me at her side. Buzzing fills my ears. I hear their voices at a distance.

"Why didn't you tell us?"

"Her mother knew the risks."

"What?"

"I can't tell you everything, but what I can tell you is we always have at least two plans when rescuing someone. The first is always preferable. It involves the individual making the choice. The second is more of a grab-the-person-off-the-streets. Her mother knew this and had planned a trip."

"What are you talking about?" My voice is screechy.

Ruth looks at me, assessing my condition and trying to decide in a split second how much I can take. "Well, had you gone away with her, she would have known it would have been a chance for us to grab you."

"So, that was the second plan?"

"I don't know, but your mum knew we would try to get you out. I didn't have any direct contact with her. I don't know the exact details or arrangements made for missions."

My mum knew about this, about the League? How come? Why didn't she tell me? Why would she hide it from me? It doesn't make sense.

"And now?"

Ruth clasps her hands and leans forward. "We were arranging for her to come here after things calmed down a bit. She knew that, but she also knew she was being watched, so getting her out immediately would have been impossible. The Diversity Commission took her in for questioning. That's normal procedure. When she wasn't released, we became concerned. The heart attack we're not sure about. It may not be true. We've been trying to find her location to get a mission operative in."

"This is Cam's mum. She had a right to know."

Ruth doesn't immediately respond, but her voice is steady when she does. "You're right. We just wanted to find her first and, at the same time, protect you both."

A surge of anger shoots into my brain as if a knife has sunk deep into its recesses. Pushing Liddy away, I can barely control my screeching voice as I jump up and fling my arms out in anger.

"Protect us? You promised to protect my mum. You said you had Watchers, that you'd keep an eye on her. You promised she'd be safe!"

"I'm sorry, Cam. It's just so dangerous out there for you." She gets up, reaching for me, but her words anger me further. I stumble back, horrified by her attempts to console me.

"How dare you decide what's right for me? You're not my mother! I trusted you, trusted you would look out for her. You said no harm would come to her." My stomach churns and my heart beats so fast I think it will explode. My mum's face appears over and over, begging me to stay safe, while putting herself in danger. This wasn't supposed to happen.

The clip of the clinic flashes into my mind – what they do to people, what they did to Vicky, Taor and Jon. They've tortured her, I'm sure. She'll die alone, and all because of me.

The thudding in my ears pounds, making me dizzy. Liddy and Ruth both try to approach me, but I move behind the sofa, grabbing onto it for support as I pant and lean forward. Great gasps of air are not enough to feed my hammering heart. Then my eyes betray me, blurring until all I can see is a rainbow of colours shooting out from everything, surrounded by a golden, white light. My hearing goes next. A turbulent waterfall crashes around the room. I strike out, using my arms to cut through the air, refusing to be lost in something I can't control.

Gradually, the room comes back into focus. The sofa is against the far wall, the Monet on the floor, lamps strewn about and Liddy and Ruth are held in time, like statues, their arms reaching out to me.

I know what this is, know I've shifted into data processing mode, that the world around me has slowed down and my brain is speeding up. I realise immediately this is perfect. They can't get to me. The crashing noise of life has gone, even my heartbeats are few and far between. This is a space they can't enter, can't interfere with. And while the world around me is quiet and I'm in control, I can calm down, think about what to do.

I can't believe my mum knew about all this stuff and never told me. Right now, that's not as important as saving her life, but it wounds me. I thought we were close. She said to stay away, to stay safe, but does she just expect me to leave her to die alone? Maybe the Commission are lying, and she's just been drugged or something. A flicker of hope opens up with the possibility of a rescue. They invited me to visit before she dies – a trap, yes, but maybe I could make a deal?

As I run through my options, the hallway door shifts. I hear the familiar humming of Tom, asking permission to enter my mind. He must be outside. I don't want him to know my thoughts. Heck, he probably knew what was happening all along and never told me. After all, he's related to the original founders. Why didn't he tell me that? How much more is he hiding? Mentally, I step up on my mountain and push him across the valley.

By the time I'm ready to pull back on my bow string, the control function that releases me from data processing and takes me back to the normal world, I have the beginnings of a plan and feel stronger. Glancing at the clock, I see I've been away for five minutes. To me, it seems more like thirty. Gut instinct tells me they won't let me leave the base. They'll tell me it's for my protection.

Vicky and her advice not to trust everything they say, comes to mind. Why are they keeping things from me and what do they actually want from us? I need to know what she's found out.

But first, I have to let them think I believe them, go along with what they say, even act distraught – which won't be hard. There are things I need to do. Even getting through their invisible offshore barrier is going to be trouble, but it can be done. I know it can, and I will find a way.

CHAPTER THIRTY-THREE

Tom stands in front of me, Liddy and Ruth are to the left. I stare around the room. Broken lamps, the Monet picture on the floor; the sofa at the wrong angle. As I return from the silent world of Processor mode, the sudden noise and movement is loud. Liddy steps towards me, but Tom gets to me first.

"Take it easy."

"Cam, are you okay?"

I need them to believe I'm confused.

I am!

Sniffing and shivering, I lean against the wall and sink down, exhausted. "What happened?"

Wide-eyed, Liddy squats in front of me. "You don't know?"

Tom has his arms crossed. "Why didn't you let me in? I could have shown you how to get back quicker."

I want to tell him to get lost. How can I trust someone who betrayed me? Instead, I shrug and pull my knees tight to my chest. "Can't remember much."

He knows I'm lying and scowls, shaking his head. "Well, I don't think it's full-on telekinesis, but you can disrupt objects using vibrational force. That's something, I suppose."

Looking around the disorder in the room, I squint up at Ruth. "Did I do this? I'm sorry, I didn't mean to."

She smiles wanly. "Don't worry, no real damage."

She and Tom meet each other's gaze for a second and I wonder what message is passing between them. Obviously not telepathy, but something's going on.

"Ruth, do you have any energy drinks?"

"No. Juice okay?"

He nods and she moves to the kitchen.

"Come on, Cam. Come sit on the sofa."

Liddy helps me get up. Tom keeps his distance, sitting opposite me. He has a peculiar expression on his face, and I hear his signature humming again, asking permission to enter my mind. I glare and shake my head. Shock spills across his face, a dart of vibration shimmering out from his body, like early morning mist evaporating across a cool river.

"So, what's going on?" He's asking me why I don't want him in my head.

"Did you know about my mum?"

He doesn't give a precise answer. "You know it's a trap, don't you?"

Liddy, who's sitting beside me, snaps back. "But did you know?"

Elbows on knees, head lowered, he mumbles his answer. "Yes."

"Why didn't you tell me?"

He looks across the room at the Monet and clasps his fingers together. "I argued for it, but they thought it best not to upset you, at least not until they'd found her and you had more control."

Liddy explodes. "Who is this *they*?"

"Both the chief executive officer of Base One and the general chief of missions. They have people out searching already."

Liddy's still screechy. "Who are these chiefs? We should meet them. Our opinions count, y'know."

"Julia and Lucette? Look, I don't even know if they're currently on base."

Ruth comes back with two glasses of orange juice, handing one to Liddy and one to me. I sip it, letting it cool my hot throat, before speaking. "So, what's the plan? What are these two chiefs actually doing?" I look at Liddy. "What are their names?"

"Julia and Lucette."

Ruth tries to reassure us. "As Tom said, mission operatives are already out there. Once they find your mum, we'll go in and extract. Bring her here."

"And what if they don't find her?"

The room goes quiet. There isn't an answer. Placing the glass on the table, I get up. "I want to go now." My voice is low, hoarse. "I'm tired."

Liddy goes with me to the door, picking up her wrap and my bag of protein on the way. Ruth follows us, opening the door to let us out.

"I'm so sorry you found out like this, Cam."

I grit my teeth and stare at her, trying hard not to show the anger. "So am I."

Wrapped together in the shawl, we say nothing until reaching the park. Liddy's the first to speak.

"So, you have a plan?"

"What are you talking about?"

"I may not be able to read your mind, but I know what you're thinking."

The wind's stronger now, strange weather for mid-July. The swing rocks, squeaking in the dark, as if a child's ghost is pushing it higher. I pull up my hood and shiver.

"What can I do? They have people out there, looking."

Liddy stops us and turns to look at me, her eyes glistening in the light. "Listen, I know we've had a few problems lately, but you can trust me."

"I know I can, but there's nothing we can do. They won't let us." I place a finger on my lips in a shushing motion. She frowns as I point at the staff building, then gesture like I'm reading a book, before finally pointing to her head. Standing under the glow of an orange lamppost, I wonder if she'll get my macabre game of Charades. We used to play it as kids, at Christmas. I'm trying to tell her they may have people listening in or reading our minds.

She glances at the building and then at me. Understanding crosses her face, and she nods and grasps my hand. "I suppose they're better at it than us, but if you need me at any time..."

I nod and smile. "Thanks, Lid. You'll be the first I'll call."

After a few minutes' silence, I speak again. "I don't think I'll sleep. Do you want to take a walk to the jetty, instead of going straight back?"

"Yeah, sure."

She knows something's going on, but we keep our talk simple.

"And sorry about your dad."

"It's my mum I feel sorry for, not me."

"You know why she puts up with it?"

"I do, but she could get a job. Support herself. Make some friends at least. I mean, she's around the same age as your mum." Liddy sighs. "I think he's spent so long telling her she's useless, she believes it. And she's afraid of him."

The training building is on our right. Moving slowly, we pass it and head to the dock area. Liddy snorts.

"Once, after he'd slapped her around, I reported him to the police. When they turned up, she said it was nothing and apologised for the inconvenience." A deep sigh gurgles from the back of her throat. "She told me never to do that again. So now, we just hide in our bedrooms and let them get on with it. Or rather, that's what I used to do. Not my problem anymore." She stops and stares upwards. I follow her eyes to see a crescent moon peeping through dark clouds.

"Pretty."

"Yeah, in a creepy, vampire sort of way."

I chuckle, even though my chest feels heavy. Liddy has always been a good friend, always there for me. I put my arm through hers. She looks down at me, smiling. "Where are we going?"

"End of the jetty has a good sitting spot."

"'kay."

The boats bob up and down; water splashes onto the lower side of quay as they sway in their moorings and strain at their ropes. We pass a gleaming white yacht, large enough to hold at least twenty people. On the stern there's a tall flagpole. It's too dark to tell the design of the flag at the top, but the clanging noise, metal to metal, as it flaps back and forth in the wind, keeps pace with our steps. Next to the yacht is a dinghy with a small petrol engine, a couple of canoes, a rowing boat with oars and several speedboats. I wonder where the keys are kept to the speedboats and whether we could manage one. "You ever piloted a boat?"

"Nope."

As we reach the end of the jetty, Liddy raises her eyebrows, pointing at a couple of jet skis. "They look fun."

"They do."

I stare out at the dark waters between us and Lymington. Liddy watches me. I can feel it, almost sense her pulse, her thoughts, as she tries to figure out what's going on. Even the idea that we can't speak freely makes me feel trapped.

"Have you ever been on one?"

"Nope, you?"

"No, but they can't be that hard."

"Wonder who we ask."

A cool north wind blows through us, causing me to shiver. Liddy pulls the wrap up over my shoulders and I creep closer to her warmth. She's my personal hot water bottle.

"There must be a safe zone."

"What?" I turn my head sharply up, crashing into her chin.

"Ouch! You're making a habit of this."

"Sorry, Lid. You okay?"

She's rubbing her jaw. "Solid head you have there."

I grin and stare out at the dark sea again. "Safe zone, as in the barrier?"

"Yeah, wouldn't want to crash into it." She gives me a silent stare and points across the water to the land beyond. I know she's trying to tell me we couldn't get through the barrier. We don't know the coordinates, but she doesn't know that Tom can sense the vibrations and move through it without coordinates. If he can, then surely I can, too.

"You're freezing, Cam. We should go back."

"Just a minute." Closing my eyes, I focus on the sea – its sound, the waves beating against the shoreline. I try to build up a picture of the vibration and imagine stretching myself across the water, to feel the magnetic barrier. There has to be a way, but nothing happens.

Damn, I need to do this for my plan to work.

"They're probably watching us." Liddy's voice has a note of warning.

"What?"

"Cameras, I would think." She's looking over her shoulder. "We should go."

I follow her eyeline and notice the CCTV sticking out at the top of one of the lampposts. "Give me a sec."

Breathing deeply and closing my eyes, I place myself on my mountain perch and demand the world around me slows down. I know it's worked when I can no longer hear the crashing waves or the screeching seagulls, still active even though it's dark. Vicky can sense magnetic fields, can tell if a ship is coming too close.

I should be able to learn this.

"It takes practice." Tom's voice enters my head.

"Get out. I didn't give you permission."

"It isn't just CCTV. They're keeping a very close eye on you, Cam."

"Who? You? You're one of them."

"I'm the only one stopping them getting in your mind at the moment."

"But you said—"

"We call them mind hackers. M-Hacks, for short. Trained to bypass blocks."

"So, you're a hacker."

"I am, but you knew that."

"So, are you hacking me for them?"

"They did ask me to, yes."

"Get out."

"I didn't tell them anything and, since your first session with me, no one can get in your mind." He laughs. "They think your block is a dark cloud."

"I told Liddy that."

"I know, and I didn't tell them any different."

His words make me pause, but then I strain to push him away, imagining a huge wall of water in the valley between us. After a couple of seconds, he steps through.

"Impressive."

"Damn! So, that veil I built, could you have got through that too?"

"If I'd tried, but I didn't."

He's infuriating, and yet I still feel comforted when he's present.

I really need to get over this!

I become more abrupt, snapping out my responses. "Why now, then?"

"I just wanted to apologise for not telling you about your mum. I should have."

"You don't tell me much."

"What do you mean?"

"Your family. The Beresfords. You didn't tell me that, either."

"Ah, that's a long story, but something I would have told you, had you asked."

"Right. You've done your apologising bit. You can go now."

His humming vibration remains. "You won't learn fast enough."

"For what?"

"Getting through the barrier."

"Damn you." I want to curse worse. "Go on then, run away and tell your masters."

There's a silence between us, but I know he's still there.

"Look, I'm not going to let you run away and get yourself killed."

I can feel myself bristling. "You can't tell me what I can and can't do."

"Sorry, that's not what I meant. Being bonded complicates things."

"What?"

"We're connected. If you die, I suffer."

"Right, nice to know you think I'm gonna die." As flippant as I'm being, and as much as I think he deserves it, I also hate that he's probably right. The suffering thing is news to me, but I let it pass, for now. There's some emotion he's holding back, one I can't quite see. "How do I know you're not manipulating me? Maybe this is a trick."

"Can't lie in telepathy, remember."

"I don't know what's possible anymore. If a person can hack into a mind, change how a person thinks, how would I know you're telling the truth?"

"I'll show you proof of what I'm saying tomorrow, I promise. Just don't do anything rash until then."

"My mum—"

"Do you think she'd want you to risk your life?"

My thoughts are getting mixed up in his reasonableness. The burning energy to get away still smoulders, but his words make sense, and I hate him for that, too. "Look, just leave me for now. We can talk tomorrow."

And he's gone. Part of me feels sad, another part is glad to have my brain free of him. I am back in the noisy world. The freezing rain pelts down on my face, numbing my cheeks. I open my eyes. Liddy's pushing me to turn around.

"You were gone again."

"How did you know?"

"I can't feel you with me anymore."

I smile as we make our way back up the jetty, our shoulders hunched. "Perhaps you have talents of your own."

"No, just know you."

I stop and look up at Liddy through the rain, shaking my head. "I think we need to give them a chance to find my mum. If anyone can, they should be able to do it. Look how they got us out."

She stares, eyes wide, confused at what I'm saying. I nod rapidly, trying to get her to agree. Her mouth forms an 'O' shape.

"If that's what you think's best."

"I do, but no more secrets. I want access to the news."

"Good idea. Me, too."

"Let's go back and call Ruth."

"I've got hot chocolate in my room."

"Good. Let's get back."

The rain's soaked through the shawl, my hoodie and my jeans. I push the shawl off and begin jogging. Liddy's soon at my side, shouting something at me.

"Eh?"

"So, how does this mind thing work?"

"Processing or telepathy?"

"That and the telekinesis stuff, I guess." She stops and I turn around to look at her, pushing back my wet fringe. "Doesn't it scare you?"

Her question surprises me. "Haven't had much chance to think about it. Everything's changed, Lid."

"You're so accepting. I'd be freaking out."

"No, you wouldn't." We move forward again. "But you're right, I should be freaking out. Not sure why. Just seems right... A part of me."

"A part that wasn't you two weeks back."

"It was probably always there. I just didn't know it."

She goes quiet. It feels wrong. I grab her arm and look up into her eyes. She stares back.

"Do you think I've changed?"

"No, not in essentials."

I snort. "What's that? Blood, guts and brain?"

"It's a phrase I read somewhere. I mean, you're still you, but there's something about you that's different."

"Different how?"

"Dunno. Come on. Let's get inside." We begin walking again. "Maybe I just need time to get used to the idea of these witchy talents you have."

"You and me both."

As we approach the training building, Liddy squeezes my shoulder. "Can people read my mind?"

"Yes, but there are protocols to prevent it."

"Does that mean they won't?"

"Yes," I say, just in case people are listening, but I shake my head again.

She gasps and coughs, as if choking on a mouthful of rain. Her shoulders drop, her eyes look at me with fear. "Good. Wouldn't want people in my head."

I grasp her hand and squeeze, trying to comfort her. "Let's go, I'm freezing."

Liddy nods. "Home it is, then."

CHAPTER THIRTY-FOUR

It's midnight when I venture down the corridor. Liddy's bedroom is to my right, and I hesitate in front of it, listening, but I hear nothing. When the motion detector lights flicker on, I wince and stop for a second, but all is quiet, and no one jumps out at me.

Having spent the last two hours tossing and turning, going through all this stuff in my head, I need to actually do something. My plan is risky, but heck, at this point I don't care. Usually, I'd be dragging Liddy along and I almost feel like this is a betrayal, but it's better this way. I don't want to get her into trouble. Vicky, on the other hand, is a different matter.

Tapping on her door, I half hope she won't answer, but she does. I notice her light is still on, so at least I didn't wake her. She raises her eyebrows, her large eyes widening.

"What's up?"

I glance around, wondering if there are hidden cameras in the hallway. I don't see any, but who knows?

"Can I come in?"

"Sure." She opens the door, and I squeeze through. "So, not a midnight tryst, then?"

"Yeah, right! No." My hands feel so shaky, I place them on my hips, but she takes my stance as some sort of power play and steps back.

"Spit it out."

"You know my mum's been taken?"

"Yes, rumour does get around."

"Well, I'm going to the mission ops building to find out what's going on."

Her response is explosive. "What, now?"

"Yes."

"Middle of the night?"

"Yes."

She paces along the length of the room before sitting on the edge of the bed and staring up at me. I notice her pink pyjamas for the first time. Weird... she doesn't strike me as a pink person.

"And you're telling me, why?"

"You said you had a way of getting in." I'm trying to keep my voice low and calm, as if I'm in control, but my stomach feels as if I have a swarm of butterflies in it.

"I might, but nothing you could use."

Striding to the door, I reach for the handle. "Fine, you don't want to tell me, I'll get in on my own."

"Wait. No, I meant it's one of my talents. I can undo locks and things."

I turn and we both stare at each other, trying to decide whether we're making the right decision. The spurt of energy that got me here is fast dissolving and I already have doubts about trusting her, about the whole thing, really.

Perhaps I should just go back to my room?

"I'll come. I was going to wait a few days, but now's a good a time as any." She begins unbuttoning her pyjama top and I turn around to give her privacy.

I hear her tutting. "Nothing here you ain't seen already."

"What?"

"Well, I assume we're pretty much the same."

Crossing my arms, I lean against the wall, my back to her.

"So, your plan is what? Get in, look around, see if you can find anything?"

"That's about it."

She tuts. "Crappy plan, if you ask me. There are security cameras, you know, and it's highly likely most of the stuff you want is on a computer with passwords."

"Mm..." I slump and take a deep breath.

What was I thinking?

"What, you thought they'd conveniently leave their plans lying around for you to find?"

"I just want to know if they're telling the truth about searching for my mum. They said they were." She's moving around the room as I speak. "But they kept it from me... and wouldn't have told me at all."

Suddenly, she's next to me, thrusting something woollen into my hand. "Put this on," (it's a balaclava), "and these."

"Gloves?"

"Fingerprints."

My eyebrows raise as I pull the scratchy balaclava over my head. "You've thought this through."

"Well, at least one of us has." She opens the door, and we creep out. "Just follow my lead."

Once out of the training building, she scoots around the back and takes an indirect route that leads us to the rear of the playground and straight past the ops building. Only when we squat at the side of the admin building do I notice she has a mobile in her hand. It shows a green screen.

"You have a phone?" My whole face is sweating. I want to drag the balaclava off my head and take some deep breaths.

She shrugs. "You don't?"

"I thought..." A red dot flashes up on her phone. "What's that?"

"Lower your voice." She points to her screen. "This software detects security cameras. Come on, let's go. And stay down."

We double back and end up scuttling along the side of the ops building. We stop below a ground floor window.

"Although it's difficult to get on the island, their security lapses in some places." She's whispering. "The cameras have blind spots, and this window doesn't have a keypad lock, just a regular one, which I can manage."

"How do you know all this stuff?" I pull the balaclava away from my eyes, stretching the material wide. The gap allows me to take in a gulp of cold air that settles on my exposed face, cooling me down a little.

"I told you, before I commit to anything, I want to know what I'm getting into. You've got your reasons for doing this, I have mine. Whatever happens, we both get what we want."

I nod, though it's dark and she probably doesn't notice. Vicky's obviously a lot brighter than she makes out.

"Ready?"

"Yes."

She leans up and peers through the window before grasping the edge and gently pulling it outwards. I can't see what she did to get it open but am glad no alarm goes off. Once inside, she flips her phone around and switches on her torch. It's a small office with a couple of desks, computers and chairs, along with some shelves and books. At the far side is a door, which she heads to.

"Vicky, why don't we check here, first?"

"Let's just scout around. This isn't a main room, and we don't have much time."

She's already through the door, waving at me to follow, when I feel something, a presence. No, not a presence, but Tom. Tom's here, somewhere. Vicky's turning left, but I pull her shoulder.

"This way."

"What? Why?"

"There's something going on. I can feel it."

"How?"

"Shh!" My finger touches my lips as if I'm a schoolteacher. I close my eyes and focus until I sense our connection, almost like an invisible beam of light drawing me towards him. "First floor, about halfway down the corridor."

It only occurs to me then to put up my own barriers. I don't want Tom to find me sneaking around here, unless, of course, I just confront him.

"There are people in the building?" Her eyes widen.

"At least one I recognise."

"We should leave." She places her hand on my shoulder as if to turn me. I shove it off.

"You go. I'm going to see what's happening." This time, I take the lead as we creep up the stairwell.

Vicky grabs my arm at the first-floor corridor. "Cameras."

My heart's beating madly and I feel an urge to rip the balaclava off my head, as if it's the reason for my constricted breathing.

"Give me a sec," she whispers in my ear. Leaning around the corner, she taps something on her phone, before looking back. "Done."

"Done what?"

"Disabled the cameras." She's pointing to her phone. "A little hacking trick I learnt."

"It's that easy?" I'm almost impressed. "How did you learn to—"

"No time to talk now. Go, before someone comes."

She pushes me forwards before I can ask anything more. When we step out into the main corridor, the lights flicker on again. My heart beats hard in my chest and pounds in my ears as we lean against the inner wall, waiting to see if anyone comes to investigate. When no one appears, we dash down the corridor to an office with a wooden door.

I know Tom's in there and wonder if he can sense me close. There's no reason for him to reach out to me. After all, I'm supposed to be tucked up in bed, fast asleep, but he did say I made a lot of vibrational noise.

Vicky raises her shoulders and hands, as if to ask, 'what now?' I sigh and reach for the door handle, determined to find out what's going on. If we get found out, what can they do? Throw us off the island, manipulate our minds to forget? Would Tom allow that? I don't know for sure, but we're here now. Perhaps I could just stalk in and confront him, force him to show me proof of what they're doing to help my mum.

Opening a small gap in the doorway, just enough to peer through, I take a breath when I realise it's just an anterior reception room with a desk, chair and some shelving. A voice floats in from an open doorway. We slip in and scuttle over to the far wall, plonking ourselves down behind the desk. With my back against the wall, I pull up my legs and strain my ears to listen to the person talking.

"...late, but the weather prevented an earlier flight. Let's make this a quick update and get to bed. Jenny, what have we learnt?"

The woman's voice has an accent, one I think I should recognise but can't place. Jenny, I do know.

"We believe she may be in District Nine, though it's a wide area and we can't pinpoint the exact location. They must have some strong protections in place."

"Strong as in—"

"Yes, as in talents."

"Damn." I hear a thump on a table. There is another person with them. Her voice is quieter but just as forceful. "I knew they were moving fast, but how could we not have known about a new facility?"

I hear Jenny again. "Some of our operatives haven't reported in for a few weeks."

"Are we worried?"

"They are in very deep. It happens sometimes."

"And we fortified our security systems last month? Nothing could have been acquired?"

Jenny responds. "Ma'am, you know our entry tests have become more sophisticated, but it's still possible for people to find a way in, particularly those with talents. If we can plant people in their facilities, they could do the same here."

I hear someone moving around and imagine them burning tracks in the carpet, thinking about the possibility of infiltrators on the site. Vicky and I glance at each other. Her eyes are wide with fear, and I wonder if I look the same. The pulsing in my ears has gone crazy.

"And the newcomers?"

"Fully checked out."

"Okay, so we're no closer to finding Mrs Chadwick as of the last report, and we could easily have a breach we don't know about. Am I getting this right?"

Jenny's voice is subdued. "Yes, Ms Dante."

Vicky grabs my arm, and I understand why. One of the people inside must be a member of one of the founding families. The room goes silent again and I hold my breath, my whole body taut.

"And how's Cam reacting to all this?"

My heartbeat speeds up and prickly heat dots my forehead.

She knows I exist! Have I already been reported to a higher level?

Tom responds. "She had a bit of a meltdown when she learnt about her mother, but I think she's coping well, considering everything that's happened over the last week."

"Good."

I can just hear the tapping of nails on a wooden surface.

"Tom, we need a change of plan. I know you were not due to ship out for a while, but I want you and Cam gone. If we have a breach, the talents you both possess – and now this bond – put you and Cam in great danger." It's the one with the accent speaking again.

"What? No!"

My face heats up. I want to storm in and agree with Tom. I almost get up, but Vicky presses my shoulder as if to stop me moving. Her eyes warn me to stay still, to listen.

"Jenny, I'm redirecting your immediate efforts. You're to get Tom and Cam off the island. You have thirty-six hours to get them to Base Two. It must be top secret.

No one can know about it, absolutely no one."

"And Mrs Chadwick?"

"We'll deal with that once they're off the island. I want them on Base Two by Friday evening."

Tom interrupts. "Wait. Don't I get a say in this?"

"No, you don't."

"Cam won't leave. Not without seeing her mother first."

I feel some satisfaction in hearing Tom stick up for me, but my head is spinning. This 'somebody' thinks she can just do whatever she likes with me. I grit my teeth and pull my knees tight into my body. The Dante woman is speaking again.

"Cam doesn't understand what's going on. She doesn't know what she's capable of."

Jenny's question is abrupt. "And you do? What aren't you telling us, Tom?"

I wonder the same and wait for his answer, but the accented woman replies.

"Now's not the time for dialogue. We need to move. And if I know her mother, which I do, she'll want Cam taken to safety."

She knows my mum. How? From where?

Vicky's now gripping my shoulder. She must sense the urgency I have, the desperate need to charge in there and demand answers.

A chair scrapes back as if someone is standing abruptly. "Tom, you're a soldier and I'm your general chief of commissions. I expect your obedience in this matter, and I expect you to convince Cam to comply."

"Convince?" His voice is raised, hers is steely cold.

"I hear from Schultz that he couldn't manipulate her, perhaps you can persuade her."

"I'm not hacking her. Forget it!"

"Then convince her in any way you can. I won't lose her to the other side." She hesitates as if she's considering her next words. "It would be disastrous. Your bond is unique, something they'd want to test and use. What if it has the potential to turn the tide on this war, Tom? Have you thought about that?"

I glance at Vicky and wonder what she's thinking. Her eyes have narrowed, her body is tight. Nothing about an actual war has ever been mentioned. And as for using our bond to turn the tide... I just don't get it. I'm biting the inside of my cheek and only stop when I taste the oozing blood.

Dante is still talking. "Your bond's something we can't allow them to even know about." She breaks her lecture, as if waiting for everyone to agree.

"Sometimes hard decisions have to be made. That's why I'm in this position, and that's why I expect you both to carry out my orders. Now, let's get some rest. We all have a lot to do tomorrow."

"Yes, ma'am." I hear Tom storm out by a side door.

"Please make sure he follows orders, Officer Cooper."

Jenny responds, before exiting by the same door. "Of course."

When the two women are alone, I hear her sigh. Dante's voice softens. "Was it so hard to handle the young ones in your day, Julia?"

"My day?" The other woman is English. Her voice is frail. "So, you think my days are over?" There's a hint of joviality in her response.

"That's not want I meant."

"You have to remember these are different times. There's a balance between giving orders and ensuring everyone's on board. We can't afford for them to walk out. Not at this time."

"I know, but how much do we tell them?"

"The right time will come." I hear someone stand. "Now, how about this old lady goes to her bed. We still have an early morning."

She's mocking the Dante woman. There's a shared snickering and some quiet chatter as they leave and move down the hallway.

CHAPTER THIRTY-FIVE

Vicky and I sit there for a few minutes. What we've heard is crazy. My mind spirals with so many questions. I push the thoughts aside; I have bigger problems. They're delaying my mum's rescue to get me off the island. She could die. And Tom's right, I won't go. They can't force me to. But would they? Could they? Would Tom try to manipulate me to agree? His boss has given him direct orders. Part of me wants to believe he would side with me, but how long has he been here? Where do his loyalties really lie?

As we dash down the corridor and stairs, making as little noise as possible, I contemplate my next move. By the time we creep out of the window and back to our dorm, my body is trembling. With fear, yes, but also with anger, a torrent of emotions raging through me. Before I know it, I'm sitting on Vicky's bed, my knees jiggling. I don't even attempt to stop them. Instead, I jump up, unable to still the energy pouring through me.

It's as if fate drew me to the operations building tonight. It seems crazy and I don't believe in fate, but what else could it be? And then Tom comes to mind. Maybe he planted the idea in my head, maybe he wanted me there. I grunt and physically shake my head. I just don't know what to believe anymore.

"I'm sorry." Vicky's handing me a juice box.

"What are you sorry about?" My jaw is tight as I grind my teeth.

"Well, sorry you found out this way. They're just the same as DC – treating you as a commodity to use as they see fit."

She's right. All of them pretending to support me. I suck hard on the straw, crush the box and stamp over to the wastepaper basket to throw it in.

"What are you going to do?"

I stare at Vicky, her hair dishevelled from the balaclava. She seems so different to when I first met her.

"What would I like to do, or what can I do?"

"Both, I guess."

"I'd like to get off this island, go find my mum, rescue her and take us away from all this." I wave my arms around. "Whatever all 'this' is."

She doesn't respond immediately but rather peers at me pounding the carpet as I march back and forth. I halt and look at her, waiting for whatever it is she's contemplating.

"I think you're right. Something's going on that we don't know about. They talk about the Diversity Commission creating an army of talented people, but how is the League any different? Sounds to me as if they're doing the same. What is this war they're not telling us about? And then there's your bond. What do they want to use it for? And Tom – he didn't even get a say in what happens to him."

I walk over to the window and pull the blinds to one side. It's pitch-black outside. My hot breath forms a cloud of mist on the dark pane.

"Do you know where District Nine is?" A crazy plan is beginning to form in my brain.

"Yes."

"Tom can get off this island, y'know. There are coordinates, but he can sense the corridors."

She comes to stand next to me. "You can't trust he won't tell them."

I feel my face holding a frown. My shoulders slump. Vicky's so close, I can feel the heat emanating from her body. I know she's assessing something.

"Okay, fine."

I step back, away from her direct eyeline. "Okay, fine what?"

"I'll do it."

"Do what?"

"Get you off the island and through the corridors. I sensed it coming in. I'm good at pulling and pushing vibrations away, particularly anything magnetic. I'm sure I can find my way through."

My mouth drops open as I register her words. I don't know what to say. This is moving too quickly.

Can I really do this? Am I strong enough?

"Once I get you to District Nine, you're on your own, though. I'm heading north. Getting away from all of this." She sits in her armchair and stares at the opposite wall.

"You have a place to go?" My voice lilts a little in surprise.

"Not really, but I've heard of a place. I'm going to try to find it."

"But—"

"But what? Are you in or not? I'm going, anyway. I heard enough tonight to know I don't want to be on this team."

"I can't bear the thought my mum will die because of me."

"Even though you may be walking into a trap. You do know that don't you?"

She's right, of course. My mum wouldn't want me to do this, but what if she died before the League got to her? Now I know she's not their priority, things have changed.

"Maybe I could negotiate my life for hers. You know them. Would they do that, if they want me so badly?"

"Possibly, but your mother may be dying. Are you sure you want to do this?"

I wince, tears threaten to fall, and I turn away, blinking rapidly. Walking into a trap, giving up my life for my mum's – it's madness and terrifying at the same time.

I picture her in the middle of the road wearing her purple suit. A bus is coming up behind her, but she hasn't noticed. I see myself on the curb. Would I jump out and push her away, risking my own demise? The response is immediate and certain: of course I would. Then, how is this any different? It's so different. In a million ways. But the bus image brings a strange feeling of calm. It drifts through my body and soothes my fears, the earlier panic subsiding. I straighten my shoulders.

Decision made, I nod. "Yes."

"Okay. Meet me tomorrow at midnight on the jetty. I'll figure something out. Tell no one."

Liddy comes to mind. It's as if she reads my thoughts.

"If Liddy wants to come, that's up to her, but no one else. And remember, they can read your thoughts here. Keep your barrier up."

"Right."

How am I going to keep Tom out?

"And go to classes tomorrow. Behave normally."

"My normal would be going crazy with worry."

"You're right. Do that, then. Ask for information, whatever, but follow the schedule and do everything as expected."

"Okay, but how will we—"

"Let me worry about the details. Just be there, or I'm going without you."

Exhausted, I lie on my bed, staring into space, my mind racing. I suddenly realise Vicky was talking about 'keeping barriers up'. Yesterday, she said she was unable to use telepathy. I roll over. Maybe it's something Sally has been teaching her?

Closing my eyes, I know only one thing for certain: this time tomorrow, I'll either have made it to the mainland or I'll be on a plane under this Dante woman's orders. They said I had a choice. They lied. They said they would protect my mum, that they would find her. They have failed. And now they talk about a war and using our talents – something I know nothing about and haven't agreed to. One thing is for certain: I can't trust any of them. Liddy was right – it's just her and me.

CHAPTER THIRTY-SIX

This morning's schedule flashed by in a daze luckily, otherwise I would have been jumpy about the escape. Not about what happens after – that I'm resigned to – but more about getting caught before I even have a chance to see my mum.

The swimming was even worse than I expected. The chlorine burnt my eyes and nose, the humidity left me struggling to breathe and my slow crawl earned me last place. Taor, with his long arms and legs, casually floated on his back next to me, cheering me on as if I were a seven-year-old in a beginner's class. I tried to splash his face but lost my rhythm and swallowed half the pool before he dragged me up.

"You okay?" His face sported a huge grin.

Gulping and nodding, I waved him off.

After humiliating myself in the pool, I then went on to do the same at the track. Well, it wasn't a track, as such, more like a circular path around the island. Not even the crisp sea breeze could stop me sweating and lagging behind. As if that wasn't enough, we then spent twenty minutes in the gym. By the time we went to breakfast, my legs were trembling, and I was glad to slump into a chair, forehead resting on one of the metal tables. The only good thing about it was that it stopped me thinking about what might happen after I found my mum.

"Come on, Cam. Get something to eat."

Liddy's sitting opposite me, tucking into a bacon bun. The greasy smell makes me want to puke. Lifting my head, shaking my protein cup, I watch Vicky, Jon and Taor approach with trays of food. Vicky doesn't even glance at me. Jon plonks himself to my left.

"Green gunge for you, then?" He'd gone for the full English, Taor for egg and beans on toast, and Vicky has some yoghurt/fruit concoction. I sip the protein for the first time and gag, covering my mouth. Taor frowns sympathetically.

"That bad?"

"Think lumpy wallpaper paste with seaweed blobs."

"Ew!"

Tom's voice enters my head, startling me. "Your guard's down."

"What?"

"Back on your mountain."

"How long?"

"A few seconds."

"You're keeping tabs on me?"

That's worrying.

"A link, yes. Just keeping you safe."

"Safe from what?"

"Gotta go. Later."

"Wait. What about my mum?"

"Nothing new. Same news item rolling over."

I did my best, asking questions he'd expect, pretending I didn't know their real plan, but I feel as though I've swallowed a heavy stone. It's not just my mum, but also the fact he's lying to me, that he's willing to obey their commands; kidnap me against my will. My chest aches. I know I haven't known him long, but I feel betrayed.

Tom appears again. "Keep a lid on your emotions. People can get in."

"But who would want to get in?"

"Oh, and don't sip. Drink it back in one go."

"What?"

"The protein. You'll get used to it."

Tom's caution worries me further. I can't tell if he's protecting me from them or preparing me for something worse. Shifting, I lean to look over Liddy's head. The canteen has around twenty people, most of them under thirty, although one man with a group of four around him looks older – like a teacher, surrounded by students. Tom's nowhere to be seen.

Liddy waves her hand in front of my face. "With us?"

"Yeah… Just not used to morning exercise."

"You're not used to any exercise."

I stick my tongue out in response, only to have all of them make disgusted noises back at me. "What?"

"Green tongue."

"She's gone mouldy!"

I grin and shake my head before lifting the lid off the shaker, taking a deep breath and slugging the gloopy liquid back. It sticks to my throat and lands in my stomach like heavy, uncooked dough, but it's gone. I slam the cup down and wipe my mouth across my sleeve, as if I've been in some sort of drinking competition. The four of them stare at me in wide-eyed silence until Liddy claps and whoops. They all laugh, and I grin back. For a second, it's almost like they're my friends. Well, Liddy is, but the others I hardly know.

Vicky changes the subject. "So, Taor's the swimmer, Jon's the runner, and Liddy can lift weights for me anytime." She leans in, blowing Liddy a kiss. Liddy pretend catches it and scrunches it up in a ball and lobs it across her shoulder. Vicky grins, flicking back her spiral hair. "Hey, I have hope for you yet."

"Yeah, well, you heard that story about hope falling off a cliff and drowning?"

"Ouch! You sure you don't want to grab a coffee later? I'll pay."

I don't get why Vicky's behaving like this with Liddy. There's no reason. My fingers begin tapping on the tabletop. Vicky glances at me, her eyebrows rising. It's almost as if I can hear her saying, 'play the game'.

Liddy looks at me, a white glow emanating from her like a halo. "Sorry, can't do. Already got a date. Promised Cam I'd help her with a new wardrobe. She can't go around in the same jeans and hoodie for the rest of her life, especially now she has that green gunk all over her sleeve."

Taor jumps in. "Can I tag along? I need clothes, too."

"Sure, we're going about 4:00 p.m."

I decide I like Taor. Liddy glances at me, frowning. On swallowing his last mouthful, Jon looks up.

"I've not got much to do. Where we meeting?"

Liddy's right, he's a different person. After what I learnt last night, I totally believe someone has done something to him.

Jon raises his water bottle as if cheering some celebration. "Class outing it is, then."

I shrug and sigh. "Fine, but clothes shopping will be a boring, ten-minute thing. After that, I'm on the coffee."

Liddy stands. "First class, soon." Her face is blank, but I can read her thoughts as if I'm entering her mind. *This was supposed to be just us.* My lips form a thin line, and I nod.

It doesn't really matter. I'll be out of here soon.

She gasps as if something has hit her.

"You okay?"

"Yeah, yeah" – she picks up her plate – "sharp pain in my head, that's all."

Liddy's eyes narrow and I realise, somehow, I managed to plant the thought in her head. We're staring at each other as if we are boxers in a ring.

Her voice is low and strained. "We need to talk, bestie. Soon as."

"Er, okay."

Tom pops into my head again. "You need to put that waterfall thing up again. Someone's prodding your barrier."

"Who?"

"Trying to locate the vibration now, but you're safe. Just a precaution."

Immediately, I picture myself on my mountain. Producing the wall of water is easy. In the distance, I see a dark, shadowy figure and gulp. It jumps a bit closer, shimmering like a ghostly spirit, but I can't tell who it is. I almost yelp out loud.

Tom's still with me. "You know that old song *Ten Green Bottles*?"

"Er, yes?"

"Start humming it."

"Why?"

"To keep your brain busy and others out."

"Right."

"Got to focus on other stuff right now. See you at training."

As soon as I'm back in the real world, I begin humming the tune.

Liddy's frowning and rubbing the side of her head, but grins at me and begins singing the end of the line: "*Standing on the wall.*"

As we walk out of the canteen, Taor joins in. "*Ten green bottles standing on the wall, and if one green bottle—*"

Vicky gives me a sideways, questioning look, but then groans. "That'll be stuck in my head all day, now."

Jon tuts. "Kids!"

But Liddy and Jon stick their faces in front of each other, competing for the next line.

"*Should accidently fall, there'll be—*"

"*Nine green bottles—*"

"*Standing on the wall!*"

Liddy's gone into full 'composer' mode, waving her hands as if conducting an orchestra. By the time we reach our first class, we're all giggling and singing along, except Jon, who's lagging behind, pretending he doesn't know us.

CHAPTER THIRTY-SEVEN

Tom's standing at the entrance of the building we trained in yesterday. A warm, July sun glows off the white block walls. He's wearing khaki trousers and a navy T-shirt and has a canvas bag slung across his back. All thoughts of escape temporarily slip my mind as I notice his biceps and then his eyes – hazel, almost transparent in the bright sunlight. I want to reach out and stroke his dark hair and follow his high cheekbones with the tips of my fingers.

The thought makes me shiver until I hear him chuckle. His eyebrow raises, and I know he totally heard what I was thinking. Embarrassed, I stamp my foot and fold my arms. Curbing my yearning has to be a priority. It's not even real, just some sort of freaky DNA thing.

Looking away, I gaze at the sea glinting as waves lap towards the shoreline and remember I don't have to worry about it much longer.

"You're on time." I'm glad he's changed the subject.

"Why wouldn't I be?" My response is defensive but betrays the turmoil of my emotions. As he flashes his wrist across the security pad and opens the door, I hear his warning in my head:

"We have Watchers."

"What?" I don't know why I'm surprised, but I hesitate too long.

"Tired? Worried about your mum?" He's speaking aloud again, so I know this is for the benefit of people listening in.

"Yeah, didn't get much sleep."

"They're doing their best."

"I know. Anything on the news?"

"Nothing different to yesterday." He gently pushes me forward. A tingling sensation rushes down my arm, and he pulls back sharply.

"What's that?"

"Just our connection making itself known." He's joking, but there's a seriousness there as well.

"Will it always be like this?" I want to ask whether we will ever be able to touch each other or rather, whether I will ever be able to touch him. I sense his awkwardness as he grabs a couple of bottles of water from a small fridge in the corridor and throws one to me.

"The bond with Ivy – my trainer – wasn't like ours but, at the beginning, there were a few sparks. Mostly me, my emotions getting the better of me."

I remember his restraint after the first night we met. It seems like ages ago. "Is it painful if I'm out of control?"

"Can be."

We enter the same room as before and I stroll over to my place on the opposite wall and sit, my legs crossed.

Where's my straitjacket?

He chuckles. "Think of the padded walls as protection against hackers."

"Maybe we should just stay in here, then."

"I won't let that happen to you, Cam." He sounds sincere and I want to believe him, but after last night I know I can't trust him.

"And when Ivy died, did you feel it?" I change the subject, trying to keep our conversation on topics that won't alert him to anything.

Tom sits, his legs bent. He flicks a speck of something off his shoulder. "It felt as if my body was being ripped apart." He rubs his hand across his face, shadowing his eyes. "At the time, no one knew what was wrong. I was hospitalised and medicated. Later, when we found out about her death, they figured it out."

"So, the bond is dangerous?"

"Honestly, Cam, I don't know. A strong DNA bond is rare and not much is known about it. We're good subjects for research at the moment." He's annoyed, but not at me.

"Is there something you're not telling me?" I have to give him a chance to come clean.

He glances to the side and bites the corner of his lip. "Look, let's practice."

I nod, disappointed. His soft, melodic vibration seeks permission, and we move into telepathy.

"Now you're asking me?"

"I'm following protocol."

"And before?"

"Well, I only jump in if I think you're in danger."

"Am I in danger?"

"We're all in danger, Cam."

As it seems that's all he's going to say, another thought crosses my mind. "Are there any cameras in here?"

"Yes. Lefthand corner."

Automatically, I turn my head. "Thought it was supposed to be secure."

"Don't look."

"Why, what difference does it make?"

"I'd rather let them think I don't know."

He's off today. Not so gung-ho about the League. I want to tell him I understand what's going on, that he can trust me, but can I trust him? Where would his loyalties lie?

"Fine. So, what am I learning today?"

"Let's start with where. Back in your bedroom?"

"Sure."

This time it's almost instantaneous. I'm sitting on the floor, my back against the foot of my bed. Tom's at the door, as usual.

"I want to show you how to tell if people are lying, how to shroud thoughts and to do a massive knowledge dump."

"Sounds good."

Shrouding my thoughts is perfect.

He's uncomfortable. I've always been able to sense when people have inner turmoil, but this is different. Our bond allows me to feel a deeper connection, especially in this linked-mind state. It's as if his aura has changed colour with his mood, or maybe it's my mood and the fact that I know about last night. Maybe it's just the fact that he has to hide his orders from that Dante woman. I wonder if he can see anything strange in my behaviour. I decide to hit it straight on.

"You're odd today. What's going on?"

"I have news."

"What?"

"There's a plan to ship us out, tomorrow. A decision made last night. Someone high up has given the order."

At least he's trying to be honest!

"What? They can't do that. My mum comes first." For a second, my reaction is honest, as if I didn't already know this, but then it comes tumbling back and my stomach sinks. I don't want to play this game with him.

He smiles, a thin-lipped thing that doesn't reach his eyes. "I told them you'd say that, but I have no sway in these decisions."

The room darkens and I notice rain clouds building up outside. There's a crack of lightning, followed by thunder. The corner of his mouth twitches as he responds to my querying frown.

"You're externalising your anger, projecting the storms in your mind."

"Right." I refocus, trying not to let my emotions get the better of me. I don't want him to know I already know what's going on.

"Thought you were an expert M-Hack? You can read their minds. Find out what's going on."

"I can, but information can still be shrouded."

"They can't force me to go anywhere I don't want to."

He sighs and looks away. "They could."

"What does that mean?"

"Subtle coercion. You'd never even know it was happening."

"You mean mind control."

He sighs and nods.

"Have they used it on me?"

"No, not yet."

"How do you know?"

"Our link... I would know."

I wonder again if he already knows about tonight's plan. Would he tell them? Stop me?

"And what if they ordered you to use it on me, would you?"

He frowns, irritated by my question. "No, Cam, I wouldn't. You can trust me."

I want to. "I thought they believed in equality and freedom."

"They do." He is having a hard time justifying his mentors and bosses. "They aren't the enemy. It's just, sometimes things are done to achieve an end result."

"My history's not that great, but surely that's how the last war started." I get up and walk over to my desk. It seems so real, even though I know this is all in my head.

On the wall is the framed photo of me, my mum and aunt. In reality, that picture is now in my backpack, but my mind likes to see it on the wall. I turn to face him.

He changes the topic. "Let's go into processing mode."

I nod, returning to my bed and sitting in my self-assigned place in this imaginary headspace. The thudding in my ears gets louder, a slow panic at what I must do to allow Tom to dump information in my brain without him knowing what Vicky and I have planned. Taking a deep breath, I bend my legs, rest my forehead on my knees, encircle my legs with my arms and hold on tight, as I try to calm my fears. The world around me stops.

CHAPTER THIRTY-EIGHT

I feel the numbness first, a tightening on the left side of my brain and then a flash of coal-black, before streaks of light dart into my head, like bursts of multicoloured lightning shattering a night sky. The first hit is like a pinprick, barely breaking the skin, but by the tenth, the pain is excruciating, as if someone is jabbing a sharp knife into my skull over and over.

At the same time, I have a sense of Tom's presence softly stroking my pain after each jab, giving me a sadistic sense of comfort before injecting another piece of knowledge into my firing neurons. I become lost in a rollercoaster of pain and pleasure, fearing the agony and welcoming the loving reassurance. I lose all sense of time, motion and space – of where I am or what is happening. My universe narrows to the forces ruling my mind, until one word jolts me awake:

"Enough."

Steamy hot breath dampens my face, the floor is hard, my back stiff. An arm rests across my shoulders, a body leans in. At first, I think it's Liddy, but then his voice enters my mind.

"You okay?"

I lift my head to meet his weary, concerned eyes. The white walls tell me we're back in the real world.

"It hurt, I know, but the pain will pass." He rubs my shoulder, as if soothing the pain. "You were excellent, by the way. No fighting back, at all."

I go for a smile but can only manage thinly stretched lips. Glancing at the camera, I use telepathy. "Is that a good thing?"

"It is for me." He grins and, suddenly aware of how close we are, slithers to the side of me and leans against the wall.

"Thought it was dangerous for us to touch."

"Not when I'm controlling your brain."

"Oh!" I hadn't thought of it like that and wasn't sure I'd agreed to brain control.

"Don't worry, you have full control back and I didn't go snooping around."

Stretching out my legs, I stare at him over my shoulder, wondering if that's true. I don't want to have such doubts about him, but Liddy's right – I'd never know. He's too good at this stuff. He has years of training and experience; he could have already manipulated me.

I choose to speak, rather than use telepathy. His eyebrows raise in acknowledgement, but he says nothing. "What did you put in there and how do I use it?"

"You don't, until I show you how." I'm about to ask him what he means when he holds up his hand. "Which I will do now, if you are ready for it?"

"Give me a minute." I reach for the water and glug huge gulps, emptying half the bottle. "How long were we in there for?"

"About thirty minutes."

I nod, leaning my head against the wall and closing my sleepy eyes. "Not sure which is worse, the tiredness or hunger."

I hear him crawl over the floor to his bag, get something out and scoot back. "Eat this."

He has some sort of protein chocolate bar in his hand, and I reach out, my arm feeling like a dead weight, but instead of passing it to me, he rips off the top and shoves it towards my mouth, tapping my lips to open, like spoon-feeding a baby. I snort and grab the bar, stuffing a third in my mouth. My saliva glands work in overdrive as the salty sweetness fills my senses and my body craves the food.

Note to self: buy some of these bars.

After a couple more and another bottle of water, I'm revived enough to pay attention.

"Lying."

Is he asking me if I'm lying?

His face is neutral, no accusation.

"Okay, what about it?"

"One of the pieces of knowledge I dumped, so I'm going to show you how to use it."

"Right."

"This has no real telepathy involved, it's all about sensing changing vibrations." He narrows his eyes, waiting for my agreement.

"Okay."

"I'm going to tell you a story. Listen to my words but hear the vibration beyond what I'm saying."

I nod, sensing him breathing deeply. Tom guides me to listen to his vibration. I recognise his normal melodic purring, and then he opens his mouth.

"My grandfather was fantastic. I loved him. We used to do lots of stuff together."

While speaking, his vibration changes. Static makes it jump around, like an old-fashioned radio unable to hold onto a channel.

"What happened with your grandfather?"

"You heard it. The vibration?"

"Yes, it was wrong. Like static."

"Exactly. That's how you know someone's lying."

"As simple as that?"

"Normal people can sense a lie, but we feel the vibration."

"Odd."

I'm intrigued and feel my face flush with heat, wondering again if he can sense anything different in me.

"You'll get used to it."

"So, you didn't love your grandfather?"

He goes back into telepathy, but we remain in the padded room instead of moving into my imaginary safe place.

"Not particularly. My grandfather denounced our family, our heritage, and taught his children, including my father, to follow him. They work for the Diversity Commission, helping them to capture and experiment on people like us."

I can hear his heart beating faster.

"My father tested my brothers and I at a young age – it's tradition in my family. They don't expect anything to be wrong, so when my test was faulty, he and my mother argued about what to do with me."

I see a flash of memory in his mind. He's hiding by an office doorway. Two people inside are shouting, the woman leaning across a desk, anger contorting her face.

Tom quickly shuts down the image. "I believed I was an abomination, an embarrassment to my family, and so handed myself over to the closest clinic when I was twelve."

"What?"

"OK, enough of my dismal history."

His head hangs low and he flicks an imaginary fleck off his jeans. Sighing, he reaches for his water and spends a moment collecting himself. I watch as he drinks the full bottle before squashing the plastic between two hands and throwing it in the corner.

Something occurs to me. "Oh, that's your link to the Beresford's, then?"

"Yes, one of my great, great grandfathers was the original founder of this base. Julia, his daughter, still plays a role here, although she's really old."

I remember the name from the previous night and suddenly things are clicking into place. "But surely that means DC know what's happening here and about the League?"

"No, my side of the family haven't been here for years. The island was a sanctuary when my grandfather visited the island last, but he thought his brother's claims about gene evolution were crazy and so he never became involved in the research or the expansion of the League."

"Right." I pull my hair back from my neck and tie it with the band on my wrist. He changes the subject again.

"Do you want to learn about shrouding today, or should we leave it till tomorrow?"

As I don't intend to be here tomorrow, I figure I should learn as much as possible in case I need it. "I'm fine. What's shrouding?"

"Shrouding is about hiding thoughts so hackers can't find information."

That definitely sounds like something I should know.

He watches me, his eyes intent, his body now still. "It's a good thing to learn this early on, for your own sake and mine." He pushes his fringe back, takes a deep breath and closes his eyes. "Think of something."

Vicky jumps into my mind. I push it down and bring up the TV clip of my mum. I visualise her on the bed, wires and tubes attached to her. I can't help the tears. A sadness crosses his face, but quickly he focuses.

"Close your eyes. I'm going to allow you to enter my mind and see what I see, but let me guide you. No sudden moves."

I place my head on my knees just as an image appears in my mind. I know he's placed it there. There's a plank of wood over a brook, water spills over it. Tom stands on the other side of the bank and beckons me across, his hand held high. Behind him is a wooded area with tall, green trees, the sun sparkling through the top branches. I wonder if this is a real place from his past.

"Are you sure? What if I hurt you?"

"You won't."

I step cautiously until I'm close enough for him to grab my hand. Gently pulling me the rest of the way, he then grasps my shoulders and turns me around. I expect to see a riverbank, but instead, I see me – or at least I see me as he sees me. It's oddly disorientating.

"Stay calm. This will be quick."

I feel us flying forward, and suddenly we're both in my mind. It's like looking at myself from outside-in or watching a movie on a screen. My own thoughts are on pause, and I watch as Tom wraps a large, black woolly blanket around the thought of my mum on that bed. The area in my brain becomes nothing, just a blank space, as if the thought doesn't exist. Seeing both what's in my head and what's in his head makes me physically sway, vertigo rushing up through my body. I boomerang back to myself and lurch forward.

"Whoa!"

He's at my side again. "It'll pass and you'll learn how to cope with it." He gives me a few minutes before offering water. "Did you see it?"

"The blanket?" I sip at my almost empty bottle.

"Remember, the way this works is to use familiar images that the mind already understands and can react to. The blanket's my image. Use that, if you want, or find one for yourself."

I nod. "Does it stay there for ever?"

"Unless you consciously boost it and keep the image intact, it will gradually dissolve over a few hours. Our minds can't cope with shrouds for too long. The effort to keep the mental shroud up saps your energy, particularly when you're new to it."

"Can you shroud other peoples' thoughts? Hide things from them or from other hackers?"

"You can – or rather, I can – but we would need to be very careful." His words are a warning. "Even though the knowledge is in your head, practice is important. Think of it as forging new pathways between your neurons. The more you practice, the easier it becomes."

"Like learning to walk."

"I'll let you try it on me first. After all the pain I've caused you today, I think I can take a little from you."

After several attempts, during some of which I had to back off at his screeching, I somehow get the hang of throwing a blanket over his thoughts without harming him – although my blanket is more like a tent – and in the end I imagine it with ropes and pegs.

"You're doing well. Now, take the shroud away."

"How?"

"Imagine pulling it off."

I tug at the tent, but it bounces back. Eventually, I run around the tent, pulling at the ropes. The tent pegs pop out of the ground. Finally, I heave the canvas away. By the time I've finished, I'm breathing heavily, as if I've really done it. "Taking it away was harder than I thought it would be."

He chuckles.

"What?"

"It's all in your head, you know. But still, our brains believe what they see. Your tent image was great, very secure. It's just that in this process, it's harder to get rid of."

"Note to self: don't use a tent. Okay, so how much more did you download?"

"Energy manipulation, recognising vibrational tuning and mind hacking. Some of it will be instinctive, I think. You learn very quickly, faster than I ever did, but we'll need to keep up the practice."

I decide, after all the shared brain work, now is the time to test his honesty and whether I can trust him. "Tell me the truth, Tom. Have they been looking for her?"

He looks up, knowing what I'm asking. His eyes cloud over, and his chest rises as he takes a deep breath before responding. "They have, but she's been put in a clinic they don't know about, and the Commission have strong protections in place."

My body goes stiff as I push away the bubbling doubt and fear. I'm not even going to think about what it will take to get my mum free. A bargain of some sort? One life for another? I'm hoping the trade-off will be enough. They don't need her. It's me who's the odd one, the Apex.

"You don't have to be afraid, Cam."

"What?"

"I'm just saying. I won't let anything happen to you."

I don't know what to say. He's being so kind, and I'm lying to him. That's when

I notice a shimmering, silver light between us. It surrounds our bodies and glimmers as it slinks back and forth, connecting and reconnecting.

He chuckles at what I can only assume is the shocked look on my face.

"Spotted it, then."

"What is it?"

"It's been there since the first night. The more we share, the more connected we become."

"I'm..." The words don't form. 'Surprised' doesn't cover it. To see our connection is otherworldly, alien. A few days ago, I wanted nothing more than to be closer to him, but this is so intimate. I refocus and stare at him, trying to ignore the silver light. He's smiling, a look that shows both sympathy and understanding.

"Intense, I know."

"Part of me still can't believe it's all real, even though I can see it." I fiddle with my fingers, looking down. "Just a couple of weeks ago, none of this existed." I whisper my next words: "Maybe I'm in an asylum, imagining it all."

"Yeah? And who am I then, in this plot of yours?"

I shrug, cocking my head to one side. "A dark and dangerous doctor, who's operating on my brain to bring me back to sanity."

He grins. "If only it were that simple."

"Who are we, Tom? This isn't—" I stop short of saying 'human', but he hears it anyway.

"No, it's not the usual 'human', but we still have bodies and organs and minds. More in common with them, than not."

The *them* and *us* is hard to accept, but I'm starting to believe it's true and beginning to wonder what *they*, out there, want – the League leaders as well as the Diversity Commission.

Both talk about genes being key to survival and both want people with DNA differentiation, but where does that place people like Tom and me? Foot soldiers to battle for one side or the other? To give one side the power to make the decisions, to control people without their consent? No one should have that amount of power. Every cell in my body tingles as I reject the thought of being used by anyone to achieve such an end goal. DRL rescued us, yes, but after hearing Dante last night handing out orders – deciding who dies and who's saved, without their knowledge – I begin to wonder if the League is really any different to the DC.

Maybe I should run and hide, like Vicky. She has a point when she says we need to stick together. The light between Tom and me is still visible. It distracts my dismal, confusing thoughts.

"Why can I see it now?"

"Partially intuitive, but a lot to do with the knowledge dump and the training we just did."

"Have you always seen it?"

"Yes."

"You and Ivy?"

"Barely visible. A few silver dots when we trained together."

"Oh." I'm stupidly happy about that, especially with what's about to kick off. By tomorrow, I'll be gone. "Can other people see it?"

"Some can sense it. Those talented in emotional vibrations." He frowns, hesitating, not sure whether he can speak freely. He casually glances up at the camera and then slips into telepathy.

"They think there's a breach, and that's why they want us away from here. If we have an infiltrator able to see our connection, they'll report it back. We could be very useful to the Commission, and also very deadly. I learnt that the hard way."

I don't know how to respond. Nothing he's said today has been a lie. He must take my silence as something else and tries to reassure me.

"You're coping so well and learning fast. Some don't. If you do get scared, if other things start to happen that are beyond your control, I'll help. You know that don't you? You know how to find me."

I can't tell what he knows. With our connection, I ought to be able to, but with trying to hide my own thoughts, nothing is clear. I wouldn't even know if he's already seen the plan. "Yeah, just scream Tom in my head and there you are."

We go quiet for a second, before he jumps up, a little awkward, hands on his hips.

"So, there's nothing you need to tell me?"

"Er, no?"

Is he being too casual or is it my paranoia? I feel totally guilty, as if I'm betraying him. My face flushes and I look down. There's no way he doesn't spot it, but he says nothing.

"Don't you have clothes shopping?"

"Oh, God, what time is it?"

He walks over and stretches out his arm, pulling me up. The tingling in our fingers delights and terrifies me at the same time. I want the feeling, want to be close, but know it can never be. I sigh, feeling silly all over again as the real world comes bouncing back.

"It's 3:30 p.m."

"Right, gotta go."

"Me, too. Need to catch up with Amy." He sighs.

"Something wrong?"

"She's not too happy with our link."

"Right." I try to act the 'concerned friend'. "Well, I hope you sort it out."

He grins, his eyes narrowing. "You're awful at shrouding your thoughts from me, you know. And I can spot a lie from a mile away."

I stare up at him, only just able to meet his eyes.

"Come on *trainee*, let's go."

As we separate, I can't help wondering how much he knows; how much he isn't saying. And if he does know, will I turn up at the jetty to find security there to take us back? I mentally slap myself. I should have said I was sick and cancelled the session.

Why didn't I think of that before?

Turning around, I watch the silver light between us stretch as he walks in the opposite direction. It's like a sparkly elastic band or stretchy chewing gum – a bit like a swirling umbilical cord I can see through. Tom looks over his shoulder, his voice in my head.

"Stop concentrating on it and it will disappear."

"But it's still there, right?"

"Always."

"And how far does it stretch?"

"At least across the length of the island, maybe further."

"What if we were in different countries?"

"To be honest, I don't know."

"It's weird and—"

He finishes my thought. "Amazing? See you later." He strides towards his accommodation block, the silver glow tailing him. A sadness creeps through me. This may be the last time we see each other. A spasm hits my gut, as if my body is resisting the whole idea of our looming separation.

My mum comes first!

I mentally slap myself and turn sharply. There's stuff Liddy needs to know.

CHAPTER THIRTY-NINE

"There's something I need to tell you, Lid."

"I'm here for you, you know that."

We're in her bedroom. It smells of something floral, the leftovers of a body spray or shampoo. Her shawl is laid across the back of an armchair, her make-up neatly placed in front of a hanging mirror with a small shelf under it. Other than a few schoolbooks on the desk, nothing is out of place. Even her bed has been made. She's always liked things neat.

"Is it to do with your mum?" Her mouth forms into a thin, downward line.

"They haven't found her yet. Still looking." I grab her hand and pull her to sit next to me on the bed. She has tied her dark hair in two short French plaits. One of the bands is loose. I tighten it, sighing.

"What's going on?" Concerned blue eyes meet mine.

"Do you trust me, Lid?"

"Course I do."

I nod and lift my hand, touching my forehead and then hers, not sure if she will understand. Her eyes widen and she jumps up. Aware people may be listening, I continue speaking aloud.

"They've arranged for Tom and me to leave the island. They think we're in danger here."

She spins around. "What? Why? When?"

"Tomorrow." I shake my head, desperate to make her understand. "It'll be okay, I think."

Her eyes are wide again, the pupils enlarged. "What about me?"

"You stay here. You can make a life here, Lid. Be yourself." Again, I shake my head and touch my forehead, before placing my hand on her forehead. This time she nods, and I take a deep breath. Closing my eyes, I tentatively reach out with my mind. I don't want to pry; I just want to deliver a message that no one else can hear.

She gasps as I project an image of blankets placed over chairs with us both underneath. It's a picture from when we were kids, playing tents. I'm aware she's squeezing my hand, but I focus entirely on what I'm doing. I don't want to hurt her, and I'd never even think of doing this if I wasn't desperate.

When I'm sure our tent is secure, I tell her the escape plan as fast as I can. She can't answer back, so it takes less than thirty seconds. Besides which, I can't afford to stay very long in her head. Once the shroud is secure, I leave and open my eyes. We sit there, staring, her narrowed eyes and frown mimic mine.

Is she okay?

I touch her cheek.

I'm sorry.

She nods and stands up, striding to the door before turning around.

"What's with all this hugging and crying? You think you can get rid of me that easily? We'll see each other again. Hell, I'll swim to wherever you are, if I have to."

My brow puckers in confusion.

She shakes her head, points to her bag and mouths, "I'm coming."

I try to keep up the façade. "It's just, we promised to do this together." Shaking my head, I mouth, "It's too dangerous."

"Come here, stupid." She storms over, hugs me for real and whispers in my ear, "You're not going without me. That's final!"

Out loud, she says, "You'll need some clothes, if you're leaving. Let's go out."

Tears threaten to overflow. I selfishly don't argue with her. Having Liddy with me will give me the confidence to see this madness through. "Okay."

She grabs her bag. "Do you have your token card?"

"Yeah."

"Shopping time!" Her voice sounds excited, but her eyes are sad. Without delving into her mind, I can't tell what's going on, but everything I know about her also tells me she's readying herself, preparing for what lies ahead. Even making lists of what to pack. Is she sad at leaving, or is she afraid to go back to a world that doesn't accept her for what she is?

Maybe I ought to persuade her not to come.

That's a useless thought! Still, I won't be able to talk to her properly until we're far away from prying M-Hacks. When we can talk, I'll persuade her to turn around, to find her way back here once we're close to the clinic. There's no point in both of us being captured, and this community, independent of what their true mission is, is the only safe place for Liddy now.

She's watching me. There's been too long a gap between her last sentence and my response.

"Oh, come on. It can't be that bad!"

I play the game and groan. "My worst nightmare."

"Don't worry, we have the gang with us."

"Damn!"

"You invited them, you goose."

"You calling me a goose?" I slap her arm as we walk out of her room.

She throws her head back, laughing. "A butterfly just self-destructed, trying to batter my arm. Poor creature."

"You wait, once I've taken all this protein, I'll be so strong—" I don't finish. Her face is in front of mine.

"You've always been strong, Cam. You just don't see it." She winks, a lopsided smile not quite reaching her eyes. "Come on, let's get there before the mob meet up with us. Maybe we can finish before they arrive."

The trip and the clothes shopping work as a distraction. After about an hour spending half my tokens, we sit outside the coffeeshop, enjoying the afternoon sun. It warms the top of my head. I close my eyes and tilt my head back. I generally don't like sunbathing, but this feels soothing, as if the rays are massaging my troubled mind. There's a kerfuffle and I squint to see what's going on.

Jon has somehow managed to spill coffee down his top. Taor's sniggering, watching him soak it up with napkins, worsening the stain.

"Need a bib?"

"Shut up, you."

"Plastic or cotton?"

We all laugh at Taor's teasing, ending with Jon jumping up and chasing him around the tables, clattering the metal chairs, until the owner comes out and tells them to stop or leave.

Vicky leans in. "So, you know?" She's looking at Liddy.

"Know what?"

"Cam told you."

"Damn well did. And if you think I'm letting her go with you alone—"

"Shh! There are other types of ears listening around here than the ones sticking out of our heads."

Liddy's jaw tightens.

Jon and Taor return. Vicky goes back into her irritating mode. Who's she playing for this time? "So, Lid, don't you want company tonight?"

Jon groans. "For the grace of God, Vicky, don't you know when to give up?"

She leans back, her dark eyes challenging Jon. "I don't believe in God, and I find persistence to be highly persuasive."

Jon turns to Liddy. "Feel sorry for you, mate. Sticky Vicky's on the trail."

At that, we all laugh again, almost like normal friends. Vicky has folded her arms, her brow furrowed. "You'll be sorry for that, Jon."

"Yeah, and why would that be?"

I'm jittery about tonight and the chatter isn't helping. "Right, I'm going for a shower before dinner. You lot can stay and argue all you want."

Taor stands up. "Me, too."

As if it's a cue to move, everyone gets up and we make our way back to the training block.

"See ya both later." Vicky nods at Liddy and me.

Taor turns and shouts, "Sure, Sticky Vicky. Till dinner, then!"

The room is dark with the exception of one lamp. Its yellow glow spreads up the wall. Normally, it would be calming, but tonight it just seems eerie and foreboding. I pick up the watch I bought earlier and strap it to my wrist. There wasn't much choice, and its only function is the time and date, but it will do. I look at its small analogue face before picking up my backpack. It's 11:40 p.m. and time to move.

I'd packed my few things before dinner and so didn't have much to do when I came back but watch television. After half an hour, I'd had enough of trying to concentrate on some silly, slapstick comedy and spent the rest of the time wearing down the carpet, marching from the door to the window. After a while, I'd thought it might be a good idea to unpack and repack. During that time, Tom checked in. He said I had a nervous tension about me. I told him it was about leaving tomorrow, and he seemed to believe me.

Liddy's already outside her door. I've become so used to her skirts, wrap, make-up and nails, that her jeans, jacket, and hair hidden under a cap surprises me.

"What?" Her shoulders rise along with her hands, questioning my stare.

"Nothing, you just look odd."

She gives me a lopsided smile. "I look horrible. Even had to cut my nails. What I do for you!"

I squeeze her shoulder. "Let's go."

We creep along the corridor and out the side entrance without saying a word. Aware there must be security cameras around, we scurry along, our heads down as we keep to the shadows of the walls and avoid the orange glow of the lamp light. The air is humid and sea-salty; a sweaty film sticks to my skin.

Liddy's gripping my hand as we dash along the jetty. At the end, I see Vicky sitting in a three-metre dinghy with a small outboard motor. She waves at us. "Get in, quick."

Liddy goes first and reaches for my hand to help me aboard. Vicky leans in, whispering, "No noise." She points to the front. "Cam, sit there, and Liddy, I need you to sit with me in the middle. As you're here, you may as well help."

Liddy nods and moves along, trying to keep her balance as the dinghy sways. I plonk myself down, using my backpack as a leaning post. I notice a larger backpack at the other end and wonder what Vicky has packed for her escape. Just as she's about to untie the rope, we hear a noise and all of us freeze. Footsteps. We respond in unison, crouching low, hoping the jetty will hide us, but a voice forces us to look up.

"What do you think you're doing?" Tom towers over us, his hands on his hips. "Isn't three a crowd? Maybe I should come. Even it out a bit. Or maybe I should just call the security guard."

My heart booms in my chest as he addresses me directly.

"So, Cam, is this some sort of outing? No, let me see, a rescue effort?" He moves to sit on the end of the jetty, his legs dangling over the edge. A large military-style bag is slung across his shoulder.

"Did you think you could hide this?" His voice is low, disappointed. "Do you think so little of me that I can't be trusted?"

I find my voice. "What? No, it's not that, it's just—"

"You were both there last night, in the office." He points at Vicky and me. "If it wasn't for me, you'd both have been caught."

"You knew?"

"Who do you think has been shrouding your thoughts all this time, Cam? Protecting you from mind hackers?"

Vicky glares at me. "We can't trust him. He's one of them. Let's just get out of here."

Tom's face hardens and his jaw sets as he turns to Vicky. "You're very good at shrouding, for someone supposedly just learning. How long were you in those clinics, Vicky?"

"This is stupid. We'll all get caught. What do you want?"

"I'm not letting Cam or Liddy go anywhere alone with you. I'd rather call the guards and risk disciplinary action."

She looks at me. "Your call. You know what we saw, what we heard Dante say."

"What's all this about?" Liddy splutters. "Are we getting out of here, or what? We can't just sit like ducks on a shooting range."

"He was honest with me today, Vicky. He didn't lie."

Vicky tuts. "For God's sake. Either get in or go away. We're leaving."

Tom passes his bag down and swings into the dinghy, which is now sitting even lower in the water. I use telepathy to speak to him.

"The bag. You knew all along."

"I did."

"But why didn't you say anything?"

"Why didn't you?"

"You'll get into trouble."

"You'll get into more trouble if you go wandering off with her."

"She's not so bad. She helped me." I feel I have to defend Vicky. She got us this far. "Without her, I wouldn't have known what was happening. You'd just have let them take me away."

He says nothing. What can he say? I put up my water barrier and push him away from my mind. He sighs, his shoulders sinking. I don't feel sorry for him but, as he's sitting next to me, our physical boundary is limited. His arm touches mine and I shiver as tingling static passes between us.

Vicky gives Liddy a large plastic paddle. "We'll use these until we are at a far enough distance to dull the sound."

Glancing behind, the lights on the mainland shimmer, but between us and it, the black sea is deep and dark. Not only that, but we also have to navigate the barriers. It isn't that cold but my stomach trembles. The dinghy sways, riding waves that would drag us in a different direction. My stomach lurches, the thought of tipping over terrifying me, but Liddy and Vicky's combined strength keeps us moving forwards. After five minutes or so, Vicky stops paddling and pulls in her oar.

"This is the corridor. Tom, do you want to do the honours, or should I attempt it?"

He tuts. "Switch places with me."

I grip onto the sides of the dinghy as it pitches to one side. Saltwater splashes up my arm. Once they're settled, he grabs the tiller and flips on the engine. It purrs and Tom brings us around. I hear his vibration asking permission and allow him into my mind.

"What?"

"Watch, listen and learn."

"Eh?"

"Learning on the job. I'm going to show you how to get through the barrier. Just in case you ever need to, alone." I can practically hear him thinking, 'so you don't need anyone like Vicky in the future', but he doesn't say it.

"Okay, fine, but I don't think I'll be coming back."

"You never know."

"And what's this thing with Vicky? I know she's a bit odd, but she's helped me get this far."

He doesn't answer. I feel a tugging sensation between us, as if I am falling toward him, and then our silver connection transpires out of nowhere.

"It's there, again."

"It's always there." His face is white against the dark night; his fringe has dropped across his forehead and his jawline is tight. He's not happy with any of this.

"I didn't ask you to come."

He glowers at me and takes a deep breath. "Processing mode would be useful."

"Is it safe?" I could imagine us happily going along in processing mode as we tip into the sea and drown, unaware what was happening.

"Won't happen." He's snappy, but certain, so I close my eyes and direct my thoughts to Tom. The world around me slows down. It's as if we're the only two people in the universe.

"Tom, I'm sorry. I just can't leave my mum alone. And nobody tells me anything. What's the League really doing? Why do they need to move us? Are they creating a superpower army?"

"Now's not the time. Just listen to what I'm doing and understand."

He shows me several vibrations. Two belong to the sea. One's a deep, crooning power and the other a distinctive clash – as the waves gather momentum and crash against each other, fighting and then making peace. Another is the breeze, at the moment low and steady. A third is at a distance, a constant humming I don't recognise.

"That's electricity from the mainland."

"Wow!" I know I sound like a little kid, but I'm amazed. Suddenly, things have sounds. Sounds I'd never thought existed. "How come?"

He understands immediately. "You were never trained to sense them."

It's as if I've just had my mute button turned off. He sniggers, and I'm glad he's not so angry with me.

"It can get very noisy, but I want you to hear the barriers. Listen." He guides me to a high-pitched buzzing that screeches in my head and clears all other sounds.

"That's it?"

"Yes."

"It's so loud. Are we close?"

"Fairly. Now spot the gaps."

"Gaps?" And, as if by magic, I understand what he means. Though invasive, the buzzing isn't everywhere; there are patches of non-buzzing space. In my mind, it appears as white static against a black nothingness. "The corridor?"

"Correct."

"I can't believe—"

"The knowledge is there. You just need some training, although you do learn very quickly."

"Right, and so *not* right." I'm trying to express my surprise at all the massive things he's so used to.

His voice is gentler. "I understand." And he does, in every cell of his body. I can feel it. "Let's go back to the normal world but follow me through. See if you can guess which way."

"Okay."

Before I can do anything, I feel someone squeezing my shoulder. I open my eyes, and everything crashes into me, almost as if someone has shaken me awake from a deep sleep. The noise of the engine and the splashing sea are louder than before. The deep darkness of being on open water and the wind licking my face are harsher. Liddy's leaning towards me.

"You okay?"

I nod. "Yeah, fine."

Vicky interrupts. "Can be dangerous to come out so fast."

Liddy stares at her and then looks at me, her eyebrows rising with the same thought as I have. *How does she know?*

"I'm learning how to get through the barrier, that's all."

She shrugs and nods as I close my eyes and concentrate on Tom's lesson. At least 50% of the time, I guess correctly – which is good, according to Tom – and so, by the time we exit the corridor, I feel pretty pleased with myself, until Vicky jolts me out of my euphoria.

"Someone's coming after us."

"What?"

"While you've been in your lesson, I've been scouting."

Tom confirms it. "She's right."

"Can they catch us?" Liddy has turned to look at Tom.

He shrugs. "They're in a speedboat. Was this your doing?" His accusation is aimed at Vicky. She looks annoyed.

"Me? Why would I do that? And how do we know it wasn't you? You're the soldier here."

He snaps back at her. "I was the one who managed the security cameras. What, you thought it was pure luck you weren't caught last night, or tonight, in fact? You think you can jam our cameras with an app on your phone? We're a bit more sophisticated than that."

Vicky scowls but says nothing. I glance at him.

Was he helping us out all along?

Now's not the time to ask, but part of me hopes he was.

Looking out beyond Tom, I don't see any lights, but now I've tuned in to it, I sense the vibration of an engine.

"Can't we make it to land before them?" Liddy's lowered her voice.

Tom responds. "They'll catch up quickly, even if we do."

I glance at Vicky. She's frowning and tutting, thinking something, I can tell. And then I remember what she told me, when we'd had our little chat in my room.

"You can mess with the boat's magnetic field. Send them the wrong way."

Tom interrupts. "You can?"

We all stare at her.

"Yes, it will buy us some time. But get us out of here, fast. I don't want to be dragged back."

She grasps the handles of the dinghy, closes her eyes and places her forehead on her knees. At the same time, Tom revs up the engine and turns the boat in the direction of land.

CHAPTER FORTY

We dock at a secluded inlet. It's a sandbank of sorts – wet and slippery. My feet sink into the mud, and I hear the squelching of my trainers as I drag them out. Without lights, we carefully drag the dinghy up the bank to hide it in some bushes, hoping it will delay our detection. Once done, we gather behind a clump of bushes. Vicky pulls her rucksack higher on her shoulder.

"Cam, it's either you and me, or you and Tom. I'm not risking my escape. I don't care, either way."

I swallow hard and hesitate a second too long.

"'Bye. Good luck with your mum."

"Vicky, wait!"

But she's gone, disappearing down a narrow country road. I feel bad, as if I'm switching allegiance. I can understand she doesn't trust Tom. A niggling voice at the back of my mind asks me if I can, but I knock it back. I would know if he was lying to me. He showed me how. But he probably also knows how to hide that from me.

I'm still staring at the road, as if she'll wander back. What if she gets lost? Then I remember she has a phone. Tom's kneeling on the ground, fiddling with some straps on his bag.

"She's not everything she seems, Cam."

"She just wants to be free."

"Don't we all?"

"The League has a weird concept of freedom; forcing people to do stuff they don't want to do."

"You can't judge what you don't understand. There's a bigger picture here."

"There's always a bigger picture. Even the Commission has a bigger picture. Does that make what they do right?"

Liddy's leaning forward, hands on her knees.

"You okay Lid?"

"Yeah, it's passing. Just felt faint for a second. A bit of sea sickness, that's all. Being on land is helping."

There's a sheen across her face. She wipes it on her sleeve, takes a deep breath and picks up her bag. "So, can you tell me everything now?"

We both look up at her, confused.

She's frowning. "Well, I'm a bit in the dark. I've no idea why we trusted Vicky to start with, Cam, and why she wanted out after they rescued her. What is the League up to? Where are we going?" The questions tumble out.

Tom grunts and rubs his chin. "My plan's a bit sketchy – last-minute, really. I know there's an empty barn, not far from here. I thought we could head for it and then discuss everything."

"I just need to get to District Nine."

"And then what, Cam?" Tom stands and glares at me. "Were you just planning to find the clinic, march in and hand yourself over?"

"Basically, yes."

Liddy explodes. "Are you stupid? That was it? That was what you were going to do?"

Ignoring them both, I stride ahead. Liddy catches up with me.

"No, Cam, I won't let you do that." She grabs my arm, but I push her away. She stumbles, supporting herself on a tree trunk. "Hey, has the protein already kicked in?" She looks across at Tom. "Can that happen?"

I stop; both of them look confused.

I shake my head. "Too much is going on for this. Let's just get out of here. We can talk at the barn."

Tom takes the lead as we stride through long, wet grass and reach a small, wooded area. We crouch about six metres from a barn.

"Cam, what can you sense?"

"What? Lessons now?"

His pale face is serious and intent. "If anything happens to me, you'll need these skills."

"Fine."

Liddy touches my shoulder. She's been quiet for a while. I know she's apologising for her outburst and somehow trying to share the burden of all this with me. I concentrate on the flat land between us and the building.

"I can't sense anything." Anxious to move, I get up, but Tom pulls me back.

"There's never nothing."

Liddy moves to form a triangle between us. "We can't just sit here. What do you mean?"

Tom picks up a twig and begins snapping it into tiny pieces. "Remember, Cam, when you said everything was so noisy? Well, in our world it is. When you can't sense any vibration, someone has laid protective barriers that will alert anyone inside if we enter their proximity."

I swallow hard. I would have led us in there without a second thought. I know so little.

Liddy responds. "So, there are people in there?"

"It's one of our older safehouses. It was abandoned years ago." Tom abruptly stands up. "Let's move."

"What?"

He yanks me up. Liddy's about to protest but then she sees something over my shoulder and jumps to her feet. I glance back. Four people in soldiers' garb are exiting a side door in the barn and are now running towards us.

Liddy and I chase Tom back through the long grass. I'm surprised I'm able to keep up as we dash into the thick woods – a perfect darkness of oak limbs and long, leafy branches.

Liddy's words are choked out between heavy breaths. "If we keep moving, stay ahead of them, maybe we can find a road. Hitch a lift, or something."

Tom lashes out at a low-hanging vine. "They've got someone with them like us. They'll track our vibrations, wherever we go."

"What? Why did you bring us here, then?" Liddy's tone is strained.

Tom stops at a small clearing. "This place is on the system as deserted. I don't get it. I thought it would be safe." His hands are on his hips. "Look, we can't outrun them."

Liddy's leaning against a tree, a sheen of sweat on her face, her hair falling out from under the cap. She wipes a sleeve across her forehead. "So, we just let them take us back? That's what all this was for? Nothing?"

I'm watching their exchange. I don't know what to think. Tom glances from me to Liddy.

"Cam can tell when I'm lying, and I'm not. I wouldn't betray her. I can't—" He looks away and takes a deep breath. "Look, we'll play them at their own game." He sits against the tree. "Form a circle."

Sitting isn't quite what I expected. I notice his eyes have dark shadows beneath them.

"We're going to create an external shroud."

"We can do that?" I sit next to him, pulling Liddy down.

"We can try, but we'll be using our bond to make it happen."

"How?"

Our knees touch and instantly my legs tingle, our bond alive with fear and adrenalin. Hearing booted feet creeping closer, we all tense up as if static electricity is crackling through the air. They aren't crashing through the woods; they're more like predators stalking their prey.

"Hands on each other's shoulders."

As we form our triangle boundary, the silver light binding Tom and I glows brighter. There's a numb tingling sensation and I flinch, almost pulling away, but when I sense him going into processing mode, I swallow hard and follow. The world goes quiet, just him and me and the slow, solid thud of my heartbeat.

"An external shroud is about throwing out our own energy, combining it with vibrations external to us, and manipulating both. Imagine our bond" – he indicates the silver river flowing between us – "as a mirror or reflective surface."

I'm struggling to grasp what he's trying to explain. I feel Tom dragging other energies into our bond, energies that seep up from the ground until they slowly change its look and feel into a deep, greenish-brown colour. Our bond becomes sturdier.

"How are you doing that?"

"Remember, every living thing has a vibration. I'm turning our bond into a mirror and bouncing it off the trees, the bushes and the grass to mingle with them, to make us disappear."

"You mean like some sort of cloaking device?"

"Sort of."

"That's crazy impressive."

"That's energy manipulation."

"Right. Of course it is." I hear him snigger. "Something funny?"

"No, not really." He snaps back to being serious again as we step out of processing mode. "Learning on the job, lesson number two."

I squeeze Liddy's shoulder.

"You were gone again." She's whispering.

"Back now."

Tom interrupts. "We need to extend the shroud to cover Liddy as well."

"Keep still, Lid. We're creating a tent."

She grabs my shoulder tight as if she's expecting to be hurt.

"No talking, at all. They're getting closer," Tom whispers.

Our eyes meet for the last time before I feel our energy-blanket stretching. Gritting my teeth at the sharp pain flashing through my chest, I'm amazed as Tom stretches our bond and spreads it further out over our shoulders.

"Help would be good."

"Sorry." Not sure what my role is, I do the only thing I can imagine. As Tom pushes, I pull. My mind sees my hands grabbing the end of the woollen shawl and yanking it over Liddy's head and down her back. I feel Tom sigh with relief.

"Good. It needs reinforcement."

Nails flash into my mind and I hammer the blanket to the ground with my mum's old hammer. Tom is busy gluing down our side. Once we're sure there aren't any gaps, I return to Liddy, who sits in the real world, eyes flicking uncomfortably from Tom to me,

"Well?" she whispers.

"Done. Don't move, don't speak."

Our arms are still stretched, clasping each other as the soldiers stride into the clearing. I daren't look around, but the beam of a flashlight is near, and I hear them talking in low voices as they step closer.

"They're around here somewhere."

It's a woman's voice. I don't recognise it, but Tom tightens his grip, and I know he knows her.

A man answers. "I don't see them."

"You wouldn't. You two, scout the perimeter." I hear two sets of boots moving away. "Sue, anything?"

"Not visually. You don't think—"

"Well, Tom knows the theory of external shrouding and it's dangerous without grounding first."

"But it requires more than theory."

"He's talented, one of our best young recruits, and he had Ivy training him. Now he's got the strength of a bond, who knows what he can do?"

I don't know what to think, or how to understand what they are saying. What do they mean by 'grounding' and the 'strength of the bond'? What do they know that I don't? My body is taut, gripping Liddy and Tom's shoulders, my chest tight as I hold my breath and grit my teeth. I just want them to pass, for us to get out of here, and everything else can be sorted out later.

"What I don't understand is *why* he's doing it."

They move to the left, kicking at the undergrowth. I wonder why they're kicking when Tom enters my mind.

"The shroud isn't physical. We're just blinding them so they can't see us. If they kick one of us in the right place, we're out of luck."

"What? But they're close." I hold in a gasp.

"Two of them, three of us. We'll be fine."

My heart bangs in my chest, my throat burns and my arms ache. I go over my limited fighting skills.

Yep, none!

I think it's Sue who speaks again.

"Why would Tom betray us?"

"Who knows what a bond does to a person? Maybe this is his way of bringing her to us."

Liddy tightens her grasp on my shoulder. Her arms are trembling. My whole body radiates heat, as if the energy I'm contributing to the shroud might explode. I glance at Liddy and take a deep breath. Even though she doesn't have powers, I feel her presence like an earthing rod rooting me in the present. Tom feels it too, I know he does.

Tom's vibration enters my mind. I snap the link open. "You did this. A trap!" My voice in his head is incredulous.

"No, no. Listen. I didn't." He's trying to reassure me. A cold shiver runs down my spine.

"I trusted you."

"Why would I have come with you in the first place? I could have let them know on the base, before you left."

"I don't know! I d-don't—" I'm stuttering and, in the end, I just shut him out. Concentrating on the shroud is enough, for now. I don't know what to believe anymore. He's one of them. He must have known soldiers were here.

"Anjali, I know Tom's energy trail. It doesn't leave this patch."

"Good." I hear the swish of a coat as she turns but, with my back to her, I don't know what she's doing or how close she is, until I hear her voice directly behind. Just one step and she'll fall on top of me.

"Tom, we know you're here. It's good that you came to us. You don't need to hide anymore. We're in this together and we're not about to harm any of you, but we have orders to bring you in – all of you. It's not safe out here alone."

Liddy's arm flinches. The whites of her eyes are bright as she stares at Tom, and I know he's talking to her. I leap into his mind.

"What's going on?"

"We're going to attack first. It's a risk..."

I'm about to protest, when I feel a sharp spark splinter across my neck as Liddy quickly slips away from me. Tom moves at lightning speed and, as I turn, readying myself to help, I hear a screech. He's already got Anjali in a chokehold, one muscled arm clamped around her neck, the other fighting off grasping fingers. Liddy knocks Sue over, twists her arms behind her, sits on her back and looks up. Tom gives the orders.

"Cam, take any guns and tasers. Quickly, before the others come back."

Anjali has dark eyes and black hair tied back in a bun, though strands have escaped in the struggle. She kicks out at me as I remove a taser and pistol from her waist. Tom pulls her up tighter, leaning her head back against his shoulder.

"Keep still. Check her ankle boots."

In her boot is a short-bladed knife. Liddy has somehow managed to relieve Sue of her weapons – a knife and taser – and throws them over to me.

"Put them in my bag, Cam."

As I open side pockets, I hear Anjali's pleas.

"Tom, what's going on? We're not here to harm any of you."

"Since when did we send soldiers after free citizens?" He's sneering at them.

"Free citizens don't creep away in the middle of the night. We have a procedure for people leaving the island. You know that. Besides, you brought her to us. We were notified, yes, but when you came of your own accord, we thought you were bringing them in. Why all this trouble?"

"Trouble? I can hack your mind, you know, and find out what's going on."

She grunts and is opening her mouth to say something else, when a deeper voice cuts in.

"Let them go."

The two soldiers have returned from searching the perimeter and are pointing their guns at us. I reach for a taser, thinking I might be able to just point and shoot, but the taller man stalks over to me and puts a gun to my head.

"Don't."

My hands fly up, like some criminal from a TV show, and I rise slowly, my head spinning as if I suddenly have low blood pressure.

Tom sneers. "They aren't going to kill us. They need us."

The guard closer to Liddy points his gun at her. "True, but this one isn't needed."

"No!" I charge towards Liddy, but the dark-haired solider grabs my wrist, holding me back.

Liddy stares at me, eyes so wide the whites seem to glow in the darkness. She shuffles, unsure what to do. Anjali sounds more confident.

"Why don't we all calm down? No one's going to die. We can go back to the barn, have a drink and figure out what the next step is."

Using telepathy, I plead with Tom. "Save Liddy. Please. We can figure out what to do later."

"If we go with them, it's the end of the rescue."

"We can negotiate. I just want my mum back and then I'll do anything they want."

"And what about me? Do I get a say?"

"You can go back to Amy, to your old life."

"They want us both, Cam. And Amy and I are over."

"What?"

His turbulent emotions flood through me, entering my mind, shaking my confidence and jolting me with his pain. He's always been so calm, so careful. I shriek aloud and Liddy turns to me, thinking someone has hurt me.

"Get off her!"

The one-second distraction is enough. Sue throws Liddy off her back, pushing her so she hits the ground hard. Jumping to her feet, she kicks Liddy in her kidneys. Groaning, Liddy curls over onto her side.

"You." Sue points at the soldier on her right. "Give me your gun."

He passes it to her. Sue squats; her broad shoulders remind me of my mum. The gun is now lined up with Liddy's forehead.

"Tom, it's over. Let Anjali go now, or he's dead."

I spit out my response. "He's a *she*, and what right do you have to do this? We don't belong to you."

Sue sighs. "You can't even begin to understand." She glances at Tom. "Don't think of hacking my mind. I'm not a trainee, my blocks are guarded well."

Tom sighs, removing his arm from Anjali and freeing her from his hold. I hear him apologise in my head as Anjali scowls at him.

"There's a right way and there's a wrong way, Tom. You are a serving officer, and this is definitely the wrong way. You are out of control. What the hell's happened to you?"

Not waiting for an answer, she barks commands. "Everyone, back to the barn. Sergeant, grab their bags."

As the sergeant bends down to retrieve our rucksacks, I glance towards an opening in the woods. Dark eyes stare at me, a face peeks out. She points to her head and then at me – a signal I understand – before disappearing behind the tree again. The sergeant pushes me forward. I purposely slump and slow my pace, my heart beating hard.

What's she doing here? And how's she getting away with it? Surely, one of them could pick up her presence.

Then I hear the expected vibration, chirping like a morning bird, asking permission to enter my mind, and I know it's Vicky. I waver, unsure. She'd said she couldn't use telepathy, but obviously she can. The sergeant pushes me to move faster. Feeling desperate, I agree.

Vicky speaks rapidly. "I told you none of them could be trusted."

"Tom didn't do this on purpose. He tried to protect us."

"You're so naïve. Manipulation, that's all this is. They're controlling how you're thinking, you're not even seeing things straight."

"You're wrong."

"Fine, I'm wrong. Look, this is the deal: I can get you out of this, get you to your mother, but you have to decide now. Once you're inside their barrier, there's nothing I can do."

"You know where my mum is?"

"I do."

"How?"

"No questions. Decide now, or I go."

"But—" I need answers. Why did she come back? How does she know where my mum is? My head pounds. I reach out to Tom but can't feel him. My pulse flutters and stomach churns as I realise the world is quiet without him in it. I am alone.

"Yes or no?" Vicky is demanding an answer.

The sergeant pushes me again. "Hurry up. We're lagging behind."

Vicky's back in my head. She's nervous. "They're blocking the link between you and Tom. I can't hide this conversation much longer."

"How? What do you mean?"

"I told you not to trust everything they say. Don't you think Tom could do something about this if he wanted to? He's strong enough to stop them blocking you."

Rubbing my face and pushing my hair back, I struggle to think straight. Doubt about everything I think I know creeps in. My mum's dying in some clinic; DRL are marching us as prisoners; the Diversity Commission want to rid the world of us. Tom, well, can I be sure? And Vicky? Whose side is she on? I feel a thudding in my head.

"I'm out of here."

"No, wait."

My mum's pallid face enters my mind. Can I really offer my life for hers? I see the bus coming for her again. I see myself running out into the road, pushing her away from danger. A life for a life. That was my decision. Not Tom's nor Liddy's, not anything to do with anyone else. They shouldn't put their lives on the line for something I've decided. I know they'll both hate me for this, but it's my decision."

"Okay. Do whatever you need to do. Just get me out of here."

The soldier crashes into my back and knocks me down, forcing the wind out of me. I gasp for breath as Vicky runs out and rolls him off me. Dragging me up, she pulls me into the trees. At the last minute, I remember my backpack and grab it as we pass the pale-faced man on the floor.

"What did you do?"

"Energy shot. Knocked him out. Let's go, before the others come looking."

"But they'll easily track us."

"I have transport, but we have to be quick."

I look in the direction of Tom and Liddy, my face scrunched up, my heart pounding, and tell them I'm sorry, as if they can hear me.

"It's too late for them. They're inside the barrier now. We, on the other hand, have a chance."

Vicky's right. There's nothing I can do without getting taken myself. If Liddy was here, she'd be dragging me away. Tom would be telling me not to trust Vicky. At least they will be safer without me.

Vicky yanks my arm. "Let's go."

Within a couple of minutes, I spot a black motorbike. She hands me a helmet. "You can ride this thing?"

She swings her leg over the bike and kicks the pedal. The low thrum of the engine sends birds flittering into the skies.

"Fifty miles of almost empty motorway. We'll be there before it's light, if we get going now."

"You're too young—"

She sneers at me. "Get on, or I'm leaving."

Only as we careen out of the woods and onto a small lane do I wonder where the hell she got this bike from, but there's no turning back and, at the speed we're going, in less than an hour I'll be with my mum.

CHAPTER FORTY-ONE

Even with my hoodie up and my jacket zipped to my chin, I'm freezing by the time Vicky pulls in at a garage to get petrol. My legs stiff, I climb off the bike, rub my arms and stamp my feet. Vicky moves to the pump and places the nozzle in the tank.

"Keep your helmet on and your visor down. There's CCTV around here and a bounty on your head."

I nod as she flips a bank card across a screen. It beeps and she climbs back on the bike.

"How far do we have to go?"

"Come, we'll get coffee and have a chat."

Sitting on worn asphalt, leaning against the back wall of a pop-up coffeeshop in a lay-by, I cradle a hot paper cup, relishing the strong aroma of coffee. I sip the scalding drink, waiting for her to say something. There's a grass embankment in front of us. Behind it, the sun's rising, giving the impression of a halo around the mound. It must be around 4:30 a.m. I check my watch; the glass casing is broken. The hands are stopped at 3:20 a.m. I sigh. Must have happened when I was knocked down.

She's quiet, so I busy myself with reinforcing my mental block. I imagine a gushing waterfall and check for gaps to prevent anyone from entering my mind. Vicky interrupts my task.

"I know you don't trust me, and you're right not to, but I'm not your enemy here." She glances over at me before continuing. "The Diversity Commission took me when I was eleven. They were doing some advanced screening at our school." She's poking a twig in the gravel. "My family had no idea and no choice. I haven't seen them since. They don't even know I'm alive."

"That's sad." I'm not sure where this conversation is leading or why it's happening at this point in time. I want to get on with finding my mum.

"No, not anymore. At first, yeah, but now it makes no difference. It'll be nine years in October."

"Nine..." I do some quick mental maths. "You're twenty?"

"Almost."

"You don't act your age, or even look twenty."

"My looks are the benefit of my genes; the rest is just playing a role."

"That stuff with Liddy?"

"Just fitting in. Pretending to be a teenager in love. All part of the DC's training. If DRL had any indication of my real age, they wouldn't have rescued me." She snaps the twig, throwing it to the ground, and looks at me sideways. "Never would have acted on it, obviously. Liddy's a baby and I'm not a perv."

"What?" My stomach churns and I bite the inside of my lip. "I don't get it. Why use Liddy like that? Why even bother?" I begin retying my shoelaces, tightening them up and then sitting cross-legged. She watches me for a second. When she responds, she doesn't bother to answer any of my questions.

"It's hard at the Commission, but they taught me a lot. My speciality is how to attract and repel magnetic vibrations, but there's a lot you can do with that. You'll do well."

"What are you talking about?" I feel a slow, sickening feeling rising from my stomach. She's had nine years with the DC and managed to deceive everyone at the base. Then it dawns on me: she was a spy for the other side. I've been an idiot. My face heats up and I shuffle away from her.

She turns to face me. "So, here's what's happening. I'm trading you for my freedom."

"What? Are you mad?"

"I hand you over and then I disappear. No Diversity Commission. No Diversity Resistance League. Just me."

Jumping up, I spill the coffee over my hand and drop my cup. As I wipe my fingers down my jeans, I spit out my response. "I am not being traded."

I scan the area, wondering which direction to go in. Any direction away from her would be fine. My pulse pounds in my ears. I've made a major mistake coming with her.

"Hold up. I didn't lie. I know where your mother is and will take you to her. That's where the trade will take place."

I glare, my nostrils flaring. "You're lying... and you're working for the Commission."

"No," she snaps back at me. "I work for no one. Not anymore. I told you, I'm buying my freedom."

Tom taught me how to recognise the vibrations of people telling untruths but the static coming from her is difficult to read. How has she been able to stay under their radar? I consider using telepathy, but veer away from it. Opening my mind to her would be stupid.

"I don't get it."

"Look, they have spies, just like the League. The Commission needed someone on the inside, someone who could find the way onto the island. Everyone else had returned without any memory of their time there, but I'm stronger than most. They had their suspicions about Schultz, so brought him into the facility I was at. They waited to see if he took the bait. And he did. A successful rescue attempt!"

A wave of nauseous realisation hits me; why she seemed so familiar when we first met. "You're the girl I saw in the film."

"He filmed me? Didn't know that."

"It was all a trick. Everything about you is one big fat lie."

"Not everything." She pretends to be insulted, touching her chest and sighing. "But most of it. Clearly, I'm not new to all this talent stuff, but you were pretty easy to fool. Just a few prods and you were on your way to discover the truth."

I step back, my mind reeling. "I don't want to hear any more. I just want to find my mum."

"And I'll keep my promise. There are a few things you need to know first. It's for your own benefit, if you intend to walk in there."

Stalking over to the mound, I turn back and stare at her. She hasn't moved but she's watching me with a leopard's stealth, ready to pounce.

She smirks. "Yes, I could."

"Could what?"

"Manipulate your mind, make you go with me. That's what you're thinking, but I won't. Our kind need to stick together. I told you that before."

"How is this sticking together?"

"Why do you think I stopped at all? I could have just driven you there."

"I don't know."

Her eyes are wide and shiny. There's almost a mad glee about them. Why didn't I see any of this before?

She grins as if she's telling me an interesting story. "Hey, I'm just giving you what you want. That throw-yourself-under-the-bus, guilt trip thing you have going on made it easy. Just a few insinuations here and there and a couple of mind pushes in the right direction kept the doubts in place." She's bragging, as if she's proud of me, of her, of the whole situation.

"It was all you. You even came to my room to ask for help. I couldn't believe you had the courage, but there you were, tapping at my door, asking how to get into the ops building." A short burst of laughter escapes her throat. "You saved me a whole lot of trouble. Tom was so good at protecting your mind from intruders, he made it difficult for me to get in. I was trying to figure out how to persuade you to go with me, when you just turned up." She waves her arms around majestically. "Must have been fate!"

I feel my eyes narrowing and my jaw tightening. I've been foolish. Playing right into her hands.

"But the meeting with Tom and the others? You couldn't have known about it."

She raises her eyebrows. "I'm a pickpocket. Minds are my speciality."

"A hacker?"

"Sometimes."

"So, you did know about it. You set me up." I think back to the night and how reluctant she'd seemed to be, how she'd purposely gone in the opposite direction, allowing me to think I was leading.

She smiles. "Not at all. You pushed me, remember." Her eyebrows rise, mocking me.

Was it really my decision that night, or did she somehow manipulate me?

I stalk over and pick up my bag. My face is hot and I'm breathing heavily, snorting through my nose. She isn't the silly girl mooning over Liddy at all. I can't get over how no one saw it. I shake my head and lower my voice. "You're not trading me."

She grabs my wrist and yanks me down, twisting me onto my back. Her dark eyes lean in. "Oh, I think I am."

I feel a wall hit me and my limbs go numb, all sensation disappearing. I try to scream out, but no sound leaves my mouth. The sky above me is depleted of all colours, a nothingness, grey as the day dawns. My throat chokes up.

She's there again, face in my face.

"Calm down. You're fine. I'll finish my story and then we can go."

She has a crazy grin on her face, a madness in her eyes and, for the first time in her company, I'm really afraid. She has complete control over my body and possibly my mind. She could get me to walk out onto the motorway and I couldn't stop her.

"I know, I know, you think I'm mad, and perhaps I am. Years at the Commission can do that to you. But if you make it out, make it to the other side, then you can live." She sits back down. "And I'm going to live. The DC makes a seven-year deal with you. Learn, work, do your duty and, after a final mission and replacement, you get a huge pension and a new ID. Well, I've done my time, plus two years to find a replacement."

She leans in again. Her hair falls across my nose. "That's you, by the way. My final mission was finding out how to get on the island." She strokes my cheek. "And then you turned up. Scatty, weak, useless, but still, they want you. For you, they let me go."

Tom warned me she was not all she seemed, but I thought I knew better. I'd just gone ahead and done what I thought was right, which apparently was exactly what she'd wanted all along. The fear slowly turns into a burning anger. My brain feels hot.

She flicks her hand like a witch. "You can talk now."

I spit out my words. "Let me go! You can't keep me like this for ever."

She raises her eyebrows, amusement on her face, as if I'm an insect challenging a bird.

"You're bonkers."

"Yes, yes, I know. Isn't it delicious!" She laughs out loud, but then becomes serious. "I'm not any madder than anyone else, y'know. Just want my freedom. Done my time." She sighs deeply and looks away. Her arms are tight around her knees, and for a few seconds I almost feel sorry for her, sorry for what she must have gone through. But the feeling passes quickly. I feel the air pulled in through my throat as I take a deep breath and try a different approach.

"Vicky, aren't you already free? You could just walk away, right now."

"No, they have trackers. They'll trace me if I don't keep my end of the bargain.."

"And how's this deal going to change that? They can still track you."

"There's a technique called vibrational wiping; it clears individual vibrational information. I've seen it happen with others before. Some choose to stay, be part of the organisation, but not me."

"You're a fool if you think they'll let you go."

"You know nothing. Anyway, I'll control the wipe."

Birds have started tweeting, as if this day is just like any other day.

"Oh, you can get up now, if you want."

I sit up and stare at her again, my brain trying to sort out what she really is. Her dark face shimmers in the early light, her eyes bore into mine. She looks down for a second, not in shame, but to check the time. Pushing her spiral curls behind her ears, she takes a deep breath. "Look at it this way: I've organised the swap. Me for you. It's going to happen. The plus side for you is that this might be the last chance to see your mother alive."

My jaw aches from clenching it so hard, but she isn't finished.

"This isn't a choice, you know."

"What?"

"You know you can't escape me. There's no Tom here to protect you." She smiles, thin-lipped, her eyes narrow. "Let me show you something, prove I'm not lying to you."

A sudden blast of white energy hits me, knocking me back as it seers through my waterfall blockade, like light deflecting rain. Gasping, I squat and hold my head, waiting for my breathing to settle and the pain to pass. "What did you do?"

"The soldier got it worse."

"I said, what did you do?"

"Just a little lesson, some tough love. You know so little, but the Diversity Commission will soon drag those powers out of you." For a millisecond, her face contorts, a memory of pain flashing across it.

"Lesson?"

"Access the information I just shot into your head."

"How?"

She tuts and raises her eyebrow. "There'll be a humming noise from where the pain hit. Follow it."

"Do you think I'm stupid? What is it? Some sort of trap to get me to do as you say?"

"It might be. I could." She flexes her fingers, examining her nails, and it becomes clear she's enjoying this little show and tell; that she's planned this warped 'reveal' all along.

"Jon tried to go against me. Look what happened to him."

"Jon?"

She's off on a tangent again.

"Yeah. He remembered me from the clinic. Knew I was stronger than I was making out. He didn't exactly threaten me, but I knew he was thinking about telling." She smirks, observing my reactions. "I fixed his attitude at the same time. Couldn't have him causing problems. You should thank me. He was horrible to Liddy." She sighs and comes back to the present. "Anyway, go find that knowledge I just dumped in your brain." A smile creeps across her face as if I'm her best friend.

Not wanting her in my head more than she already is, I take tentative steps towards the humming noise. It's a bit like picking at a scab, itchy and painful at the same time but, once uncovered, the sensation overcomes me.

I can feel her, my mum. I don't know how, but I can. Tears burn my eyes. I quickly blink them away. She's unconscious and sickly. Whatever new skill Vicky placed in my head shows me her vibration. It sounds like a bee, buzzing close to my ears and then flying away quietly, before returning. I turn to my left, half expecting her to be there, but instead I see a faint pink line drawing me to it. It's my mum's aura. I know it is. It may not be a bond, but it's a strong link. Standing, I ready myself to follow.

"Hey, wait up. We're a few miles from the clinic. You'll need a ride." She's clutching the helmets.

"No, I don't. I can find her on my own, thank you."

She smirks. "Have you not learnt anything today? I can blind you to your mother's vibration as easily as I gave it to you. I can hack your brain until you don't know what you're doing. And you" – she pokes me in my ribs – "are my bargaining chip."

I ball my hands and stand my ground, seething. She watches me, a predator assessing her next move.

"Of course, it isn't what I want. I'd rather you had full control of your own mind. And look at it like this: you've just had your first lesson in tracking. I bet Tom didn't teach you that. You should be thanking me."

She's so calm, as if this is all normal. Wrapping my arms around my body, I lean against the wall. All I can think about is smashing her smug face and watching her beautiful white teeth crumble. I look up from under my fringe. She meets my eyes, waiting for a decision.

This could a trick, one big lie, or something she's put in my head to confuse and trap me. Maybe that's not my mum's aura. I can't tell, can't get any read on Vicky. Not even a static vibration to tell me she's lying. It's as if she isn't even here. How did she learn to do that?

I wonder if she's like Tom's father and grandfather – working for them, taking me in – but why go to all this trouble? Why not just drive me straight up to the front gate? If I knew for certain, I'd risk walking away, assuming I could actually do that. The clinic can't be far from here, Liddy and Tom could help me find it. I call out for Tom, but he doesn't answer. Why is the League blocking us? I stare at the mound, unsure of the truth. Maybe it's Vicky, maybe she's the one isolating us. How would I even know?

She's grinning a big toothy grin with sparkling eyes. "Make up your mind."

"Why should I bother, if you can force me anyway?"

"Think of it as a kindness. Better we both have our full capacity when going in."

"You mean, you."

She nods. "I don't want to be focusing on you when facing them, and you don't want to be fighting me."

Aware I'm making one of those 'no going back' decisions, I take the helmet she's holding out to me and slam it on my head.

"See, not so hard, is it?"

Scowling, I stand by the bike, waiting for her to move. At the same time, I reach out for Tom. It's a habit. I don't think she'll allow it, but the silver river connecting us appears. My pulse quickens as I rush to tell him what's happening, let him perceive my mum's vibration and the direction we're heading in before our connection is blocked again. I don't even know if it will reach him, but I have to try.

She laughs out loud, a deep, throaty noise. "Oh, do contact Tom. I won't even obstruct you this time." She's swinging her leg over the bike. "Get on."

"You're the one who stopped us?"

She looks back at me as I balance myself behind her. "I'd love to be there when he charges to the rescue, a courageous knight on a white horse. Valiant unto death. But I'll be far away by then." She flicks up the bike stand. "Commission will be happy. Apparently, you're the duo to have. All those combined powers to play with."

I reach out for Tom again to tell him it's a trap, but the silence is back. I have the urge to pummel her back, put my hands around her throat and throttle her.

"And you're a funny child."

"I'm not a child."

She revs the engine and swivels the bike around. As we enter the motorway, I grip the sidebars to steady myself. We hurtle along at top speed, heading for the one place that fills me with terror and yet draws me to it, to my mum.

Life for a life!

I have to keep telling myself this. This is my choice. I decided this. Not Tom, not Liddy and not even Vicky. I put myself in this position and now have to accept the consequences. The Diversity Commission are my enemy and if I can get away, I will. I won't spend seven years in their service and be driven mad. I can't do what Vicky has done, can't swap my freedom for someone else's imprisonment. I'd rather die.

And the League? What are they, really? I don't know anymore, don't know what's real, what Vicky has twisted, what she's even influencing now, but I know that meeting happened. Dante – whoever she is – ordered them to stop the search for my mum.

Everything's becoming a confused mess of uncertainty, but, frankly, it doesn't matter anymore. All I can do is trust what I believe to be my own instincts and, right now, they tell me to follow the pink aura and find my mum. Whatever happens after that, I'll have to deal with it.

CHAPTER FORTY-TWO

We're at one end of a large car park, surrounded by expansive farmland. To the left is a large, flat-roofed building with dark glass windows and a sign in blue: Fibres Clinic. I notice an ambulance and a line of cars, but my focus is on my mum.

Without a doubt, she's in this building. It's as if I can smell her standing next to me – flowery, like roses after summer rain. A breeze blows her scent in my direction, but then I sense a bitter aftertaste. Maybe it's the sickness. What have they done to her? I want to dash to the entrance, run down corridors and follow the vibration to her bedside. Stupid tears flood my eyes. I sniff and wipe them on my cuff.

Vicky glances at me. "Don't get all weepy and weak. Now's not the time."

A short woman with thick-rimmed, red glasses walks through automated doors. Three men in green scrubs follow her. The woman's close enough that I can see the corners of her mouth twitch as she looks at me. Vicky puts her hand up.

"Don't come any closer."

They obey her order, though I can see hatred in the woman's eyes. She's not used to being told what to do. Vicky crosses her arms and squints in the early morning light.

"We have an agreement." It isn't a question. "I need access first."

The woman casually places her hands in her grey trouser pockets, ruffling up her jacket. "Go ahead, Vicky. It's all yours."

The woman's aura suddenly appears. It's dark and shadowy and, immediately, I know what it means. Deceit. I turn to warn Vicky.

"Don't—"

Vicky's high-pitched scream causes the air around us to quiver. She reaches out to grab me, to steady her balance. Before I can catch her, she pitches forward, her head crashing on the hard tarmac. Her dark eyes roll upwards, showing the whites of her eyes, and I hear her weak thoughts in my mind.

The woman's grinning. "You think we'd just let you walk away? Such a highly prized asset."

Vicky's trying to regain control of herself. "How's this happening? It's not supposed—" There's an internal screech. "...binding me. Double-cross. Someone in there—" Her thoughts hit me in blasts. "Access this. Free yourself!"

And then a massive burst of pain shoots through my head like white lightning. I fall to my knees, holding my head in my hands. The woman's voice is distant.

"Bring them both in."

Part of me burns with anger at Vicky's stupidity. Surely, she should have known this would happen. But then, what if they just manipulated her mind? Made her believe the whole 'freedom' story?

I don't give it that much thought. Self-preservation kicks in and I dive into processing mode. The world around me is silenced.

I slow my thoughts, compel my mind to focus, to acknowledge this story has no knights in shining armour. Panicking is not the way to go. I need to think. Tom put stuff in my head. What did he say? Energy manipulation, vibrational tuning and mind hacking. There must be something I can access, something I can use to protect myself. How do I find it?

Aware of Vicky's last insertion, I cautiously unpick her latest scab, trying to understand what she's given me. As it opens up, I see vibrations. Not just those linking human to human in a rainbow of colours, but trees, animals and plants; all have signature tunes, wrapping around each other, connecting and converging like electricity fields. Loud, clashing and uncontrollable. I don't understand how Vicky thought this would be useful, but then I sense something else, and the melody of living things fades into the background.

At first, I don't get it. It looks like the Aurora Borealis streaming from the sky; hues of stunning greens and blues. Then I realise I'm seeing a different kind of vibration. As the light hits the ground, another reaches up to meet it, burning reds and yellows bursting upwards from the centre of the earth. The clash of colours mingles to create brilliant purples and various shades of emeralds, ochres and orange-reds. The vibration dances, joyous and alive, humming a constant resonance so full of power.

I wonder at it, want to become part of it and leave the painful world behind. I reach out and gather strands, whipping it up into a ball of silk-like threads. In my mind, I throw it back, watching it explode – a strange, volcanic magma – before reforming and resuming its place as part of the earth's vibration.

In some deep part of my mind, the words form: energy manipulation. That's what this is. I know intuitively, as if the knowledge is there. And, of course, it is. Tom downloaded it. I feel the pieces of a puzzle locking into place. If an internal shroud can be externalised to hide behind in the real world, why not energy manipulation in the same way?

A silver river pulls me back, grounding me. A desperate voice enters my mind.

"Cam?"

"Tom?"

"You can hear me?"

"Yes. I thought they'd taken you to the warehouse."

"No. Once I got your message, they knew I could lead them to the clinic. We're on our way."

I show him everything, all that has happened.

"Stay where you are. Don't do anything rash."

"They're close."

"We'll get you out."

"It's a trap. They'll bind you."

I remember Vicky, everything she told me and how they bound her. He sees what I'm thinking.

"We'll find a way."

"Tom, I see it, see the energy fields. I don't know how, but I think I understand what energy manipulation is."

"No, Cam, you don't understand it. Seeing and using it is different."

He's right, but also not. There's a new sensation within me, uncurling – something that's been hidden for a long time. It feels powerful and strong.

Tom's last words fade into the background. "Just try to hold on."

Coming out of processing mode, I'm still standing in the car park, but now I feel calm, almost ethereal. There is so much energy out there, such amazing vibrations, a whole other magnificent world, one I've only just come to understand and see. And I'm a small part of it. But, more importantly, a small part that is connected, that can draw on that strength. For the first time in my life, I feel potent. My heartbeat slows as I rise and face my aggressors.

Two men are picking up Vicky. A third, broad-faced and sturdy, stands in front of me, hatred in his eyes.

"Let's go."

"I want to see my mum." My voice is low and steady.

"Your mother?" He smirks and flicks his head towards the door. "She's inside."

I nod and step forward without hesitation. The woman with red glasses is standing at the door. Another female stands with her.

"Sakiya, bind her."

Sakiya looks afraid, but nods assent, and I feel the unwelcome intrusion in my mind. To test my theory that I can use the implanted knowledge – that everything I need to manipulate energy is already within me – I visualise a small ball of the earth's vibration forming into a red and yellow shield and push her away. She tries again, but I shove harder, and she gasps and shakes her head at the woman who's now standing next to me. The frown and thin-lipped smile betray little, but her aura spikes in surprise. I feel elated, relieved and grateful at the same time.

I move to the right to allow the two men carrying Vicky to pass by. Her vibration is dulled, but she's alive.

The woman gives more orders. "Take her to cell four." She then holds out her hand. "I'm Professor McCallister. I run this facility."

Ignoring her, my words are clipped. "You know who I am. So, take me to my mum. Or should I just find her myself?"

She hesitates, before conceding. "Follow me."

We walk down a narrow corridor which is illuminated with sensor lights above us. On the right-hand side are glass doors with numbers, some with names. On the other side are doors with security pads and viewing hatches, reminding me of a prison. Sliding my hand along the left side, I sense nothing, which is impossible. Everything has vibrations. The spaces inside must be like the training rooms back on base. I realise they are cells for people like me, Tom and Vicky; cells that can't be escaped from.

Professor McCallister leads. I hear several steps behind me and glance back. Sakiya has been joined by three others – two men and one woman. Again, I feel prodding as they try to enter my mind.

I don't feel fear. I know I should, but I don't. No sickly stomach, no shuddering, just an absolute calm. I wonder if Vicky placed more than understanding in my brain. The image of the universe's energy flashes in my mind again and my waterfall mind barrier turns into a vibration of colours, resistant to all who try to pass. I hear groans and turn to see their fearful faces. I can't help smiling.

Professor McCallister tuts. "Are you all so useless? Get the soldiers in."

I skip into her mind and become aware of her contradictory emotions. She's both jubilant, and wary, eager to begin my testing but afraid to anger me. She believes giving in to my demands will help. When she notices me prying, she stops and stares at me.

"Please don't do that. You may be powerful, but you understand nothing of what we do or why we do it."

"I don't need to understand."

There are footsteps approaching us and, from around the corner, a group of four approach. One man stops in front of Professor McCallister, the others stare as they pass by. Professor McCallister stands to attention. The man is tall, with dark hair greying at the sides. Probably around fifty.

"This is her?"

"Yes, sir."

He narrows his eyes at me, snorting. "This little thing is what all the trouble has been about?" He steps towards me.

McCallister reaches out. "Mr Beresford, please take care."

The name hits me like a slap across the face; my cheeks heat up as he looms over me.

"What, she can't be more than thirteen, and this is the thing my wretched child has bonded with? How can that be?" His words explode from within him. He's a man used to scaring people into submission.

He looks across to McCallister for an explanation, so my response is unexpected – even to myself.

"For a start, I'm nearly sixteen. And if you're Tom's father" – and now I see the resemblance – "then—"

He cuts across my words. "Tom is not his name." He then turns to McCallister. "Will he follow?"

She responds quickly as my brain reacts to the knowledge of Tom not being Tom's name. *What is his name then?*

"We believe so, sir. From the quick read of Vicky's mind, he's already off the base. If the bond is as it seems, he should be here shortly."

What! They already know?

"Vicky?" He frowns just like Tom.

"Subject 497."

"So, she succeeded. A debrief and the base's entry coordinates as soon as possible, please." He points as me. "And I want a daily report on this one. If my son turns up, bring him to me immediately."

"Yes, sir."

He folds his arms, sneering at me, his voice is deep and scarily monotone. "I told my son what I'm telling you now: there's a fine balance in this world of knowledge and truth, security and chaos, and war and peace. The Diversity Commission are the only ones holding up that balance, protecting our society, making sure normal people like us survive freaks like you and my son, like your mother and friend."

He sighs. "It was a sad day, when I realised my son was one of you. I loved him most of all. And when he joined us, I was convinced he'd shown his loyalty to our cause. And then, he betrayed me, his family and everything we strive to achieve. My own flesh and blood." His eyes narrow as he leans in. "All your kind are a minority, soon to be wiped out. We will re-educate you to understand that the only way to live is through the Holistic Law. The world agrees with me and so will you – eventually." He stands tall again. "Your genes pollute the majority. Your DNA, left to run wild, would eventually destroy the human race. It nearly did. Surely, you understand that by helping us, you'll save our world. Your sacrifice will mean we can all go back to what we were naturally born to be: human. For all our faults, just human."

I stare up at him, unable to break the hold his black eyes have on me, as if he has me in some vice-like grip. He's close enough that I easily pick up his minty breath.

"You're an abomination – a blip, a stain, that is all. One we're cleaning up. History will thank us for the hard choices we're making now."

I think he's finished but, no, he still has one last comment.

"You think you'll get out of here, that those friends coming to rescue you will get in. Well, you're wrong. You're ours now, and you'll do as we say, or that parent of yours will die."

With that, he storms away. I already hate him. Hate him for his smug conceit, hate him for his beliefs and what he's doing here, but most of all because of what he and his father did to Tom. That little speech – calling his son an abomination, a stain on society. And the worst thing is, he believes what he's saying.

I can't imagine what Tom went through, but my chest feels restricted, and my breathing is heavy. I push my shoulders back, grit my teeth and ball my fists. I can't become weak now. I imagine punching Tom's father in the face and seeing blood pouring from his nose. Pity he's already left, as I might have actually done it.

"Come." McCallister smirks, crossing her arms over her chest. "You're with me."

She has an odd way of speaking. There's a slight Scottish accent and her intonation is peculiar. I reach out for Tom, but he doesn't respond. What bounces back is a vibrational block, like a wall surrounding the building. He likely knows where I am and will know of the dangers, but not of his father's presence. I wish there was a way to warn him.

By the time we reach the second floor, the pink energy is so thick, it's like a magnet drawing me closer to my mum. I want to rush to her side, but I doubt the uniformed soldiers toting loaded guns would allow that. As we enter a padded room, the person lying on the bed eliminates any other thoughts.

"What have you done to her?"

My mum's face is so pale, it's almost blue. The beep of a machine tells me her heart is beating, but her stillness rips pain through my chest, and the calmness I felt disappears as I throw my arms around her, my face falling into the crook of her neck. I want to shake her, scream at her to wake up. Instead, I stroke her dry cheek and reach out, entering her mind as if we've done it all our lives. There's a shroud so dark, I pull back, shocked, and stand upright. That's when I notice her beautiful hair has been cut short.

"What and who is in her brain?" Anger ripples through my body.

"The shroud places him in confinement, a coma of sorts. As long as you cooperate, he will live."

"He?"

She smiles. "Oh, yes. That's the thing. Your mother was born male. Didn't he ever tell you? Must have had the operation illegally. Black market pills, I would think as well." She relishes the shock that appears on my face. This has been her plan all along to weaken my resolve.

"You're telling me you never noticed the Adam's apple scar?" She folds her arms and laughs. "Perhaps you're not even related. Tests will tell us more."

She's saying something else. They're all snickering. I stare past them. It makes no sense. None of it. Why would my mum do this to me?

Trembling, I reach for the bed and lower myself to the floor. If she isn't my mum, who is she? No, it can't be. This is just one of their mind tricks, to fool me. Pain shoots through my chest, causing me to inhale sharply. Wrapping my arms tight around my stomach, I lean forward, cooling my forehead on the metal frame of the bed.

It's a lie. All a lie!

McCallister's giving orders, but I don't react.

"Take her to cell fifteen and ensure maximum security. Bind her, if you can."

I'm being carried, someone strong has me in his arms. There's more laughter around me.

"You have a go."

A prodding in my brain. The colourful waterfall maintains the barrier, but it isn't as strong.

"What if we all did it at the same time?"

"Good idea."

"Okay. One, two, three."

A barrage of stabbing hits my head. There must be at least five of them, over and over, trying to break me. I can't be this pathetic. No matter what they said about my mum, I have to do something to save us.

"Tom!" I scream his name, unsure if I'm using telepathy or not and, to my surprise, I feel our bond. He must be near, maybe already in the building. "Tom, help me!"

I can't hear him but can detect his energy like a silver river, flowing into me. I tug harder, demanding strength and the knowledge it contains. Remembering the blanket he created in the woods, I imagine the cool shadow of our bond enveloping me with power and protection.

They're still trying to bring down my barrier, laughing like a pack of baboons and encouraging each other to try different methods. Tom is somewhere, but now I know I'm connected to more than just him. Without giving it too much thought, I reach into the earth's resonance and gather strands of the vibrant reds and greens. The opposing forces of cold, metallic silver and molten fire combine. I imagine them hardening like a sheet of steel and coil the energy around my body and mind until I become unassailable.

Breaking free from the soldier's grasp, I flip over and stand before my captors, like an athlete bouncing off a high bar. They're surprised. So am I. I've never done that before, so not sure how I did it or where it came from. How the heck did I even land on my feet? It's almost as if I bounced off the energy. I don't have time to think about it. Guns are raised to shoulder height and several clicks let me know they're ready to shoot. Sakiya steps forward.

"Don't shoot to kill."

The man in front of me keeps his eyes on mine. "Do you need her knees?"

My mind is alive, as if all neurons are bursting at once and I picture every detail: the door to the left with a coffee stain; the peeling paint in the corner; the flickering light; the shock on each of their faces; the flinching; the smell of sweat on their foreheads, the nervous handling of guns. Instinct takes over.

Closing my eyes, I block out the physical and focus on colour. Vibrations like a thermal heat sensor light up the corridor. The walls are blue, their faces orange, their internal organs red. Below them, the earth sends spears of light through the floor and up through the ceiling.

"What's she doing?"

"I don't know."

"Stop her, whatever it is, or I'll shoot."

Spreading my arms wide, I gather an armful of the earth's vibrational strands and stretch them like a wall of multicolour threads. They feel soft and malleable and yet strong, as I weave them together to form an object I can use to protect myself.

"Is she dancing?"

"She's mad as a hatter, this one!"

"No, she's not. Disable her, now."

My mind forms eight glowing arrows with poisonous tips. Without considering the impact, I send them forward with lightning speed. At least four of the men drop to the floor. I feel nothing for them. Their fading energies are irrelevant.

"What's happening? I can't see anything." The man at the front is screeching, clinging onto a bleeding thigh. He looks at Sakiya. "Stop her!"

Sakiya steps back, turns and runs down the corridor. At least three follow. I focus on those remaining, once more gathering vibrational energy to produce a silver net. Throwing it out, it snatches their guns from their hands and smashes them against the far wall. They scream and try to fight back, pulling out knives and tasers. Some use talents, but I reject everything and use my growing power to send their weapons flying. They clutch at their heads in agony, but I don't care.

Pulling more strength from the bond with Tom and trusting on a baser instinct to claim the knowledge planted in my mind, I use the earth's energy field and slam it down the corridors. It's a surge of electric power, ready to find and destroy enemies. I follow it with my mind. Its vibration is loud, like several trains echoing down a tunnel. As it bounces off walls, it's like an earthquake erupting.

Ceilings crash, every door in the corridor flies open and the glowing energy of people I don't know dissipates. Those still standing dash towards the entrance of the building. There are others like me, young, with talents. They have a different vibration, indigo and white light streaming from the top of their heads. I let them go – they deserve their freedom – and, instead, search for Professor McCallister's signature.

She bound my mum, I'm sure of it. I hate her, I want her destroyed. It's the only way to free my mum and, deep down, I'm convinced McCallister deserves to die for everything she's done here.

My head burns, my body shakes, but my physical awareness fades and is of lesser importance. It is a vessel from which boiling energy erupts. The colours swirl, burning like molten candy dripping, turning darker and darker, blasting outwards, exploding into anything and anyone that gets in the way.

A tiny voice reminds me that there are innocent people in this building, but the will to rein in the power has long gone. The force has taken on a life of its own. A sonic boom detonates outwards and the building shudders. The ceiling above me cracks and the corridor goes dark as sparks skitter across the walls. I smell burning and hear a piercing fire alarm. Water spears down from a sprinkler system. The world is in turmoil around me, but I'm blind and deaf. Vibrant colours spike in front of my eyes, the noise of gushing energy deafens me.

It's only when I fall to my hands and knees that the physical pain slingshots me back to the real world. Finding it hard to breathe, I slump to the floor, coughing, blinded by smoke. My head pounds and my heart struggles to keep up with the physical needs of my body. I know I have to come back fully, to release the energy from my hold completely in order to register what's going on, but I still feel it charging through me.

Rolling onto my back, I crash into another body – one of the guards, trapped under a fallen post. He smells of burnt flesh and sticky, congealed blood. I see half a bloodied cheek and a glassy eye. He looks familiar, he looks like Liddy's dad, but surely it isn't. Part of me thinks I should care, but even when I'm fairly certain it might be him, I just can't summon up anything vaguely resembling concern. Not after everything he did. I try to get myself up but slip in the gunge on the floor. I need to reach my mum. That's when I hear a clattering of footsteps.

People are coming around the corner. I spin around on my hands and knees, readying myself, dragging my body to obey, pulling on the energy strands again. Someone tries to get into my head, but I push them out and toughen my defences with fire and metal.

A dark shadow appears around the corner. Smoke and water make it difficult to see who it is.

"Cam, it's okay."

But I know this is a trick. They're playing with my mind. It's not okay. Nothing's okay. I won't let them take me and I have to protect my mum.

The shadows get larger and there are more of them. More soldiers. I ready myself to attack the enemy, fire balls at the end of my fingers. From a kneeling position, all I can do is fling out tiny, bright orange energy darts, but they're sharp enough to do some damage.

Her face appears through the smoke and shadows. A sad smile as she reaches towards me. "It's okay, Cam. We're here."

It can't be her. It can't be. But it's her face, her voice.

Liddy?

My mind is a blur. I don't realise my mistake fast enough. She can't even see the energy darts heading for her heart.

No, Liddy, no!

I scream at her, but she can't hear. My voice doesn't exist anymore. I am no longer part of this world. I am vibration and light, molten rock and green earth. Everything is swirling around me like a tornado of colour, protecting and encapsulating me.

Another body dives forward, knocking her sideways and removing her from danger. Relief lasts less than a millisecond. Her saviour, Tom, takes the full blow of my attack and crashes to the floor. Our bond flutters and the silver tie that connects us fades.

No! No!

My head hits the floor as the pain crushes me. I can't breathe, I can't speak, I can't think. There are just the rods pressing into my brain, my body, needle-sharp, over and over again. One long, howling scream racks my mind, endless insanity. Wave after wave of despair is crushing me, pressing me into the cracks of the floor, dissolving me into a thick sludge of liquid nothingness, as I seep down a dark, impenetrable trench.

CHAPTER FORTY-THREE

I hear a ticking, a mumble. Someone picks up my hand. A dull ache in my arm. The smell of roses. A flash of light. More muffled sounds. Footsteps. A beeping. Someone weeping. Someone holds my hand. Who? My eyes are sewn shut.

It's dark. I lie still, listening. A sound like a suction cup close by, in and out, in and out. I open my heavy eyelids. The lamp in the corner blinds me and I squint, trying to lift my head to look around the room, but my neck is weak, my head's in so much pain, my eyes water.

There's a rail to my left, a grey plastic curtain drawn across it. I hear a snort. Someone's in a chair to my side, her head on her chest, a book flopping over on her knee.

"Mum?" My throat is sore, the whisper not loud enough. I try again. "Mum!"

She jolts awake, looking around, the book falls to the floor.

"Mum?"

She sits up and leans towards me. "Cam!" Tears spring to her eyes. "Oh, Cam. Thank God."

I squint, unable to think beyond the excruciating agony in my head. The room seems to float and a wave of nausea pulses through my stomach.

"You're all right, you're safe now."

"Safe?"

She sits on the side of the bed, stroking my forehead. "You're just a bit confused."

Frowning hurts, so I just stare, waiting for answers.

"Let me get the doctor."

I try to tell her not to go, but she scurries away and comes back with a dark-haired woman.

"I'm Dr Aisha. Good to see you awake." She smiles. "Do you know your name?"

"Cam."

She nods. "Your full name?"

The question's odd. Of course I know my name, but the words are slow and slurred. "Came_ia Camden Chadwick."

"Good." She has a clipboard in her hand and a stethoscope around her neck. "And where do you live?"

"District Five. Yellow Block. House fourteen."

"Good. And how old are you?"

I look at my mum, noticing how pale she is. Her eyes have black moons underneath them, but she nods to encourage me. I glance around the white walls, the one opposite me has a framed print on it – all square boxes in shades of grey and black.

"Fifteen."

She takes out a small torch and shines it into my eyes. "When's your birthday?"

"20th of December."

"Perfect. Just look to the left for me." I do as she asks and she examines both eyes. "I think you'll be okay, but I want you to take it easy." She looks at my mum. "Nothing strenuous. No long conversations. Small sips of water. Lots of rest. I'll send the nurse in."

"Thank you, Doctor." My mum sits on my bed and strokes my head again. I'm missing something. It's as if my brain has a thick, damp fog in it.

"Is this a hospital?"

"Yes, but you're okay."

I frown, confused. "What happened?"

"You were in an... an accident."

"I don't remember." Tears fill my eyes. The world blurs.

"Oh, Cam. Don't cry." Her own eyes fill. She leans over me and strokes my forehead. "You'll be okay. You just need to get well. Have some water." She picks up a cup with a straw. "Not too much."

I sip a little, watching her, watching me. Something's going on. I hear a beeping and the suction cup again, behind the curtain to my right. Someone's over there. Liddy comes to mind. Was she in the accident? The sickness rises to the back of my throat.

"Where's Liddy?"

"She's safe. She was here with you yesterday."

"How long have I been here?"

"Five days."

My eyes widen. A clinking noise to my right startles me. I turn my head too quickly, causing a pain to shoot down my back. Breathing in, I notice my nose and ears are blocked, as if I'm on a plane with sinus problems.

"Who's over there?"

My mum looks up. She tightens her lips, her eyes water again. "Rest, Cam. We can talk tomorrow."

"Mum?"

A nurse comes in. He smiles at me. "Good to see you awake, but I'm going to give you something to make you sleep now."

"But I don't want—"

My mother squeezes my hand as he turns a plastic key attached to a bag of fluid. A pink liquid moves down the tube into my hand. I feel the coldness entering my bloodstream. My eyelids betray me. I fight to keep them open but can't resist the sedative as it shuts down my mind.

When I open my eyes again, the room is bright. Sunlight comes in from the right, but I can't see a window. The print has taken on shades of grey-pink and now looks almost three-dimensional. Liddy is in the chair. She drags it closer and leans her elbows on my bed.

"Cam!" She grins. "'Bout time you woke up. Lazing around all week." She strokes my arm, and I smile weakly. "You thirsty?"

I nod as she picks up the cup with the straw.

"Your mum's gone home to shower and change. Said I'd sit with you for a while."

My head's a bit clearer, though it still hurts. "Where are we, Lid? What happened?" My throat is raw, my voice barely above a whisper.

"We're back on the island."

"The island?"

She frowns. "Yeah, y'know, the place we escaped to and then ran away from." She grins and shrugs, waiting for the information to creep into my brain.

"Oh, yeah, right..." Everything's a bit foggy. "But my mum?"

"We rescued her, too."

Infinitely slower than I'd like, my brain connects dots. My mum comatose, dying. "How? She was so sick."

She looks around as if someone might be listening in. "Look, you got hurt, but I'm not supposed to tell you anything, yet."

"Why? How did I get hurt?"

"They don't want a relapse."

I frown. "But you'll tell me, right?"

She grits her teeth and sucks in air. "Promise me you won't panic or do any of that weirdo stuff."

As I have no idea what she's talking about, I nod.

She leans in, whispering. "You destroyed the clinic. It's all gone. Your mum and the kids in the cells were brought back here. Hey, there's loads of them, just like you, all in reception." Her voice lowers. "Ruth said they're having a hard time adjusting." Her eyebrows raise. "They even brought back some of the creepy scientists and that McCallister person. They're in custody, being questioned, I think."

Her words still confuse me.

"Destroyed the clinic? What clinic?" A flash-image comes to me. My mum lying in a bed. "Is my mum ill?"

"Not at all. It was all a trap. Once you knocked out that Sakiya woman – and she's here as well, by the way – the bind Sakiya had your mum in vanished. That's good, though, isn't it?"

I fight my mind to reconcile everything she's saying. The pieces are not clicking together properly. I have a vague sense something else happened.

"Vicky scarpered. Good thing she did, otherwise—" she hesitates, fiddling with the covers. "Sorry, maybe this is all too much for you. Should I stop?"

"Er, no. It's helping, I think."

"Jon's gone back to his normal, hysterical self, but I'm ignoring him, and Taor told me to tell you to get well soon."

"Right. Okay. To be honest, my mind's a bit of a blank." I feel I should know the people she's talking about, but I can't picture them.

"Well, you did have a wild time. Still not sure how you did it."

"Did what?"

Her forehead crinkles and a thin-lipped, sad smile crosses her face. "The doctor said the memory loss is only temporary, Cam. It'll come back." She hesitates, weighing up whether she should tell me something. "And Tom's in the bed next to you." She's pulling at her hair as if to make it grow longer. "He's in a coma."

"Tom? Oh Tom, of course, yes, I remember him now. How could I forget?" My chest rises, a sharp pain catching, like a muscle spasm. "Why's he in a coma?"

"Please don't panic. They say as long as he comes out of it, he should live. He's a good guy, he saved my life, you know." She looks down, smoothing the covers. Her tormented face and dark blue eyes are hidden, her hair pushed behind her ears. She's wearing a green plaid skirt with black tights and a white blouse. The woollen shawl has fallen from her shoulders onto the bed and I reach out to touch it. It's soft and warm, full of striking colours that seem to bounce off the bed. It strains my eyes, so I close them. But the colours are still there, dancing in circles, twisting in formations, connections within connections, flaring up from the ground like flickering fires, into my fingers, my body, my head.

I gasp and sit up, dragging tubes and wires with me. My head pounds and my heart hammers as my mind is flooded with images: Vicky, unconscious in the car park; the clinic; my mum; people dying; my attack on Liddy and the blinding energy bursting from my body.

My chest heaves as I drag thick air into my lungs, unable to fill them. I hold my stomach, rocking and sobbing as more details return, filling in the whole picture. Smoke. Fire. Fallen ceilings. A soldier with glassy eyes, lying next to me. Liddy's father? Maybe! Tom and silver darts. What did I do? My mum. Is she my mother? Liddy almost dead.

Tom's bond... I can't feel it. Where has it gone?

Liddy clings onto me. "It's okay. It's okay. Oh, Cam, please stop."

The curtain to my right swishes open. I hear Dr Aisha's voice. "Not the best way to remember, but now she knows, it will be easier."

I hide in Liddy's chest, ignoring the comment.

"She's still too weak."

"In a couple of days, she'll be ready. We can't risk waiting any longer."

She walks away, leaving Liddy to comfort me. In the bed next to mine is Tom, his face the deathliest shade of bluish-white I've ever seen. The suction noise is his life support machine.

"I'm sorry. I shouldn't have said anything."

Wiping my face with trembling hands, I glance at Tom and then back at Liddy.

"No. You did the right thing. Please, Lid, what did she mean about 'risk' and 'waiting'?"

She leans in, as if she didn't hear, but lowers her voice. "Something to do with your connection and waking him up."

I nod. "Yes, yes, of course. I can do that. Can I?" I lean back, exhausted. "I'm a monster."

"Don't be daft. You're just some weird, witchy person. Told you that before! And when you're well, I want the full story. How the heck did you do it?"

I can't smile this time. Looking up at her, I know there's something else I need to know. "Can you get my mum?"

"Yeah, sure. Do you want me to stay?"

"No, but can you come back soon?"

"Bring you some stash?" She grins and I try to grin back but feel my dry lips cracking. Tears fill my eyes and my body begins trembling.

"It's okay, Cam." She pulls me close to her chest and I reach my arms around her waist. She smells of something like cinnamon. "We're still together."

I hiccough, trying to control the gulps. "Lid, I'm not sure, but your dad might have been in the clinic."

She pulls back and looks at me. For a second, she's undecided. I sense her conflict.

"If it was him, at least my mum's free now."

She clings on to me tighter and I feel her strength grounding me again. I'm not sure I ever really appreciated how much Liddy has always been there for me.

"I can't feel the bond anymore, Lid. Is he dead? Tell me the truth."

"No, no. I swear, it'll be okay." She's stroking my back. "You're still worn out, Cam. Sleep for a while. I'll stay with you until you nod off."

I don't notice anyone administering it but feel the sensation of the cool liquid running through my veins again and the sleepiness overtakes me.

CHAPTER FORTY-FOUR

By the time my mum returns, I'm still in a half-stupor. My eyes feel heavy as I try to wake up my mind. The ceiling creeps down on me and, for a few minutes, I fight the vertigo. Eventually, it recedes, and I sense there is someone else with my mum. Not the doctor, someone new. I hear a second chair being dragged over and then my mum's voice as she holds my hand.

"Liddy told me you remembered."

"Yes." The word sounds like a gasp.

"Do you want more painkillers?"

"No." I need a clear head. Opening my eyes, I look at my mum's pale face, her dark blonde hair short and spiky, as if it's been hacked at. She has a scarf around her neck. I glance at the woman next to her. She's slim, has dark brown hair, almond-shaped green eyes, and is wearing smart clothes. She smiles, reminding me of someone, and then it hits me.

"Aunt Lucy?"

I look at my mum and back at her. She's smiling, tears in her eyes.

"My brave child."

I remember now she has a drawl. It's strange I didn't remember that before. Something flickers at the back of my mind, some connection I'm not making.

"But you're dead." I look back at my mum, my voice tight. "Isn't she?"

"No, I'm not. I'm sorry, we had to keep me a secret, but we can tell you everything once you're well."

"What? No, tell me now."

She sighs and looks at my mum as if for permission. My mum nods.

"Your mum and I were never sisters. We were very good friends." She looks across at my mum, her eyes steeped in doubt, before turning back to me. "My full name is Lucette Dante – of the Dante family, one of the Diversity Resistance League's leadership team."

Okay, I get why I might have called her 'aunt', a friend of the family, but why did my mum say she was her sister and why tell me she was dead? Memories of the fun we had on my birthdays flash through my mind. My mum somehow got permission to travel outside our district. The last time we'd met was at an aquarium. We'd been standing in front of the shark tank when Aunt Lucy had told me she had to go away and wouldn't see me for a while. I still remember the tears in her eyes as she knelt before me.

"Why, Aunt Lucy?"

"My job, darling. Just my job."

She'd clutched me to her and breathed in deeply, as if she could for ever inhale my fragrance and take it with her. "I'll see you again. I promise."

But she hadn't returned. Ever.

Nothing they're saying matches with what I thought I knew.

"Mum, you knew about the Diversity Resistance League? You know one of the leaders?"

"Yes. Lucy and I met seventeen years ago. It's a long story. When you're well—"

And then the memory resurfaces of Vicky and I slipping into the mission operations building; the woman in the meeting room speaking with Tom and Jenny. They were Lucy's words. It was her.

"Mum, I need to tell you something. Alone."

"Anything, of course, but Lucy's a good friend. I trust her completely."

I glance from one to the other. Both lean forward, encouraging me to continue.

"Fine, if that's the way you want it." I give Lucy the cold shoulder, twisting slightly so I face my mum. "You do know this 'good friend' of yours was ready to leave you to die? She was going to drag me off with Tom, just to fight this war of theirs."

Tom!

I'd forgotten Tom. I look over at his bed. He's still there. Still alive. I need him.

Aunt Lucy notices. "We're doing everything we can to help him. I promise you that."

My mum takes my hands in hers. "Cam." I notice her fingernails are short, like her hair. Something they did to her at the Commission's clinic. "What your Aunt Lucy did, I would have wanted. I'd gladly give my life to keep you safe. Lucy did what she had to."

Lucy interjects, her voice defensive. "We don't force people to fight our battles. It was about keeping you both safe."

"That's not what it sounded like." I scowl at her. The words I really want to say falter. I don't trust her. I want her out of the room.

"Mum, I want to ask you something."

"Of course. Go ahead." Her eyes are kind, encouraging.

"Alone."

She looks at Lucy, who nods, gets up and steps back, though not far enough to be out of earshot. I turn to my mum again, swallowing hard. "Are you... I mean... are you my real mother?"

"Yes, I am."

"It's just, at the clinic, they said you're a —" I stumble over my words, unable to ask the question that's foremost in my mind.

My mum frowns and glances at her friend.

"She needs to know, Sonia." Lucy has moved back to the foot of the bed. I wonder what she knows that I don't. I can't think of her as my aunt anymore. She isn't related to me and she's a leader of the League.

"What? What do I need to know?"

"Darling." My mum sits on the edge of the bed, stroking the side of my face. Tears swell in her eyes. "We'll tell you everything when you're stronger, but perhaps a shortened version of our story's best, for now."

A thudding in my ears tells me my heart's speeding up. *Our story?* My face flushes. My spine stiffens. Lucy moves to the other side of my bed.

"Don't worry. You're loved very much."

What right does she have to say that?

They nod at each other and my mum speaks. "We're both your mothers. Lucette's your birth mother."

I feel my heart thudding, speeding up as if I'm chasing a dangerous tornado when, really, I should just turn back.

"So, I was adopted or something?"

They look at each other again, as though the tornado has a thunder cloud twisted in it and it's about to hit ground level. I realise they're both holding one of my hands. My palms are sweaty, though my fingers remain slack. I can't bring myself to reciprocate their gesture of comfort.

"What? Just tell me."

My mum's biting the inside of her cheek. "There isn't an easy way to tell you this, Cam, but I was your birth father."

"What?" A storm has exploded in my brain. "No. No, that's... impossible." I pull my hands away from them, flapping like a bird with broken wings. "No, no, that can't be true. You told me I had a dad, who died."

I wait for her to confirm what she's told me all my life, but the pause is too long. She glances away.

I yank on her sleeve. "Mum?"

My whole body is heating up. I feel as if I'm sitting next to a furnace in an old-fashioned steam engine, only the driver has lost control of the train and we're about to run right off the tracks into a deep ravine.

"He did... in every meaningful way." She fiddles with her scarf, straightening the knot. "It was what I wanted. Cam, it was my choice."

"What they said in the clinic is true. You were really a man." I suck in a deep breath and let it out slowly. "How could you hide it from me all these years?"

"It was for your safety."

"But, Mum." I hesitate. *Should I even be calling her that?* "All those things you said about Liddy, insisting on calling her Lou, saying she would adapt... that she would learn to accept who she was..."

Tears come to my mum's eyes. She wrestles in her bag for a tissue, blowing her nose. Lucy leans across my bed and squeezes my mum's shoulder.

"It isn't how I wanted you to find out. I'm sorry." She grabs Lucy's hand. "Lucy and I met when she was on a mission. I didn't know who she was at that time, but we b-became close." My mum's stammering. "I was a young man then and—"

Lucy helps her finish, her voice more matter of fact. "We had a short relationship, and you were conceived. It was afterwards that I learnt of your mother's inner conflict – of how she suffered trying to hide her real self from the world – but, by that time, I was pregnant."

There's a gripping pain in my chest. I massage the area while staring at the foot of the bed; a normal hospital bed, with a grey, metal frame and sides that lock in place. There are some scratches in the middle bar where the clipboard has been hastily fastened.

I look at Lucette Dante, a DRL leader, my aunt, my mother's lover and my real birth mother. I don't know what to say. It's all too fantastical. There's nothing in me, an emotional emptiness. Surely, I should feel something. The white walls glare back at me. Such a whiteness, it expands into the air, surrounding me with its nothingness, seeping into my breath, my veins, my blood. I swallow hard.

"I'm sorry I couldn't tell you before now. We intended to, once we got you away." I look at my mum, fiddling with her scarf – the scar, the bicycle story flits through my mind. Was any of that true?

"Away?"

"Remember the trip I arranged? It was to come here."

Lucette takes over. "We set into motion two plans. We knew it was a risk. We knew you were being watched."

"Two plans?"

Schultz had told me that before. At least that part tallies. I fiddle with the sheet on the bed when a thought occurs to me.

"If you knew about this place… er, Mum" (never has saying the word 'mum' seemed so strange), "why didn't we just live here? Wouldn't it have been safer?" I'm surprised at how steady my voice is. When they don't immediately answer, I look up.

"Tell her, Sonia. She has a right to know."

My mum nods. "We lived on Lucette's family base for the first two years, over in the Americas, but I'd made an agreement, one I was happy to make: my gender change for service. I became a mission operative. When they decided to send me on a long-term mission – to infiltrate the Actuate Energy Fields Company – my only condition was that you came with me. I couldn't bear to leave you behind."

"And my condition was that I should be allowed to visit, once a year," Lucy adds.

They each, in turn, fill in parts of the story.

"We gave you both a new identity, a chance to live as normal a life as possible. Had you been here, you would have been tested much younger and taken into training. Some start as early as seven."

My mum tuts. "Too young. We both agreed it would be better if you were with me. But once I became the CEO's secretary, the security became tighter. They would have noticed Lucy's visits. You were ten when they stopped. Do you remember?"

I glance up and nod, before returning to my occupation as sheet-twister, my fingers knotting and unknotting the corner. A few seconds later, Lucy continues.

"I'm sorry. We had to put the mission first. We were so close to finding the answers we needed. We couldn't risk any suspicion. That's why we left the arrangements so late. In hindsight, we should have picked you up earlier."

"Pick me up?" *Mission? What was my mum up to?*

"When your Change process halted, we could have taken you in, but we needed a little more time. There was high level, international exchanges going on that only your mother had access to. And yes, they were watching, we were sure of it, because of your age. We thought we had enough resources in place to manage any situation, but they moved faster than we expected."

My mum sighs. "When we found out your test results, Lucette arranged transport for our escape off the main island, but you ran away. You'd already gone for plan A."

My eyes feel dry from staring at one spot. I blink several times. Lucette tries to reassure me again.

"Thank God Schultz spotted you first. It was our mission operatives that picked you up, although I only learnt that later on." She clasps her hands, glancing at the wall behind me. "I wanted to tell you your history face to face, but I promised your mum we would do it together. Had I known you were listening in that night—"

"So, no one else here knows?"

"No."

I turn to my mum. "And we've been living a lie?"

I want the words to sound accusing, but they come out as a murmur and fade into silence. They've both gone quiet. I look up from under my fringe. Tears trickle down my mum's face. She wipes them away with another tissue and I notice her large, familiar hands, the scarf on her neck, and her slightly deeper voice, all confirming the outlandish tale. I finally believe what I should have realised all along: she was a *he*. My mum was a man. My birth mum was my aunt, and now a DRL leader.

I want to shout, to accuse them of betrayal even though a very small part of me actually gets what they're saying and why it happened. Shock turns my body cold, my limbs begin trembling, and then an infusion of heat travels across my brain. I hear them trying to soothe me but know I can't cope with them fussing.

All I can think is that my whole life has been a lie. And they knew. They knew about the Diversity Commission, they knew about Diversity Resistance League, they knew what HGS was, how it affects a person and the danger it put me in. More importantly, they chose to hide their true identities.

None of these thoughts help me calm down, so I dive into processing mode, my silent world into which no one can enter. I need time to think.

CHAPTER FORTY-FIVE

I'm sitting in my bedroom. The curtains are drawn, the orange lamp's glowing, my desk and chair appear with my laptop, followed by my single bed. It has my favourite blue duvet cover on it. I stroke the cover and glance at the wall. From my seated position at the end of the bed, I glare at the framed photo of mum, my aunt and me. I want it to disappear, but it won't. I focus on setting it on fire. Smoke coils up, the paper falls to the ground and turns to ash, but when I look up, it's there again, as it was.

"So, you've had a shock?"

The voice startles me.

"Tom!"

I leap over and wrap my arms around him, never wanting to let him go. He sniggers as I lean back and stare at him.

"At least we now know why they were trying to get us off this base so quickly. Mum number two has influence."

I ignore his comment. "Tom, are you real or a figment of my imagination?"

"You ask this now?"

"Well?"

"Any normal psychiatrist would tell you you're imagining me."

"But we're not normal."

"No, we're weird." He grins.

"Oh, Tom, I'm so sorry. Everything that's happened—" Tears roll down my face.

"Stop the tears. This is your safe place, remember."

We sit opposite each other, me near the bed, him with his back against my dressing table drawers. I cross my legs and lean my elbows on my knees.

"None of it was true. All lies. My whole life."

"Dramatic! Not everything was a lie. Sure, this is a shock, but, hey, there are worse things. You had two loving parents, Liddy had none of that."

He's right, of course.

"You're in a coma."

"I know."

"I did it." My face heats up with guilt. He smiles at my squirming and reaches out with both hands to steady my quivering shoulders.

"And you're going to get me out."

"Am I?"

"Hey, after what you called up at the clinic, this will be easy." His eyes shadow and I feel his worry, but he jokes, anyway. "Told you you'd be learning on the job."

"Can't you get yourself out?"

"Too weak."

"I'll do anything, I promise."

His green eyes hold mine and he gives me a lopsided smile. "I know, but it needs to be now, Cam." His voice is level, but there's fear in his eyes.

"Tell me what to do."

"Our bond's still there. If it weren't, I couldn't be here, but it's getting weaker due to physical failure. My neurons are slowing down."

"What does that mean? I don't know what to do."

"Go back. Get as close to me as possible, physically. You need to somehow speed up my electrons to stimulate vibration. You'll need to do this through our bond to wake me up."

"Tom, I don't know how to do that."

"You've done it twice, now. You know what it feels like. That first time we met. You almost merged into me. I had to hold you back. Remember?"

"Yes, but—"

"You did the same when you pulled the strands from the earth and used the strength of our bond to destroy the clinic. You pulled me in."

"You felt that?"

"Yes. Now do the same, in reverse. Give me your strength. Avoid using other vibrations and energy fields, though."

"You mean, don't cause an explosion."

"Not a good idea."

A pain shoots across my chest. "I can't lose you."

He leans over, touching my face tenderly, his thumb following my jawline. "Please don't."

A shiver radiates through my body. I hang on to its silvery foundations. Our bond, I can feel it again. But Tom is fading.

"Don't go."

"Find me, quickly."

"Please, I love you, Tom." I feel silly, but what if he died and I never told him? "I know it's just the bond, but I couldn't bear losing you."

I hear a snigger. "Hold on to that thought until I wake up."

"Thought you said no emotions?"

"Not this time."

I look away, but his now almost invisible image holds my chin gently, meeting my eyes again.

"Two mums. Cool."

And he's gone. The room is cold and dark. With a quick glance at the framed photo, I dive back into the world, holding on to the silver thread he gave me. I have to pull him back. I can't fail. I won't lose him.

Words I never thought I would say pop into my head. Tom's a part of me. I'd break without him. Acknowledging that truth is a relief, even though my heart pounds with fear at what he's asked me to do. I realise it doesn't matter if he doesn't love me the same way. I can get over that. I can't get over him dying.

CHAPTER FORTY-SIX

"She's coming back."

Lucy's voice is the first to reach me. The next is my mum's.

"Cam?" She's holding my hand. I feel her trembling fingers. "I'm so sorry. Please can you forgive me?"

"Forgive us?"

Gritting my teeth, I just don't know how to respond. My mum's shoulders sag. Lucy's frowning, but their worries are unimportant.

"Can you help me?"

"Of course," says Lucy.

"Anything," breathes my mum.

"Move my bed next to Tom's."

Lucy's smile is condescending. "I understand the bond, but I don't think—"

I raise my voice. "I don't care what you think! He's dying and he needs me." I flick my eyes to my mum. "Are you going to help me or do I need to get Liddy?"

"Let me speak with the doctor."

"No, it has to be now." Lifting myself to a sitting position is hard, but I do it anyway. I can't hold in the explosive groan as my throbbing back pain sharpens.

"No, Cam. Stay where you are. We'll move your bed."

"Sonia?"

"Lucy, there's no harm in it. If he's dying and she needs to be close to him, I don't see what difference it makes." Their eyes meet and I wonder what information is passing between them. "I know you've explained it, but let's deal with that later. After."

Whatever is left unsaid doesn't matter. They nod their heads in agreement. The distance between Tom and me is no more than two long strides, so dragging a bed on wheels isn't hard. Coordinating the monitor and saline bag I'm hooked up to causes the difficulty, even with two of them. The alarm goes off and Dr Aisha appears.

"What's going on?"

My mum pushes the bed another inch. "She needs to be close to Tom. If it helps her, I intend to do it."

"You will not. This is my ward, and I decide what happens." She looks at Lucy. "I would expect more from you, Dr Dante."

Lucy's in charge of moving the monitor and the saline bag. She stops what she's doing and pushes her shoulders back. Only then do I realise she's as tall as my mum.

"Dr Aisha. This may be your ward, but I'm in charge of missions and Tom is a trainee missions operative. Therefore, his welfare is my concern, and I make the decisions."

The doctor folds her arms, a look of contempt in her eyes, but she doesn't back down. Instead, she stands in between both beds.

"They could both die. I can't allow this, until we have contingencies in place."

I push myself up further. My mum rushes over to help me.

"I spoke with Tom." This gets all their attention, but I focus on the doctor, my tone flat and low. "If we don't do this now, he'll die. So, either help or get out of my way. You know the damage I can do."

She flinches. "You spoke with him?"

I glare at her; my voice is demanding. "We need to be as close as possible. His neural vibrations are failing."

Lucy gasps. "They could both die." She turns to me. "Cam, to agitate his neural vibrations, you'll need to merge at the deepest bonded level, almost cellular."

"I know."

I don't actually understand what she means by 'cellular', but I don't want them to know that, plus I'm sure, if Tom is there, he'll show me.

My mum frowns. "Lucy, explain this to me."

Lucy's hands are on her waist as she considers the situation. "Their junk DNA is almost identical. That's the reason they can create such a strong bond. It's hereditary, but not something we understand, as yet. I do know it is deep within the cellular structure, within the atoms." She turns to me. "Cam, we can't help if it goes wrong."

A gasp explodes from my mum as she grabs her chest. "No, Cam. I can't lose you, again."

"Losing Tom would kill me, anyway – at a cellular level." I say this even though I don't know if it's true. No one contradicts me. "So, we either do it, or we both die."

The doctor calls in a nurse to help. The four of them push the beds as close as possible and unlock the bed rails, but still, there's a gap. I stretch out to touch him, but only the tips of my fingers reach the edge of his bed. As the team discuss what to do, and I'm thinking about getting up and crawling over, Liddy appears with a bag in her hand.

"What's going on?"

"He's dying, Lid. I need to do something about it, now."

She drops the bag on a chair, moves to the head of the bed and leans over, wrapping her arms over my shoulders and squeezing tight. Tears fill my eyes.

"Can't get close enough, Lid."

"Course you can." Her voice is loud in my ear, as she addresses the crowd at the foot of the bed. "Well, move her."

My mum answers. "We are."

"No, move her into his bed."

"But—" My mum doesn't finish as Lucy interrupts.

"No, it's a good idea." She pushes my bed aside and begins giving orders. "Aisha, move the monitor and saline to this side. Nurse, can you move Tom a little to the right? Make enough room."

Two more nurses are called in and three of them help carry my body across the gap, gently placing me on my side, next to Tom, my head at his left shoulder.

Instantly, I feel his tingling warmth against me, and shiver. Lifting my right hand, I touch his ribcage; his heart beats beneath it to the tune of the life support machine. Breathing in his scent, I know it's wrong. Not fresh and spring-like, but sickly and damp, like a winter's death. Inhaling sharply, my chest heaves and my eyes prickle with fear. I can't sense our bond again. If he were to die because of me, I couldn't live with myself.

I lift my head a little. The many eyes watching, waiting, as if I'm about to produce a magic spell, make me feel exposed.

"Can you all leave, please? I can't do this with you watching."

The doctor responds. "Someone needs to be here in case something goes wrong."

"Liddy can stay."

Lucy takes over again. "We'll all be outside. Liddy, anything happens, shout for us."

My mum comes over to me, stroking my hair. "Are you sure you don't want me here?"

I shake my head. "I just need quiet."

The doctor makes some final checks with the machines. "Do you know what you're doing?"

"I'll find Tom. He'll show me."

As they leave, Liddy pulls up a chair next to us, taking my hand.

"I'm here. I'll watch over you both."

"Thanks, Lid."

I feel calmer with just Liddy here. Even though she doesn't have any real talents, her gift to me has always made me feel more in control. Turning back to Tom, I stroke his pale face.

I'm coming for you, Tom. Wait for me.

I rest my hand on his chest, close my eyes and jump into processing mode.

The first thing I note is the absence of Tom in my room. I dart over to his place by the door and sit, knees bent, head in my hands.

"Tom? Are you here? I need you to tell me what to do."

I strain my senses, listening, reaching out. He has to be here. The silence extends until I can bear it no longer. Leaping up, I walk over to the window and look out. I see a memory of our street. The yellow flats opposite, the road. It's morning and my mum would be on her way to work – or, rather, her *mission* – but not here and not today. The streets are empty.

"Right. Think. What did he say?"

Follow the bond, give him strength, kickstart his neurons to vibrate.

"Three steps. Easy."

I move to the mirror, squinting at myself, ignoring the rest of my body as if I'm just a floating head. Watching as the *she* in the mirror touches my cheek where Tom's thumb stroked it. My face flushes warm and an ache in my chest recognises the intense love of the bond. As I remove my hand, a tiny silver strand sparkles at the end of my fingers, tingling and growing into a thin piece of threadbare cotton, leading away from me.

Tom! He's somewhere, but where?

Stuffing my hands into my pockets, I sink to the floor and close my eyes. I need to make the bond stronger. At first, I think about a fisherman's thick rope, but it's too stiff. Lightning comes to mind, but it's too strong. Intuitively, I understand it will break the tenuous hold. But then I remember a picture from when I was a kid. Sitting at the kitchen table, I'm pouring silver glitter from a plastic tube onto glued paper. Fragile, but solid and something I can shape.

Imagining a litre milk bottle, I fill it with the glitter and then begin pouring it over the line of our bond. I visualise the bond accepting the sprinkled dust and watch it widening, like a river receiving a sudden downpour of rain. And then the bond turns into a sparkling brook, weak but stable, and something I can hold onto.

"Tom?"

I don't understand why he can't answer. If the bond is here, why isn't he? I should be able to sense his mind, his thoughts, but the bond's drifting into nothingness. How can I follow it into emptiness? The fear of floating around, lost in dark space hits me.

I open my eyes. The dressing table is still opposite me. Rubbing my face, I pull my hair tight behind the base of my neck. My pulse pounds in my ears as I look around the room. Cosy, calm, quiet, but it's my mind creating this. If I can conjure this space, surely I can follow the bond and summon a safe place for both of us?

Clasping my hands together, I close my eyes and dive in, imagining myself swimming along the bond, looking for the end and my partner. The bond is cool, and the more I move through it, the thicker it becomes, until it feels like sludge, and I have to wade, forging a pathway. I remind myself this is all in my mind; that in reality I am in a hospital bed and Liddy is sitting next to me. If it's my mind creating this, I should be able to change it.

I think about the brook again, but the sludge turns to thick mud with gassy bubbles breaking on the surface. At either side of me are banks of burnt grass and trees. I try to bring them to life, but although one or two leaves turn green, most remain stubbornly black.

I don't get it. Why can't I change it? If I'm creating it, why doesn't it do as I want? There's something odd, something I'm not getting.

The sludge is not the worst of my problems. Looking up, I see a mist, crawling its way around a corner. At first, it moves slowly but gradually it increases speed. I turn to head back to the safety of my room, but my feet are stuck. I wave my hands, waggle my hips, pull at my thighs, fight to get out, but it only makes it worse, and I sink to a crouch. My heart's thrashing so hard that all I can manage are shallow gasps.

The first wisps touch my cheeks and the smell of death washes over me. Sickly, dark, dank and cruel, so cruel. I can't bear the horror, the pain. My body trembles as I plunge to my waist. The air smells of something worse than bad eggs. I cover my nose with my top but, as the terror and the fog envelope me, I realise it makes no difference as I am pulled further into the mire. My chest, my shoulders, my neck. Soon, I won't be able to breathe. I'll die here.

I hear a gurgling, then a wailing which becomes an agonising scream, followed by great waves of sobbing, and ultimately silence, as I'm sucked into some underground cavern of hell.

"Now, Cam! Now!"

Tom's voice above me makes me look over my shoulder.

"Tom?" I'm laid out on a flat mud bank. I don't know how I got here. "Is that you?"

I can't see anything through the fog, but feel a dragging on my body, like a forcefield pulling me towards it.

"What's happening?"

"Help me get out of this, Cam."

It's only then I realise that this is not my mind, not my image. I've stepped over into Tom's current reality and it's horrific. It's how he's picturing death, how he feels as his life force diminishes and all vibrations leave his body.

"How? Please tell me how," I plead, desperate to get out, desperate to get Tom out.

"Give."

"Give what?" I wait for an answer, but nothing comes. "Give what? Tom?"

The dragging sensation pulls on me again, but this time, weaker. I resist, frightened something evil is taking me away, terrified I'll never get out of whatever his mind has created. I reach out for Tom, but all I sense is dank mud and rotting vegetation. I look for any vibration, anything alive, but even the earth's reds and oranges are gone. I wonder how he could imagine all this. I've never seen such a place. But if these are Tom's images, his thoughts, maybe he's still here somewhere.

I'm about to scream his name when I see a sparkle. It's so tiny, I almost miss it, but after a few tries, I manage to grab it. A tiny piece of glitter, our glitter, our bond. I stifle a whimper. There's only this one tiny piece left.

I curl over in pain, the weight of loss crushing me, splitting me in two. Tom's leaving me. He's saying goodbye. I know it. I've failed. I close my hand around the last morsel of us and weep. Excruciating pain shoots through my chest. Heaving, I gulp the last words I'll ever speak to him.

"I'm so sorry, Tom. I don't know what to do." And then the only words I can think of spill out. "I love you. Take that with you, wherever you're going. Take my love."

I reach out into the darkness, imagining my love as a golden light spreading outwards, hoping it will help him pass through this dark place to wherever he's going. I don't want to say goodbye, so I cling on to the silver memento in my hand and try to strengthen the light, powering it up like the sun coming out from under an eclipse. I feel its vibrations whirring around me, beneath my body.

"I'm with you. You're not alone. Don't be afraid."

The light turns from orange, to gold, to white, as if I'm smelting a glass vase, heating it more and more. It burns my body and my face, running down my right arm and into my hand, until I can't bear it. I open my eyes and see my clenched hand is glowing; my fingers are blistered, as if I'm holding hot coals.

Mechanically, I let go, releasing thousands of silver stars of glitter. Each one darts in the direction of the light I tried to send to Tom. I want to hold on to my last piece of Tom, but he needs them more than I do. So, I relinquish my grip on it, on our bond, on everything that is Tom, and crawl into a ball, pleading for a safe place to return to.

CHAPTER FORTY-SEVEN

Whispering. Beeping. A ticking. Someone checking my blood pressure. The world around me is alive. I don't want to be part of it. I don't want to wake up. I force myself to sleep.

Someone's shining a torch in my eyes.

"She's fine. She'll come round, when she's ready."

I'm not ready.

Another voice. My mum's – worried, stressed. "But it's been so long."

"She's been through a lot."

And then I hear Liddy. "Do you think she knows?"

And Lucy responds. "We can't be sure until she wakes."

I know, I know. Shut up, everyone. Go away.

I take myself away, determined not to face up to the world.

Minutes, hours, days – who knows? – go by. I land in my bedroom. Not sure I even planned to be there, but I realise I must be in processor mode. Maybe I slipped into it in my sleep.

I walk around, touch the silky duvet cover, stroke the wall, pull the curtains shut and move over to my dressing table. I glance at my brush and comb, the glass paperweight, the ceramic donkey – gifts from my mum that I'll never really hold again.

I stare at the mirror. My face looks the same. Angular, pale, brown hair. I scrutinise my body. It hasn't changed: flat-chested, straight up and down. But it isn't important anymore. I am what I am. Not male, not fully female, but something other. What did Tom say when we first met? 'I accept my body for what it is. I don't need fixing'. Something like that.

I stand back to see the full picture. Short legs, though in balance with the rest of me, narrow waist. I'm dressed in blue jeans and a black hoodie. This is me. It's as if my whole body has been locked down for so long that now something inside lets go and frees me. I almost smile at the reflection. I know I'm not quite there, but perhaps I'm not so odd. I'm exactly what I should be right now. Maybe that will change in the future. I realise I'm okay with that, too.

"Thank you, Tom!" My voice hitches, but I swallow hard. No more tears. I move to the lamp to switch it off. This will be the last time I come here. It no longer feels right. It isn't me anymore.

"When are you going to wake up?"

Startled, I reach out to balance myself on the chair. I daren't even swing around to look, sure he'll disappear if I move.

"Well?"

"You're a figment, aren't you?"

"Of your imagination? Don't think so. Though I do like figs." He snickers.

"My imagination—"

"Yeah, that's what we DNA weirdoes do, imagine stuff."

I spin on my heals. "Tom?"

He's sitting in his usual place. I want to run to him but am afraid he'll disappear.

"I mean, are you back? Really back?"

"Well, I'm not gone. Wasn't sure for a while. Where are we, in the real world?"

I don't know where to start. "Hospital on Base One."

He nods, rubbing his forehead. I want to fill him in on everything that's happened, but my mind is spinning, and I just spit stuff out. "Lucy told me that our extra genes are identical, that's the reason we can have this connection. She also said we're somehow related."

He looks up, the frown disappears. "Very distant cousins, then?"

"I have a theory on that."

"Do tell."

"Aliens, neanderthal or elephants? Take your pick."

He chuckles. "I think I like aliens – something cool would be good."

"What, like ten arms or something?"

He snorts. It's good to hear him laugh again.

"Does it even matter? Isn't everyone distantly related in some way?" I go for a smile, but it feels false on my face. I can't keep up my chirpy façade, throwing witty comments back and forth. I slump in my chair and look at my fingers. Tears well up in my eyes.

"Don't be sad, Cam. This is a good day." He leans his head against the door; his fringe falls across his forehead, his hazel eyes sparkle, and his mouth has a perfect smile. I want to run over to him and hold on, never let go.

"You know I can read your mind, don't you?"

I stand and grip the chair back, wishing this to be real. A tear rolls down my cheek. I wipe it away, blinking hard. The ghost of Tom gets up and walks over to me. He stands so close I feel the vibration burning off him as I look up.

"I'm real, Cam. You did it."

"But this is not real."

"Okay, let me rephrase. I'm as real as we can be, here. And I'm physically still alive, thanks to you."

My limbs begin trembling. I can't trust this spirit in front of me, I can't trust I'm not making it up. He pulls me towards him, his arms tighten around my back, holding in everything that wants to burst out, as he whispers in my ear. "Time to wake up!"

"No!" I cling to him, my cheek close to his heart. "I want to stay here with you, like this, for ever."

I throw my arms around him and clasp my hands behind his back. I know I sound like a love-sick puppy but, after almost losing him, I'm beyond embarrassment. He steps back, gently removing my arms, but holding my hands for a few seconds before sitting on the edge of my bed.

"You're young, Cam. The bond still controls your emotions."

"So you keep saying, but isn't that what saved you?" I hate that he's so level-headed, after everything we've been through. I walk over to the windows and open the curtains, just for something to do.

"Now you're angry with me." His long fingers ruffle through his hair, lifting his fringe off his forehead.

"No. Yes. I don't know."

"It's not real, you know. Not this." He gestures around the room. "Not us, not the feelings you have. You'll see. The real world is out there, waiting for us, and we have our lives to live."

"It *is* real." I stalk over to him and plonk myself down, shoulders slumped. "This room exists."

"You know what I mean."

"Okay, none of it's real. Fine." I throw my arms around his neck, smiling. "Don't worry, this isn't real."

His eyebrows rise, he already understands my intent, but doesn't say anything, so I continue, pulling his head closer to mine. My heart pounds, waiting for him to resist, waiting for him to do something to stop me. His lips are so close, I taste his warm breath as I mumble words.

"It isn't real."

As our lips touch, soft and sweet meets hunger and need, gentle at first, then more demanding and forceful. For a few, dizzying seconds, I am me, I am him. I know his thoughts, feel his love and know he wants this, too. He can't hide it from me.

As we both lie down on the bed, staring into each other's wide eyes, I truly believe this one, delicious moment is worth giving up my entire life for, and perhaps even my soul.

"This can't happen."

I smile. "What are you talking about? This isn't real."

He smiles back. "It's coming."

"What?"

"Brace yourself."

I'm thrown against the far wall, a bolt of electricity between us. Tom's against the door. He's rubbing his head and groaning. "Jeez..."

"Tom?"

"I'm okay. You?"

"Mmm..." I sit up. "The bond?"

"Told you it can't happen, cousin."

"Cousin? But you wanted it. I know you did."

He grins. "We can't always have what we want. Time to wake up, my little warrior."

CHAPTER FORTY-EIGHT

My eyes open to low lighting. I'm on my side, a warm body next to mine, a sheet close to my chin. There are noises around me, soft footsteps, machines beeping, quiet voices. An antiseptic smell burns my nose and, even though I know where I am, I feel disorientated.

Tom's humming asks permission to enter my mind, and I joyfully agree.

He's really alive!

"The bond makes it impossible, Cam. We can't be together. Not the way you want."

"For now. Things could change. And is that your first thought on waking up from a coma?"

His chest rises in a tired chuckle. "Jeez, I hurt."

"Sorry."

"Stop apologising."

I lift my head to meet his eyes. He somehow manages to put his arm around my shoulders.

"You're tough, for someone so short." He smiles.

"I'm not that short. Tough is good."

"It is. Stay still. Rest with me for a while."

I snuggle closer, my head rests on his chest. "I don't want them to come."

He knows I mean doctors, parents, even Liddy. I just want a few more private moments with him, before all the questions and demands begin. After a while, I breach a topic that I'm not really comfortable with.

"Tom, I met your father." My mind relives the one-way conversation I'd had with him. The words 'abomination', 'sacrifice' and 'freak' pop up. Tom sees the image in my head. His mind is immediately full of black, spiking anger and scorn.

"Did he really say that to you?"

I can't hide the disgust I feel. "He also said your name isn't Tom."

He sighs, his chest rising and falling.

"I was just twelve when I handed myself in to a clinic. I believed in the Diversity Commission, the purity line and everything they said about wanting to cure the human race."

I see the memory in his mind. His parents arguing about the early testing; his mum wanting his father to hide Tom until they could find a way to fix him; his father slamming his fist on an office desk and refusing to even consider it. As leader, he had to set an example. Tom is creeping away, getting on a bicycle and 'doing the right thing'.

"I thought my father would be proud of me. I thought he would come and visit, but I never saw my parents again, and slowly, I learnt the horror of what they do to people like us."

I feel his deep sadness, the resentment and the horror he faced, but he cuts the image quickly.

"So, he's one of their leaders?"

"He's the son of the founder and chair of the Global Diversity Commission, as well as the most senior leader in the UK. Crawled his way to the top with his barbarism."

"You didn't tell me."

"I didn't want to think about it."

"So, you had a different name?"

"My birth name was Tonia Tobias. My mother wanted a girl after two boys, so she named me."

He breathes deeply. I sense the pain he still feels when thinking about his parents.

"When I came here, I wanted a complete change and I didn't want them to find me. I chose Tom after a relative in the past who went to war."

"The 'Thomas' this island was set up for?"

"Yes."

I look up at him. His eyes are closed, his jaw tight.

I still use telepathy as I don't want anyone to hear us. "He – your father – wants us both."

"Oh, yes, we'd be such an asset to him." The sarcasm is tinged with hurt.

"Don't be upset."

"You don't get it. He's the real enemy, Cam. He wants us either dead or working with them to battle for power and control of a world that just doesn't exist anymore."

"Isn't that what the League's doing? Creating an army of talented people to battle for their way of thinking? Vicky had had enough, y'know. She was running away from it all, to some place up north. She just wanted freedom, to be off grid."

"How can you compare the League and the Commission? We'd live in peace if the Commission didn't come after us, if they allowed others to live as they choose. But they see us as a deadly virus, to be used or exterminated. We're evolving and all they want to do is destroy us and anyone who's different or doesn't conform. And that includes people like your mum and Liddy. It's nothing to do with purity or protecting the human race from extinction anymore, it's about military power and global influence. It's corrupt and I'm ashamed my father heads it up." There's fear and anger in his voice, but also frustration.

"And, thanks to Vicky, they know too much about this island. Although we can change security, it's no longer a safe haven. Imagine if they have ten, twenty or thirty Vickys, all trained to infiltrate our islands. What will happen to our people?"

I know he's being serious but, having just got him back to the land of the living, this is not the conversation I saw us having. I try to head him off in a more playful direction.

"Given this a lot of thought in your coma, haven't you?"

He chuckles. "My coma didn't do this. I've watched the Commission building its network for years. But not everyone believes as they do. They fear them, yes, and follow the Holistic Law, going along with them because there aren't any other options. We need to give those that would oppose them a different option. That trick you pulled at the clinic will give them hope."

My brain must be a bit fried, as I'm having difficulty following him. "What trick? Hope for what?"

"We have allies who would work with us. People will fight, if they think we have a chance. Destroying that clinic showed we could really make a difference. We can take on the Commission and win."

"I didn't do it alone, y'know. Vicky helped me. She downloaded stuff into my head. I couldn't have done it without that knowledge. I'm not even sure what that knowledge is or how I used it. It just called to me, or I called it."

"I knew you learnt quickly, but now I think it's more than that. It's as if you assimilate knowledge."

"What?"

"We'll test the theory later, when we're back in training." His thoughts move to Liddy. "She's a good friend."

"Always been there for me."

"There's a vibration about her that's very calming, when she's not angry with me."

"I thought it was just with me she was like that."

"I could sense something in her when we made the external shroud. Almost an absence of vibration."

"But vibrations are everywhere."

"Yes, and she has vibration. I don't quite understand it myself."

His mind wanders to Vicky again. "Y'know, she had a choice, Cam. She was here. She saw what we're trying to do. She could have joined us but chose not to."

"She didn't want to be controlled or used anymore. She knows of a place—"

"Is that what you think we do here?"

"Those new kids – the rescued ones – will they be given a choice?"

"We hope they'll join us, but everyone has a choice. You know that."

"And what if they choose not to help?"

"Look, I know you've got a lot going on, but the world's changing and we are part of that. Hiding or doing nothing may as well be siding with the Commission."

"Tom, I'm only just getting my head around a world that's already changed, for me."

"I know." I sense him sighing, trying to relax his tense body. "Our talents are needed, Cam. That clinic is just one of many. There are also orphanages where they test kids as young as five years old. The take them away if they believe their parents aren't adequately training them on the right path, or if they see potential for talents. Imagine what we could do to help them if we combine our strengths. What you did was untrained, but if we harness that ability, show we have the power to defeat them..." He stops again, aware a lecture is not the way to convince me. "Eventually, you'll need to take a side."

He makes it sound as if I side with the Commission, which I don't. How could I? I rattle off a list in my head. Home's gone, Liddy's a female, I have two mums, HGS, freaky DNA, talents, a bond – heck, less than a month ago, I was just this schoolgirl worrying about her flat chest and grey school uniform, who daren't mention the

'Golem' word – and now? Well, now, I've....

"I've actually killed people, Tom." Liddy's father jumps into my mind. He sees it but makes no comment. "I know I didn't mean to, but isn't that manslaughter still? Why's no one mentioning that?

He goes quiet. I sense him sighing again, an acknowledgement of my distress.

"I know. I'm sorry, I'm ranting. I'll stop now."

"And, even worse, I think I'm in love with this boy, who's witchy weird like me, and who tells me none of my feelings are real, and who now wants me to join a club to exterminate the Commission's global dominance. Have I got this right?"

I hear him stifle a chuckle and groan in pain as he does. "Everything's happened so quickly, let's not deal with any of it now. No matter what, at least I can promise you one thing: I'm here for you and there'll be no more secrets between us."

"So, I just had to blow up a clinic to get the truth out of everyone."

He snorts, his chest rising sharply. "Ouch. Rest. We can talk later."

"Stay with me?"

"You think I can move?"

A warm sensation creeps through my chest. I smile and close my eyes. "You know you're stuck with me for life now, don't you?"

"Mmm..." He's drifting into sleep.

"The bond, I mean."

"Yes, *cousin*. We're stuck together for life."

"Good."

I sense him smiling as he slips away. He's so sure about the League. I guess he does have experience of both sides – and his family, too – but this whole thing about two sides, of power and control, of battles and war, of the end justifying the means, is frightening and alien.

As alien as my DNA?

My chest rises as I breathe deeply. Maybe I'm not angry enough yet. Maybe if I were enraged, like I was at the clinic, I could channel that energy and use it to fight. But fight what? I still don't know the exact nature of all missions and the work here. Is their plan to go around blowing up clinics? Is that what they'd want me to do? Become a killer?

Tom's right about one thing: things have happened so fast. All I really want, right now, is a little time to rest by his side. In some ways, I understand Vicky. I'd happily hide away from them all in my safe place with him and go back to the pretend kissing.

I mentally slap myself. Need to stop thinking about that. Need to be stronger. Because, somehow, when I wake up tomorrow, I'm going to have to face everything – my mum, Lucy, the lies, the consequences of what I did out there. And then what?

Then I'll have to make that decision. Stay with Tom and become one of them or decline their offer. Defend or hide. Could I leave Tom, if I wanted to be like Vicky and not take sides? I snort and tut at myself, knowing the answer to that question well enough.

Reaching out, I touch his chest. The silver bond between us drifts around my fingers as I raise them up and down. Content for now to watch his chest rise and fall naturally, I close my eyes.

"For life, then."

THE FIVE TENETS OF THE HOLISTIC LAW

1. Intention

Liberate us from fear, ignorance and self-deception. Trust the Holistic Law. Only it can lead to our salvation!

2. Responsibility

Accept responsibility for everything we are, everything we have done and the consequences of those actions and decisions of our predecessors. Commit to working together to change the disaster we brought upon ourselves. Do not let your children suffer from the errors of our past.

3. Expulsion of Evil

Know without question that pure genes are the ONLY safe genes. We are all in danger of conversion. Reject evil and report difference!

4. Embrace Change and Exercise Control

Understand great change requires individual sacrifice. Our world needs our sacrifice so future generations can live freely and without fear. Let no one person ever lead you astray with impure thoughts or behaviours. Reject difference. Reject those beliefs and emotions which would corrupt our society and breed doubt. And remember, we are all in this together.

5. The Whole

Accept our lives are part of the whole – a journey we all take to improve our existence and the security of our future as humankind. For the sake of the whole, for our continued liberation, and the transformation of the world, be a good citizen.

The Good Citizen

We are born to serve. We uphold integrity and honesty with unwavering determination, and we act fearlessly against all who would destroy the purity of the human genome and the natural world.

The Pledge of Allegiance

1. I promise to observe the five tenets and never misuse them for my own or other's benefit.

2. I promise to respect and obey my elders and those in a position of knowledge and greater understanding.

3. I promise to champion purity of humankind and the natural world.

4. I promise to serve my country and free it from disease and corruption by rooting out evil and the forces that would destroy us.

AUTHOR'S NOTE

Major universities and research laboratories are researching the so-called junk DNA as the 'dark matter' of all mammals. The University of California, Berkeley, and Washington University led a study that shows how this DNA has evolved in our bodies and how it has a critical role, not yet fully understood.

"If 50% of our genome is non-coding or repetitive – this dark matter – it is very tempting to ask the question whether or not human reproduction and the causes of human infertility can be explained by junk DNA sequences." – Andrew Modzelewski, UC Berkeley.

Furthermore, organisations across the globe are experimenting and researching the application of gene editing, racing to be the first to show it is necessary for the optimal performance of the human body. It is already a multi-million dollar industry and fortunes are being made.

In 2017, Horizon Discovery Group, one of many businesses exploring this potential market, had an income of £36.5 million ($46.532 million). It saw a 52% jump in revenue, and a transformation wrought by its acquisition of Dharmacon from GE, giving Horizon Discovery gene-modulation capabilities and global cross-selling opportunities.

ACKNOWLEDGEMENTS

I first wrote this book in 2019, based on my work in the field of Inclusion and reading about research into DNA. Since then, the story has evolved and been rewritten several times. So, I want to thank my family and friends for their continued support, patience, and for reading various versions.

I particularly want to acknowledge the support and advice of two people. D. Scott-Jones, Scriptwriter, and Dr. Lukasz Chrobok, Lecturer in Neuroscience at the University of Bristol, who allowed me some of his precious time to ensure I understood human biology.

If you enjoyed this book, please leave a review!

ABOUT THE AUTHOR

Tracy Todd is an accomplished writer and author, having dabbled in everything from short stories to business books. With a series of published short stories and novels, her work has also featured in Indigo Dreams, Hammond House and Mslexia. One of her novels was longlisted for Mslexia's Novel Competition, and the first draft of *The Apex Agenda* was well received by the Penguin Random House Write Now Competition. From a pool of 1,700 applicants, Tracy was one of the 150 writers invited to attend a workshop in Nottingham. Currently, she is working on *The Apex Agenda* TV script with co-writer D. Scott-Jones.

Outside of writing, Tracy runs a non-profit social enterprise, The Equality Practice, which promotes the idea that everyone, independent of their gender, age, background or personal circumstances, should have the opportunity to thrive and live a life that is fulfilling and meaningful to them. Since 2016, The Equality Practice has worked on projects, conferences and programmes that promote inclusion, value, respect and belonging.

www.tracytodd.co.uk

@tracy_todd_still_writing